CHURCH CHOIR
MYSTERIES

A Crossings Omnibus

GUIDEPOSTS

CHURCH CHOIR MYSTERIES™

The Highly Suspicious Halo

The Coin Conspiracy

The Doubtful Doctor

Eileen M. Berger

CROSSINGS®

Garden City, New York

CONTENTS

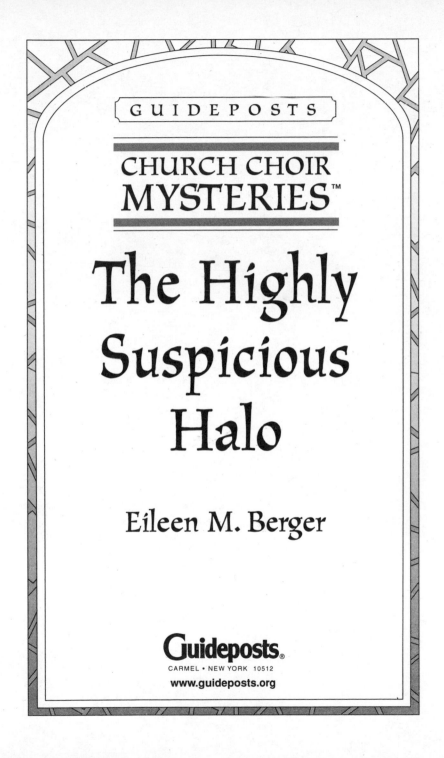

GUIDEPOSTS

CHURCH CHOIR
MYSTERIES™

The Highly
Suspicious
Halo

Eileen M. Berger

Guideposts®

CARMEL • NEW YORK 10512

www.guideposts.org

"Help Me to See Thee, Lord" was written by Eileen M. Berger.

Series Editor: Michele Slung

Cover art by Robert Tannenbaum

Cover design by Wendy Bass

Interior design by José R. Fonfrias

Interior cat illustrations by Viqui Maggio

Printed in the United States of America

The Highly Suspicious Halo

To VICKI, JIM, AND BILL

Our wonderful, now-grown offspring
whom we enjoyed and fretted over as children,
worried about as adolescents and teens,
and admire and appreciate
ever more and more as adults.

We think of you often, and always with love,
and with prayers for
and blessings upon you,
and with gratitude for God's grace in granting us
the privilege of being your parents!

One

THE ELDERLY MAN with the pruning shears was holding on to his aluminum walker with one hand as he stared at the overblown chrysanthemums. Grinning, he then asked his red-haired niece, Gracie Parks, to join him in the attack. "You brought your pruners with you, right?"

"I was tempted, Uncle Miltie, but didn't succumb—not this time. There are a dozen things I should be doing, but it's such a lovely day I couldn't stay inside."

"I can understand that." The eighty-year-old man moved his walker enough to allow him to snip off more of the flowers. "I've seen countless autumns when we've had frosts, *killing* frosts by now, so I'm trying to keep things blooming as long as possible."

"You're doing a great job—as always." That was no exaggeration. Her uncle, George Morgan, called "Uncle Miltie" for fifty or sixty years because people claimed that his jokes were as unfunny as those of the comedian Milton Berle, certainly did have a way with flowers!

Gracie's husband, Elmo, whom she missed terribly, even though five years had passed since he'd been killed in an accident, had not had that knack. Still, he had cheerfully always kept the lawn mowed and was willing to help her plant bulbs or move a shrub or whatever else she needed.

He had been nearly as devoted to his many responsibilities around town as he was to her. Not only had he served as Willow Bend's sanitation engineer, but also was elected mayor for several terms. Yet what he'd enjoyed most of all was acting as unofficial pastor's helper at their Eternal Hope Community Church.

The truth was that it had been Elmo's special way of drawing people to him, of supporting them—and her—that made her widowhood so hard to bear. And yet, as one of the most active citizens of Willow Bend, Indiana, Gracie herself could lay claim to only a few genuinely solitary moments.

She shook her head to bring herself back to the present, and had just started to praise Uncle Miltie further when the phone rang. He turned back toward her as she pulled her cellphone from her pocket. "Hello?"

"I'm sure glad you're there, Gracie, 'cause we do have a major problem."

This was not a call she'd looked forward to, but she tried to be upbeat. "Hi, Barb, isn't it a gorgeous day?"

There was the slightest of pauses before, "Wel-l-l, yes, it is, but I've got to talk with you about that rehearsal last night."

Oh, dear. . . . It wasn't that Gracie was surprised—she'd have to agree that things had not gone as well as she'd hoped. "There were some rough edges."

" 'Some rough *edges*'?" Barbara Jennings' voice scooted up the scale with incredulity. "It was awful! They didn't get the notes right and the timing was beyond belief. There's no *way* we can be ready for Sunday—and in front of all those people, too!"

"Oh, Barb, we weren't that bad."

"Yes, you—yes, the choir was! We'll be the laughingstock of Willow Bend—of the whole *area*, if we go ahead with that dratted choir contest!" She drew in a loud breath. "There's no way we can fix everything that's wrong—what were we *thinking* of, putting ourselves up against Waxman Tabernacle again—and all the others in this ministerium?"

Gracie ran her left hand back through her short, curly red hair. "It *was* discouraging to have Amy unable to sing. . . ."

"It certainly would have helped, but even that wouldn't have been enough."

"It might have been. I was the one to insist she not practice with us this time. I wanted her to get completely over her laryngitis—for her not to try singing those high notes. I was afraid it might make her lose her voice entirely, like what happened last winter."

There was a sound from the other end, but Gracie was trying, as usual, to be a peacemaker. "I talked with her this morning, and she claims she's better—that her throat doesn't hurt as much, and the huskiness is nearly gone. And remember, Barb, Rick Harding hadn't moved here yet at this time last year. With both him and Amy, we can handle it."

The response to that positive outlook seemed more a grunt than a sigh. "I do hope so! I hardly slept a wink all night, what with fretting about this. . . ." Barb, a first-class worrier if there ever was one, went on and on, until Gracie was forced to hold the phone away from her ear as, with raised brows, she looked at her uncle.

However, by the time she hung up, Barb was in a slightly better mood. Aware of this, Uncle Miltie smiled crookedly. "Well, Gracie, I take it your worthy organist/choir director's all het up about that choir concert."

"Afraid so. But then she's 'het up' about a lot of things much of the time."

"Isn't that the truth? That bantam hen's so constantly clucking about possible troubles that she can't see past the immediate *now*."

Gracie moved closer, placing her hand on his denim-shirted arm. "Well put, Uncle Miltie, an excellent analogy. Being so busy with all her fretting, she has trouble seeing those many kernels of blessings all around her."

Her pumpkin-colored cat, Gooseberry, came strolling across the yard to rub against her leg, leading Gracie to pet him and tell him again what a fine specimen of feline grace and friendship he was.

Turning back toward her house, she declared she'd better get inside and start preparing for her Sunday school lesson. Normally she started that at the beginning of a week, yet here it was, Thursday already, and she didn't even know what the Scripture was, let alone what part of the text should be emphasized!

Gooseberry followed slowly—but knew to be quick enough so that, tail curved up over his back, he could slither through the opening just as the door was closing. Heading for his food bowl, he checked to see if Grace might have placed some special tidbit there, then padded over to where she was sitting at the kitchen table. With an effortless leap he was on the chair next to hers, and, after turning three times, curled up and went to sleep.

He gave no sign of being aware of it when Marge Lawrence, Gracie's best friend, crossed their adjoining yards, looked through the screen door and, seeing Gracie at the table, walked in. "Can you spare a few minutes?"

"Of course!" She pushed back her chair and, having kicked off her shoes, walked barefoot to turn on the heat beneath the shiny copper teapot. "How do you happen to be free this morning?"

"One of the blessings of owning my own business." She gave a satisfied chuckle as she fiddled with the jacket of an outfit Gracie hadn't seen before. "Things are sorta slow today, and I was caught up with all the paperwork, so I told Nan I was leaving for a while."

"Great!" Gracie set mugs and small plates on the table before taking pink depression-glass plates from the cupboard and placing cookies on one of them.

"Ummmm. Your famous ginger cookies!" Marge reached out her perfectly manicured hand for one of the delicacies.

"Grandma's recipe—Uncle Miltie's mother's. I've always liked them, and *he* practically inhales them."

"Probably brings back a host of memories for him."

"For me, as well." Gracie nodded. "I didn't get around to making these very often after Arlen left for college, then took that job in New York." She wished that her son and his family would get home more often. "Then, after Elmo died, there seemed little reason to make them—until Uncle Miltie came to live with me."

The teakettle was giving its familiar little hum signaling that the water was ready, so she brought her assortment of tea bags in the ironstone sugar bowl. Marge checked them all before choosing the green-tea-with-mango she'd looked at first.

Gracie still preferred plain orange pekoe. She opened one of these packets and waited for her friend to let her know if there was some special reason for this visit. She could only hope, after Barb's agitated call, that it would have nothing to do with the competition coming up in just three more days. Marge was a second soprano which, in their choir, meant she'd sometimes sing with the sopranos and sometimes with the altos; she, also, had been present for last night's rehearsal.

Instead, they discussed instead the beauty of the season, commenting on several church members who were in the hospital or recuperating at home, and praising Uncle Miltie's care of Gracie's flowers and the advice he'd given Marge about hers.

It was only as she was getting ready to leave, after a second cup of tea and sixth cookie, that Marge mentioned choir practice. "Personally, I thought things went fairly well. Sure, it would have been better if Amy could have sung with us—but I appreciate the fact that she even *came*, which was more than most of us would have done with such a sore throat."

She straightened the little jacket as she got to her feet and headed for the door. ". . . Especially since she already knows by heart all the lead-in's and stuff."

"Yes, she does. And I encouraged her to not strain her voice; we can't have her unable to sing with us on Sunday."

"Yeah. Let's keep praying that her laryngitis will be completely gone by then. . . ."

Gracie was putting away her books when Uncle Miltie came in the back door and laid three perfect long-stemmed roses on the table. She picked up a deep, almost-maroon one to hold close to her nose. "Want me to get a vase for these?"

"No, I'll find something." He returned from the pantry with a tall glass vase and went to fill it at the kitchen sink before bringing it to the table and inserting the blooms. It was amazing how well he managed with his wheel-fronted walker.

She cocked her head thoughtfully. "Would you mind if I were to give these away? I'd planned to go see Joe and Anna Searfoss this afternoon. . . ."

"We've got lots more, just as pretty, still on the bushes out there," he said. Then he started back to the small, off-the-kitchen room. "I'm getting something else to take them in—so they needn't worry about sending this back."

For lunch, she made up twice as much tuna salad as they'd eat. The extra would go into her basket, along with the flowers and some cookies. She was pleased when, at the last moment, he decided to join her. It had been two years since her uncle had come from Ohio to Willow Bend, Indiana, with the understanding that he'd stay only through the winter. Thus, at first, he'd made no effort to put down roots.

Aunt Doris, his wife of fifty-six years, had recently died, and he was insisting he *would* not "butt in on his kids." But his osteoarthritis had become worse and he was having enough trouble getting around that he seriously considered selling his home and entering a senior-citizen complex.

That's when Gracie, inviting him to visit for several months, put the bed and dresser in what had been Elmo's office, off the living room. This arrangement had worked out very well, since the downstairs bathroom was the one with the walk-in shower.

His physical condition, however, began to improve, and each year saw him participating more and more in the life of the community and of the church. He even volunteered to read to kids in the local library, and sometimes drove for the Meals on Wheels deliveries, with Gracie or one of his friends doing the actual carrying-in of the food.

As they pulled away in her trusty ten-year-old Cadillac—affectionately known as Fannie May—on their way to visit their friends, Gracie took in her two-story clapboard house with the huge rhododendron bushes in the front. She couldn't help admiring the flower beds that lay not only close to the house and garage but also along the post-and-rail fences bordering both streets.

With the exception of the years he spent overseas during World War II, Joe Searfoss had been on one or another board ever since the Eternal Hope Community Church was founded in 1945—on the very day that the war ended! Anna, too, had served in many capacities, though she'd gradually relinquished responsibilities as her sight became more limited, and her over-forty-years' battle with diabetes continued to give her constant pain, due to nerve damage.

They weren't always able to go to church, so Gracie was pleased to hear Anna say, "I'm looking forward to being there for the contest on Sunday. I think our choir has a good chance to win, don't you?"

"We're doing our best, Anna. You may have heard that Amy's got laryngitis, but we're hoping she'll be in full voice by then."

"Isn't she a sweet little thing?" The older woman's voice and face revealed her affection for the young singer. "I look forward to her solos, and often make out her voice when you sing those anthems.

"And isn't it nice that Sunday's choir-meet will be held in Waxmire Tabernacle?"

Gracie herself had been concerned that the host church would be given an advantage. She hesitated just long enough for Anna to explain, "It's not only handicap-accessible, but its pews are farther apart, so it's easier to get in with a walker—not like in our over-a-hundred-year-old structure we took over when the Presbyterians moved to their new one."

Uncle Miltie agreed. "That narrow spacing bothered me, too, at first. I finally learned how to go in sideways without tripping myself—or incapacitating someone else."

"I'm spoiled, you see." Anna smiled. "I guess I should use my walker more at home, so I'd get more used to it—but I know where everything is, and I'm usually in reach of counters, or doorways, or furniture. . . ."

"Hey, I wouldn't use *mine* if I didn't need to," Uncle Miltie reassured her. "I can stand for a while, like when pruning bushes or something, but I keep my security blanket nearby—my walker's always ready to get around with."

They talked about the eight area choirs that had signed on—especially Eternal Hope's, much smaller than the one from Waxmire, yet larger than several of the others. There was a crooked grin on Joe's face when he commented, "Way back in high school, the actual dress rehearsal for any production, whether a skit or band concert or drama, always seemed to show us at our very worst despite however many weeks or months we'd worked on it.

"None of us ever actually wanted to believe the old theater adage about the worse the final practice, the better the opening-night would be—but you know what? It *did* seem to hold true."

"Then we've nothing at all to worry about, Joe. We're a shoo-in!" Gracie sagged down in feigned relief as the others laughed. "I'm gonna hold on to that—but, in the meantime, I'll feel better if we can work in just one more rehearsal, perhaps tomorrow evening. . . ."

With that thought uppermost in her mind, she took her uncle home before going on to stop at a small, cream-colored, aluminum-sided house near the end of Main Street. There she found Barb even more upset, if possible, and convinced that their choir was going to "bomb."

"Uncle Miltie and I stopped at Joe and Anna's a little while ago," Gracie told her, "and Joe reminded us of the old adage about 'good rehearsal, poor production. Poor rehearsal, *good* show.' "

"If only that were true—but it's *not*, and you know it!" The other woman was distraught. "We should just drop out."

Gracie, having expected Barb's pessimism, now made a counterproposal, "Or what would you think of calling one more rehearsal?"

"It's a waste of time, Gracie, *that's* what I think!" She ran her hand back through her already tousled salt-and-pepper hair. "You were there—you know we had all kinds of problems. And some of the music is just too convoluted, especially that required one, *Hallelujah, Save Us, Lord*. I'm already kept much too busy to work in any more special directing for the contest."

She frowned. "Besides, some of our members still have no sense of counting out the beat, or where to come in when the accompaniment's different from their notes. . . ."

Gracie couldn't deny any of that, but still: "Maybe if we went over it a couple more times—not necessarily the whole thing, you know, just working on problem areas . . . ?"

"Oh, Gracie!" Barb sighed very slowly and deliberately. "Honestly, I wouldn't even know where to begin."

"But—the thing is, it's already in the paper—Rocky gave us such wonderful coverage, far more than he had to—even sending the photographer to take those pictures of each of the choirs. I—I'd really hate not to follow through." Rocky Gravino was more than just *The Mason County Gazette's* editor-in-chief, he was a cherished friend of Gracie's, someone she could turn to with problems—and with whom she could also share joys.

"But. . . ."

She had to be firm with Barb. "Remember that the name of our church is already on the printed program—and we're in the sixth position, which, in fact, I think is a good place to be. . . ."

"It's—too much pressure, Gracie. I can't *handle* this—I really can't!" That was getting closer to the truth.

"Would you consider it if I were to assist with the directing?" How had that slipped out? Gracie had had no intention of making such an offer, but now it was too late to wonder about the wisdom of getting so involved.

"Wel-l-l, that *might* help. . . ."

Barb had started to look somewhat more cheerful, and Gracie decided that a bit of flattery still might be advisable. "I'd be starting at square one—I'd need an *awful* lot of help. . . ."

Barb crossed the room to bring two pieces of music from her baby grand. "I've been trying and trying to make it simpler to get them started at the exact moment, but nothing so far has worked consistently."

"So how about sitting here on the sofa with me, and we'll see if we can maybe figure out some way to get them coming in together better."

It wasn't an easy task—but Gracie hadn't expected it to be. They began with the song each choir was required to sing, the one with which Eternal Hope's choir had experienced trouble right from the start.

She asked to see the rules for the contest, and checked them carefully. "Well, it appears to be the same as for other years, doesn't it? The choir's size is immaterial, and the words and melody of any music must be retained. But just about anything else—rhythm, beat, use of solo or duet or multi-part sections, can be altered. . . ."

She struggled to keep the smile from her face as she again read the hymn's name: *Hallelujah, Save Us, Lord*. Rick Harding had earned a glare from Barb when he suggested wryly at the last practice, "There can't be a more apt request, considering what we're doing to this music tonight!"

She couldn't now risk making such a joke but, treating Barb as her mentor, asked questions and tried to be constructive when it came to putting advice into practice. She was also grateful that their headstrong organist didn't seem to be feeling threatened, for after working on the first selection to their satisfaction, Barb suggested that Gracie also be the one to lead their "anthem-of-choice."

The decision-making for this piece had been difficult, as they hadn't wanted something too simple or too familiar, like a variation on *Amazing Grace*—nor did they want a piece no one would recognize or enjoy. They finally settled upon one Marge suggested, saying she'd heard *Help Me to See Thee, Lord* sung as a solo while visiting her elderly mother the year before.

"I especially like the words and the *feel* of this one," Barb remarked now.

"Me, too. It's not *deep* or anything, but it's good to be reminded that no matter what happens, God still loves us. Even when things don't go the way we think is best, He's there—though we sometimes have to make a conscious effort to look for Him."

"I confess this has been one of those times when I sure haven't been feeling His presence." Barb shifted position. "I guess I should have been working harder at *seeing* God in all of this."

Up until now, almost all of it had been sung in four-part harmony, but today they played around with various possibilities for different portions. Perhaps the men alone there in the middle section, with several brief duets and solos? The women could then take care of the part immediately prior to the closing, when everyone would sing softly, repeating the title words twice. Then Amy would take it one more time, alone.

They began calling the choir members, Gracie using her cell phone to speed the process. They'd anticipated groans from one and all at the thought of scheduling an emergency, unexpected rehearsal tomorrow night, Friday, at 7:00. However, after the very first call, they obligingly changed the time to 5:30, since Amy told them about a 7:30 program at the high school to which several choir members, including herself, would be going.

"That should be fine," Gracie assured her. "And I'll tell you what, I'll bring meat, cheese, and bread for sandwiches, and two kinds of soup for anyone getting there by 5 o'clock or a little later. If we've already started rehearsing before some arrive, they can eat after practice."

Almost unbelievably, every single choir member told them he or she could be there for all or most of the practice! "Talk about the Lord providing!" Gracie exclaimed, tucking her handy little phone back in her pocket and heading for the door.

She started for home, but then, changing her mind, she pulled up instead in front of the *Gazette* office. Going inside, she could see Rocky busily working at his big desk, which took up almost a third of the glassed-in area. However, in order to make her way back there, she first had to stop and exchange greetings with several other friends on the staff, and by then he'd seen her.

"Welcome!" He came around the desk to hold both of her hands in his for a moment before seating her in one of the two straight chairs. He took the other, instead of going back to his own. "To what do I owe the pleasure of this visit?"

She gave a pretend-frown. "Can't I just drop in to say *hello*?"

"Any time you choose, Gracie. You know you're always welcome." He gave her a slow, warm smile. "Unfortunately, you don't take advantage of that opportunity very often. Ergo, I suspect you have something on your mind."

"Transparent as a fresh-cleaned window, that's what I am."

"And I like freshly cleaned windows, even though," indicating the big ones between him and the rest of the staff, "some make my life an open book."

"In a town the size of Willow Bend, *most* people's lives seem to be that way."

"True. Very true," he agreed. "But I suspect you came for a totally different reason other than discussing glass and gossip. Is everything okay with you?"

"I—hope so. I guess I'm not too bright, however, or I wouldn't have volunteered this morning to take over for Barb at the competition on Sunday."

"So they're sending in the relief pitcher," he teased. "I'll look forward to that."

"Just so you—and others—aren't disappointed." She was beginning to wish she had not made that impulsive offer.

Rocky was about her age, but stockier, and four or five inches taller than her five-four. "Knowing you, Gracie, I have no doubts that you'll do your very best, and so will everyone else." He shrugged. "So how could I be disappointed?"

"Thanks, Rocky. That's what I needed to hear today—some sane person encouraging us just to do the best we can."

"Sounds like you've been having a rough time."

"Well, we haven't done an especially good job on one number all along—and did even worse on both of them at last night's practice. Barb even got upset enough to try to convince some of us that the wisest course was to walk away from Sunday's contest. You know how she is, but somehow that didn't seem like the right thing to do."

"So—I'm assuming that's when you made your generous offer." He lifted his eyebrow quizzically.

"It was obviously a moment of insanity."

They laughed together, but she pretended to take offense. "I don't expect us to do *that* poorly."

"I don't expect you to do poorly at all—and you know it Plus, you know that wasn't why I was laughing."

They'd been friends for years, ever since he arrived from Philadelphia to take over this eighty-year-old paper. Elmo had met him when he'd been just considering the purchase, and Rocky often reminded her that his first meal in Indiana had been eaten in their home.

It felt good to sit here, talking comfortably. However, before long she was obliged to say, "I must get home—and you need to be freed so you can do your writing and editing and assigning and whatever else you do."

She was already at the door when she turned to ask, "You're coming to hear us Sunday? To hear all of us?"

"I wouldn't miss it. And I'm bringing Ben Tomlinson, our ace shutterbug, to capture what I hope will be a special triumph!" He had walked to the door with her. "I'm going to be rooting for you, my friend."

"Is an editor allowed to be partial to one choir over another?"

"I *am* human, dear girl, even though you may not have noticed. And there could be no rules as to my having feelings and interests, so yes, I may root for my friends."

"I'm glad." A glance out into the editorial department made her realize that some of the employees had been watching. "There are people wondering what's going on in here."

"So be it."

"Thanks for letting me steal your time, Rocky. I'm supposed to be such a great *coper*, but I'm not always. So I came to see you, someone not directly related to the choir, to make me think about other things, and yet I was the one to bring up the topic! Ah, the inconsistencies of being a woman."

His hand rested for the briefest of moments against the small of her back. "Ah, the inconsistencies of being a member of the human race. . . ."

Two

GRACIE WENT OUT for her usual brisk walk the next morning, Gooseberry accompanying her. But she didn't talk to him much, as she often did when using him as her sounding board, for she had a book-on-tape she'd borrowed from the library. It wasn't that she was bored, for she loved nature any time of the year, but sometimes she just felt like doing things a bit differently.

Her niece, Carter Stephens, had recommended this book to her. "You'll love it, Aunt Gracie. It takes place in a town remarkably similar to Willow Bend—it even has as many zany characters per block!"

"Zany characters?" Gracie repeated in mock dismay. "You think we have zany characters?"

Carter laughed. "How could I ever have entertained such a thought?"

"Present company excluded?"

Her eyes were sparkling. "But of course. How could you possibly think otherwise . . . ?"

Gracie adored her niece, but with her working as hard as she did in Chicago, Carter didn't get to visit very often. She reminded Gracie that it was equally distant in whichever direction one traveled, and made clear that she'd love to take her aunt around the city, to the museum and the zoo and whatever else suited her fancy.

But Gracie seldom drove up there anymore, for it wasn't the same without Elmo. When he was still living they'd make it a special weekend or more, going to the Pump Room for their wedding anniversary or getting tickets for a concert or a play.

21

Maybe she *should* go, however—perhaps for Christmas. But that was an almost-*less*-than-fleeting thought, for Christmas was one of the busiest seasons in the church and community. And since Uncle Miltie had been with her, there was someone else to consider. Not to mention Gooseberry.

Where *was* that cat? He could disappear faster than. . . . Oh, there he was, crouched down in checkmate-position in front of a big German shepherd. The dog was straining on its leash, nose less than a foot from Gooseberry's, apparently having no idea what a force he'd have to reckon with should the cat decide to slash out with its long, sharp claws.

Gracie hurried toward the face-off. A slender young woman—a girl, actually, maybe sixteen years old—was tugging with all her might and yelling for the dog to back off. He, however, employing canine selective-hearing, chose to ignore the panicky human voice.

"Come on, Gooseberry," Gracie urged soothingly. "Let's go back home."

He kept his eyes on the dog, making no move to obey—which she had to admit was wise under the circumstances. "Make sure you hold your dog," Gracie told the girl as she reached down, placed her hands around the cat's muscular body and picked him up. As Gooseberry hissed his contempt of the other animal, the dog's attempted leap ended in his crashing back down on the sidewalk, then scrambling back to his feet, yelping the entire time.

"I'm very sorry," the girl apologized, now with tight hold of the collar. "I'm supposed to be dog-sitting for the Berkmeyers this weekend, and they told me to take Fritz for walks—that he listens well. . . !"

"This is the first time you've tried it?" Gracie was still holding Gooseberry in her arms. "They may think he does obey, whereas it's only the *master's* voice he recognizes as an authority—it's only the master he obeys."

"I assumed when they said he listens, that he *would*."

"Well, no harm was done."

"And there won't be any, either," she stated firmly. "Once I get him back in his run, he's staying there!"

They walked together until the dog and his sitter turned off on their side street. Gracie then finished her three-mile circuit, trying harder now to keep Gooseberry in sight at all times.

She wasn't listening to the tape anymore, however, too busy

thinking of what she'd just said to the girl. *Help me, too, Lord, to listen to Your voice, my Master's voice. Sometimes I don't seem to recognize it as well as I should.*

One good thing about preparing to eat at her own church tonight was that she could use the plates and silverware already there, rather than buying disposable items. As spur-of-the-moment as it was, this rehearsal still counted, to Gracie, as a church function!

She'd checked her supply of vegetables when getting the large chuck roast from the chest freezer and had put the meat in the slow-cooker before she and Gooseberry went for their walk. It was safe to leave that simmering until mid-afternoon, when she'd cut up the meat, removing all fat or gristle. And since she had a good supply of fresh carrots, potatoes, and onions, these vegetable-soup makings could be thrown together later.

Gracie also prepared chili, using ground turkey instead of hamburger, as several choir members were currently shunning red meat. Since she was using dried kidney beans, it would take very slow cooking in order to blend the full flavor of the seasonings with all the other ingredients. So that, too, she prepared before lunch.

It seemed that everything she did wound up being interrupted by phone calls. Sometimes this could be annoying, yet she realized that many people, particularly older ones, were lonely and felt the need to make contact with someone. She told herself she should feel grateful to be able to help in this way—but sometimes that was hard, when she was aware of how much she had to get done.

One call was from Anna Searfoss, telling how much they'd enjoyed the food Gracie had brought. "And it was so good to talk with you! Joe and I realize how busy you are, Gracie, and I know I shouldn't be bothering you, but it's just not that easy for me to talk with people now that I can't see their faces—to know how they're reacting to whatever I'm saying."

"That—would be a problem." Gracie tried to imagine just how different that would be, how difficult.

"Well, at least it's not too bad at church, anymore. People there understand how bad my vision is—but at a store, or elsewhere, they often just back away, as though blindness is catching, or something."

"Maybe they're just trying to make it easier for you, Anna. Just trying to get out of your way."

"Oh, yes, for *some* that could be the case, but not for most." She then gave what sounded like a little chuckle. Yet Gracie recognized it wasn't entirely humor she was expressing when adding, "And many talk louder, as though if I don't see well, I probably don't *hear* well, either. . . ."

Later in the afternoon, shortly before she left for church with the food, the voice she heard on the other end when she picked up the phone sounded very young. "Hi, Miss Gracie. This is Patsy. I just wondered how Gooseberry's doing?"

Ah, Patsy Clayton, from Vacation Bible School last June. "Hello, Patsy. Gooseberry's doing very well, thank you, and he and I want to know how *you* are."

"Pretty good—now. The doctor operated on my leg again, and it doesn't hurt so much as it did."

"Is there a cast on it?"

"Um-hmmm, but the doctor says he's going to take it off next week if everything's okay."

"Are you using crutches?"

"Sometimes. Mostly my walker. And Mrs. Johnson comes to my house two times each week, so I'm keeping up at school even if I can't go to classes. But I'll sure be glad to get back again after Thanksgiving. . . ."

"I'm sure you will, Patsy." This child, a gentle fourth-grader, had never called before, and Gracie couldn't help wondering what had led up to it now.

"You and Gooseberry went past my house today, but you were going so fast I couldn't get to the door to call to you. I thought maybe if—well it would be nice if you could stop sometime. I'd like to pet your cat again."

She'd almost forgotten having taken Gooseberry to Vacation Bible School one day. Patsy had been very quiet, almost unresponsive during the first session, but had immediately bonded with the cat, holding him on her lap and stroking him and telling him how wonderful he was. "I'm not sure where you live, Patsy."

"Right next to Amy. She's on the corner, and I'm right next to her house. That's how I went to your church for Vacation Bible School—she brought me."

"That's nice, dear. And does Amy bring you to Sunday school, too?" If so, Gracie hadn't seen her.

"No, but she asked me. Maybe after the cast comes off."

"I'll look for you there, dear." She glanced up at the clock. Now she'd really have to hurry to get to the church in time to get everything done. She closed the conversation with, "Gooseberry and I will stop at your house soon, I promise."

Unexpectedly, it was times like this that Uncle Miltie sometimes chose to feel sorry for himself. "If only I could help you carry out all that food!" he grumbled. "It's *awful* that you have to make trip after trip to the car, while I sit here like a lump!"

"You're a lovable lump," she teased lightheartedly. "And I'm glad you're here."

He tried to ignore that with, "I came to spend one winter, as you remember—and look at me! Talk about overstaying one's welcome!"

She was crossing the kitchen with the large electric slow-cooker filled with hot vegetable soup. "If *you* aren't happy with the arrangement, Uncle Miltie, all you have to do is say so. As for me, you continue to be a blessing." And she went out, letting the screen door bang shut behind her for emphasis.

She'd left a container of chili for his supper and would have put out an entire meal had she not been so sensitive to his determination to "be no more trouble than absolutely necessary." She wondered what had put him in that mood this time, though she realized from experience it would soon pass.

She could appreciate how difficult it had to be for such a previously active person to be unable to do all those things he'd formerly done, and suspected she'd be worse than Uncle Miltie should she be restricted that much.

He had been a successful builder who could do just about anything from masonry to roofing, from drywalls to driveways. And now, even with his walker, he'd quietly made many repairs to her house and garage, many of them things she'd not even recognized as needing attention.

Even more important was just having him here. After being married to and living with her beloved Elmo all those years, her home had become incredibly quiet, unbelievably *empty* with just her and Gooseberry in it.

She was the first to arrive, as she'd hoped to be. Of course it would have been nice to have someone there to help carry, but she was used to it. First, she took in the cold sandwich and salad makings, then the hot soups and, after that, everything else. Gracie had always enjoyed cooking, and during these last years had been called upon more and more to cater luncheons, dinners, brunches, and picnics.

She didn't have to, though, because even if she wasn't wealthy, Elmo had enough insurance, in addition to stocks and bonds, to let her live comfortably. But she *liked* preparing meals and planning parties.

She'd certainly had enough practice behind the scenes here at the church, for festive occasions, and at all of Arlen's Boy Scout meetings, church camps and school activities she used to be so involved with!

Back in the early sixties, when their church bought this aging wooden building, there had been only the big sanctuary, a small chapel room and bathroom, plus the space beneath it. This consisted of a small kitchen and furnace room, and a large room split into classrooms by homemade dividers, which could be rolled back against the wall for dinners or wedding receptions or meals following a funeral.

But when the huge addition was added about thirty years ago, they finally gained adequate classrooms on both floors, as well as the large Family Activity Center. *This* time the women, the ones who'd be using it the most, got in on the planning and design of the first-floor kitchen. What a blessing that was, and how Gracie appreciated it! Although it wasn't terribly large, everything was now so well organized that it was a joy to work in.

Gracie was grateful that they'd retained the old flow-green glass in the sanctuary windows, which contrasted beautifully with the white vinyl siding that unified the old and new portions of the building.

Used to working alone, she buzzed around getting the jugs of cider in the refrigerator, the coffee perking, hot water ready for tea, and everything laid out and ready by the time the first singers arrived. It took only minutes for them to move three long tables end-to-end and get chairs in place so that as others arrived they could dish up their soup, make a sandwich, and find a seat.

Gracie was amazed and grateful that even Barb seemed in good spirits, and that there was so much relaxed joking and having fun. Amy arrived too late to eat before practice, but her voice seemed much better. Both Gracie and Barb, having every reason to believe she'd do her usual good job on Sunday, cautioned her not to strain for those very high notes tonight.

They gave a three-minute-warning just before 5:30. After this, the choir entered the sanctuary, with latecomers knowing they could eat afterward. Gracie wanted all sixteen of them first to get in the order in which they'd be singing on Sunday afternoon. Having checked and found there'd be three levels of wide risers placed on Waxmire's platform, she had them practice the procession so everything would go smoothly. By the third try, everyone successfully crossed the platform to end up in proper configuration.

For the sake of the few later in arriving, Barb explained again that Gracie would be taking over the directing for tonight and on Sunday, as well. There were a few raised eyebrows but no negative comments— after all, she'd led them for several cantatas and when Barb was on vacation, and they knew her capabilities.

They began with the required number, the *Hallelujah* one, but this time—with Gracie stressing that she and Barb had together made the changes—several of the most difficult passages for the entire choir were marked for solos and two-part harmony.

Don Delano, the thirty-year-old chemistry teacher, one of their baritones, asked if that meant they were still observing the rules. "We won't be disqualified or penalized if we do this, will we?"

Barb was the one to reassure him, "We've gone over everything, and there's nothing in the information we received that says we can't make these changes."

Estelle Livett, overly conscious of being the only member of this choir who'd ever studied under a *real* singing teacher (albeit twenty-some years previously) now volunteered to take Amy's place in the solo—because of the girl's laryngitis, of course, to help save her voice.

Gracie glanced at Amy to see her reaction, and found the teenager was smiling. "I appreciate your offering, Estelle," Amy told her, "but I really think I'll be okay."

Realizing that all of them were aware that Estelle's "operatic" tones and pretentious manner would do nothing to help them win, Gracie courteously thanked her for making the offer. She managed to get through the difficult moment by saying they'd have to wait to see how Amy got along before making additional changes—and struggled to keep a straight face when Marybeth Bower, another soprano, winked at her.

Don and Amy were asked to take the first short duet, about a third of the way through the number. Rick Harding, the only African American in the choir—although there were two other black families in the congregation besides him, his wife, and two-year-old daughter—was given the eleven-bar tenor solo near the middle. Amy then would begin the one near the end, with Rick joining her.

As the practice got underway at last, first with just the chosen ones going over their parts and then the whole choir running through *Hallelujah, Save Us, Lord* from beginning to end, Gracie felt relief. Not unexpectedly, there were some rough sections, but everyone worked at going back over the difficult bits again. After singing through it one final time in its entirety, they all agreed it was excellent.

And then it was time to start their second number, the one everyone liked best, *Help Us to See Thee, Lord*. Here, too, modifications were made and several solo and duet parts given out. They started out very well:

> "I know that You are with me,
> I know You really care,
> But sometimes it is hard, God,
> To feel You with me there.

> "When days and nights are dreary,
> Or. . . ."

As their voices joined together, with Amy well into her solo part, suddenly, unaccountably, she went *way* off pitch!

The sound of it was so unusual that Gracie stared in amazement. She became even more concerned when she realized the girl was standing there with her hand pressed to her head, a look of distress, then fear, taking over her expression. Gracie dropped her music and raced up the steps. Amy's eyes had rolled upward unseeingly and her knees seemed unable to support her as she started to crumple downward. "Grab her, Rick! Amy's falling!"

Don helped Rick ease her down upon the maroon carpet. Murmurs of alarm rose agitatedly around her. What happened? What's wrong? Is she going to be all right?

But, at that tense moment, answers were in short supply.

Gracie handed Don her cell phone with, "Call 911!" and was down on her knees on one side of the unconscious Amy, prepared to help Rick, a volunteer EMT with the Willow Bend Volunteer Fire Company. "I've taken Red Cross courses, Rick, but never had to use them. Tell me what to do, and I'll try my best."

She was dimly aware of Pastor Paul Meyer arriving and of hearing someone filling him in about what happened, but she was much too busy even to look around. It seemed forever before the ambulance got there, and only then was Gracie able to get to her feet, letting a better-trained professional take over.

Suddenly she realized she herself was shaking and Marge was putting her arms around her, while Lester Twomley, one of the tenors, had come over to help lead her to the front pew. "Lean forward," he urged. "Put your head down."

She was suddenly thoroughly annoyed with herself. How could she, Gracie, be acting like some stupid little Victorian female who collapsed at the least upset? "I'm fine," she assured them, sitting bolt upright. "I've never fainted in my life, and I'm not about to!"

"Glad to hear that, Gracie." Lester was smiling down at her. "You took over like a pro when you were needed, and I'm proud of you."

"Hmmph!" She wasn't so proud of herself right then, and forced herself to get up on her feet. She wasn't too prideful, however, to murmur, "Thanks, Don," as his arm went around her waist, and they walked over to where Amy was being lifted onto the gurney to be wheeled to the ambulance.

Rick left with them, so someone familiar might be with her on the way to the hospital. Looking around, Paul suggested, "How about you folks going on with your practice? I'm following the ambulance to Keefer Memorial—and will start the prayer chain as soon as I get there."

"You'll call us, too, won't you?"

"Of course, Gracie." He patted her shoulder. "Just as soon as I learn anything."

He was going out the door when she called after him, "Are you going to notify Amy's parents, or should I?"

"I'd appreciate your taking care of that. They'll have questions, of course, and I just got here."

She nodded and, taking the cell phone from her pocket, made the call. It was awkward not being able to tell Linda and Roy any more than that Amy had had some sort of attack or seizure and passed out. Yes, the ambulance was on its way to Keefer.

29

She also told them who was manning the ambulance and that Pastor Meyer had followed it and would soon be starting the prayer chain.

Hanging up, she informed the anxious choir members that Amy's parents were leaving immediately for the hospital. "And before we start singing again, I think we should pray for Amy and her family and all those working with her. . . ."

They made a circle, holding hands as they prayed, then went back to their *Help Me . . .* anthem. It seemed to go well, especially considering the frightening interruption, and Gracie even made a few additional changes. Always in the back of her mind was the need for constant attention to each individual voice, especially the tenors.

She already knew that Rick had a remarkably wide range, but Lester and Don did beautifully this time, also, so she asked them to please stay after the others were excused. Should Amy not be able to sing with them Sunday, which seemed likely, she explained that Lester would have to be ready to take her place in the required numbers, while Don and Rick would handle that part for *Help Me to See Thee, Lord.*

They went over these sections several more times, and through the entire program twice before making arrangements to come early on Sunday morning to practice both anthems in their entirety.

Still having heard nothing from the hospital, Gracie remembered to call Uncle Miltie to tell him not to worry if she got home very late since she wanted to stop and check on Amy's condition and talk to her parents.

Having learned that Amy was in the Intensive Care Unit, Gracie went directly to the ICU waiting room. Putting her arms around Linda Cantrell, who was sitting on the three-cushioned couch, crying, she learned that the parents and pastor had heard nothing more than that Amy was considered to be in critical condition.

Was there any way to make sense of it? Could it have been something she'd eaten? She'd been a little later than usual coming home from school, but had told her mother only that she'd been hanging out with friends. No, she'd not mentioned them by name.

She'd then sat at the kitchen table, as she often did, to finish her calculus assignment, but refused a cookie or an apple, which she'd normally have eaten while doing this. Linda said she *should* eat something, but Amy told her she'd wait until getting to the church. She did, however, have a diet soda—which led to her father's comment that she certainly didn't have to watch her weight, as thin as she was!

Amy had mentioned the possibility of meeting someone after practice, and maybe going to a movie. No, she hadn't said which friend that was, but her mother assumed it was Francine Barton, with whom she frequently went to youth activities at the church or for a pizza or to the mall.

This reminded Linda to call Francine to let her know what had happened. The girl was a bit hysterical at first, then informed Amy's mother that she intended to come to the hospital right away.

The teen was just entering the waiting room as Dr. Floyd Jennings came through the door from the Intensive Care Unit to talk with them. Amy was still unconscious. The test results weren't in, but her vital signs were improving. He also asked a number of questions, particularly as to what she'd eaten and drunk. Then he said it would be fine for her parents and the pastor to go in to see her for a few minutes.

Gracie used this opportunity to talk with Francine. "We're always together during our last class of the day," she was told, "and, though there are a couple of other students between us, we're in the same homeroom.

"But we didn't walk home together like we often do, my house being just a block before hers. Today Amy said she had to make a stop on the way home."

"Do you know what this stop was?"

Francine shook her head, frowning. "Come to think of it, maybe she said she had to meet someone. I'm not sure about that, but I *do* know she seemed okay, and was looking forward to the practice at the church and eating there."

"Can you remember anything else you talked about?"

"Well, some stuff about the all-day Youth Fellowship project eight days from now. We've volunteered to do interior painting at the new Habitat for Humanity house, since that's almost ready for the people to move in. And I asked if tonight's singing could hurt her throat—but Amy insisted it was already much better.

"She was really looking forward to singing this Sunday!"

No, there had been no mention of feeling ill or of any other problem. Amy had been very much herself—if anything, she was *more* cheerful and "up," probably because of the upcoming concert.

But Amy's not having mentioned the possibility of going to a movie following the rehearsal did seem strange to Francine, since they usually told each other everything.

The Cantrells were wiping their eyes when they returned to

report that their daughter hadn't responded to their presence. Pastor Paul, looking very serious, borrowed Gracie's phone to call the church to inform the chairman of their diaconate board to go ahead with the scheduled meeting, since he felt he should stay with the Cantrells at the hospital.

Amy's mother tried to release him with, "Really, Pastor, it's all right for you to leave. . . ."

Gracie had decided that she, too, should remain with Amy's parents. However, she did think to inquire if there was anything Paul had planned to bring to the meeting in addition to what was already on the agenda—or if he'd planned to handle any particular matters in a certain way. Learning that this was the case, she asked him to come out in the hall with her, where they discussed her attending as his emissary. After all, his presence was needed here more than hers was.

She was a little surprised when arriving at the church to find the meeting hardly begun. Instead, they had spent time in prayer for Amy and her family.

"And not only our own prayer chain has been activated, but that of the other four Willow Bend churches, which have chains like ours," Don told her. "So if you have anything additional to share about Amy's condition, we'll get that out, too."

She shook her head. "No, nothing more as of now. I just wish there were."

They finally got the business of the evening attended to, but it took longer than usual since the group kept speculating about possible causes for Amy's blackout, and also about her prognosis. Gracie confessed, "I've been going over what happened ever since I saw her start to fall. It was so *sudden*! So unexpected! It's true she had laryngitis several days ago, but this is—I don't know—something else altogether. It's . . . suspicious even."

Rick shook his head reprovingly. "Just because you read so many mystery books and enjoy watching mysteries on TV doesn't mean that someone in Willow Bend is capable of such a devious thing."

"Well, it was just a thought . . ."

"You're not Miss Marple, my dear Gracie. Nor do we have here Cabot Cove's requisite murder per week—not even an occasionally attempted one. Maybe before you start hunting for clues, you'd better first consider reading other things."

This was too much! Indignantly, she defended her taste in literature. "Look, Rick, a good mystery is refreshing; in what other genre can you routinely find right triumphing over wrong in today's world?"

She knew she shouldn't rise to the bait but, really, how could she keep from it? "No matter how rotten people can be, no matter what moral or ethical or spiritual rules are broken and seem to be gotten away with, by the end of most mystery novels the doers of evil get their comeuppance—they do get their just desserts."

All around her were fond grins, which she tried to ignore, but in a few more minutes they were all again deeply involved with the meeting, everyone apparently determined to stick to the agenda since they were running so late. Things from this point on went smoothly, and nearly all of the business was concluded when Paul phoned.

"Amy seems about the same to us, but the doctor and nurses seem certain she's *stabilized*."

Gracie, who'd taken the call, heard this news with gratitude. "Good! Maybe it was our prayers. Anyway, the meeting's nearly finished, so I'm planning to come back there. Is there anything I can bring—or do?"

"Thanks, Gracie, but I can't think of a thing we need. And, since I've decided to stay here with Roy and Linda for the rest of the night, there's no need for you to come."

"I'd be glad to, Paul—to relieve *you*, if for no other reason."

"Thanks for that, too, but you go home and get your rest. You may be needed even more in the morning."

"Oh?" She wasn't sure she liked the sound of that. "Why did you say that?"

"I'm—not sure, but the doctor's just been in again, this time asking questions about the possibility of Amy having been 'given something,' and that has her parents really upset. I'm hoping it turns out to be just some kind of a 'bug,' some virus or something, but at the moment, not knowing for certain just what they're dealing with, everyone's concerned."

"Yes," she said softly. "I'm sure they would be."

She didn't mention what their pastor had just told her, however, to the board members.

Gracie had been too tired to bother taking all of her leftovers home, but she did carry out the containers of soup. Now, returning to the peace of her own house, carried them into her kitchen. There wasn't enough refrigerator space for both, so she transferred the contents into smaller dishes. She'd divide them into portions-for-two packets tomorrow, and place them in the freezer.

Uncle Miltie was already in his room with the light out, so she tried to be quiet. Gooseberry, on the other hand, must have had enough sleep, and kept trying to lead her to the door for a walk or to his bowl to beg for a treat. "Sorry, Gooseberry, but I've had a big day and am not as spry as you right now," she told him, keeping her voice low. "Try me again in the morning, when we'll both be ready for a jaunt."

Three

A ND SHE WAS. It was another gloriously beautiful day, cool and crisp, but not cold—a perfect day for a four-mile power walk, with Gooseberry accompanying her. She often thought that her seven-year-old cat acted more like a puppy in some ways, going at least twice as far as his mistress by circling her, walking between her feet, and checking out cans sitting along the street awaiting the arrival of the garbage man.

He was fascinated by everything, scraps of paper, a styrofoam cup, a small sock—and, today, something in the shrubbery. He soon caught up with Gracie and laid a no-longer struggling, very dead gray mouse in front of her. With the toe of her shoe, she nudged it over to the inner edge of the sidewalk—then deliberately paid attention to other things as Gooseberry disposed of it.

One important advantage of coming out so early was that only the serious walkers were about, matching her obvious briskness. This made it easier to just wave or call a greeting to them and to those leaving for work, instead of having to chat.

Another benefit was that she was able to do some of her best thinking at this time—this morning's, not surprisingly, largely concerning the young choir member for whom she'd been praying.

To the best of her knowledge, everyone liked Amy—or at least, didn't *dis*like her. She was quiet, good-humored, and never pushy—or at least that's how she seemed to Gracie. She had to recognize, however, that a girl *could* be different at school or other places.

Amy recently had been helping in the Sunday school nursery, or so Gracie believed. She hadn't been checking on her, so she couldn't be positive. Could there be a clue there?

Amy's mother was the high school librarian, and had been ever since they came here, which must have been at least five or six years by now. Her dad was a manager with Ace Electronics, a high-tech company on the edge of town. Gracie had hardly spoken to Mr. Cantrell until last night—and felt she still didn't know much about him.

According to Pastor Paul, what had seemed to disturb him most was the physician's questions about the possibility of someone wishing her harm. *If* there had been intentional injury done to Amy, which still seemed most unlikely, when might it have taken place? At school? It couldn't have been accomplished at home or at church—could it?

But *supposing* it had been at church, who there might possibly have a motive? The only person who could conceivably have one would be Estelle—and Gracie was not about to even think of that! It was too ludicrous to imagine, even if she obviously longed to sing Amy's solo.

Estelle, after all, was a good woman. They'd known one another for years and Gracie couldn't think of any really "wrong" thing she'd ever done. (Of course, to any reader of mystery novels, that alone could qualify her as the prime suspect—but for the moment Gracie wasn't going to give that idea any room in her mind!)

Or, still considering what she kept reassuring herself was impossible—that the choir rehearsal was the scene of the crime—might whatever happened have been meant for someone else, with Amy *not* the intended victim?

It wasn't so easy following in the footsteps of Jessica Fletcher! Here she was, thinking of others who might have done something, but what were they thinking, in the meantime, about *her*? Remember, she told herself, it was you who prepared the soups in your own kitchen. And in the church she had not only fixed the beverages, but also laid out all the ingredients for sandwiches. Might she be considered as much a suspect as anyone else? Perhaps *more* so?

Or, what was much more bearable, perhaps there had been no foul play at all? Wasn't it possible that Amy simply had fallen victim to some peculiar, not to mention *rare* virus, like those that keep manifesting themselves suddenly and making headlines? One of these had been reported in their own paper not that long ago, so that's probably what it was.

It was a relief to come up with that thought—but only insofar as Amy was concerned. That would be the good news. The *bad* news was that, should that prove to be the case, there'd almost certainly be a number of others coming down with it, too.

Wouldn't it be incredible if this case should end up in the province of some national clearinghouse, like the CDC, the Center for Disease Control, which collects and disseminates such information so word can get out to physicians and hospitals?

She walked quickly back to her own street and saw a car parked in front of her house. As she got closer, she realized it was the pastor's, causing her to hurry even more, eager for news. Paul was in the kitchen with her uncle, who was just plunking down the big crockery cookie jar on the table after having gotten each of them a can of cola from the refrigerator.

"And we were so thirsty that our throats were like sandpaper. . . ." Uncle Miltie was sharing one of his World War II stories—which still surprised her. Until the last five or ten years he'd refused to talk about these memories, and still wouldn't get drawn into any discussion or description of his long stay in a prison camp.

This time he was going on about his experiences during the Battle of the Bulge, and Paul was listening respectfully.

But Gracie knew how tired their pastor must be, after staying at the hospital all night, and soon managed to interrupt. "Can I distract you long enough to offer French toast or omelets?" Paul declined, saying he'd be leaving in just a few minutes; he'd got no sleep, and was looking forward to dropping off for several hours before a scheduled interfaith luncheon.

He'd simply wanted to reassure Gracie with the report that Amy appeared to be somewhat better, though still not herself. "She seems confused," he reported. "To me, she even seems scared of something, but of *what* I just don't know."

As Gracie walked with him to his car, she tried out on him some of her recent thoughts, and he didn't make fun of her or tease her about amateur detecting. He even nodded and said he'd come up with similar explanations, himself. However, he didn't share any additional theories, which made her feel guilty, as though she'd been gossiping or something.

At least she hadn't mentioned the only person she'd thought of who might conceivably harbor a motive. Estelle truly could be difficult, and her feelings easily hurt, yet she could be almost saccharine-sweet at other times, especially when dealing with the younger singers. Like Amy.

Gracie tried to push this thought out of her mind, to erase any suspicion as to Estelle's jealousy trying to do away with solo or duet competition. She even felt her conscience pricked for not giving Estelle even one of those spots for Sunday.

But how could she? Every single person in the choir had been so generous with time and effort that it would hardly be fair to allow Estelle, with all her airs, extra opportunity to mess things up.

She hoped, of course, that the woman wouldn't drop out of the choir again, as she had two or three years ago when showing her displeasure at "being passed over again." It had taken a lot of effort then, especially on the part of Gracie and the thirty-five-year-old Turner twins, Tish and Tyne, to smooth her ruffled feathers.

Barb, in order to keep peace, had deliberately allowed her a few solo parts since then, and in July and August, when the choir as a whole was "off," Estelle had been asked to sing a solo each month. That opportunity would have been more rewarding had she not tried so hard to show off what she felt certain was her superior talent and ability. As it was, the smiles on the congregants' faces or behind their hands and bulletins seemed to sometimes be more of humor than appreciation.

Gracie drove Uncle Miltie to Barry's Barber Shop for a trim of his still-thick gray hair, and while he waited for his turn, she crossed the street to see what might still be warm from Abe Wasserman's ovens. She'd been hoping for a special coffee cake—but the cheesecake looked pretty tempting, as well.

As usual, she sat up at the counter while talking with Abe about many things: books they'd read recently, the price of cheese and other ingredients, the beauties of the season—and, of course, the emergency situation involving Amy Cantrell.

Abe had just removed crisply thin honey cookies from the oven and, walking around to sit, perched one stool away, so the plate of still-hot treats was within easy reach for both of them.

She'd remembered that Amy had occasionally worked part-time for Abe. "She's been a big help to me these past two summers, and sometimes on Saturdays, and I've come to care a lot for her," he said. "Like a sort of granddaughter to me," he told her, "sweet and lovely with a rosebud air—and just as easily crushed."

She waited for him to continue and, focusing past her left shoulder, toward the front door, he finally did. "I did notice in her something continually a little tense, a kind of low-level anxiety. I couldn't figure out the reason, though it was always there. And she has this—this *need* to be liked, to be loved—yet at the same time seems afraid to open herself to people."

He then looked directly into her eyes. "Why is this, Gracie? Do you have an explanation? Am I crazy?"

"Now that I think of it, I suppose I noticed it, too, but tried to tell myself I was imagining things. So I didn't pursue the matter, though perhaps I should have."

He nodded in agreement. "Why not now? Before it's too late."

Amy was only seventeen. Could someone be merely trying to scare her? To kill her? Or, could the problem stem from something within herself? Were Gracie and Abe worrying about nothing? Maybe, going back to the virus theory, there *was* no "problem" as such, and they were headed off the deep end, just two overprotective snoops.

Suddenly remembering that Uncle Miltie might be waiting for her across the street, Gracie smiled in amusement at the thought, and told Abe she had to go. He asked her to wait a few seconds and, going back around the counter, he took a paper from beneath the cash drawer, but held onto it saying, "You know, Gracie, Amy was always punctual. But during the last week of summer, just before school started, she was barely making it on time. And she seemed to be more nervous, more uptight or edgy than before.

"I tried talking to her—but got nowhere. Then I figured it might have something to do with her boyfriend, which would be none of my business, except that it *was* my business she was being late for."

"Oh? I never saw her with a boyfriend, certainly not at the Youth Fellowship or its group activities."

He nodded to show he'd heard, even if he had not responded directly. "Well, it wasn't actually a boy. I got a few glimpses of him, and he's dark-complexioned and of medium height and weight—and obviously older. He'd sometimes drop her off here, and also pick her up after work. He'd never come in, though, and when I told her I'd like to meet her friend, she got real flustered—and asked me not to say anything to anyone about him."

Gracie frowned. "I don't like the sound of that!"

"Me, neither. That's why, when she was ready to leave that Saturday, I sneaked out the side door to check him out—but all I could see was the fairly new, gray Ford. And *this*," laying the paper on the counter in front of her, "is the number on the license plate—a Florida license."

She reached across to remove the pen from his breast pocket, and copied the series of digits onto the corner of her napkin. Tearing it off, she then carefully placed the paper in her wallet and after asking a few more questions, said she must pick up Uncle Miltie.

However, suspecting that he was making the most of this time to try out some of his newer, but still awful jokes on his friends, Gracie hurried down a side street, intent on making another very important stop—at the police station—before getting him.

&

When she got back to the barbershop, her uncle was busy with one of his jokes: "A man asked his pastor if it was a sin to play golf on Sunday. The minister replied, 'Sir, the way you play golf, it's a sin every day!' " No one laughed more than her uncle.

She never actually told him that she'd gone nowhere but Abe's and didn't feel guilty when he presumed that. Anyway, the fact that she'd brought with her a dozen freshly baked honey-almond cookies helped take his attention from the time he'd waited.

She parked in her driveway and they went inside—and were almost relieved to find no messages had been left on the answering machine. Gracie considered calling the hospital but, not being a relative, feared she wouldn't be given any meaningful information about Amy's condition.

She also momentarily thought of calling Phyllis Nickolson, who was probably on the switchboard, for she seemed to know just about everything that went on at Keefer Memorial. She didn't, however, deciding instead just to drive on over to the hospital. It was likely she wouldn't be allowed in to see her young friend, but it might be harder for them to refuse her request if she just showed up there.

Everything would depend on which nurses were on duty.

She went back to where she'd parked Fannie Mae, wondering if she had subconsciously planned to go see Amy when pulling into the garage as she almost always did. She just loved this dark blue, shiny oversized vehicle that Elmo had bought for her right after some dear friends were killed in their small economy car.

"They didn't stand a chance against that pickup truck the drunk was driving," he'd insisted. "You're the most important person in my life, Gracie, and I want to keep you forever. . . ."

She'd had no idea that *her* "forever" of keeping him with her would be just five more years. And his death had happened in an accident, not with another person's vehicle, but on a deserted stretch of road only five miles from here.

To the best of her knowledge, he had never before fallen asleep when driving. Yet, coming back to her from Chicago at almost two in the morning, with an almost-full moon and that stretch of road in good shape, with nothing to obstruct his view as he came around that curve. . . .

Might it have made a difference had *he* been driving Fannie Mae? But she would not, could not let herself dwell on that.

She turned on the radio to the station featuring Golden Oldies and started to harmonize along with those songs she knew well, humming when she forgot some of the words. It didn't really matter if the selections were from the fifties or the sixties or seventies or even later.

Or earlier, for that matter: She liked almost all of them.

She was taking the long way to the hospital, along rural roads she and Elmo had often wandered. There were times like this when he still seemed so very near, so close that she could almost touch him, or at least talk with him.

Both of them had been strong willed, so there were of course some disagreements, even an occasional flare-up—but there had not been a single day after they first had met that she hadn't loved him.

They often went for drives, or for long walks together, and they had such big plans for their future, for his retirement—but all of these were based on the assumption that they would be doing things *together*, not having one of them left alone!

How I wish we could talk things over, El! This situation with Amy has me so upset, so worried. You were the one who could look at things from a dozen different perspectives while I was hung up on just one or two. How I need your wisdom now, dear.

You didn't know Amy and, anyway, she'd have been only twelve when you were killed. Come to think of it, I guess I didn't know her then, either, but have had the chance now to see her grow and develop, and I do care about her. . . .

She was almost there, going down the street on which the hospital stood. Gracie believed wholeheartedly in what she was doing, yet recognized that she was instinctively still looking for the right path to take. As she turned into the parking area, she sent up a silent heartfelt prayer for Amy—and also for herself, that she would say and do whatever was best for her young friend.

She couldn't, in fact, have asked for a better nurse to be on duty than Nancy Bixler, who had known Gracie all her life. "Amy doesn't seem to be in any pain, but just wants to lie there," Nancy told her. "Even sipping water or juice through a straw or from a glass is apparently just too much trouble, and she can't be persuaded to try to eat a bite. Not of *anything*."

"Would you let me talk to her?" Gracie asked. "I don't know if I can get through, but I'd sure welcome the opportunity. . . ."

There was only a moment's hesitation before the nurse opened the ICU door. "You might as well; you can't do worse than we have." But then, as they started inside, she added, "She did seem to perk up a little when her parents were with her for a few minutes. Perhaps seeing another familiar face will help."

Amy looked so young, pale, and vulnerable that Gracie ached for her. Turning to the nurse, she whispered that maybe they should just let her sleep—but at the mention of her name, Amy's blue eyes slowly opened and looked right at Gracie.

Gracie reached out and took her hand—she couldn't help herself. She sat on the thin blanket next to her and stroked her arm gently. She was sure she felt a momentary responsive squeeze before Amy's eyelids closed again. Gracie told herself it might have been an unplanned or unintended sequence, but suspecting it to have been a deliberate decision not to communicate, she sent up another quick, inaudible prayer for help.

She told Amy how sorry she was about what had happened, then talked about her parents and her pastor staying with her throughout the night.

None of this got any response so, remembering Amy's love of animals, she related some of the silly things Gooseberry had done recently, and how Gracie sometimes thought there must be a dog's soul inside of him. "After all, he follows me everywhere, and he loves dog biscuits—and tussles playfully with Charlotte, Marge's shih-tzu!"

That finally earned the shadow of a smile from the silent patient, just a small flicker of response, but enough to encourage Gracie to think of other Gooseberry-inspired anecdotes. She even admitted her own squeamishness at witnessing the ultimate end of that gray mouse this morning, confessing that she'd had to turn away!

Having allowed Gracie to chatter on, Amy finally made a comment of her own, and her hand again seemed to squeeze back. "I like

Gooseberry's coming right up to me. He rubs against my legs and lets me pet him."

Just at that moment Nancy came back in and tilted the top of the bed upward, something Gracie gathered had previously been protested. She understood that any cooperation they could get on Amy's part indicated improvement.

Gracie assumed that Nancy's arriving at that time was a reminder of her own promise to stay for only five minutes. Upon leaving, she still knew nothing more about what brought on the "attack" last night. She'd not even dared to bring that up directly, for leading questions, no matter how carefully worded, were difficult to frame so they didn't sound prying, had been ignored.

But at least she was now more confident about Amy's recovery. Their prayers seemed in the process of being answered, for Gracie sensed that Amy, deep with herself, was struggling to return to her previous state of mental and physical health.

Gracie closed the garage doors, and, as she walked back toward her house more slowly than usual, realized that Uncle Miltie had been out doing more pruning. She felt exhausted, and had even considered not stopping at the church to pick up the leftovers that had been left in the refrigerator there last night.

She normally enjoyed meal planning and preparation, whether it was a simple snack for herself, a dinner for Uncle Miltie and herself, a Sunday supper for friends, or a Thanksgiving banquet. But right now it was good to just re-heat some of the vegetable soup and make them each a sandwich.

Uncle Miltie had jotted down a phone number for her to call, but couldn't say who it was. "He didn't give his name, Gracie, but it sounded sort of like Herb Bower. He said he needed you to call as soon as you got back."

Needed? She didn't want to ask if that was the exact word used, but punched in the numbers right away. A woman's voice answered after the very first ring, then Herb Bower, Willow Bend's chief of police, was on, asking, "Have you mentioned to anyone that number you brought me?"

"No, I haven't." She resisted asking why. "Have you been able to make some identification?"

43

He didn't answer that. "Look, Gracie, I'd appreciate this remaining just between you and me at this point, okay?"

"Of course, but. . . ."

"And the same goes for Abe's mentioning and describing the man interested in Amy. But please, if there's anything else you think of—if you get *any* more information, even the smallest, seemingly inconsequential things, I'd appreciate your passing it on."

"I don't know what that could be, but yes, I'll do that." She started to ask another question, but it went unanswered or, rather, since she'd heard that tiny click, she realized he was no longer on the line.

For a moment she stood there looking down at the phone. She knew Herb better socially than professionally, but felt sure he'd not deliberately go around trying to antagonize or upset people by hanging up on them. Perhaps he'd been interrupted by someone coming into the office, or maybe he had so much on his mind that he didn't even recognize that this could be interpreted as rudeness.

Could his abruptness have anything to do with Amy's case? Could things be getting even more complicated, rather than simpler? Had he learned anything about the identity of Amy's mysterious so-called friend? Could drugs possibly be involved? Murder? Espionage?

Or have my years of devoted reading and watching mysteries done something to my senses—caused them to sort of kick in suddenly, making me suspicious of everything and everyone?

She snorted in annoyance at even having those thoughts, and also at the unknown factors that were making her think them. None of it made any sense at all in friendly, peaceable Willow Bend!

Tomorrow, she promised herself, *I'm going back to the hospital and I'm simply going to find out from Amy who and what this friend is!"*

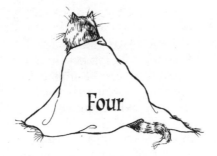

Four

BUT A DIFFERENT NURSE, one she didn't know, was on duty when she turned up the next day, and stated authoritatively that only the immediate family could see Amy while she was still in intensive care. And that was *another* something to mull over. For Gracie had telephoned the Cantrells shortly after getting around that morning, and they'd been convinced Amy was much improved.

She returned home and got a load of laundry running while she swept, dusted, and worked at clearing away some of the other tasks that had been set aside in all the excitement, though not the sort of excitement one welcomes, she thought.

Finally, by early afternoon, she and Gooseberry were ready to start out on their walk, but with her mind on so many other things, Gracie wasn't paying much attention to where she was going until she noticed she'd headed off to one of the older parts of town. Begun some 150 years earlier as an area of residences for tradespeople and other upper-middle-class citizens, it was a longer route she seldom took.

Though the section had deteriorated in earlier years, during the last two or three decades most of the weathered old wooden houses had been given new windows and plantings and were re-sheathed with aluminum or vinyl siding, making it now one of the prettier neighborhoods of Willow Bend.

She always enjoyed having Gooseberry with her, even though some people looked frankly amused at seeing the big, Halloween-orange cat not only accompanying, but trotting right along with—and around—a red-haired, sixty-plus woman who was out there exercising so briskly!

She made a point of smiling at each of them; the problem for most of these folks was that they didn't have a cat like hers—as though anybody *could*!

Ah, yes, there was Amy's house up ahead, that large corner one with the wraparound verandah across the front and partway back on either side. It was all-white, white-on-white, trim and all—as were also the houses on either side of it.

Gracie slowed a little as she went by Fifth Street, then turned on Maple. There was the short driveway leading to their three-car garage; all of its doors were closed—as tightly shut as her mind seemed to be when it came to unraveling the situation with Amy!

She recalled having dropped off the girl off a number of times before she was old enough to drive—and even a few months ago brought her home after choir, when the car she sometimes drove was being repaired.

But she couldn't keep her mind on those past moments when she remained so obsessed with what had happened to Amy the other night. It had to have been just a bug, or some viral thing that hit her so suddenly—didn't it?

Yet she still had this odd feeling she was missing something—and she didn't like that one bit! *Is Amy in danger? Can there be some reason other than her physical condition, which could account for her still being in ICU when they say she's so much improved?*

She sucked in a deep breath of the morning shower-cooled air and deliberately stopped to look at a trellised rose at the edge of the Cantrell property, forcing herself to give it her full attention.

But this was no way to get the exercise she felt her body and mind needed! Straightening to her full height—she hoped she hadn't started getting shorter, as many people do as they age—she took several steps before realizing she was alone. At first she was almost amused, fully expecting Gooseberry to amble out of one of the plantings where he'd been checking for whatever he could find that might appeal to him.

She hoped it wouldn't be something alive or recently alive, like that mouse, which he'd obviously considered to be worthy of her praise. He'd been known to bring her chipmunks and moles or even (though more rarely, thank goodness) small snakes—which she'd informed him he need not do again, thank you!

Gracie retraced her steps for a short distance, but he didn't come bouncing out from behind the massed yellow coreopsis or the large bed of sturdy marigolds even when she called his name—something she recognized as an exercise in futility. Gooseberry did not feel obligated to come when she called—that being, she reminded herself, one good argument against her "theory" that, in spite of appearances, he was actually a dog!

She was annoyed. Time passed very quickly when she was striding along, but standing still or moving just a few steps made it almost stop. She should go on home without him—but knew she wouldn't, even though old-timers often told of cats finding their way home from miles away, even hundreds of miles.

And who was she to be thinking of others as old-timers? Even twenty or thirty years ago she thought people in their sixties were either already in or dangerously near being in that category. *Fortunately, I don't feel like anything that term indicates,* she thought. *And I don't believe I look or act like it either!*

She felt a rueful, self-disparaging expression creep across her face. Probably every reasonably healthy, fairly active person her age thought of herself or himself as being an exception to the description "elderly."

And that word set her mind off in another direction. She must remember to tell Rocky that she didn't appreciate one of his newspaper staff—undoubtedly quite young—writing of an "elderly" man hurt in an accident last week, then finding as she read the article that the injured person was sixty-one! *Come on, Rocky! Don't let them make us "elderly" before our time!*

Although her thoughts had been wandering, she'd also been keeping a vigilant eye out for that missing member of her household. Suddenly she saw him meandering down the very middle of the Cantrells' front sidewalk! There was something light-colored in his mouth, but it was only when he came closer that she realized it was a shell, a rather large one, actually, but not of a clam or oyster or mussel or whelk, which made up her entire familiarity with shells.

She reached down to take it from him, but he backed away, then deliberately kept beyond arm's reach as he preceded or walked behind or beside her on the way home.

Gracie was annoyed with him—and with herself for letting him get away with acting like this. It felt like condoning an act of thievery, except that her cat couldn't understand that concept—and she could only guess from whose property it might have come.

She'd assumed when first seeing him that he'd emerged from the plantings in front of Amy's porch. However, he'd been gone long enough that he could have been at any of the neighbors', then come back that way.

"Where have you been, you curious cat?" she demanded. "Where did you get that? Is it one that somebody brought back from a visit to the seashore?" She hoped that wasn't the case, for that would mean it was treasured as a memento. *I'm going to hope someone bought fresh seafood, then threw out the shells.* "But, of course, you know the adage about what kills cats."

That it had been part of meal preparation surely was the answer, wasn't it? If so, it wouldn't hurt for Gooseberry to carry his rather unusual trophy back home if he wished. It seemed strange for him to bother with something like this, yet he'd done the same with certain other inanimate objects like going off with Uncle Miltie's screwdriver when he'd been right in the middle of fixing the garage door last week. And Gracie had long ago discovered that she couldn't leave a dust cloth lying around and expect to find it where it had been left.

She couldn't tell for sure, but assumed there was nothing within the shell. She smelled nothing rotten from this distance—however, *should* it be there, she supposed that might partially account for the cat's so proudly bearing it home.

They'd been walking along Maple Street for well over a block when a smooth-running gray Ford passed them, going in the same direction. With almost disbelief she saw—and she took out the torn-off piece of napkin to make sure—that the license plate had the same numbers as those she'd copied at Abe's!

What were the odds that the one car she'd been thinking about would pass by her here?

Uncle Miltie was more intrigued by Gooseberry's find than she was. Having been quite a fisherman, he knew most of the freshwater mollusks that could be found in the lakes and streams of Ohio and Indiana—but this was new to him. He was curious enough to look it up in the seashell guide he had on his shelves, along with other volumes about nature.

Gooseberry had marched right in with it and willingly gave it to her uncle—earning for himself a, "What a good cat you are!" and extra petting, which he obviously enjoyed. He even sat there beside Uncle Miltie at the kitchen table, as though interested in the search being conducted.

"I can't find any pictures *exactly* representing this one, Gracie, but these periwinkles look something like it." He read aloud the accompanying information, which mentioned a caveat about some of them being poisonous. "I wonder where he found it."

"Me, too. All I know is that he wasn't carrying it as we approached the corner of Fifth and Maple, where Amy lives." And that reminded her again of the gray car, which had to have passed that house shortly after she did.

Feeling rather foolish even while doing it, she made a phone call as soon as Uncle Miltie went back into the other room to watch a science fiction movie on one of the cable networks. "Hello, Herb, this is Gracie, and I'm sure this isn't at all what you had in mind when you told me to call about anything which might be unusual or suspicious. . . ."

She waited for his assurance that whatever she thought was worth calling about was, indeed, bound to be significant. "Well, I was out for my daily walk—I went this afternoon, since it was raining this morning." *Oh dear, he's so busy and I'm just rambling, giving unnecessary information.*

"My cat went with me, as he usually does. We were going past Amy's house when Gooseberry disappeared for a while, then came back carrying a strange whitish shell."

Get to the point, Gracie, she scolded herself. *That's not what you were calling about!* "And then as we were coming up Fifth Street, maybe a block or so from Amy's, I saw a gray Ford—actually, *the* gray Ford, the one with those license numbers I gave you."

There was silence for a moment before Herb's voice asked, "And . . . ?"

"Well, uh—I didn't know if it was of interest that the mystery man may have been driving past Amy's house to check on her, or to . . . I don't know . . . it's like I just said, it was probably silly to call about such a minor thing."

"We can't consider anything 'silly' or 'minor' as of now, Gracie, so I'm glad you called—I really am."

"Do you suppose it's possible he was the one she'd planned to meet for a movie after the rehearsal? If he's on the level, I suppose he could be worried about her, and was cruising around trying to see her. . . ." But it was that "if" that was unsettling.

"That does represent a possibility," he replied, his tone giving no indication as to whether he thought that plausible.

She did not go on with the reverse of her supposition: if he were *not* on the level. "Have you heard anything recently about Amy's condition?"

"She's supposedly doing very well."

Supposedly. Everything with qualifications! "Will she be getting out of the hospital soon?"

"I'm not sure just when—but then I'm not the doctor."

"Something seems strange, Herb. Don't they usually, nowadays, take people out of ICU as soon as possible? Is she sicker than we've been led to believe?"

There was a small chuckle. "Remember me, Gracie? I'm a policeman, not a physician. I'm not about to get drawn into the usually's or what should be's of medical care."

She laughed, too. "That brings us back to the old saw about a little knowledge being a dangerous thing, right?"

"Right!"

But that wasn't the end of their conversation. He wanted to know, "Did you get the impression that the man might have noticed you?"

"From the time I saw his car, he kept looking straight ahead, not paying any attention to me nor turning toward me. But he probably did *see* me. How could he keep from seeing this red-haired woman and her pumpkin-colored cat striding along?"

Although Herb was good at asking questions and expecting a response, it was evident that it didn't work that way with her queries. Thus, she wasn't expecting it when a police car stopped in front of her house within the next half-hour and Herb appeared at her door to ask more about the shell, and to see it.

"It's probably not significant, Gracie," he told her—but despite saying that, he asked to take it with him. Uncle Miltie was the one who emphatically informed him that they wanted it returned. After all, he was still trying to find out what it was!

Gracie made an effort to relax, but received a number of calls through the evening—from nearly every one of the choir members, in fact. There seemed to be more and more nervousness, and mounting uncertainty, about tomorrow afternoon, especially, but about the morning service as well.

"Everything's going to be fine," she assured Tyne Anderson, one of the altos.

But Tyne wasn't easily convinced. "I just got off the phone with my sister, and we can't remember everything that was changed on those two numbers, like when we come in."

It wasn't surprising that this was a problem for Tyne, who never seemed able to count out the rhythm, the beats. "I remember seeing you penciling in the changes on your music, so I'm sure you'll do fine once you have that in front of you. And I'll be right there, like at rehearsal, helping you know when to begin."

"I—just don't know. . . ."

"Please don't stew about it. We're all going to be at church early tomorrow, remember? That way we'll go over *Help Me to See Thee, Lord*, and we'll also be using it as our choir anthem in the morning.

"If people get there as soon as requested, I'm hoping we can run through that twice. And remember that we're staying long enough after Sunday school to sing through *Hallalujah, Save Us, Lord*—so we'll be able to work on anything that might still need a little polishing."

Tyne and Tish were now thirty-five years old but still known throughout the church and community as "The Turner Twins," probably because they were both blond and blue-eyed, were usually seen together, always wore girlish dresses and shoes, and liked the same things. They'd been married for perhaps seventeen years—Tyne to Bill Anderson, and Tish to John Ball—and were both giggly and unsure of themselves.

Gracie had tried several times to have Tish move into the soprano section. Although she might need some help in developing the top of her range, that section more often than not carried the melody—a big help for someone who couldn't get the hang of reading music!

However, Tish would not change seats, choosing to remain with her sister, also an alto.

When Gracie picked up the phone the next time, however, the caller's attitude offered a welcome change of pace. "Hi, Gracie, it's Rick. How are things going for you this lovely evening?"

"Hel-*lo*, Rick. It's great to hear your cheerful voice—a wonderful contrast from those in the choir who are so worried or pessimistic about tomorrow."

He laughed. "Did you tell them that faint hearts ne'er win awards?"

She was so relieved by his attitude that she sank onto a kitchen chair. "I would have had I thought of it. Okay if I steal it?"

"That's impossible, Gracie! It's given to you. Be my guest."

"I'm glad you called, Rick, I wanted to tell you how much I appreciate and thank you for taking on the special music. It was sorta thrust upon you, but we had to do something about those sections."

"No problem at all. You know I love to sing." Rick Harding had been sent to Indiana by his computer company when they were opening their new division here. There weren't a lot of other African Americans in Willow Bend, but the new dentist practicing with Dr. Comfort had come with his wife, a nurse/anesthetist, and there were two teachers and at least a dozen students now in the school system.

Gracie couldn't speak for the whole community, but there didn't appear to be any prejudice, and everyone here in this church had come to love Rick, his wife and their two-year-old daughter. Of all the voices, his was the most exceptional, and he could not only read music but had previous experience in choirs much larger and more prestigious than theirs.

Unlike Estelle, however, he never tried to throw his weight around. Even now, he didn't appear worried or troubled. He just asked, "Is there anything I can do to help you tomorrow, Gracie? I know you have things under control, but I'm available if there's anything that needs done."

She sighed, this time from thankfulness, not tension. "I didn't realize how much the downheartedness of some others was beginning to get to me. Thanks for the pick-me-up."

"Anytime." He chuckled. "This is great. I'm not used to receiving two thank-you's in one day."

"Well, let's really make your day, then. I want especially to thank you for not only knowing what to do with Amy last night, but doing it. She might not have made it if we'd had to wait for the ambulance."

She thought his momentary hesitation was going to lead to his saying he hadn't done anything that special but, instead, there was a question. "I wasn't sure what was happening—I *still* don't know, do you?"

She shook her head, even though he couldn't see that. "I know they've been doing a number of tests, but if they have significant results, I've not been informed."

They talked about several other things before Gracie asked, "Do you do much research on the Web?"

"Sure—quite a bit."

"Well, I'm practically computer illiterate, so could I ask a favor?"

"Of course. What is it, more recipes?"

She laughed, remembering that at one of their rehearsals a year ago somebody had mentioned a craving for her grandmother's "light dumplings." When none of the women had been able to come up with a recipe for them, it was Rick who had solved the problem by going on-line. The whole choir thanked him when, the following week, Gracie surprised everyone with this unexpected old-fashioned dish.

"No, not a recipe this time—it's for a shell Uncle Miltie thinks might be a winkle, he says, or a periwinkle. My cat, Gooseberry, is always finding things and bringing them to me—but it's my uncle who's intrigued by this particular one, which he can't find in his field guides."

"Bring it with you to church in the morning, so I'll know what I'm looking for when making the search. I'm sure we can come up with something."

That sounded so simple—but she'd never tried to do it herself. "If you succeed, your reward will be more light dumplings, okay?"

"It's a deal!"

"But don't worry if you can't find it—I'll make them again soon because I'm getting hungry for them, too."

It was after hanging up that she remembered lending the shell to Herb.

Later, after supper, Gracie began going over her notes for her Sunday school class the next morning, but errant thoughts kept creeping into her mind. She tried disciplining them, but when they continued to intrude she got up and headed for the living room. "How about some ice cream?"

Uncle Miltie looked over the top of his glasses. "What flavors are there?"

"We always have vanilla, but there's also Cookies 'n' Cream, and Butter Pecan. Take your pick."

It was no surprise when he chose the Cookies 'n' Cream—he usually did when it was in the lineup. Since he was in the middle of watching a nature program, she joined him in the living room for the end of the segment on seals. Although not one for watching football, golf, game shows, or science fiction, all of which he was partial to, she did sometimes join him for history, travel, or nature ones.

She and Elmo had had much more similar interests.

She went back to the kitchen when the phone rang again. This time it was Marge, somewhat gloomy because, "There's not a thing to *do* here in Willow Bend on a Saturday night—not when you're unattached!"

"Oh, I don't know." Gracie knew if she let Marge start, she'd cry on her shoulder for a good chunk of what was left of the evening. "Uncle Miltie and I are sitting here in front of the TV finishing off bowls of ice cream. What more could anyone want?"

"Oh, Gracie! You, too, must get lonely!"

"If you mean missing Elmo, of course I do, and always will. But I don't wallow in it, dear friend. There are too many things in life—good things, I'll have you know—for me to lose out on if I allow myself to stay in the dumps!"

What finally happened was that Marge came over for "one game of Scrabble"—which became "just one more" when Uncle Miltie joined them at the kitchen table. This was his favorite game—and he almost won this time, too, but had a "Q" left to be played—and no available "U" anywhere.

Marge's win got her out of the doldrums, and she only partly in jest said they were poor sports when Gracie, yawning openly, started to put things back in the box. "I'm bushed, Marge," she explained, "and I'm heading for bed within the next ten minutes."

Marge pretended offense. "I thought we were friends, and here you are, practically pushing me out your door!"

"And if you leave peaceably and soon, the 'practically' will remain in that sentence," Gracie responded, putting their cups, bowls, and spoons in the dishwasher.

Marge shook her head ruefully as she started for the door. "Well, so much for friendship. I finally win one game and get thrown out of the house."

They could hear her still laughing as she stepped off the porch and started across the yards. "You're an excellent niece, Gracie," Uncle Miltie said as his arm circled her shoulders. "And you're one terrific friend to many people."

She felt humbled at his saying that. "I have such wonderful people as friends, Uncle Miltie. And as relatives."

He nodded. "It takes one to recognize others, my dear."

Five

SHE'D EXPECTED TO READ a few chapters of a new mystery before going to sleep, but made it through only part of the first one. It was with amazement that she opened her eyes to daylight. Those numbers on the digital clock couldn't be right, could they? 7:42?

She looked at her watch, and got up immediately. She was expected to be at church in forty-eight minutes and she still had to shower and dress! Thank goodness her hair was naturally curly and that she still had enough natural color so her skin required only the lightest cosmetic emphases.

Tish and Lester were pulling into the parking area at the same time she got there, and Don arrived right after them. Gracie looked around as she entered the church, seeing excitement in everyone's eyes and hearing it in their voices. Somehow, thankfully, the negativity with which the last rehearsal had been conducted seemed dispelled. Instead, an enthusiastic we-can-do-it attitude permeated the place.

Paul didn't sing with them; as he'd put it when asked to join them, he had enough to do as pastor on a Sunday morning. But he was in and out of the back room as Barb played and the choir went through the anthem for the morning.

Gracie beamed at them. "You're wonderful! Positively marvelous!" she cried, bringing her palms together in applause. "There's nothing that I saw or heard that needs further work, but—well, I didn't tell you I was doing it, but I recorded this run-through on tape."

She glanced at her watch to make sure they had time for what she was about to suggest. "I'm going to play it back to you now. Pay special attention to your own parts, but also to others. *If* we need to go over one or two specific sections before we sing it straight through one more time, we will do so."

Don Delano did ask Barb to play one short passage, in order to make sure he was getting his baritone part just right, and then Rick requested help with the four-part harmony—which Gracie was quite sure was a request being made more for the altos than himself.

"In the beauty of Your world and in a baby's smile,
Whether I am far away or at home for a while,
Whether I am rich or poor, with pennies or a hoard,
Whatever my condition, help me to see Thee, Lord. . . ."

It was the final, FINAL rehearsal of *Help Me to See Thee, Lord*—and not one person missed a note and nobody came in at the wrong time. "We are READY!" Gracie cried, clasping her hands above her head in a victor's stance.

And the others responded, "We are READY!"

Yes, God, I do see that only You could have changed the outlook, the mood of all these people overnight! Thanks . . . !

Gracie hoped and prayed this enthusiasm would hold through the Sunday school period, which was to begin in a few minutes with her class meeting here in this room. Somebody had taken care of making the coffee and heating water for tea, so a number of people had already filled their mugs and were seated in a large circle.

Amy's father had come with his wife today, a first for Sunday school, although he was almost always there for church. Gracie asked Linda and Roy Cantrell to fill them in on their daughter's condition, and everyone was pleased to hear that Amy was apparently much better.

No one else seemed puzzled at her still being in intensive care, and Gracie didn't feel she should raise that question. They were all concerned, though, so Gracie led a brief prayer before getting into the lesson.

Jim Thompson was in her class today, too, along with the Cantrells and nineteen others. He was often on police duty on Sunday mornings, or else admitted to being in bed at that time, following an extra-long Saturday shift.

Gracie briefly brought up to speed those who had not been there for the study of the very beginning of the Christian church, the book of Acts—one of her favorites.

She'd read it many times, and now shared with the class the way each reading could offer new understanding and insights. Today's lesson was a continuation of last Sunday's, when Stephen, one of the seven deacons chosen by other followers of Christ, was giving his defense in the Temple.

Gracie filled in some of the background before getting a discussion going about how to know what *is* right—especially when everyone else thinks you're wrong. What must it have been like for Stephen's parents, his friends, and those who loved him?

Today's portion dealt with his being stoned to death—not for something he had done wrong, but because he'd tried to do what was *right*.

Several in the class were outspoken, but she was concerned about others who withdrew, looking down at their hands, or at a corner of the room, or out a window. Amy's mother reached out to touch her husband's sleeve, but he drew away, not acknowledging her gesture, nor looking at her, just holding in both hands the quarterly, thirteen printed lessons for adults, covering a three-month period. Gracie didn't have time to think about it right then, though suspected she would later.

The class was drawing to its close, a time always accompanied by prayer, so Gracie included a number of known needs—including Amy. ". . . And we know that nothing like this affects only the patient, Lord, any more than Stephen's murder concerned only him. So please be with her mother and father, and surround them and all the others we've prayed for, with Your love, Your protection, and Your peace. In Jesus' name, Amen."

Several members made a point of inviting the Cantrells to stay for the worship service, but they said they must go: ". . . We want to be with Amy."

"Give her my love, and assure her I'm continuing to pray for her," Gracie requested. "I'll be there to visit either today or tomorrow. . . ." But by then she had to hurry with preparations for the worship service, since Barb had already gone into the sanctuary and was playing the organ.

Gracie heard Estelle say, "Poor dear Amy, to be missing this day she worked so hard for!" and quickly felt guilty for being judgmental. Her very first reaction had been that the woman was exhibiting her sugar-wouldn't-melt-in-her-mouth persona again—that she was trying to show everyone how generous and wonderful she was.

She wanted to banish this unkind thought, but it just would not fade away. She even had a mental picture of Estelle reaching her arm up in an alluring manner, adjusting the halo, which she so assiduously tried to keep polished.

However, following Paul's brief but meaningful prayer with the choir, it was easy for her and the others to let the smiles within their hearts show on their faces, as robed and *ready*, they lined up and processed into the stained-glass brightness.

ᴥ

Gracie wasn't quite as calm as she wished, and suspected some of the others were nervous, too. The service, however, was going smoothly, as usual, for Paul, who had come to serve here three years earlier, had a knack for organization, and everything fit together beautifully—the call to worship, the congregational singing, the scripture, everything.

It was time for the tithes and offerings to be received, and two of the older men and two teens slowly went back to the aisles. Then came the time for everyone to rise and sing the *Doxology* and for those who'd collected the offerings to return to their seats. And everyone else was seated, also.

Usually the choir members rose as one at this point, with no announcement, but today Paul mentioned that the number they were about to sing, *Help Me to See Thee, Lord*, was their anthem-of-choice, which would next be heard at the competition that afternoon at Waxmire Tabernacle. He hoped everyone would try to be there in support of these faithful people who used their talents and time to provide the excellent music these congregants got to hear each Sunday morning.

As Barb played the first note, Gracie, sitting in the front row, stood up, as did all of their choir members. They moved forward, positioning themselves so the back row was on the platform, the middle row on the wide steps, and the last ones in front of them, on the sanctuary's carpet. Just as rehearsed.

Gracie had moved over to stand front and center before them. So now, looking forward, she gave an encouraging smile, moving both hands close in front of herself to give a double thumbs-up.

She nodded to Barb, and there was an immediate change in

melody and tempo as the organist swung into the first bars of their anthem.

The singing started off perfectly, everyone in unison, the music and the words clear and easily understood. Most of it was in four-part harmony, but there were those several breaks when only one or two voices were featured. There was not a missed beat or muffled word.

And then there was the final, harmonious *Amen.*

There was a moment of silence, without so much as a rustling paper, and Gracie wondered if maybe they hadn't done as well as she'd thought. But then someone started clapping, then more and more as spontaneous applause rang out from their own congregation!

This did not happen very often in the Eternal Hope Community Church, and Gracie had a moment of wondering whether it was due to people responding to the message of their music or to their delivery—or possibly to the pastor's having mentioned that this was one of the two numbers they'd sing this afternoon.

Whatever the reason, every member of the choir was beaming as they returned to their seats.

Thank You, Lord, she breathed silently. *Even if we don't place in the competition, this has been a most wonderful, memorable experience today!* And she surreptitiously blotted a tear from each eye as Paul began his sermon.

Some members came up front after the service, telling individual members and the whole group how splendid the music had been, and that they were rooting for them. What was most thrilling to Gracie was how many promising, after hearing them this morning, that they were definitely going to be at Waxmire Tabernacle, on the other side of town, for the competition—despite not having considered that earlier.

No one thought it necessary again to go over the number they'd just sang so beautifully, but they wanted to run through the other a couple of times. It was, therefore, a little later than usual when Gracie and Uncle Miltie ate lunch. Afterwards, she called the hospital.

"Oh, that's great!" She was delighted to learn that Amy was no longer in intensive care. "What room has she been moved to?"

There was a slight pause before the person said, "Just a moment, please."

She heard the murmur of voices, then a briskly efficient voice was asking, "May I help you?"

"I understand that Amy Cantrell has been discharged from ICU, and I just wanted to know what room she's in."

"This is Mrs. Jackson. To whom am I speaking, please?"

What difference does that make? But she answered the question, "I'm Grace Parks, a friend of Amy's. I've visited her in ICU, and just asked to what room she'd been moved." There seemed to be another pause, a longish one, which made her wonder why.

"I believe she is no longer a patient here at the hospital."

"What do you mean, she's no longer there? Has she gone home—been transferred to another hospital—what? How *is* she?"

"She seemed to be doing well."

Only one answer out of the three! "Then . . . ?"

"I'm sorry, Ms. Parks, but that is the only information I can give you. . . ."

There was a click on the line, indicating that Mrs. Jackson had hung up. Gracie felt light-headed. *I'm not catching the same virus or whatever Amy had, am I?* No, she was sure she wasn't. In fact, she recognized that she'd had this sensation before—when more upset than she was willing to acknowledge.

What is going on? The only thing she knew to do under this circumstance was to call the Cantrell home. She dialed—and became even more agitated at receiving no answer. There was not even an answering machine.

Well, they'd said they were going to see Amy right after Sunday school. Gracie would have thought that if they found that their daughter could leave the hospital, they'd have taken her home. On the other hand, considering how ill she'd been, and how little she'd eaten since being admitted, if Amy asked to stop for a snack on the way back to her house, they might have done so. Yet that scenario just didn't seem to fit with what she knew of this family.

On the other hand, *should* Amy be in trouble of any kind, Gracie could never forgive herself if she didn't at least try to help, even if she was pretty sure the Cantrells wouldn't welcome her intrusion.

She drove to their house, noting that the garage doors were shut again, and everything looked the same as the last time she saw it. She parked at the curb, got out, and walked up the sidewalk to the door, but no one came in response to her pressing on the doorbell a second and third time. She'd heard the ringing, so knew even as she then pounded on the door that such an effort was futile.

Still, she decided to walk all the way around the house. If the parents did any gardening, it was possible they might be out back.

They were not.

She even knocked on the side door of the garage but, as she expected, there was no answer.

So what should I do now, Lord? I'm still trying to do what I think is right, but if there's something more, please show it to me.

She went back to her car, and just sat there, thinking. *I don't want to make an ocean out of a mud puddle, as Uncle Miltie would say, and I don't have an awful lot of time because of the choir contest, but I'm here now, and available. Please, Lord, help me know what to do.*

Well, she supposed she should first of all call the police station. Thank goodness she had a good memory for numbers: She punched in the right one and Herb himself picked up on the first ring. She blurted out that she believed Amy to be missing, and how she'd failed when trying to reach the girl's parents, and. . . .

"Gracie—just a minute, Gracie."

"But. . . ."

"I know that she's left the hospital, and that you were making inquiries."

How did you know I was asking questions? "Is she okay? Do you know where she is?"

This time his response did not come as quickly, and even then it was not an answer: "Where are you right now?"

"In my car, in front of the Cantrell house, and. . . ."

"Could you drive over here to the station?"

"Well, sure, I can. But why?"

"Just come, as soon as you can."

"Okay, but. . . ."

"Park in the back, please—and tell no one where you're going, or why. . . ."

Maybe I've been transported to Cabot Cove or St. Mary Mead after all! And wouldn't Rick get a kick out of this particular scene? The director of their choir in the middle of what had all the earmarks of something cloak-and-daggerish—though it probably wasn't! "All right, Herb. I'll be there within two minutes."

And then, as she turned the ignition, she almost wished she'd not been quite that specific, timewise. Patsy, the little crippled girl who lived next door to the Cantrells, was coming out onto her porch, using her walker. She was waving at Gracie, and it looked as though she was beckoning her—but all Gracie had time for was to smile as she waved back.

She pulled away from the curb and kept going, watching Patsy recede in her rearview mirror. Although not understanding the rationale for such precautions as Herb had indicated, she came down the alley behind the station and parked there, where her car would probably not be seen.

Gracie was surprised to see the inconspicuous rear door of the building open as she got out of her car. She'd never had occasion to come back here before, but would hardly ever have noticed that, as there was no knob nor doorstep. And here was Herb, using the same motion she'd seen only a minute before, beckoning for her. "Come on in."

She glanced around as she walked toward him. "I feel like I'm in some suspense thriller or something."

"Or something?"

"I'm to come secretly, park here . . . and even come in through an unmarked door!"

"Well, yes." He reached for her arm. "But I'm not the ghoulish figure your fertile mind is probably conjuring up. Just a town policeman trying to do my job."

It was her turn to smile encouragement. "And there are many of us who sleep well at night for exactly that reason."

They turned left, into a medium-sized, neatly organized office she'd never seen before. But she wasn't looking at that right now, for Roy Cantrell was getting to his feet. "Thanks for coming, Mrs. Parks."

She looked from him to his wife, whose eyes and face looked as though she'd been crying. "You're welcome." *What more can I say when I haven't the faintest idea of why I've been asked to come?*

Herb indicated the third chair facing his desk, and went back to sit in his own as she took her seat. "Amy has disappeared, Gracie. We don't know how she got out of ICU with nobody seeing her, nor how she could have walked out of the hospital without raising suspicion and being stopped."

Gracie turned toward Linda. "She was still wearing one of those flimsy hospital gowns?"

"Not since yesterday." And the tears started again. "She'd been complaining about them, and got permission for us to bring her sweatpants and sweatshirts. Last night she was wearing the royal blue set, the one with colorful winter birds—cardinals and grosbeaks. I suppose she might be wearing the marigold-yellow one now . . ."

Herb was already punching in numbers on his phone, and asked the ICU nurse who answered, "What was Amy Cantrell wearing this morning? Yes, please *do* inquire—and also check on whether she left anything there, anything at all!"

Covering the mouthpiece with his hand, he muttered, "I can't believe I was that stupid—assuming she'd be dressed like a patient . . . !" But then he was listening to what the other person was telling him. After asking another question or two, he hung up.

"Okay, she was apparently wearing the blue outfit, since the yellow one's still there, along with her underclothing. There are personal toiletries, but no money—do you know if she had any?"

"Not much, a few dollars at most. She said she felt like a three-year-old if she didn't have at least some quarters. I tried to explain that the nurses would give her a soft drink or crackers or anything she wanted—but did end up giving her what change I had." She looked stricken. "If only I hadn't—but I never expected she'd do *this!*"

Gracie reached over and took her hand, then tried to warm it by holding it between her own, rubbing the back of it. "I suspect the nurses keep some record of ICU visitors, don't they? Do you know of any others besides the four of us, and our pastor?"

"They told me we were the only ones."

"She had to make contact with someone outside in order to sneak out of there—perhaps the man in the gray car?"

Herb started to shake his head as Roy demanded, "*What* man in a gray car?"

She let the officer explain what little they knew. Oddly, the part that seemed to bother Roy the most was that the car had a Florida license plate. "Have you checked out who it belongs to?"

"It's registered to an Andrew Hively and. . . ."

The man's face suddenly changed color. "He's—*here?*" The shock caused his voice to break.

"We're not positive of that. The car's make and model match the license plate, but we still don't have a good description of the man who's been driving it—and the car itself hasn't been seen since yesterday, although we've had an APB—an all points bulletin—out for it."

"Why didn't you tell me?" Roy demanded.

Herb was asking at the same time, "Why is his being here so important?"

This last query was the one answered. "He hates me! He's threatened me, hounded me and my family." Roy sank back into his seat, his voice little more than a moan, "Now he's back at it. Again."

Gracie asked, "Why does he hate you so much?" She realized as soon as the words came out that it should be the officer asking questions, but either way she wouldn't have been prepared for his reply.

"He accuses me of killing his father. He apparently believes that I did."

She was afraid she might have given an audible gasp, but nobody apparently noticed. Herb was asking, "And *did* you kill his father, Mr. Cantrell?"

"Of course not." He was so agitated that he was on his feet, but there was little room here in which to pace. "His dad, Tony—Anthony, that is—was my partner in a financial planning group, in Florida."

Linda was not even attempting to blot the tears running down her face. Herb started to reach for the box on the corner of his desk, but Gracie picked it up, pulled several tissues from it, and handed these to Linda as Roy continued.

"I trusted Tony implicitly—he was my best friend, and we did everything together. By the time I found out we were in trouble—when I first even suspected that things weren't as they should be, Tony was on a month's vacation, which was the first time he'd taken off for an extended period of time.

"I started noticing some—what I considered discrepancies, so tried to figure what was wrong. And then I brought in the best accountants in the state, hoping against hope that he—that Tony had not been stealing us blind!

"But he was! It turned out that even on that vacation, in Atlantic City and Las Vegas, he was using more of our money to try to win back his massive losses.

"He lost that, as well."

Gracie saw him pause behind his wife's chair, and her head leaned back against his chest as his hands came to rest on her shoulders, and her left hand, bare of any jewelry, rose to cover his.

"I had no choice but to go to the authorities and—by the time he got back it had become a certainty. At first he tried to bluff us, to use his carefully fictionalized records to confuse people.

"And when we began looking for it, we discovered a paper trail so wide that at first it appeared to everyone that I had to have known about his embezzlement earlier.

"But I didn't! He was the one who took care of special accounts, and the elderly widows and singles adored him, and placed all their faith in him. They were the primary ones who were taken advantage of—multimillions of dollars siphoned off into supposedly safely secured accounts—with his name on them, so he could 'better take care of it for them.'"

Roy now looked physically ill. "He was of course not allowed near the accounts after that—though he tried desperately to get me to find some way of giving him access. He kept saying he could straighten out everything, that none of this was his fault.

"I felt almost as terrible about having to refuse him as in having been the one who started the investigation."

"So then he tried to pin it on Roy!" Linda was indignant. "Though *that* didn't work at all."

"Except with his family." Roy's voice had gotten lower and lower, until the last word was barely a whisper.

It was Linda who, in a pain-filled voice, added that, "If only Tony had toughed it out! Yes, there would certainly have been jail time, but . . . he'd always been the Golden Boy, the one on whom the sun would always shine.

"But when that light of adulation was shut off, his life, as he saw it, was over. He wrote a letter to his family, insisting he was innocent—and shot himself."

Gracie sat there stunned, staring at this woman and her husband. Herb looked down at the pen in his hand, then laid it down precisely, lined up perfectly with the edge of his pad. He looked straight at Linda, then Roy. "What happened then?"

He cleared his throat. "We saw it through as best we could, salvaging as much as possible for those who'd suffered such severe financial losses."

Linda nodded. "Most of what Tony stole proved to be unrecoverable but, again using his own records and investigating further, the authorities were able to prove where some of the stolen money went, in addition to what he used for gambling.

"But Andrew just never believed his father could have done what he was being accused of," Roy said. "Somehow he convinced himself it was all my fault—that I'd called in the accountants after I'd doctored the records to make Tony the fall guy for my thievery."

"Once he began denouncing his father's denouncers, the people Tony blamed, it wasn't long before he started threatening us."

"How?" Herb asked.

Roy clenched his jaw. "Mostly it was vague—that we'd be sorry. I thought at first it was just bluster and pain until our place at the lake burned.

"But how that got started could never be proved."

Roy brought his right hand, fingers splayed, up to his face, as though trying to rub away something repugnant. "Then it got more overt. Notes started arriving, with only a couple of words like, 'Your Daughter' or 'Think Safety' or, the last one before we left Florida: 'Amy. Love. Ha-ha!'"

"They came through the mail?" Gracie asked, knowing that would comprise a federal offense.

Linda nodded. "Some were; but others arrived in a variety of ways, like fastened to an SAR lapel pin left on a porch stand. Roy's been a member of the Sons of the American Revolution for many years, and has held a variety of offices in the organization.

"How Andrew got hold of Roy's pin is still a mystery, but it was definitely his! However, the engraved initials on the back, the 'LJC'—that's L for Leroy, then James Cantrell—had deep scratches across them, as though he—as though my husband was being—deleted!" She almost choked on that word.

Gracie could see Herb open the top right drawer of his desk and take something out. She drew in her breath sharply at seeing what it was, but knew it was hidden from the eyes of the other two. The officer asked, "Were there other ways in which he threatened you?"

Linda twisted around so she could look up at her husband, but waited for him to answer. "Yes, there was." One hand again rubbed down across his face. "He and his father used to like walking together along the beach when he was little, and they'd made a collection of seashells, especially mollusks, which won awards for Andrew in Boy Scouts then, later, even in college.

"That last note I mentioned, with the *Ha-ha*—that was left on our doorstep there in Florida, taped to a shell."

Herb's hand came up on top of the desk, Gooseberry's shell across his palm. "Did it look something like this?"

Gracie needed no vocalized answer to that—Linda began sobbing and Roy's face was frozen in shock. He finally managed, "Where—did you get that?"

Herb nodded toward Gracie, who understood she was to tell about Gooseberry's discovery—which she did. Roy demanded, "Was there a note with it?"

"Not by the time he brought it to me. Perhaps there might have been one—but is it possible he could have figured that the shell, itself, was all that was needed?"

There was a slow nod. A long, drawn-out sigh. "Yes, that's all that would have been needed. . . ."

Six

GRACIE WONDERED ALOUD, "If your families were so close and did things together, why wouldn't Amy realize who Andrew was, or what he was up to?"

"Actually, our families didn't know one another very well, and besides, Amy was quite a bit younger than he," Roy admitted. "It was Tony and I who did things outside of business, anyway. Especially golf—and that reminds me of something else: Andrew was an excellent golfer, expecting—at least hoping—to become a pro.

"He graduated from college with a degree in golf—"

I must have misunderstood. "A degree in golf?" Gracie asked.

"It had some sort of more-official-sounding title, like golf management or administration or something. Anyway, he'd had many interviews and offers, but finally chose to stay there in Florida with one of those super-exclusive golf courses."

"Ah, then that might be a starting place, Herb," Gracie suggested.

"I agree." Herb cleared his throat as he picked up his pen again. "Can you give me the name and address of that course, Mr. Cantrell?"

He not only gave its name, but the location, and manager. However, "He's no longer there—which is another reason he hates me; he lost that position when it was discovered that his father frequently made up the foursome when the wealthy and famous played there.

"When the scandal broke, some of them testified that Tony used those hours to talk them into investing with him—with *us*. By then he was apparently taking bigger and bigger risks, and some of those golfers lost appreciable amounts.

"And were among the first to file for restitution!"

Gracie thought aloud: "That club would still have all the information in their files somewhere, wouldn't they? His full description, likes and dislikes, if and where he was competing in tournaments and if there was a particular chain of motels or hotels he stayed at when away? It might even tell where he's living, and could possibly say if he was married. . . ."

"He wasn't when we knew him," Linda put in. "He had many women, but marriage was not on his mind."

Gracie nodded to show she'd heard, but went on with what she hoped they might learn from a call. ". . . And they could send his picture electronically." But then she noticed the wall clock—and verified the time with her watch. The minutes were passing much too quickly!

"I'd like you to describe Andrew for me," Herb told them, "in as complete detail as possible."

They did so, their description much like that Gracie had received from Abe. The major difference, however, was that the Cantrells thought he must be around twenty-eight, perhaps even thirty. Linda frowned. "He always used to look young for his age, but we haven't seen him for a while. Intense hatred of that kind just could have eaten away his youthful appearance. . . ."

It was a severe shock to learn that not only had he followed them now to their new home, but that their daughter had been meeting Andrew Hively secretly. Linda fretted, "Maybe it was our fault for not having told Amy more, but she was just a child and all we wanted was to protect her. How could we have explained and not made her fearful?"

Gracie tried to make her feel a little better, "Even that might not have helped, though. We don't even know if Andrew was using his correct name."

". . . But that she'd go behind our backs—not tell us she had a new boy—er, man-friend!" Linda tilted her head around to look up at her husband again. "We thought we were sparing her, letting her make new friends in a new community, a new school, and a new church. And she seemed to be happy. . . ."

". . . And almost never mentioned Florida anymore," he finished for her.

Herb looked into the eyes of each of the three in turn. "If *you* were Amy and wanted to get out of ICU to meet someone, how might you go about it?"

There was a brief silence before Gracie suggested, "First of all, it wouldn't be enough to just get out of that unit. I'd first have to make contact with my friend, who'd apparently not been able to see me—if he even knew I was in intensive care. . . ."

"That's true," Herb agreed. "We don't know if they have friends in common—friends of hers from whom he could learn where she was."

". . . So I'd have to somehow call him, and in order to do that I'd need money for the pay phone in the hall, which I'd try to get from someone. And I couldn't be wearing a hospital gown to make that call, for any nurse or cleaning lady or anyone at the hospital would recognize from the color-coding that I belonged in ICU, right?"

He nodded, and she continued, "So—I'd have to be in 'civilian clothes' and wait for just the right moment, perhaps when some other patient needed the attention of the unit. If I left immediately when that happened, got out into the hallway and made a quick call to a number I'd memorized, I could keep going to someplace where he could pick me up."

"But why wouldn't she have told us. . . ." Linda began, then stopped. "But she's only seventeen and—and I guess . . . I guess that's the answer. Teens think no one understands."

Gracie placed a hand on her arm. "Look, it's not going to do any good for any of us to blame ourselves—for anything. What's important is figuring out where she is."

"And if she's all right!" Roy himself seemed to have aged ten years in these last minutes. Linda used the arms of her chair to help push herself to her feet and into his arms, where they clung sadly to one another.

Gracie started to get up, too, wanting to go to them, to put her arms around them and offer her support, as well. But Herb must have realized that, and gave a tiny negative movement with his head, then a slight frown. "We've got people calling every motel and rooming house in the area, starting with Willow Bend and working out from here. I'll phone Florida right now," his finger touching the pad on which he'd written what the Cantrells had told him, "then get all additional information to those involved in the search."

He was standing, turning toward the open door, then back again.

"Is there anything more you can tell me, anything at all that might help us identify him?"

"How I wish there were!" Linda cried, and the others grimly nodded agreement. She and her husband were almost to the back door when she added, "We'll go home and get some snapshots of Amy, recent ones, and bring them back here."

Gracie didn't want to look at her watch again—but couldn't keep from glancing at the big wall clock. In just a little over one hour the concert, the contest they'd been preparing so hard for, would begin at Waxmire Tabernacle, so she must get going soon!

However, God, I'd better check in with You again. That last answer of Yours was a doozy, if You don't mind my saying so—having me call the police station, and all. But is there anything else I should be attending to before going home for Uncle Miltie . . . ?

She'd been driving back the same way she'd come, so was nearing Amy's again—which reminded her of Patsy Clayton waving at her, beckoning. *Well, if she's outside, Lord . . .* but she'd hardly thought that when she glanced to her right, and there she was, right there to the left of the sidewalk, at the beginning of the temporary ramp, which had been built for her convenience.

She's such a plucky little thing, God. Just look at her there as she pushes the walker forward, using those front wheels, then setting down those nonskid hind feet, or whatever they're called, so it won't roll backward, then take a step forward. And another. Gracie pulled to the curb and got out, but wasn't noticed by the child until the car door slammed.

She looked around, seeing Gracie hurrying across her lawn. Surprised, Patsy lost that rhythm she'd been using and, forgetting to press down on the rubber-tipped legs, realized in a moment that the walker was starting to roll backward.

She grabbed for the railing beside her just as Gracie came running to pull her close, safe against herself. "Oh, Patsy, I was so afraid you'd fall!"

She turned, her thin little arms around Gracie's waist, the binoculars hanging from a black band around the child's neck digging into her abdomen. "I was scared! Thanks for catching me."

"I'm afraid I distracted you." Gracie steadied her as she got back in position to use the walker. "I'm sorry I couldn't stay when I saw you before, but I had to be somewhere else right away."

"I figured that must be it." The child moved another slow step up the ramp. "And I'm glad you came back."

"I'm glad, too, Patsy, but I can't stay for more than a few minutes. This is the day we have the choir contest—do you know about that?"

"Um-hmmm. Amy was going to sing special parts, but now she can't, since she's in the hospital."

Gracie didn't think she'd better tell her that Amy was no longer there—she wouldn't have time to make detailed explanations. She was glad she'd kept silent when Patsy said, "That man was real worried when I told him she was there."

She sucked in a quick breath, but forced herself to speak calmly. "What man was worried, dear?"

"The nice man who brought her presents." But then she giggled. "But I'd rather have candy, or a toy, or a book."

It can't be what I'm thinking of, but. . . . "What kind of presents did he bring her?"

"I—don't know about other times, but I saw him two times bring a big seashell. Isn't that a silly present?"

Gracie shivered, although the day was mild. "Maybe—Amy likes silly presents."

Patsy sobered. "Oh, I forgot; I should have told him she didn't get one of them. Gooseberry picked it up in his mouth from beside the front door and carried it away."

Does Patsy spend all her time watching over there? "What about the other one? Do you know if Amy got that?"

"I s'pose." She shrugged her thin shoulders. "But Mama called me for breakfast, so I didn't see who found it."

"So—both shells were brought early in the morning?"

"Not real early." She was finishing her slow advance up the slope. "Her dad goes to work early, before I get up; it's later when Amy and her mama leave for school. Did you know her mama gets to work with books all the time?"

"Yes, I understand she's a librarian there." She'd responded to the question, but her mind was much more on the fact that Amy may have found the shell first, before her mother could have. Or, was it possible that Gooseberry had made off with both of them on different mornings? It was not beyond him to have carried it some distance, then laid it down.

Like Uncle Miltie's screwdriver; they didn't find that for a week, not until, while clipping the thickly growing, cinnamon-colored chrysanthemums by the garage, he happened to see the handle sticking out from beneath the plants.

"Did the man leave notes with his presents?"

Her curly brown hair bounced with the shake of her head. "He took the shell out of a bag—but I didn't see a paper."

"Did you talk with him more than that one time, when you told him she was in the hospital?" But then she heard someone approaching, and the screen door opened.

"Well, hello, Gracie," Marilyn Clayton exclaimed, stepping outside. "I thought I heard Patsy talking to someone, but didn't know who it was. Sit down and stay awhile."

"Thanks, but I can't this time. Patsy was outside as I drove by, and I just stopped to see how she's doing. I must get to the Waxmire Tabernacle for that choir concert this afternoon."

"Oh dear! What with everything else, that slipped my mind."

"Can we go, Mama?" the child urged.

"It will be all singing, Patsy—a bunch of choirs all singing the same thing. You don't really think you'd enjoy that, do you?"

Gracie laughed. "It's a little better than that. There is one 'required' piece—but we're allowed to make changes, so none of them will be exactly alike. And each of the churches also has the opportunity to choose its other number, which can be anything—so there's bound to be a variety."

"Can we go, Mama? *Can* we?"

Marilyn looked at her watch. "I—guess we can make it."

Gracie had also checked—and barely squelched a groan. "I've got to be there within the next half-hour, but you'd have at least forty-five minutes. And, as an added incentive, there will be delicious refreshments following the competition!"

"*Can* we?" Patsy was tugging at her mother's arm. "Please?"

"You do realize, dear, that if we go we won't leave until the concert's all over, right?" The young mother wanted to make sure of this.

"Right!" she repeated. "And I want to wear my new red jumper and the white blouse with the red flowers . . . !"

Well, there were now two more going to the concert—but Gracie couldn't help wondering if the very fact of its being such a glorious fall day might keep many away. *Now stop this, Gracie Lynn Parks, stop right this minute thinking in terms of the first year or two, when the attendance was so low.*

It's been increasing each year—which is the reason Waxmire got to have another turn at hosting it, and we were skipped. I'd be happy if their huge auditorium is filled to overflowing . . . !

Dear God, please help us win at least something.

She consciously corrected that last part, for she did know better than to pray so selfishly. *Okay, Lord, I know that each choir has worked really hard at making preparations for this, and we're all hoping to win. So just do, please, help us—help all of us to do our very best—and help the judges to do their best, too, and to judge with no prejudice as to size or position or anything other than our music and our presentations.*

She was still a minute or two from home when she looked around to make sure there was no traffic before calling on her cell phone to let Uncle Miltie know she'd be there in a few minutes, but would be leaving again right away. "Since I have my choir robe and music with me here in the car, I don't have to go back to our church."

"Good! But you do have a couple of phone calls."

"That shouldn't surprise me! But who were they—and must they be dealt with right away?"

"Well, not right away—except for Anna's. She wants to know if you can pick her up, to take her to Waxmire."

"Are you about ready to leave, Uncle Miltie?"

"I sure am."

"Then could you do me a favor? Call her back, and say we'll be there within ten minutes."

"Okeydokey—it's as good as done."

"Great!" But she had to ask, "Who were the other calls from?"

"Two are going to call back, but the other was from Estelle—and I told her you weren't here, but that you would definitely be at the concert, so she could talk with you there."

"Well done, Uncle Miltie. Keep this up and I'll have to double your salary!"

They both laughed; doubling zero was not about to make him a rich man.

✒

Uncle Miltie had never seen the Tabernacle parking lot this full, and with another quarter-hour yet to go! Looking around, he exclaimed,

"I'm sure glad we're no later. Many of the best seats must already be taken, and I'd hate having to climb up into the balcony—many of the best seats must already be taken."

But he led the way with his walker, and Anna, one hand on his shoulder and the other wielding her cane, walked slowly up the aisle with him. A number of attendees spoke to them, but finally they settled into the last aisle seats in the sixth row—with Rick's wife and daughter cheerfully moving to center seats to make room for them.

Uncle Miltie leaned over to whisper in Anna's ear, "Hey, there *are* advantages to being the halt and the blind."

And Anna laughed. "You're right, George Morgan. And it's good to be reminded of that. . . ."

Gracie had seen them start down the aisle, and considered going with them, to make sure they found seats together, but one of the ushers assured her, "I'll keep an eye on 'em for you, Gracie. I know you're directing your choir, and I'll bet they're getting mighty nervous about you not being with them."

Seeing the twinkle in his eyes, she laughed. "I wouldn't be one bit surprised. So thanks," and she hurried to where all of her choir was already robed and standing around nervously.

"Where have you been?" Estelle demanded. "I called, and you weren't there, and your uncle wasn't sure where you were or when you'd get back."

"Oh, I had an errand to see about, then picked up someone who wanted to come hear us." Gracie was not about to get upset. "I understand my uncle assured you I'd be here on time, and I am."

She'd put on her robe while talking and now slid the stole over her head and patted the V-shaped front into its proper position, knowing that the longer "V" in the back would take care of itself.

When one member of the choir mentioned that she'd been too nervous to eat lunch, Don grinned. "Remember last year? I think these churches make a deliberate effort to outdo one another with all the goodies they prepare for us to eat after the singing. I don't doubt for a moment that we'll all make up for any starvation at lunchtime."

Then Rick turned to Paul, who'd just joined them. "And *you*, Pastor, plan on getting in on all the goodies afterward without even singing a note, don't you?"

"But of course!" The young minister laughed. "You couldn't possibly think I'd pass that up."

Several of the women appeared to be quite tense, but it was hard to tell with some; Tish and Tyne, not surprisingly, were whispering to each other. Gracie could see and appreciate the effort Barb was making to appear relaxed and carefree, and noted that it helped to draw her into some of the informality and fun the rest were having.

It was the responsibility of the host church, along with the choir directors, to arrange the seating of each choir. As the organist was playing and the five-minute-warning was given, everyone lined up in prearranged order, ready to march in, hymnals in hand, to sing along with the congregation.

Gracie always loved this—Willow Bend's finest singers, Willow Bend's saints from all the churches, all in one accord as they lifted their voices to "make a joyful noise together" while entering one of the sanctuaries of the Lord!

Her chest felt so full that for a moment she wondered if she really could sing at all, but then it was time for her alto voice to meld with all these others—and it was good. Very good! Whether Eternal Hope Community Church won or lost in the competition, she knew that every person here today had already won a wonderful reward— singing the praises of the Lord together.

There were many ahead of them, quite a few behind, and all were taking their seats in order, with no mix-ups. *Thank You, Lord. I don't think that You, either, would want any of these wonderful people to be embarrassed as they congregate here in this church today.*

Even as she sang, she'd glanced around. Back there on the left was Abe. And Rocky and his photographer were in the very front-center of the balcony. He gave her a thumbs-up, and she couldn't keep from smiling back at him. And there were Uncle Miltie and Anna, and oh, so many others she knew and loved!

As they finished singing, the host pastor came to the podium, welcoming all who had come to bring their gift of singing, as well as those who had come to listen to and support them. There was Scripture and prayer—and then it was time for the first choir to come forward.

Their order had been chosen by lot—with the stipulation that no church would be in either the first or last position in consecutive years. So this year's opener was the Bethesda Methodist choir, an average-sized group of fifteen, which, with Amy not here, was the same size as Eternal Hope's.

Gracie listened attentively, for the excellent and for any less-than-perfect parts. She, as well as anyone else who was interested, had access to the scoring sheets that would be used by the judges, so she now tried to assess what she'd give this group had she been one of those who had to make this decision.

Yes, they were good—but Gracie didn't think they'd probably be among the winners. Next came the choir of the Trinity Episcopal Church; she knew some of these people as soloists, and their choice of music was wise for them—showcasing two of their superior voices, belonging to the physical education teacher from the high school and Suzie Frantz, who home-schooled her three children.

By the third and fourth choirs, however, she was already confused. *If I gave number one an eight on this part of the scoring, then maybe this one should be a nine—but on the other hand, on the next part I don't think this is quite as good, so. . . .*

By the fifth choir, from Evangelical Free, she gave up on estimating possible scores and thanked God she wasn't a judge—from then on she settled back to enjoy to the fullest the rest of the program.

It was always a well-guarded secret right up until the bulletins were made as to what each church choir picked for its anthem-of-choice—and what a variety there was, far more than she'd guessed even when seeing those titles on the program! Of course that was to be expected: *We Sing of Hope*, turned out to be quite a jazzed-up rendering, while *Joy in the Morning* was comparatively subdued, dealing as it did with pain and heartbreak, yet getting through it with God's help. . . .

How can the judges possibly give meaningful scores when comparing the rendition of a Medieval chant with a Spiritual? Or a moody, a cappella rendering of a nineteenth century English ballad with a modern rap-type, rhythmic chanting in unison?

And then, at last, it was time for number six, Eternal Hope's presentation.

Barb walked to the organ, and as she played the first note they all arose. Yes! Everyone took the right position and processed exactly as done in church this morning. They approached the risers and those who could use help were given an unobtrusive hand—and Gracie knew that the others, also, must be missing Amy's presence right there in the middle of the front row.

As Gracie took her position, facing them from in front of the center aisle, the smile on her face was genuine, coming as naturally as her quick, close-to-the-chest thumbs-up before she looked at Barb and nodded.

They moved into their rendition of *Hallelujah, Save Us, Lord* perfectly. The solo parts went well—as flawless as the harmony! And the ending, that ending, which they'd changed so many times, even at the final rehearsal, was a worshipful and meaningful "Amen."

She looked toward Barb, and saw her beaming as she exchanged her sheet music for the piece they'd sung earlier in the day. The whole group must know that was the very best they'd ever sung their required number—and now were without doubt ready for *Help Me to See Thee, Lord.*

The beginning went well, the solo and duet portions were on target—and the ending equal to what they'd done in the morning service! Every member of the choir was beaming—they, too, knew they'd done their best, and that that best was very good.

They came back to their seats, only Tish nearly stumbling as she stepped down from the riser. Even that was probably not observed by most, however, as Lester was right there to steady her. She looked somewhat embarrassed, but proceeded the rest of the way without incident.

Gracie walked across in front of them to extend her hand to Barb, returning from the organ. "Wonderful! Absolutely fantastic, Barb!" she whispered as they sat down next to one another.

And Barb whispered back, "Thanks for making me go through with this—and for all your help."

Gracie simply could not have stopped smiling had she tried— which she wasn't about to do. "Thanks be to God . . . !"

The next group went up. It was painful to hear them flub their timing at one place near the beginning, but the rest of their performance went well.

Actually, all of the groups were good, but Gracie was sure her own choir was better than at least some. *If only we can win second or third place—even an honorable mention would be a major encouragement,*

God! But then, again, she realized this was not a "proper" prayer; every group here had the right to, and probably had prayed something similar to that.

So she rephrased—no, she changed that to, "Thank You, Lord, for being with us during all the practicing, and the altering, and the making-do we were involved with. Thank You for the courage to try this, and the strength to hang in there. . . ."

The very process of praying reminded her of the girl who would have been such an important part of today if only—if only what? *Where is she, God? Is Amy all right? Please, please take care of her—don't let anything bad happen to her.*

She's still alive, isn't she? She must be so scared if he took her away—although maybe not. For if she left the hospital with him, as we're assuming, of her own volition, perhaps whatever he's told her made her trust him more than she does her parents.

Does she know who he is—or is this just some "romantic fling" as far as she's concerned? But why those shells, God? Was this to be a message to Amy, or to her parents? They believe it was meant as a threat, which only they would recognize. But might he have had her believe that for him they held a totally different significance? Perhaps "eternal love," or something like that?

I've never heard of any romantic notions such as that, but what do I know? Anything's possible.

Indeed, Lord! What do I know . . . ?

She sighed, sitting there in the front row of this huge, practically new sanctuary, and consciously decided it was time to turn this whole mess with Amy over to God. *She* certainly had no sure answer to apply to a single one of the many questions she'd been asking. But God did!

She was a bit reluctant again to offer the other part of what she'd previously prayed, that God might act through her in any way He chose. He'd taken her up on her willingness before and, though Gracie was glad she'd obeyed, what now might be His call to action?

She started to close her eyes but, realizing she mustn't let anyone think she was bored or going to sleep, focused on the stole of the soprano in the middle of the front row of singers now up there—Presbyterians.

Okay, God, I'm here again. I didn't want to confess my hesitancy—but that's dumb, isn't it? You already know my thoughts even before I recognize them as such, so I guess I wouldn't have to put this in words for Your sake.

But for mine, it is necessary. Once having made the offer, I can't weasel out of it, telling myself I didn't understand the possible consequences. So here we go again—I'm willing, even if not as eager as I should be, to serve as Your hands and feet and mouth. . . .

Seven

GRACIE HAD HALF-EXPECTED to be zapped with some earth-changing thought or message almost immediately—and was relieved that didn't happen.

At least now, having already made the commitment, she could just sit back and enjoy the rest of the concert—which wouldn't take much more time, seeing that the last choir, which happened to be Waxmire's, was now on the platform.

The organist, on his home-church instrument, was superb, and Gracie thought that he, alone, could so entrance the listeners (and the judges?) that they'd be tempted to give megapoints on that! But the choir, also, had a number of trained voices, especially Roberta Bennett and Chuck DeLancy. Both numbers appeared to be flawless, their music-of-choice being contemporary, with sections of definitely rap quality, with rhythmic chanting, often in unison.

Well, I can't fault the judges if this church proves to be the winner—yet I'm almost hoping it isn't. With their getting first prize year before last, and a third last year, some of our smaller choirs may decide not to even try again. She tried to search her mind to see if that was the real reason she hoped this—and thought it was.

The competition was finally over, and Dr. Kenneth Ebersoll, Waxmire's pastor, commended and thanked everyone who had participated and the many who'd come to hear this marvelous concert. He asked everyone to rise and join in singing all verses of *Amazing Grace* while the judges finished calculating the scores.

And then it was time for the announcement of the winners, also being done by Dr. Ebersoll, who first wished to state, on behalf of the judges, that this had been a remarkably close contest. "Three of the four winners to be announced are separated by less than thirty points out of the maximum of four hundred, or one hundred from each of the four judges.

"I shall in just a moment be announcing those winners, and ask that one member of that choir come forward to receive its award. I'll be starting with an honorable mention, then third, second, and first.

"We understand that you will want to applaud, but are asking that, as hard as this may be, you wait until the end, then clap to your hearts' content—applaud these four church choirs, but also *all* those you heard today, for every single group here is a winner."

Heightening the dramatic tension, the organist achieved a most satisfactory drumroll, and the pastor tore open a large, off-white envelope and brought out a matching document. "For the position of honorable mention, I have the privilege of announcing—Trinity Episcopal Church!"

Their music director came forward and accepted for the choir, all the while accompanied by another very l-o-n-g drumroll.

Well, perhaps we'll be third, Gracie thought, but with another drumroll, Dr. Ebersoll announced that this award was going to the Evangelical Free Church on the edge of town. It was only the second time this choir had joined the competition, and Gracie tried to be generous in thinking that recognition would be especially appreciated.

She found herself wriggling a little, and sat up straighter. She knew she couldn't keep from being at least a little biased, but it did seem to her that Eternal Hope just might rank up here somewhere. But the drumroll this time, signaling second place, was for—and she could hardly wait for the intentionally delayed announcement—Waxmire Tabernacle!

Gracie wiped her forehead, aware that she was actually perspiring. There was only one slot above Waxmire's—and four below Honorable Mention. Did she have the assurance—or the pride—to believe that, though they'd done as well as they ever had, they'd been able to top Waxmire?

It now had to be either first prize or nothing. And the answer was already in that envelope, which Ken Ebersoll was opening so very, very slowly. Then the announcement: "And the first prize winner is . . . *Eternal Hope Community Church!*"

After church this morning, Barb offered to let Gracie go forward to collect their award, if they won one—but Gracie had insisted she was just one of the choir members, one who'd already been blessed by having had the opportunity to help with the directing this year.

Even as Barb went for the foot-high statuette of four singers, two men and two women, Dr. Ebersoll spread his arms and, with partially bent elbows, brought his hands within ten or twelve inches of one another and raised them, palms-upward. The people rose to their feet, and he was leading the applause, which went on and on.

Rick, beside Gracie, slipped a folded handkerchief into her hand— which was the first she realized that tears of unadulterated happiness were running down her cheeks. She put the white cotton square to good use, even while apologizing for needing it.

"Never has my handkerchief been so blessed." Rick was grinning. "What an occasion!"

Lester was hugging Barb, and the Turner twins were actually jumping up and down and laughing out loud!

When Ken again raised his arms, the applause finally died down and he reminded everyone of the invitation printed in the program, "Come on back to the social hall and join us for a time of fellowship and for snacks. What a wonderful day this has been; let's extend our time together!" And with that he gave the benediction.

Although there was a steady stream of people heading for the very large area behind the sanctuary, most choir members made their way more slowly than the others. Gracie, who'd lived in Willow Bend most of her life, was amazed at how many people she *didn't* know who said hello, or offered congratulations. Some were familiar-looking and she was sure they were from the general area, though she couldn't exactly place them.

She waved to friends who, deciding not to wait to speak with her now, were heading for the back; she hoped she'd see them there. She became aware of some of these relatives and friends of singers, who'd come from Ohio, Michigan, Illinois, and other states.

One Pennsylvanian commented about how rare such an ecumenical event was, and Gracie was pleased to share with her some of the other joint projects and services of this ministerium.

"That's wonderful," the woman approved, then added, "And now you can rest on your laurels until next year's competition."

She shook her head. "Oh, no, there's no resting yet. Waxmire and Eternal Hope now have the opportunity to go on to a regional event."

"Have you done that before?"

"*I* haven't—but this is the year. . . ."

She'd finally started to head for the back room, wanting to have the chance to speak to Paul before he left, but was still being stopped repeatedly by well-wishers. Yet, with the contest behind her, she now needed to seize the opportunity to tell him of Amy's disappearance. She finally excused herself, promising several people that she'd see them later.

Paul was near the outside door by the time she finally got to this room. Looking around, she saw that Uncle Miltie and Anna were thoroughly enjoying themselves—but then, as she again started toward where her pastor had been, she could no longer see him. She got to the back door as quickly as possible, in time to see him step into his car halfway across the large parking lot.

Rushing out, she started to run diagonally across the large macadamed area, toward the exit. *Oh, God, please let him see me and stop! If only I were wearing my sneakers, like usual—I can't go any faster in these stupid heels. . . .*

And yes! He did glance in her direction and stop, rolling down his window. "Gracie! Are you okay?"

Her hand reached to brace herself against his car. "I—I have to talk with you, Paul—before you leave. . . ."

"What a day, Gracie!" He sounded exuberant. "I'm so proud of all of you!"

"I'm proud of them too. We did have some problems along the way, but every single person really came through."

"They—and *you* certainly did."

But she had to give him her message. "Paul, what I need to tell you is that Amy's no longer in ICU. . . ."

"Great! I was just heading over there to see her."

"But it's—not great, not at all!" She was panting, so drew in a big breath before explaining, "She somehow got away from the hospital during mid-to-late morning, and the reason I was late getting to the church this afternoon is that her parents and I were at the police station."

"*What?*"

He sounded as shocked as she'd been. "No one apparently knows anything for sure. She'd coaxed her mother to bring in 'civilian' clothing, sweat pants and tops, and also to leave her some quarters—so we're guessing she called the guy in the gray car. And that she's with him now."

"You—met with Herb?"

She nodded, still breathless. "They've traced the ownership of the car and it's registered to the son of an ex-partner of Roy's who committed suicide after his embezzlements were discovered. The son, Andrew Hively, sounds as though he has a serious mental problem—at least an all-consuming hatred for Roy, which may not bode well for Amy."

"So—what can we do?"

"I'm not sure there's much any of us can do. Except to pray—pray a lot!"

They each had many questions, but their attempts at making sense of such extraordinary events fell flat. The conversation couldn't have lasted more than a few minutes before Gracie remembered to tell him, "We think it's best not to talk to anyone else about this right now—though I'm going back in to speak privately with Abe, if I can, since he's already involved."

"Thanks, Gracie, for doing all this. I'd have assumed she was much better had I gone to the hospital and they told me she'd left." He pressed his arms out against the steering wheel, pushing himself back into his seat. "What do you think about my going to see her parents?" His face was lined with uncharacteristic tension.

She hesitated. "I suppose that's a good idea—though I don't want them to think I'm going around talking about the situation. So, when you see them, please explain my coming to you."

As she went back inside and walked around visiting with people, she was suddenly startled when Rick asked if she'd brought the shell with her, so startled that she spilled some of her hot spiced cider. This mishap, however, did give her something to do while figuring out how to respond.

As she wiped up the liquid with her paper napkin, she simply said that she'd neglected to bring it—and she didn't think it was too important to know just what it was, anyway. Unfortunately, she didn't get away with that, for Uncle Miltie was nearby and stated that he most certainly did want it identified. "Where is it, Gracie?"

She avoided answering that by speaking to Anna, mentioning to her friend about having carelessly spilled her drink. "And it was so good. This early cider is the best of the year, isn't it?"

"I certainly enjoy it the most—but I've never been sure if that's because it's best, or if I'm so thirsty for it that it seems especially delicious."

And that led to Anna, Uncle Miltie, and several others talking about gathering apples of all kinds in the past, including macintosh, winesap, and smokehouse, and taking them to a family-run cider press. There were also remembrances of neighbors getting together and having a party with everyone working at making big copper cauldrons of apple butter, which was then shared by all.

From that moment on, Gracie made every effort to keep her distance from Rick and his curiosity, hoping he wouldn't again bring up the subject of that marine specimen she'd last seen being removed from Herb's desk drawer. She even wondered, now, if it would have been worthwhile, even possible, to check it for fingerprints.

She decided that would have been difficult, what with Gooseberry carrying it in his mouth, and Gracie and Uncle Miltie handling it, then Herb—and who knew how many others?

Herb! She'd better soon tell him what Patsy said about there being a second shell.

She'd seen Abe earlier across the crowd, but now she turned as a hand was placed upon her arm. "Oh, Abe, I'm so glad you came!"

"I'm glad too, Gracie. And I want you to know that I think you did a masterful job with your directing—especially on such short notice."

"Barb had it well under way before I sort of took over."

He was only two or three inches taller than Gracie, so with her wearing those unaccustomed heels, they looked straight into one another's eyes. "But you are very different people, with different talents, my dear Gracie. You are the optimist, the one who can help them see their capabilities and their strengths.

"They were not only singing for the contest today, they were singing for you."

She was flattered. "What I was hoping for was that they were singing for God."

"That too, Gracie." He grinned. "That too."

She reached for his cup. "Could I fill it with hot coffee?"

"That's not necessary. . . ."

"For me it is. How often have you refilled my cup of tea as I've sat in your deli and taken up your time with my problems—and the problems of those I love?"

"I'm not counting. For true friends, such times are always never enough."

She saw the warmth in his eyes. "I treasure our visits, also, Abe. And I may come to see you in the morning."

His hand had remained where he'd laid it, and now she felt a gentle tug as he nodded toward a table across the room. "I would like that, but perhaps now is the time to talk?"

She nodded, and took a step or two in that direction before stopping. "I just offered you a refill, and am now heading the other way. . . ."

"Better a refill of friendship than of coffee, Gracie."

"I'll second that." But they didn't exchange another word until they were seated.

"Our dear little Amy is missing," she said somberly.

His dark eyes widened, but he waited for her to continue. "She left intensive care without anyone seeing her. . . ."

"How did she manage *that*?"

"We have theories, not facts—as is true of almost everything connected with this case." A twitch of the corner of his mouth alerted her to having used that last word. "And don't you dare tease me about reading mystery novels!"

"I can't, not really. I, too, read mysteries."

She cocked her head. "You know, Abe, I thought I knew you very well, but we must never have got on that topic. Isn't that strange?"

"Not strange at all. Each of us has many facets, so many likes and interests that we wouldn't get bored even with conversations each day." But then the smile disappeared as he asked, "Do you have any idea where Amy could have gone?"

She shook her head. "Nor do we know the whereabouts of Andrew Hively, the owner of the gray car. But we suspect that when we find one, we'll find the other."

"This is not like the Amy I knew. She'd have to realize how terrible her family must feel, and how they'd worry. As well as her friends." He was frowning. "What would make a girl like Amy run away?"

"I don't know." Her gaze seemed fixed upon the reflected gleam of a big electric coffeepot, but she wasn't actually seeing it. "That's what makes this so hard. To the best of my knowledge, she got along well with her parents—that is, as well as a normal seventeen-year-old of today will let herself get along with them."

But then she wondered aloud, "Did she ever tell you why she was working? Why she wanted or needed the money?"

"Not really. When she first came to see me she indicated that she wanted to work as many hours as possible, and I asked if she was working toward something. What she mentioned was education, and possibly, sometime in the future, a car.

"But she never seemed to spend money on herself. The clothes she wore were all right, but she didn't appear to have a large wardrobe—not like I see with other girls her age—or think I see." He shook his head. "But I was not blessed with a daughter, so perhaps I do not have the clearest vision where teenaged girls are concerned."

"I suspect you see more clearly than you know, my friend." She shifted position. "Apparently there have been serious money problems in that household."

"Yet both parents are employed, and neither is in a minimum-wage position—they're far above that."

"I—don't know just how bad things are in that regard, whether they still owe a lot of money, or anything like that. But I did notice that her mother wears no jewelry, not even a wedding ring—so I suppose that's a possibility."

"Which could account for many things. . . ."

It was then that Uncle Miltie came over to them, teasing. "Talk about being stuck-up, Gracie Parks! You direct a choir that wins this year's trophy, then hide out over here in the corner!"

She reached to lay her hand on his, on the walker. "It's been a very big day, and I've talked with an awful lot of people. It's a relief just to sit here with a good friend and quietly visit."

"Well, I'm not trying to rush you or anything, but thought I'd let you know that if you were staying because of Anna and me, we're ready whenever you say the word."

She pushed back from the table. "Frankly, Uncle Miltie, I'm bushed. I'd appreciate going home and relaxing."

Abe got to his feet first, and reached to help her up. "I hope you will have a calm, quiet evening and get a good night's rest."

"Thanks, Abe. I do need that."

"I'm sure you do. . . ."

꒦

Uncle Miltie, though professing to be stuffed, still was willing to consider the possibility of a dish of ice cream later. After he shared that with Gracie, he headed for the living room TV set and settled into his recliner.

As soon as he was engrossed with what was on the screen, Gracie phoned the police station, leaving a message for Herb, who was away from his desk, to call back. In the meantime, Marge dropped in, excited at the choir's success and not noticing her friend's distraction.

"Hi, Herb," Gracie said with relief, when he finally rang her, moments after her neighbor had left. "Anything new—that you dare tell me?"

"Not much, not for sure, anyway. How about with you?"

"Well, I'm not certain this is important, but did you have any idea that more than one shell was involved?"

"*More* than one?" He paused, though obviously interested. "Involved in what way?"

She filled him in on what Patsy had said, and realized she should have asked more questions. "I don't know if she spoke with him more than that once—and I hope the binoculars hanging from a cord around her neck won't make him skittish. Is it possible he might fear she saw too much?"

"Who knows?" Even over the phone, she could sense the coiled anxiety behind the police officer's caution.

"May I ask if you've been able to find out where he is, or was staying? Or anything about his recent activities?"

"We know where he was staying for a couple of nights—and he's been there other times, as well. But he's not there now. We also know he received one call prior to leaving, but not who it was from."

"Isn't it possible for phone records to show that and also outgoing messages from the phone outside of ICU?"

"Good suggestions, Gracie. And, yes, we're waiting for callbacks as to those. In the meantime, maybe you could check again with the child—Patsy, you said?"

"Um-hmmm. Patsy Clayton. She's been disabled all her life, and is now recovering from another orthopedic surgery, getting around with a walker." She didn't want to even think about the possibilities concerning her safety. "Herb, you don't think she could be in danger, do you? I don't need to tell her parents anything about what's going on, do I?"

She heard his deep intake of breath and subsequent release in a drawn-out sigh. "I wouldn't think so, Gracie—but reading about abnormal psychology and watching it in action are two very different things, so I wouldn't dare give an unequivocal, no."

"Then I'm going over there right away. I'm already so upset about

Amy; if anything happens to Patsy, too, I—won't be able to live with myself!"

"Gracie . . . ?"

She was blotting away a tear. "What?"

"I don't think she's in danger, but I do think you've made the right decision here. Still, I *never* again want you to say that you won't be able to live with yourself!" It was only a split second later that his voice added, so softly she could hardly hear it, ". . . Although I do know, only too well, how easy it is to feel that way."

Her own voice became a little stronger. "Thanks, Herb. . . ." And she meant it.

Uncle Miltie was so involved with his program that she wasn't sure he'd even remember that she told him where she was going. Instead of walking, she decided to drive the familiar route in case she should need to go somewhere else afterward.

Just as she was heading up the walk to the Claytons, Linda Cantrell burst out of her front door, having spotted Gracie. She was obviously upset as she demanded, "Have you heard anything yet about Amy?"

"Not yet, dear." She spoke as gently as possible. "I was hoping that perhaps you had."

"Well, we haven't." She stood there wringing her hands, face showing her strain. "And I think it's time to call the radio and TV stations, so people know about our daughter's being kidnapped."

"We don't know that she has been, Linda." Gracie was trying to keep her voice calm and reasonable. "She's the one who voluntarily left the unit."

"But Amy would have come home." Her voice grew louder, as though volume alone could make her words true. "I know she would have—she probably expected him to bring her here, and he didn't!"

There was no point in arguing what would not, under the circumstances, probably have taken place. And Gracie didn't feel free to tell her that the police had determined where Andrew had stayed prior to receiving that phone call. "Do you keep close tabs on her friends and acquaintances?"

Her head moved slowly from side to side. "Not too much—not recently. We did at first, though. Then we seriously considered Andrew's threats. But it's been five years now—why would he wait for five whole years to make a move? To kidnap our Amy?"

Gracie would have had an answer to that had it been Herb or Abe asking, but she couldn't say to this distraught mother that the man could very well be mentally ill—that his continuing hatred could have finally pushed him over the edge of sanity. "I don't know. Could he possibly have been in prison? Or institutionalized?" She wished she'd thought to find out about this from Herb. They must have considered such a thing and checked it out.

Linda asked more questions, and then Roy emerged from their house to join them. By then, Gracie wasn't too surprised to have Patsy's mother and father appear at their door, looking out to see what was happening. *This is like old home week—or a movie-of-the week when the writer doesn't want someone to tell someone else something.*

But this was real life, and she chided herself for making that analogy. Besides, she had no way of knowing whether or not the Claytons even knew what the Cantrells were going through.

It turned out that all they knew was that Amy had been in the hospital. When Roy and Linda, arms around one another, had returned to their house, Gracie casually attempted to learn if Patsy had told her parents about the man in the gray car.

But her calm tone didn't fool them. "Why didn't you tell us, Gracie? How *dare* you not let us know about this, so we could protect her?" They were now nearly as agitated as the Cantrells.

"That's why I'm here," she tried to explain.

"That was hours ago when you talked with Patsy. Anything could have taken place during that time and it would all have been your fault!"

How could she respond to that? A little matter of getting to the church on time—a minor thing like winning first place in the competition paled in significance against a mother and father's possible loss of their daughter.

She was still attempting to get in a few words when an unmarked black car pulled up and Herb, in casual clothing—jeans and plain navy sweatshirt—got out and strode toward them.

Gracie introduced them, learning that the Claytons and Herb knew one another by sight, but little more. It was the police officer who asked, "Do you suppose we could go up on the porch or into the house instead of standing out here?"

That was one thing, at least, on which they could all agree, so they entered the house and went into the living room. In the next room, where Patsy was sitting in her wheelchair, the television was on, but

Gracie decided not to interrupt, stopping only to wave and smile at her young friend before settling herself with the other adults. Looking around, she waited for Herb to take the lead.

He asked first how long she'd been here and, learning it had been only a few minutes, said, "Then I guess we'd better start from the beginning."

He ran through the facts he knew and was willing to share with the Claytons: Amy's leaving ICU, the shell found by Gooseberry, and, most importantly, Patsy's account of the second shell left next door. "Did either of you see this second one?"

When they replied in the negative, he asked permission to invite their neighbors back, to continue the exchange of information.

Linda and Roy, both stiff with anxiety, walked in, confirming they'd seen neither of the shells until he'd shown them that first one at his office. And it was difficult enough for Patsy's mother to believe her daughter had seen one mysterious shell, let alone an additional one. Perhaps Patsy had merely seen the same one on two different occasions, or got her days mixed up.

But when she learned that her little girl had not only spoken with the suspect, but had innocently informed him that Amy was in the hospital, she grew even more upset.

Again Gracie was under fire—"You should have told us! It would have been your fault had she been kidnapped, too—had she had something horrible happen to her. . . ."

Eight

A S HERB TRIED TO CALM Patsy's mother, Gracie realized to what extent she'd been caught in the middle; from now on, she'd better check back with him before snooping independently.

It was certainly obvious that neither set of parents thought much of the way she'd handled things!

To defuse the situation, Herb asked for help in suggesting theories as to what could have taken place—even knowing that some of these would quickly be proven unlikely, or shot down right away.

Speculation one, that Andrew had only just now located the Cantrells and, discovering that Amy was in the hospital, decided immediately to make his move, was discarded since he had been "dating" her—or at least seeing her off and on for at least a couple of months.

Speculation two, suggested by Roy, fared little better: Amy, either on her way to the rehearsal or after her arrival, had eaten or drunk something that made her ill. (Better, of course, would be if she had just contracted some fast-acting virus.) Then, after she'd been taken to the hospital, Patsy told the strange man where she was, and he somehow managed to sneak in and see her there, talking her into getting out and leaving with him.

Linda insisted that her Amy had too much sense, and that she loved them too much to do something like that, especially when she knew how worried they were about her. Besides, she was much too weak, just recovering . . . and she began to cry.

Roy tried to comfort her, and other scenarios were mentioned, none of them answering all the questions they had. Herb put in quietly, "These are all suppositions based on her knowing who he really is. Suppose for a bit that he might have used an alias. . . ."

"Why should he?" Roy demanded. "I'm sure he wanted us to know—to worry and suffer. And how do we know he wasn't the one who gave her whatever it was that made her so sick so quickly."

Linda Cantrell groaned, putting her hands to her face in horror. "How much more we'd suffer if everything could be kept hidden until he'd accomplished—whatever he had in mind to do. . . ."

Gracie murmured, "Perhaps he didn't know how much she'd been told, what she knew. Is it possible he started out just feeling his way—and discovered she was truly a trusting young girl who hadn't yet lost her faith in other people?

"Maybe it took him this long to—to poison her mind against her parents—to make her choose him over you. Couldn't that be his ultimate revenge?"

By now, Linda was holding on to her husband's arm, as if to keep from drowning. "I can't stand this, Roy—this not knowing. . . ."

Nobody had the heart to remind her that she had no alternative.

"You've still not located the car?" Gracie asked.

Herb's eyes flickered slightly, as though he was unclear as to what he should answer, how much they ought to know. After a moment of hesitation, he said, "Yes, Gracie, we did find the car, in a Chicago suburb, but. . . ."

"Then where's Amy?" Linda strained at the edge of her seat. "She's all right, isn't she?"

". . . We don't know where either of them is. We're checking every motel and hotel in the whole area, as well as car rental and public transportation places."

"Then isn't it time to call in the experts?" her father demanded. "If he's taken her across state lines—and she *is* still a minor, you know—this is an FBI matter, right?"

Linda reminded them, "I've been wanting to call the TV stations, get her picture out there all over the place, so someone who's seen her will call!"

"And yet," Herb continued, still speaking in the same controlled voice, "supposing there's too much publicity and he becomes scared, afraid she will be recognized. Can he then keep her hidden? Or will he feel forced to . . . ?" He left that sentence unfinished.

The room all at once seemed airless and silent, quiet enough for Gracie to become aware of the music from the Disney tape Patsy was watching in the next room. It was the delightful tune sung by the Seven Dwarfs as they whistled their way home from work—its mood of cheer utterly incongruous with this room's atmosphere.

"May I propose that we let the law continue doing things its way for at least another twenty-four hours?" Gracie offered.

Linda glared at her. "The law has let that man take my daughter out of the state already. We don't know how she is or what he's doing to her . . . !"

Herb put in, "I sympathize with your wanting to take quick action, Mrs. Cantrell, but we don't even know if Amy is with him. If she is, then this man's mental state. . . ."

"He's a horrible man, a kidnapper, and—he's already threatened us, frightened us—we don't know what he's capable of!" She paused no longer than it took for a quick breath. "I *am* going to call the TV networks!" And she jumped up from where she'd been sitting beside her husband on the couch.

"Mrs. Cantrell!" Herb's voice was firm, commanding, the first time Gracie had heard that tone from him. "Be seated!"

Linda was so startled that she actually did what he told her. He was still seated in his chair, both feet flat on the floor and with no evident movement having taken place, but he now looked, even out of uniform, like someone to be obeyed.

His gaze stayed on her. "I haven't wanted to say this to you, not wanting to worry you more, but the reason you've heard nothing from or of Andrew Hively for five years is that he's been institutionalized in Florida. . . ."

She stared at him, eyes huge; it was her husband who demanded, "What kind of institution?"

"A mental hospital. Had you kept up your ties back there, you'd undoubtedly have heard that he'd, in fact, been doing many peculiar, even destructive things. He'd been arrested and finally was going to trial when his lawyer appealed to the court, necessitating a series of psychological evaluations.

"The result: He was determined to be unfit for trial."

Gracie knew to ask anything else might prove even more traumatizing for the Cantrells. Still, there was a real chance the answer might make things better. "Herb, would it help us to know what *kind* of strange and harmful things Andrew had been doing? Did he become a danger to people, or just property? Was he ever threatening or harming any women?"

He shook his head. "Not that we know of—not as far as I could find out. One of his earliest episodes involved his going up and down a rural road, in the middle of the day, shooting the connections—the insulators—off electric poles. Another came to light when perfect strangers began reporting calls from him, in which he insisted they were close family friends, and left really weird messages, like the date and time on which their deaths would occur—always within ten days!

"Also, he'd start out with a bucket of paint and a brush, covering with huge, brush-wide smears of brilliant red paint every bit of graffiti he could find. . . ."

"There was nothing—aggressive? No actual physical assault against anyone?"

"Again, not that we know of. That's not to say it's an impossibility."

Gracie felt it was time to ask, "So what do you think the odds are, Herb, that he might have her with him for—well, just for company? That he's obsessive but not really violent?" She could sense the Cantrells stiffening with fear as they awaited Herb's reply.

"I'd never hazard a guess like that, Gracie! Not ever! There are too many personal variables, and situational ones to allow me to figure out what will happen." He glanced around the group before again focusing on Gracie. "I, personally, have been doing a whale of a lot of praying for her and for all of you—and suggest you do likewise."

He pushed himself up by pressing down on the arms of his chair. "I'm leaving now. I was officially off today, but I have been on during the night and since mid-morning. You can leave any messages on the station answering machine. I'll check them at least every hour, because I'm also expecting answers to several different queries. . . ."

Gracie realized how exhausted he was—and would have liked to leave when he did. But Patsy had let her know she'd like company for the end of *Snow White,* and Gracie wanted to keep things as normal as possible for her in the midst of this stressful situation, which Patsy thus far was not aware of. Gracie knew that the two couples were still in the front room talking, and was relieved when, a short time later, she heard the Cantrells depart.

As the credits began to roll, she chatted with the child about the story and characters and asked, "Don't you think Snow White should have known better than to eat that apple?"

Patsy considered for a moment, then said, "Well, I'd maybe have liked to just taste it, 'cause it was sure a beautiful apple, and I. . . ."

"Patsy! Don't *ever* eat things given to you by strangers!" Her mother had entered the room just in time to hear that reply, and was clearly agitated. "That may be why Amy was so sick—maybe someone gave her something bad."

"I know, mama. You've always told me, but why—would Amy do that? Didn't her mama tell her not to?" she asked, wide-eyed.

Mrs. Clayton threw up her hands. "I don't know what other mothers tell their children, but you know I want you to be careful. That's what's most important."

The child nodded. "All right. I'll only eat it if I know the person who gives it to me."

Her mother again left the room, and Gracie wished she could add to that. She had the feeling that Amy would not have taken anything from someone she didn't know, either, but by this time she did know Andrew—or whatever he might have called himself—very well.

If he gave her something to eat or drink, she would probably have consumed it. What reason would she have to suspect him of wanting to harm her?

∽

Uncle Miltie reported that he'd just answered a call on the fourth ring, and was sure the line was open, but no one spoke. "I've been promising myself to buy one of those gizmos that automatically records the phone number of all callers, and I'm definitely going to get one tomorrow morning!" she informed him. But now she was going to take a shower and head for bed. She needed it!

Another call came while she was in the bathroom—but once again there was no answer when her uncle picked up the receiver. Could this be a form of harassment? Or was it someone who wanted to speak only to her?

Could Amy be trying to reach her? That possibility kept her tossing and turning a long time before she went to sleep. How she hoped that, if that was the case, Amy would do it again. And talk to her. *Please, Lord, be with Amy and her family and friends. Even if she deliberately left with Andrew, even if for some reason she's angry with us or wants nothing to do with us in the future. If Amy is still alive, God, please get her in touch with someone here.*

There were no more calls throughout the night.

Gracie awoke even earlier than usual, her first thoughts on the missing girl. Picking up the Bible from beside her bed, she held the soft-bound volume between her palms, riffling through the pages with her right thumb. She knew the words, and said them to herself—yet had to see them printed, had to read them.

Near the end of *Matthew*. After the resurrection. Jesus there in Galilee with His disciples, about to leave in that physical form of His strong, earthly manhood in which they all knew Him so well. He was giving them the Great Commission—they were to tell everyone the good news of His being the Messiah. It was the message meant for not only those throughout the then-known world, but throughout the entire world.

Yes, here it was, at the very ending of Matthew's account: *Lo, I am with you always, even unto the end of the world.*

She lay there looking at those words, reading them again, and praying. She'd been praying all along that Amy would not be too frightened, but now Gracie qualified that. *Please help her to recognize if she's in danger, and give her the opportunity to get word to me—or to someone else who can be of more assistance than I know how to be.*

Only You, Lord, know if notifying the media would make things worse for Amy—if so, please don't let her mother do that. And that goes for all of us, me, too—help us to do only what will make things better. I hope my going to Abe and to her parents and their neighbors is what I was supposed to do—it seemed right, but how am I to know?

Please do let me know what to do, Lord.

She was reminded of their anthem yesterday, *Help Me to See Thee, Lord.* Yes, *that was so very fitting right now,* so apropos. *Even in a mess like this one, You are here. But I so often don't look for You, or pay attention to what You're doing. Help me, Jesus, to see You in everything and everyone I see today.*

She got out of bed and went to the window. There were glimmerings of morning light, enough for her to fit in her walk before starting her day, with all the surprises it might hold. She smiled, remembering Elmo's comment about going five days a week to his business, while Gracie kept involved with her *busyness* seven full days and then some.

The last thing she did before leaving the house was to take the phone off its hook and lay it on the stand; she wanted to be there should there be more calls.

She was still thinking of her husband as she and Gooseberry started off for their walk. *Oh, El, I miss you so terribly. What I wouldn't give to have you here beside me, to hold me and help me and BE me. I never fully appreciated until we were married what was meant when at weddings, especially, there was the emphasis on "two becoming one."*

But we were. We really were—which is why sometimes I now feel so incomplete. How I wish I could talk things over with You, like now with this Amy problem. You had so much common sense—not just book learning, though you did have that—but wisdom. And you had so much patience, in so many ways....

She kept on walking, ignoring Gooseberry, who was sometimes underfoot but more often wandering around checking under bushes, around fences, even under parked cars in driveways. She was confident after all their walks together that he knew better than to go out into the street.

When they got as far as the Cantrells, it seemed to her as if he was giving this property a more thorough examination than most. She couldn't help but wonder if he was hoping to find another shell.

They walked on to the police station, where Gracie learned that Herb should be arriving within a few minutes. Feeling unusually restless, she told the woman on the desk that she'd walk around another block or two before coming back. She got only as far as the sidewalk when he arrived.

He had learned nothing more overnight. She figured it was worth mentioning all those "message-less" calls at her home, and told him she intended to buy, as soon as the stores opened this morning, one of those machines to record phone numbers of incoming callers.

"That's wise, particularly under these circumstances," he told her. "I've had one for a long time—and it's certainly good for cutting down on crank calls."

"I—hadn't realized. . . ."

He looked at her. "You're learning about all the cranks and crazies out there, aren't you, Gracie."

She looked up at him, this handsome, strong, wise man, this public servant she'd so taken for granted, not even wondering what his work—his life must be like. "How do you stand it, Herb?"

The crooked grin he'd flashed her was gone, but now a slow smile, more sad than happy, took its place. "I love this town and its people. If I didn't, I wouldn't still be here."

Gracie found she couldn't speak right then, and he added, "And, like you, dear friend, I try to help matters out by praying."

Gracie had asked Uncle Miltie to leave the phone's receiver lying where it was until after she'd come back from the store. But it wasn't long before he was able to tell her, on her return: "That's it, Gracie. Your new device is connected and should be operational."

He looked at her for approval, and his niece gave him an immediate hug. "Thanks for taking care of this for me."

"For *us*," he corrected. "I don't enjoy this kind of shenanigan any more than you do!"

They ate breakfast together, and he went outside to check on his flowers. Gracie was restless and worried and found herself moving around aimlessly. In an effort to distract herself—more important than the fact that the last ginger cookie had been eaten—she decided to make up a batch of snickerdoodles.

This cookie recipe had been handed down for generations—at least back to her great grandmother, possibly before that—and she hardly needed to look at the somewhat yellowed card on which the ingredients were so carefully handwritten.

She smiled, remembering her daughter-in-law wanting to copy it and many other old favorites on her last visit, and asking about this one, "How do you know how much flour to add, Mom?"

"Doesn't it say?"

"'Use enough flour to stiffen' is what's written here, but. . . ."

Gracie laughed. "I'm afraid you'll find that on many of the old recipes, dear. Those earlier cooks didn't have the measuring equipment that we're familiar with and use today, and their flour wasn't always made of the same kind or quality of wheat.

"So women used what they had, their eyes—what the dough or batter looked like—and their fingers to feel it. To be honest, I still do that to gauge the amount of flour I use for cookies and breads."

I guess when you come right down to it, that's the way I am about a lot of things, particularly relationships—friendships. My favorite people aren't at all alike, some seeming unlikely, or a bit rough around the edges, and yet. She removed a bit of dough from the small ball she was forming in her floured hands, then rolled it in the dish of sugar and cinnamon before placing it with others on the cookie sheet. *I can't imagine not having Rocky and Abe and Marge and Herb as friends.*

As well as so many others!

By the time Uncle Miltie came back in with his walker and washed at the sink, the first warm snickerdoodles were being placed on a saucer for him, the rest on the counter. He took his first bite where she could watch his enjoyment. "It's scrumptious, Gracie! As always . . . !"

She still enjoyed watching through the oven's rectangular window, seeing the cookies puff up at first, then gradually become flat again, with crinkled tops.

Her smile gradually faded as she thought of Andrew Hively's father; he must have been puffed up like that, too—appearing very big and important. But then the hot air all leaked out, leaving him in the reality of his flatness. A state in which he could not endure.

Was this true of the son, also? She could only pray—again—for him. And even more for Amy.

The phone's attachment was working fine—three telephone conversations by mid-morning, and each of the numbers was recorded. It was then the first questionable call came through. Gracie recognized the area code as a Chicago one, though the number itself was strange to her. But no one responded to her, "Hello . . . hello, who is this? . . . Is anybody there? . . . Hello?" She tried again and again, but when there was still no answer, she finally said, "All right, then, good-bye."

This was repeated within the next three or four minutes—ah, yes, three minutes and thirteen seconds, according to the recording device. She again tried to get some response on what she knew to be an open line, from the same number; she desperately wanted to connect if it was Amy—but wouldn't she answer if *she* called?

Gracie grabbed the telephone directory and looked up 773, confirming it as a greater Chicago exchange. There was no sound at all coming from the other end of the line—unless, this time, there might have been something like a heavy exhalation, perhaps a grunt—and a strange bumping sound. Or had she imagined that?

Gracie kept talking even while stretching the coiled phone wire as far as she could. She banged on the kitchen table with the sugar bowl to get Uncle Miltie's attention in the other room and he looked around, startled. Seeing her frantic beckoning, he used the remote control to shut off the TV, got to his feet and hurried as fast as possible, mouthing the question, "Amy?"

She was saying, "Perhaps you can't talk, but if this is you, Amy, please let me know. If it is, please make a noise—any sound will do, but just make it once for a *yes*, or twice for *no*."

They waited for what seemed a long time before there was one small, weak thump of some sort—and Gracie couldn't know for sure if that was an answer. In the meantime, she was indicating to Uncle Miltie the number showing clearly there on the device he'd just installed, as she was writing on the phone pad, "Use cell phone to call Herb at police station—or home. Chicago number. Will try to keep on phone." She then carefully wrote the entire number before scrawling in big letters, *HURRY!!!*

She kept asking questions, but only occasionally got that same dull thump, done just once. "Amy," she finally said, "this time, if your answer is 'yes' please give two of those sounds, okay?"

Everything was quiet.

"Amy, are you still there?" *Oh, God, please don't let me have lost her—please, PLEASE, Lord. . . .* Gracie felt almost sick to her stomach. *Help me to be calm. Don't let me panic her!* "Amy, dear, I've talked with your parents, and they are very worried about you. You are in Chicago, aren't you?"

She waited for what seemed forever before she heard a small bumping sound. *Only one? But then there was another, fainter still.*

YES! She answered me. "Are you restricted somehow? Perhaps tied?"

BUMP—a very small sound, then an even tinier one.

"Are you well, and . . . ?" She'd almost asked if she was injured or in pain, but, if she were somehow restricted, or gagged, she could very well be in discomfort merely from that. Before Gracie could decide how to fix that question, make it into one Amy could answer, giving more information, she heard a different sound, perhaps someone opening a door.

And the line went dead!

Uncle Miltie was coming back into the kitchen from the other room, stage-whispering, "Herb's calling Chicago right away, then he's coming here. . . ." He stopped short, staring at her, then pushed his walker faster. "Gracie, are you all right?"

She stared at the silent phone in her left hand. "I lost her—I had Amy on the line and I *lost* her . . . !"

"Sit down, Gracie!" He was dragging a kitchen chair in her direction. "Sit down now."

She did as he said, too numb to argue or to even answer his questions. *I had Amy on the phone—I'm sure I did. But I lost her. I couldn't keep Amy on the line . . . and if that was, indeed, a door opening and Andrew was coming in and found her on the phone. . . .*

Oh, God, dear Lord, help Amy!

She knew Uncle Miltie was upset, that he was trying to help her, but he and this house and the whole world made no sense right then. He stayed there right beside her, pushing his walker to the side so he could pull her to him, his arms around her, holding her close, her head against his chest. "Gracie, dear, you did your best. . . ."

"It—wasn't enough. She *needs* me, needs *help*. . . ."

"We have no way of knowing, here where we are, but maybe, Gracie, your talking to her might have given her even a little more courage, a little more hope. . . ."

She'd begun to shake, and there were tears starting down her cheeks, wetting the front of his shirt. *Where are you, God, when Amy needs You so? I can't see You anywhere in this mess, in spite of that anthem.*

I know You must be—I do know You're out there, but—but please help me to see Thee, Lord! And—even more than that, be with Amy in a special way so she knows she has Someone on her side. That You are with her.

Nine

IF THE RED HAND OF THE CLOCK had not been going around so visibly, Gracie might not have believed that only a few minutes had passed before Herb got there. He didn't knock this time, just walked in when seeing them in the kitchen. "Any news?"

"I had her on the line, Herb—I'm sure that's who it was, but I lost her."

"How long ago?"

Uncle Miltie answered, "While you and I were on the phone."

"I tried so hard. . . ." She couldn't get over the enormity of her failure. "The only facts I got for sure were that she is in Chicago and she's restricted in some way.

"Oh, Herb! She was trying. . . . I know she was!"

"So were you, Gracie." He came to stand right in front of her, looking down at her.

"I wanted to find out if she was hurt, if she was in pain—but she didn't let me know. And I don't know why she called me instead of her family, but there must be some reason."

He looked at the numbers of the recorded calls, then fiddled with some buttons on the apparatus. "I've adjusted it to make it record all calls for playback, and to let us all hear."

"Never read instructions unless you're stumped!" Uncle Miltie was chagrined, and let them know why. "I used to get so provoked with workers who tackled anything new that way, yet here I did the same thing!"

She squeezed his hand. "As it turned out, there would have been nothing to record." *At least I don't think those "thumps" or "bumps" would have given any clues, but what do I know?*

"I've made contact with Chicago," Herb now told them. "They could even be at that address by now, if there happened to be a patrol car nearby—and if the call wasn't from a cell phone."

"I doubt that it was. I suspect she was having trouble even pushing buttons to get through to me. But what scares me most is that the last thing I heard sounded like a door opening."

The phone rang.

Herb looked at the local numbers on the display as he picked up the phone and handed it to her. "Hello?"

"Hi, Gracie. Is everything okay over there?" It was Marge. "I saw Herb come, and he looked as if he was hurrying, as though something might be wrong—"

Gracie swallowed the retort that first came into her mind—she knew Marge was genuinely concerned, not just being a busybody. "We're expecting a call, Marge—hoping to receive some information. We thought perhaps this was it."

"Oh. Well—then I guess I'd better hang up. I'll talk to you later."

Her words had come through clearly, crisply, for all of them to hear, so they now knew Herb's adjustment of that part of the new device worked also. "Thank goodness she understood the importance of our waiting for a call," Uncle Miltie exclaimed. "That woman can run on longer than anyone in the world!"

"But you know she's good-hearted," Gracie reminded him. "I'd be concerned, too, and curious, if I saw Herb hurrying up to her house."

"But you wouldn't nose into her business by calling her about it before the screen door barely shut behind him."

Still they waited, hardly tasting the fresh snickerdoodles and coffee. They talked about Marybeth, Herb's wife, who'd taught second grade during the first several years of their marriage, was now a stay-at-home mother but, he told them, was considering the possibility of returning to work next year when their youngest would be in first grade.

"I admire Marybeth's priorities," she told him, "especially since a law enforcement officer's salary isn't all that great."

He nodded. "Her pay as an elementary school teacher would be more than mine—but we agree that these first years are so very important. Believe me, the price many families, even in our own community, pay for spending too little time with their kids is far higher, in many ways, than what their extra income ever brought in!"

They also talked about the choir. "I'm pleased that Marybeth started singing with us this last year."

"Me, too, Gracie. Since I'm the one to make up staff schedules, I can usually arrange to be home on Wednesday evenings, since she enjoys it so!"

"She has such a sweet, clear soprano voice, but we can't persuade her to sing a solo, no matter how *small* a part it would be."

He reached out his mug for the refill of coffee she was offering. "I love her voice too but, well, you know that when people speak of a church's "war department," it's all too often the choir they're referring to.

"This way," he went on, "being just a member, we feel more comfortable—that there's less chance of becoming involved in the . . . shall we say, personality conflicts?"

Gracie herself had gone down that same path—but that wasn't the only reason she hadn't wanted to be considered for solo parts. In the first place, she wasn't certain she'd be good at it and, secondly, she was most satisfied listening to the others. "When you consider the range of human types, social positions, and musical talents we have there, it's a wonder things are as calm as they are."

He tilted his chair back on its rear legs and grinned at her. "And you were thinking that during the middle of this week, right?"

Uncle Miltie responded to that teasing. "I was here. I know she was shook-up."

They were trying hard to pass the time, but there was still no call. When Uncle Miltie invited Herb to come outside and see the chrysanthemums, the younger man at first demurred, then changed his mind when the other assured him, "This is a fairly good-sized lot, but you'll easily hear the phone from any part of it."

Gracie was relieved they were gone; keeping a conversation going under these circumstances had been more difficult than she'd have expected. *I know, El, you used to kid me about never running out of things to talk about, but filling up time for the sake of just filling it is not as easy as it may seem!*

The phone finally rang—and yes, it was a Chicago number. She didn't pick it up until the beginning of the fourth ring, wanting to give Herb the chance to at least start for the house. "Hello?"

"Is this Ms. Parks?"

It was an unfamiliar male voice. "Yes, it is. And to whom am I speaking?"

"Officer Mark Jameson, calling from Chicago. May I please speak with Chief Bower?"

"One moment please." She was only slightly surprised to see that her hand was shaking as she laid down the phone. She wanted more than anything to ask how Amy was, to demand information—but she'd follow the rules as she saw them.

She hurried toward the door. "Herb, the phone—it's for you."

He was already coming in. "The one we've been waiting for?"

She nodded. "It's an officer, from Chicago."

He grabbed her hand, giving a small tug, which she took as his reassurance that it was all right for her to listen in on the conversation. She followed him, standing there in the kitchen holding on tight to the back of a wooden chair.

"This is Herb Bower."

"Mark Jameson here. I'm sorry it took so long to get back to you, but we've been very busy."

"Is Amy all right?" The crucial question.

Time seemed to freeze before the answer came, with Gracie holding her breath for what seemed *too* long, as if she were underwater and struggling for the surface. Officer Jameson's inflections remained the same, "As far as we know, there was no major physical assault, but she's been through a lot. Right now we're in the emergency room. . . ."

The emergency room!

". . . They've just taken her inside to check her over, to make sure. We'll know soon, but thought you'd want to have this much, anyway."

"What condition was she in?"

"The perpetrator must have a real thing about duct tape—it was around both knees and ankles, and around her wrists, binding them together, her arms behind her back. And not only covering her mouth, but going all the way around her head."

Oh, Amy! How did you ever manage to call me? But that wasn't nearly as important to Gracie right now as, "Ask if we can talk with her."

Her stage-whisper had evidently been loud enough so that the Chicago policeman said, "Tell Ms. Parks that would be fine with us, but Amy Cantrell has so far refused to speak with anyone."

She reached for the phone, which Herb relinquished readily. "Is she capable of speaking?"

"Physically, she is, as far as we know—but she acts scared to death, and won't say anything."

"Could you please tell her I really would like to speak with her? That it's important." But why should the officer trust her? "I'll make every effort to not say or do anything that could make matters worse."

"The doctors are with her right now, but I'll try that as soon as . . . hold on a minute, one's coming out. Docto*r* . . . Doctor Davison, may I speak with you? I'm on the phone with people from Willow Bend, Indiana, Amy Cantrell's hometown. Would it be possible for a special friend to speak with her?"

"She won't talk to anyone!"

That sounded like irritation, but could be something else she didn't even try to identify. "This is Gracie Parks. I'm the one she tried to call from—from wherever she was when the officers found her."

"That would have been impossible, Ms. Parks. . . ."

"But it *was*n't impossible. She *did* try."

Herb's head was near hers as he verified that, "Amy did attempt to communicate with Gracie. All she got was bumping sounds or grunts—but she did the best she could."

"Well . . . we can let you try—if she's agreeable to that, but just for a moment."

Gracie endured another wait in the almost-silence of faded, indistinguishable words and activities. And then the first voice, that of the city policeman, became louder and was speaking to Gracie, "I think she understood when I asked her, though at first she just lay there."

"Is she that sick—or hurt?"

"Not as far as we know, though we don't have reports back from the lab to compare with those your Indiana hospital is faxing here. It's more like she closes her eyes—and shuts out the world." He cleared his throat. "However, she did give a little nod when I asked if you could speak to her, so just hold on a few seconds."

She pulled a chair closer to the phone, and sat down as the voice said, "Here, you hold the phone, Amy. It's your friend, Gracie."

Amy said nothing, so Gracie did. "Hi, Amy, how are you feeling?"

No answer. "I'm pleased that you called earlier, but we did seem to have difficulties, didn't we?"

I'm not getting through to her at all! "Were you hurt, dear? Did he do anything to hurt you?" *Please give me wisdom, God, something to latch on to so I can get through to her!* "We miss you, dear, and your beautiful voice. I'm sure you'd like to know that our choir—your choir won first place in the contest. Everyone did a good job, they did everything just right. You would have been so happy, along with us!

"And now I'm hoping you'll be coming back soon, so you can sing with us for the district competition. . . ."

She waited, then, still getting no reply, heard herself asking, "And Andrew, where is he?"

There was a gasp. "They—killed him."

"They . . . ?" She couldn't even repeat that next word, just looked at Herb, who reached for the phone.

"This is Herb Bower, Amy. Are you sure someone killed him?"

"They killed him," the weak voice repeated. "Like my father did his."

"But your dad did *not* kill his father." Though that one word was somewhat emphasized, he had spoken softly.

"Andrew told me. That's why. . . ."

He tried to get her to continue, "That's why *what*?"

"Had to show how it hurts. Now he's dead—too."

Gracie felt she should help somehow. *But what can I say, God? Is Andrew really dead? What happened?* Herb had offered her the phone again, so, "Where *is* Andrew, Amy?"

"Took away. In the other ambulance." Still that slow, almost emotionless voice.

Gracie had a million questions, which she didn't feel she could ask: How had Andrew found her? How did he make friends with her? What sort of lies had he told her? How had she managed to use the telephone when her wrists were taped behind her back?

"Amy, dear, I'm going to ask a favor: please talk to the officers. Tell them exactly what happened, and why."

No response, so she tried again, this time already knowing the answer, "Are you there, Amy?"

"Um-hmmm."

"Okay, will you tell *me* about it?"

No agreement—but no discernible negative response, either. "Did he say you were going to Chicago when you left the hospital?"

"Just drove."

"Were you afraid?"

"Didn't want to come here, or go home. My father *killed* his."

Gracie looked at Herb, who was shaking his head, and mouthing, *That's not true.* "How did he prove that to you?"

"Told me. Showed the papers."

Logic will probably not work here.

"My father framed his—changed records. Shot him before proved innocent."

Herb was again shaking his head, so Gracie figured everything he'd checked out supported Roy's story. But Amy was convinced, and wouldn't be able to accept the truth without proof. "Are you in love with Andrew?" She couldn't help herself, now that she had Amy speaking to her.

There was a lengthy silence before, "I thought so."

Thank You, God, that she used the past tense! "What did Andrew do to you?"

There was again no answer. Wondering if someone else could do better, Gracie held the phone out a little, toward Herb. He raised his brows and shook his head, whispering in a very low voice, "Stay with it—if they want you to stop, they'll interrupt."

Maybe it is I who wants to stop, because I'm not accomplishing much. "Why did you leave the hospital, Amy?"

"Couldn't go home—Daddy killed a man."

At least she's now referring to him as "Daddy." "Was Andrew going to marry you?"

"Said so. . . ."

I don't even know if Illinois requires a parent's signature for the marriage of seventeen-year-olds. "Amy, did you see Andrew after school, before coming to the church the night you got sick?"

That little sucked-in breath again. "He didn't hurt me."

That's too quick a defense! "Did he give you something to eat or drink?"

"He brought me—no, NO! He *didn't* make me sick! He loves me!"

"But today he tied you up with duct tape," she reminded in as gentle a voice as she could manage.

"Wanted to go back—Indiana. He tried to change mind, but—ran away.

"Dragged back in room—grabbed phone. That's when used tape. Had to get food and—couldn't trust me. . . ." The next words were the most forceful, "Was *my* fault."

Did he keep telling you that all the while he was applying that tape? You must have believed what he said that time, too. I'm going to have to tell you the truth. "The reason you didn't hear of Andrew all these years, dear, is because he's been in a mental institution. . . ."

"*Not* crazy. He's not!"

"The tests they gave. . . ."

"No! *My* fault—it's mine! *Mine.* . . ." There was a high-pitched, drawn-out scream, and a loud crash followed by a rush of indistinguishable, excited voices and . . . sobbing?

Herb took the phone from her hand, and in moments was speaking to someone else. When he put it down, it was to tell Gracie that Andrew was very much alive, although he had been shot in the right shoulder—while using Amy as his shield.

The Chicago news was sobering, but the important thing was that Amy was safe now—and the authorities were notifying her family, so the Cantrells could probably be with her soon.

Gracie fretted, "What do you suppose those papers were, Herb, that Amy said Andrew showed her to 'prove' her father killed Tony Hively?" She couldn't help reverting to her sleuthing mode, especially with so much surprising information to digest.

"Perhaps Roy could have written some sort of a threat, or something," he suggested. "But that seems unlikely since Tony was on vacation when the authorities were called in."

"But—Amy referred to *the* papers. Doesn't that sound more like newspapers or documents, rather than a letter or note." She was now pacing the kitchen while trying to figure it out. "He didn't go to trial, did he?"

Herb leaned back against the refrigerator, "Not in the sense of being there in body, but there was, of course, a thorough investigation that was covered by the papers. Andrew certainly would not have shown those to her."

"That place where he stayed while in Willow Bend, did he take everything with him?"

"We'll find out." He punched in a number that was answered immediately. "Hi, Celia. Things fairly quiet there?"

He's calling the police station and Celia Pelton is giving him information about a number of calls, and of people in to see him. Herb listened intently, made a few notes in the book he pulled from his shirt pocket, asked a few questions, gave some responses, then put down the phone.

"I'm heading over to where Andrew stayed. You know the

place—Cordelia Fountain's home. There's always a chance that Andrew left something that can shed light on this."

Without asking permission, Gracie followed him out the door and got into his car. She herself wouldn't have even thought about the necessity of a policeman having to stop at the magistrate's office to get a search warrant before going on to the big brick house on Main Street. A small sign on its front porch read, "Rooms for Rent," and Cordelia Fountain, the seventy-ish woman who owned this old-fashioned tourist home, was soon greeting them.

"No, that nice, quiet young Mr. Hively hasn't checked out, but he left a day or two ago, taking only a small suitcase or carry-on or whatever-you-call-it." And when Herb questioned further, she told them, "As far as I know, most of his things are still in his room."

She was troubled about taking them upstairs, and remembered only after being on the third step that she might need her master key to let them in. It turned out that Andrew rented by the month, instead of by the night or week, and had come and gone a number of times during the last two or three months. No, he never told her when he'd be back, and she'd thought nothing of it when he'd departed this time.

They stopped just inside the doorway and looked around. There were two windows in this corner room, one facing the street, and the other overlooking Blackberry Alley. The furnishings were comfortably older, sort of like their aproned owner, making Gracie feel at ease. A laptop computer was on the table directly across the room, and a number of papers and manilla folders were both there and on the four-poster bed.

Cordelia was worried about them going through her renter's things. Herb showed her the search warrant—but that made her even more uneasy. "Does that mean he's a *criminal* or something?"

Once she'd begun fretting, she wasn't much calmed by Herb's saying he didn't think she had to worry about that, and his pointing out that he was taking full responsibility for their being there. She was clearly hesitant about leaving them in the room when her phone rang.

"I'm too much like that, too," Gracie admitted. "I always have to answer my phone when I hear it. But it's a good thing for her sake and ours that she left when she did."

He nodded, but said nothing as he continued quickly going through the folders, page-by-page. She was doing the same with the ones on the bed, then got down on her knees to check beneath it. Pulling out a large suitcase, she was surprised to find it unlocked.

Inside were underclothes, several shirts, socks, and a pair of sweatpants. Lifting these items out, however, Gracie saw a small pile of what looked like fairly expensive paper. "Herb?" He looked around, eyebrows raised in question. "Come see this."

There were three copies of almost the same thing, in each only a word or two changed. It was a hand-printed apology for ruining someone's life—with no salutation nor signature on any of them.

"Was he—practicing?" she wondered. "Maybe something to show Amy, saying it was from her father?

"Possibly." His lips were straight across, pressed together. "Whichever one—or a different one—he showed her was probably all the 'proof' this unsophisticated seventeen-year-old needed." They searched the rest of the room, but found nothing else they considered suspicious. Gracie, however, realized she could be looking straight at some crucial clue and not realize its significance.

From the police station, where she'd returned with Herb, she called home: Everything there was under control, according to Uncle Miltie, so they could no longer put off going to the Cantrells' house.

Linda looked haggard, as though she hadn't slept for a week, but invited them inside, reminding them that Roy was at work. "He's never here at this time—though it shouldn't be long now. I just got a call from the authorities in Chicago and—and I phoned for Roy to come home right away. They'll talk to both of us then. . . . "

Gracie nodded. "And we wanted to tell you that we did get to talk to Amy."

"You did?" Wide-eyed, she stared at them. "Why didn't they let me talk to her then? Is she all right?"

"Herb and I both. . . . "

"What's she doing in Chicago?"

"I'm not sure why, but that's where Andrew took her."

"*Andrew.*" Fear, contempt, and hatred were wrapped up in that one word. "That awful, beastly man! They'll send him to jail for kidnapping her, for taking her across state lines, won't they?"

Gracie let Herb answer, who only said that it was for the law enforcement officers and courts to decide. Though, of course, this did not satisfy Linda. She'd jumped to the conclusion that Amy was safe, so became perturbed all over again upon finding out that her daughter had been in an emergency room when they'd spoken to her.

How badly was she hurt? Would she be admitted? When could she come home? She was sure Roy would take off work and go with her to bring Amy home.

Herb suggested that they make no definite plans right away—it was too early for that. He did give assurance that he'd get back in touch as soon as he heard anything more, but they left Linda far less than happy. Gracie sighed as they went down the walk. "I don't think I'd like your job, Herb, if it's always like this."

"This is a *good* day, Gracie," he told her. "It's when I must tell someone that a loved one is dead, or mixed-up with a gang, or over-dosed and never coming home that it's really bad."

Gracie nodded. That would, indeed, be much worse—something she hoped she'd never have to experience.

Ten

I MUST HAVE LOOKED at that clock twenty times since getting back! She'd told Uncle Miltie about the stop at the Cantrells, but when Marge showed up a little later, Gracie kept the conversation on the subject of the choir, Anna's continuing loss of sight, and a mutual friend who'd been taken to the hospital with a heart attack.

Since their neighbor didn't come right out and ask any questions about Amy or mention Herb's being there, Gracie, surprised but relieved, was not about to give her an opening. Only as she was leaving did Marge say, "Well, I hope things straighten out—and that Amy comes back soon."

"We're praying for that." Gracie closed the kitchen door behind her friend, then sagged back against it. "Well, Uncle Miltie, we got through that—though not very well, I'm afraid."

"At least we did get through it—and without stretching the truth or telling her off." He smiled crookedly. "We could have done worse."

It was after he went back into the other room that she acted upon the idea that had been tugging at her mind.

ﻉ

"Aunt Gracie!" It was a cry of delight over the phone lines. "How wonderful to hear from you!"

"You've been inviting me for a long time now, Carter, to visit you in Chicago, so I'm wondering if that's still a possibility."

"Of course it is! How soon can you make it?"

"What about late this afternoon—or is that too soon?"

116

Carter Stephens laughed. "Just about right—but something tells me you've got more in that fertile mind of yours than just making a visit to me."

"Well, now that you mention it, yes, I do," and she briefly filled her in on the situation with Amy, and with Andrew.

"Ah, so you intend to do some amateur sleuthing."

"I need to be there, to talk with Amy if I can—to try figuring out what's going on now, as well as what took place some five years ago—and this last couple of months."

"And you're hoping I can help."

This wasn't a question, and Gracie was honest enough not to respond as though it was. "I have a responsibility, dear. I'm the one she called, not her father at work or her mother at home or her pastor at church.

"And I'm the one she talked to while in that Chicago emergency room, even when she wouldn't say anything to people there. I'm not a psychologist or anything. . . ."

Carter put in dryly, "You may not be a psychologist, dear auntie, but I challenge that anything. You forget that I've seen you in action—that I know when you're out to get information."

"I'm that notorious a busybody?"

She'd let her voice sound as though her feelings were hurt, but Carter's voice showed amused love when responding, "If you used 'noted' rather than 'notorious,' and 'concerned friend' for 'busybody,' you'd have it just about right."

"Ah, these lawyers, nitpicking over getting exactly the right word! This isn't a billion-dollar lawsuit, dear, nor a capital crime—at least as far as we know." But then she had to get back to Amy's situation. "Herb has been doing a lot of checking, and seems convinced that the story as told by her parents is the truth. However, we suspect that Andrew is deluded enough to believe his own version of what happened, no matter what proof there is to the contrary.

"And Amy doesn't understand that?"

"Apparently not, so that's why I need to come right away, hopefully before her parents get there." She almost stumbled over asking, "Are there any skids you could grease for me, dear? Any way of helping your small-town aunt—not a police officer or lawyer or licensed private eye—to get to see her?"

"I'm—not sure. . . ."

"I don't want you to do anything that could get you in trouble," she hastened to add. "It's just that, being in the DA's office and know-ing people. . . ."

"This isn't Willow Bend, dear."

"I'm aware of that." She sighed. "Well, so much for that idea."

There was a moment of silence before, "Why don't you come any-way, Aunt Gracie? We'll just have to see how things work out."

The first thing that worked out differently took place while she was still in Willow Bend. "But I don't expect to stay long, Uncle Miltie," she told him when he stated that if she went, he was going, too. "You can stay here and take care of Gooseberry for me."

"No way, Gracie! That cat can very well take care of himself, what with that automatic watering thing and that special feeder you bought."

"But if I need to stay more than a day or two. . . ."

He finished her sentence in his own way. " . . . Then Miss In-quisitive next door can come over and refill both containers."

He'd gotten to his feet to face her, as though that gave him more authority than sitting there in his recliner, and it suddenly struck her as funny. "You always have an answer, don't you?"

He grinned at her, obviously realizing she was weakening. "Only when I'm right."

"Which you always think you are!" But she was laughing as she reentered the kitchen, calling back from there, "I'm leaving in about an hour—at the very latest."

"And I'll be sitting there right beside you," he called back, head-ing for his bedroom, off the living room. "Carter's my grand-niece and I haven't seen her for far too long a time."

They did meet her timetable, walking out together after she'd al-ready transported their two suitcases and two "care packages," as he called them: sturdy plastic containers of chocolate cookies from the freezer and of snickerdoodles. They made excellent time and, earlier than expected, got to the waiting room on Carter's floor, in the de-partment of the District Attorney.

Gracie's niece was a graceful, blonde, attractive five-nine, with legs and ankles still as slender and shapely in those flat pumps as they'd been ten years earlier when she graduated from high school. She crossed the room to meet them. "It's so good to see you," she ex-claimed happily, reaching out for her aunt.

Gracie embraced her. "It's been much too long, dear."

And Uncle Miltie pushed his walker to the side so he could take her into his arms. "Carter! You look great—and feel that way, too."

"So do you—both of you." But then she turned toward the three men in the room and made introductions.

The oldest, Jim Riley, smiled pleasantly as he shook Gracie's hand. "Carter's been filling us in about you."

"Uh-oh! That doesn't sound good at all." She tried to sound and look worried. "That's why all four of you are here to greet us, right?"

"Only in one sense." He laughed. "We think a lot of this young woman, and any relatives of hers are welcome here."

It was on the tip of Gracie's tongue to say they could prove their welcome by helping with the Amy problem, but was extra glad she hadn't uttered anything that flippant when he added, "We've even helped her find some information for you."

Carter nodded as Gracie looked toward her, but spoke to the others. "And it's now time for you guys to get back to work covering for me as I take my aunt and uncle into my office."

"Slave driver!" Jim grumbled, but there was a twinkle in his eye as he looked back at Gracie—and winked.

Once inside, Carter sat down in her wheeled office chair as Gracie and Milton settled themselves across from her. "I'd planned to spend some time visiting before getting into Amy's situation, but since my big-mouthed friend and coworker jumped the gun, I'll fill you in on what we've determined thus far."

Andrew had maintained a small apartment locally for over a year, despite his history, landing a job at one of the area's country clubs as a companion or special caddie or something for some of the best golfers—and as golfing coach for advanced adults and older teens.

She'd learned nothing there of a negative nature, with the possible exception of his never having socialized much with other employees. He'd insisted on having two days off each week, scheduled at least seven days ahead, though not necessarily the same ones. He had proved unreachable on those days, for members of the staff had tried on a number of occasions to contact him.

"That must be when he went to see Amy," Gracie murmured, then sat back in her chair and resolved to just listen when Carter nodded and went on with facts. There were few phone calls on record, but he did keep in touch, though sporadically, with his mother, who still lives in Florida, and occasionally spoke with his sister, who's married to a doctor in Paris. He appears to have no close friends, but did spend some evenings in a bar not far from where he lived.

Uncle Miltie asked if anyone had implied that he'd been acting crazy or strange. Carter shrugged. "Some thought so, but let's face it, if an official came to—well, to your neighbor Marge, for example, asking questions about someone she knows in Willow Bend, isn't it probable she'd find the situation odd enough to make her think the person being discussed was, in fact, a bit strange?"

He frowned. "I can't really picture many folks reacting that way, Carter, but yeah, the one you mentioned just might."

Gracie would have liked to defend her friend, but it wasn't the right time, so she left Uncle Miltie's comment unchallenged. "What sort of professional reports did you get about him?"

"They commended his natural golfing skills and his ability to help people work at improving their own games. He obviously made the most favorable impression on the wealthy doctors, lawyers, and others he accompanied around the course—but many found him hard to figure out. As one coworker put it, 'I feel I know Andrew less well today than I thought I did the day we met.'"

"What does he himself have to say about bringing Amy to his apartment—and confining her the way he did?"

"Nothing."

"*Nothing*?"

"Not about that. His having been shot in the right shoulder has him terribly upset; he fears he'll never play golf again—or not as well."

Uncle Miltie sat there shaking his head. "And that's apparently the one thing at which he excels."

"Or did, Uncle Miltie," Carter corrected. "And he places all the blame for that on the police."

"Is surgery required?"

"They've already removed the bullet and taken out some bone fragments—and predict he'll be fine, given time and therapy."

"Have you talked with him, Carter?"

She shook her head. "No. The person who did just got silence most of the time, and hatred—abhorrence, actually, for anything connected with law enforcement."

Gracie was desperate to learn more about her young friend. "Is there anything new concerning Amy? Is she talking about having been brought here—and other things?"

"Very little. Even when told that her parents were on the way, she just rolled over on her side, facing the wall, and pulled the covers over her head."

"I presume that this hospital's been notified about her disappearance from ours . . . ?"

"Of course."

"And with Andrew?"

Carter's eyes flashed. "He's not going anywhere."

Gracie let out a sigh of relief; she'd feared a possible repeat of what had so recently taken place. "When can I see Amy?"

There was a slight pause before, "You're not going to like this. . . ."

"I *can't* see her after coming all this way?" Gracie tried to hide her disappointment.

A slight smile. "There's only one condition."

"Which is?"

"Well, it's two, really. We'd like you to pay close attention to everything she tells you—but the guard must remain in the room with you."

"Oh, Carter! I'm afraid she won't talk if there's anyone else there!"

"You're our major hope right now for getting anything out of her, and that's extremely important as to our helping her—as well as to determining what to do as far as Andrew's concerned. Besides, once her parents arrive, they'll certainly want her to rest rather than answer our questions."

"At this moment," Uncle Miltie put in, voice and manner stony, "I don't have much concern for that young man."

"I understand your feelings, but at this point the only thing we have on him legally is his use of that duct tape. As you recall, it was Amy who called him from the hospital, and she sneaked out of there to be with him.

"We have no proof that she objected to leaving home and coming to Chicago."

Uncle Miltie leaned forward, arms on his walker. "He certainly wouldn't have had to keep her there by using all that duct tape if she *wanted* to be with him."

"That seems logical to you and me, but his lawyer could come up with any number of possibilities to be considered—like her trying to kill herself or their having a lovers quarrel or ever her threatening to kill him."

"Carter!"

"By the time a defense lawyer presented Andrew's side of the

121

story, with whatever asides or embellishments were considered necessary, at least some on the jury wouldn't be sure he'd done anything more than he had to in order to protect *her.*"

At the hospital Gracie found she had been cleared by both the legal and medical authorities. She had no worries that Uncle Miltie would want to go upstairs to Amy's room with her, but was nonetheless relieved when he assured her, "I'll wait down here in the lobby for however long it takes."

"Thank you," she said, and meant it.

He was looking through the *Guideposts* magazine on one of the tables as she got on the elevator. It was a short ride, but the only time since her shower and getting dressed this morning in which Gracie had been alone.

Dear Lord, please give me the words to say and the wisdom to tell the difference between what might be my own thoughts and what You're giving me. And please make her receptive to what I'm saying, and willing to share. And, oh, yes, do help me to remember—exactly!—any truly important parts of whatever I may learn.

The doors opened, and she drew in a deep breath before stepping out and approaching the nursing station. An older woman wearing an oblong white pin indicating she was a volunteer came to the counter, smiling, and Gracie introduced herself with, "I'm Grace Parks, and have come to see Amy Cantrell."

A look of caution came over the attractive face. "I'm sorry, Ms. Parks, but Miss Cantrell isn't. . . ."

"It's all right, Marie. Mrs. Parks has permission to go to her." A middle-aged nurse had overheard, and came to place a hand on the arm of the volunteer for a moment before leading Gracie back down the corridor. Just as they reached the room at the end of the hall, however, she paused to ask almost apologetically, "Just for my records, Mrs. Parks, may I see some photo identification?"

"Of course." Gracie reached into her large purse—and almost gasped as her fingers touched the small tape recorder she'd forgotten to remove following Sunday morning's taping of the run-through of *Help Me to See Thee, Lord!* Even as she was pulling out her wallet and flipping it open to show her driver's license, she was silently thanking God, *So this is how You arranged for information to be retained exactly.*

"Surprise, Amy," the nurse greeted as they entered together. "Look who's come to see you."

Amy had been lying flat on her back, staring up at the ceiling, and for that first moment looked pleased. But then her gaze flicked from Gracie toward the blue-uniformed woman sitting between the bed and door and she seemed to—to what? To freeze in place, like that tag-game Gracie and her young childhood friends used to play.

Gracie paid little attention to the nurse's almost inaudible murmur to the guard that this was the woman who'd been okayed by both the police and Amy's doctor. She bent over the bed to give Amy a hug and to kiss her. "I've been really worried about you, dear."

The girl's arms had started to rise, as though to return the embrace, then dropped down again on the bed; her eyes shifted just enough to almost meet Gracie's, but not quite. "I know."

That acknowledgment's at least a start. "Are you feeling better now, Amy?" Gracie had already made the decision not to upset Amy by mentioning her parents.

As the silence grew longer, it was all Gracie could do to keep from rushing on to another question. The room seemed loud with silence, faraway indistinguishable voices only emphasizing the lack of words here.

Be still, and know. The words were as clear in her head as though Amy had spoken them, and they calmed Gracie's nervousness. Then Amy said, in what was no more than a raspy whisper, "I'm s-o-o-o tired."

As Gracie's one hand moved along Amy's forearm, trying to soothe with her touch as well as keeping her voice as soft as her young friend's, her other hand slipped back inside her purse to press that ON button. She also walked around the bed, to be on the window side of the room so Amy might not be as conscious of the guard's presence. "You've been through so much, dear. It's bound to have taken a lot out of you."

The barest hint of a nod. "He said he loved me."

"And you loved him, too." She must have, to come with him to Chicago.

"I did."

Good—she used the past tense! "Andrew is going to be all right, Amy."

Her eyelids closed and Gracie was sure that the strain on her face was an indication of the girl's dealing with intense pain. "They shot him—he fell down on the floor and they carried him away." Her head moved from one side to the other, tears forming. "Andrew is dead. . . ."

"No, dear. Andrew is very much alive."

"Have you *seen* him?"

"No, but. . . ."

"You believe *those* people, the ones who were out to get him."

Gracie was about to deny that, but there was that persistent little voice again: *Be still. . . .* She argued inwardly that this was the time to make Amy realize the truth, but. . . . *Okay, God, I'll try to do it Your way—even if it doesn't seem to make sense.*

Perhaps the silence was making Amy edgy, for she shifted position. "I didn't want it to be secret, but it was too dangerous."

"Dangerous for whom, dear?"

"For Andrew. People were after him, people from before, whom my father knew—they all wanted him dead. "Daddy, too." Tears were flowing from the outer corners of her eyes, down to her ears, and Gracie tried to blot them with tissues from the box on the bedside table.

"It's *my* fault." Amy's voice was a bare whimper. "I shouldn't have tried to run away, I shouldn't have tried to call you, but I—was so scared."

Gracie wanted to reassure her that she'd done nothing wrong, that she'd had every reason to be scared. "What did Andrew say he was going to do after you got to Chicago?"

"We wanted to get married."

"What did he want to do before getting married?" *I hope, God, that I'm asking some of the right things—at least she's giving answers. Don't let me bungle this!*

"I—don't know."

"You said he had to leave you for a while. What did you think he was going to do when he left?"

Amy shut her eyes again. "He said he must get food. . . ."

Gracie tried again. "Was this his usual apartment—where he lived most of the time?" *I didn't even realize I had that question in mind!* "Or did he take you somewhere else?"

She looked puzzled. "I—assumed it was where he lived but—there was no food, not even crackers, or cans of vegetables—or milk. Not anything. . . . And I was so hungry."

She finally said, managing only a whisper. "Why did he take me?"

At least she's finally beginning to question his actions, his motives! "What was the apartment like?"

"Old. Dirty. Small. He said it was just for now, that he'd rented it furnished, saving money so we could look, together, for the one we wanted."

The phone was already there, or the police couldn't have found her—even if it hardly seemed like a home. "How was it laid out? How many rooms were there?" *I never asked Carter that.*

"One room. And small bath. A tiny kitchenette in one corner—and the couch pulled out to make a queen-sized bed. I said we shouldn't— sleep together before we got married and—and he laughed, and said we'd work something out. But he did put a blanket on the floor to sleep last night.

"He put it right in front of the door, so I wonder, now, if, even then, he didn't trust me to stay."

There was another pause before, "He locked the door and took the key when he left this morning, saying he was going for food."

Again a lengthy silence, as she moved restlessly on the high hospital bed. "I got—scared. I didn't *want* to be locked in, and I was so hungry. The phone was working, but I couldn't call home." The words had become a wail, like those of a child. "Not after leaving like that, and besides, Daddy . . ." Her head turned from side to side on the pillow. "I knew if I did, they'd do something *awful* to Andrew."

Gracie continued to stroke the girl's arm. She was relieved to know that the guard was writing something over there, and wondered if any of this was getting recorded on the tape hidden in her purse.

Amy went on, "I remembered your number and—and your helping on Friday night, and staying at the hospital, and coming to see me."

Amy again looked straight up at the acoustic-tile ceiling. "I didn't expect he'd come back so soon, to check on me! I should have waited longer before trying to use the phone, because when he came in and saw what I was doing he—he was furious—not just mad, but disappointed in me, and hurt. He said he'd thought I loved him but saw now that, like everyone else, I had turned against him.

"That's when he got the duct tape from a drawer, and started to use it, first fastening my wrists behind me, then covering my mouth when I started to beg him not to. . . ."

Gracie was almost overwhelmed by bone-deep sorrow. "And you let him do it to you. . . ."

"I *had* to. So many in his life had proved unfaithful, especially my own father—and here I was, too, having been proved untrustworthy.

"Don't you see? I couldn't let him be hurt anymore."

Gracie looked at those youthfully rounded cheeks still reddened and splotchy from the removal of the duct tape. "And then you called me."

She nodded. "He left again, and the longer I lay there on the floor the more terrified I got. It seemed like hours—though I now know that it wasn't—I thought he'd been so upset with me that maybe he wouldn't ever come back.

"So—I tried banging my feet on the floor, but he'd taken my shoes off—and then I rolled over and over to get to the door, but nobody came when I kicked against that, either."

Reliving the experience was traumatic, but Gracie had to let her go on. "I figured I had to try something else, so flopped myself back close to the table and—and finally managed to get up on my feet—then sort of inched sideways till I could lean against the table, where the phone was. But I still had an awful time trying to get the right buttons with my wrists fastened together behind me."

Your poor wrists, too, are cut and bruised! They must be very painful.

"Then, just when I tried for that last digit, the phone fell off the table. So I had to get *back* down on the floor, and get it shut off so I could start over."

"But you did get me, dear. You got through to me, but I couldn't get a response from you."

"I—couldn't hear you, not till there at the very end, after I'd tried and tried and *tried*. And by then I was crying, and my nose was running, and I was so terribly afraid!"

Thank You, God, for making her keep trying—and for our finding out the number—and for getting word to the authorities in time. . . . "You did very well, Amy, with your bumping noises, your answering my questions."

"I had to sort of bang the phone to do that—and I think I messed it up. . . ."

"You did fine!"

"Then Andrew came! And he—he was so angry, and I got even more scared, for I'd never seen him like that. He—finally calmed down enough to make a sandwich for himself—cold meat in a roll.

But I couldn't have any of that, or even water, because he couldn't trust me not to yell or scream or anything if he took the tape off."

"He *loved* me. . . ." It was a cry of agony, of loss, and Gracie stayed with her, holding her close for the time it took to work through what had happened. She also attempted to explain to Amy why her parents had kept from her the extent of the problems in Florida—that they'd wanted her to have a more normal childhood in Indiana than they'd felt she could have if they had stayed where they were.

It was then that Gracie was asked to come to the lounge.

Eleven

LINDA AND ROY HAD ARRIVED shortly after Gracie did—but weren't "cleared" to see their daughter until after meeting with the police and one of the doctors, who finally sent the nurse to request Gracie to join them.

She shared with them what she considered the most important parts of her lengthy conversation with Amy, saying she felt the girl was at least beginning to understand not only her parents' situation, but also the mental state of Andrew. "I doubt, however, that she even yet comprehends the danger she was in—and she still feels guilty about not helping Andrew more."

Carter accepted from Gracie the recording, which they hoped would cover much of the early part of her talk with Amy, holding it as carefully as though it were a most fragile piece of antique glass. "At least this is a start."

"Does she have to know right away about my taping our conversation?" Gracie asked. "I don't want her feeling betrayed by me, too."

Jim and the Cantrells assured her this would be avoided if at all possible so, after going back in to say good-bye to Amy, Gracie felt comfortable leaving with Carter and Uncle Miltie.

"You are staying for a nice long visit, aren't you?" Carter asked as they walked together to the parking lot.

"Probably a day or so," Uncle Miltie told her. But Gracie just said, "We'll see."

Carter laughed. "I'm not about to push my luck any further—I'm just glad you're not heading back for Willow Bend at this very moment!" She invited Uncle Miltie to ride with her to her townhouse complex while Gracie in the other car would follow. "You and Aunt Gracie get to talk to each other all the time, so I demand at least a little of your undivided attention."

He was obviously pleased, and Gracie felt relieved to be alone right then—though she wouldn't have admitted that. When she arrived at Carter's condominium, decorated somewhat sparingly but in excellent taste with mid-to-late nineteenth-century furniture, she couldn't help but compare this with her mental picture of where Amy had been taken.

Uncle Miltie insisted that they choose anywhere they wanted to go for dinner, on him—but Gracie suggested they defer that option to the following evening. "I appreciate the offer, but I'm exhausted. Speaking only for myself, I'd rather Carter would just heat up a can of soup."

"I'm sure you are tired. What a time you've had these last few days!" Their niece looked from Gracie to her uncle. "How about it? Shall we go along with her suggestion to eat here tonight?"

"To be honest, that would suit me better, too." And then, pretending to keep Gracie from hearing by tipping his open hand over his mouth, he stage-whispered, "And this way we'll know that she's going to stay at least until day after tomorrow."

"Good thinking, Uncle Miltie!" she responded in the same fashion and, laughing, headed for the kitchen.

In remarkably short order she was serving them a delicious chicken/broccoli/carrot stir-fry with rice, and her great-uncle was telling Gracie that postponing their restaurant jaunt was one of her best ideas ever.

It was after eating that Gracie asked Carter if it would be all right for her to call Herb about what took place today. "I know he'll get an official report, but I'd sort of like talking to him, if that's allowed. He's been so very concerned and. . . ." Her voice trailed off.

Carter looked thoughtful, then nodded slowly. "Ordinarily, I'd have to refuse, but it should be all right if you want to tell him just the bare bones of what took place. He'll be learning the whole story soon enough."

So Gracie did phone the station and left a message. He called back from home within a few minutes, sounding worried, "Are you all right, Gracie?"

"Very much so, Herb—and I think Amy will be, too. I had a long talk with her, and then her parents went in to see her. I don't know how they made out, but at least the groundwork was laid."

"She wasn't—hurt?"

She hesitated before replying. "Emotionally, she is—as well as psychologically. But not too much physically, thank God! Not seriously, anyway."

Then, changing the topic, he asked, "So when are you coming home?"

"I'm not sure, but—probably day after tomorrow."

Apparently realizing the question to which her aunt had responded, Carter spoke quite loudly, "But I'm going to try extending that, Herb."

Gracie grinned at her, even telling Herb, "Gooseberry will be missing me, and he's apt to run out of food or water if I'm gone too long."

"Tell ya what, Gracie," he offered, "I'll personally tell Marge that she's delegated to see that doesn't happen."

She laughed. "Never mind, Herb. Should I happen to stay an extra day, I'll gladly take on the assignment of alerting Marge."

෯

She and Uncle Miltie prepared to leave on their second morning, at the same time as Carter. "We had a wonderful visit," she assured her niece, "and I can't possibly express how much I appreciate all you and Jim and the others did to help Amy.

Carter gave a mock curtsy—"You're welcome. You did so well that we might call on you some other time when having problems getting people to respond."

And Uncle Miltie suggested, "At the same rate of pay, right?"

She raised her brows. "Of course!"

"That's just about what it's worth—nothing!" Gracie agreed. "But I'll always be grateful for having had this opportunity."

෯

The return trip was uneventful. As they entered the outskirts of Willow Bend, she heard the whisper of a sighed, "Home! We're home again."

She smiled across at him. He had never suggested leaving her and Willow Bend, but to know that it was truly *home* to him pleased her. "Indeed, Uncle Miltie, it's good to be home—especially now that we can be almost positive that Amy, too, will be back soon."

There were no more words exchanged—none needed. Then she caught herself humming *Hallelujah, Save Us, Lord,* which they'd sung last Sunday. *We had no idea when we got that music, God, how desperately we'd soon be calling upon You. Thanks for "saving" Amy, and for letting me be a part of that. I pray that You will continue healing her and her family, and that they will become more conscious of Your holding them in Your hand.*

But that wasn't enough, was it? *Please forgive me for not having prayed for Andrew, too, for he has obviously been miserable. And for his family, who must be every bit as heartsick about all this as Amy's. Only You can heal such long-standing pain, such misunderstanding. . . .*

They were coming down Main Street; although they'd been gone such a short time, she was noting individual stores and fire hydrants and trees. And right there was the tall, stained-glass clock on the corner of Main and Cherry Streets, the one the Lions Club and Rotary Club and Volunteer Firemen had joined in erecting in honor of all the public servants who'd given so much of their lives to Willow Bend.

Everything was clear and distinct, uniquely *home,* and she couldn't keep from smiling. She was coming down her own street, pulling into the driveway, when she happened to glance over to see Gooseberry looking out the window over the sink, raising one paw to the glass.

He wasn't supposed to be up there, but she was as eager to see him as he obviously was to see her.

To *see* one another. *We kept singing that we wanted to see You, Lord, in everything. Well, You certainly took us up on that, didn't You? Only You could have pulled this off with Amy—so that now she can get help, and so can Andrew.*

And now that we're back, that we're home, even in the "busyness" of our lives please help us to make the concerted effort to keep seeing You in all that's good.

She got out of the car and helped Uncle Miltie set up his folding walker. Gooseberry was no longer in the window, but was undoubtedly waiting right inside the kitchen door. She didn't need to rush but would walk beside her uncle, who was stiff from the long ride.

He stopped halfway up the walk, looking around at the massed chrysanthemums and asters and other autumn beauties. "I'm glad there was no frost while we were gone."

She nodded, and the last two lines of their anthem suddenly came to mind:

> *Let me always choose to be*
> *With You in one accord,*
> *Then and only then will I*
> *With Your help, see Thee, Lord.*

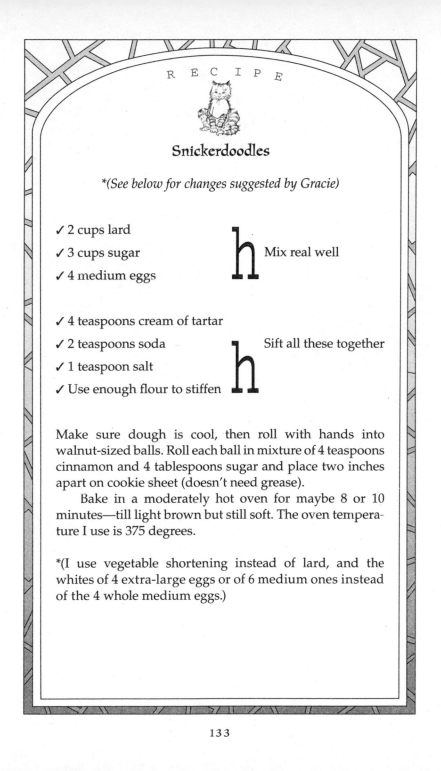

R E C I P E

Snickerdoodles

(See below for changes suggested by Gracie)

✓ 2 cups lard
✓ 3 cups sugar   h   Mix real well
✓ 4 medium eggs

✓ 4 teaspoons cream of tartar
✓ 2 teaspoons soda   h   Sift all these together
✓ 1 teaspoon salt
✓ Use enough flour to stiffen

Make sure dough is cool, then roll with hands into walnut-sized balls. Roll each ball in mixture of 4 teaspoons cinnamon and 4 tablespoons sugar and place two inches apart on cookie sheet (doesn't need grease).

Bake in a moderately hot oven for maybe 8 or 10 minutes—till light brown but still soft. The oven temperature I use is 375 degrees.

*(I use vegetable shortening instead of lard, and the whites of 4 extra-large eggs or of 6 medium ones instead of the 4 whole medium eggs.)

GUIDEPOSTS

GUIDEPOSTS

CHURCH CHOIR
MYSTERIES™

The Coin Conspiracy

Eileen M. Berger

Guideposts®

CARMEL • NEW YORK 10512

www.guidepostsbooks.org

Series Editor: Michele Slung
Cover art by Stephen Gardner & Edgar Jerins
Cover design by Wendy Bass
Interior design by José R. Fonfrias
Interior cat illustrations by Viqui Maggio
Printed in the United States of America

*This book is dedicated to all those everywhere
who faithfully and joyously sing in church choirs—
especially to those with whom I've participated for years
in the choir of the Hughesville Baptist Church.*

Acknowledgments

THANKS TO THOSE special people at Guideposts Book and Inspirational Media Division who make these novels possible by keeping us writers encouraged, even while incorporating those changes and adaptations that make our work better.

I salute you, Elizabeth Kramer Gold, Michele Slung and Stephanie Castillo Samoy! I've appreciated getting to know you by phone and with written words, and hope someday to meet you personally.

And a hearty "bravo" to Brigitte Weeks, editor-in-chief of Guideposts Books. What varied responsibilities you have, and how capably you serve! We are all indebted to you.

The Coin Conspiracy

One

THE OUTSIDE TEMPERATURE had officially hit ninety-eight degrees, but nobody had turned on the air conditioning in the sanctuary of Eternal Hope Community Church—this would have been regarded by some as unjustified expense for an under two-hour choir practice. That didn't stop people from griping, however, so Gracie Parks tried to change the subject by asking, "Have any of you been out Ferris Road recently?"

Lester Twomley looked at her and grinned, understanding her diversionary tactics.

She smiled, realizing he knew exactly what she was doing, then she sobered again. "Gooseberry and I went that way this morning," she said—everyone knew how her cat accompanied her on her early praise-walks—"and I was appalled by all the junk along both sides of the road. Uncle Miltie says no one has taken over the responsibility for picking up along that stretch since Harry Judson took ill last winter."

Barb Jennings, Eternal Hope's choir director and organist, now commented that she believed Harry still hadn't improved much. It was Amy Cantrell, their high school soprano, who suggested, "How about our doing it a time or two—you know, unless Mr. Judson's church or some other group decides to take over?"

Estelle Livett, their indomitable diva, sniffed. "Around here, if you offer to do something 'a time or two,' you're stuck with it forever."

"Well," Amy replied gently, "it does seem like a worthwhile

project—and it would be best to do it now, before the stuff's covered with leaves, then snow."

She realized that Estelle was about to argue, and quickly added. "I'd be willing to help one of these Saturday mornings if Abe can give me time off from the deli—or if we can start really early on another day."

Enthusiasm for the clean-up project wasn't unanimous. Some choir members were frankly uninterested. But enough of them agreed to meet there Saturday morning that Amy looked around at her friends and beamed. Les said he'd make sure they had the proper supplies, and Gracie agreed to approach the other church.

"I'll encourage someone in Harry's own congregation to head up a crew more permanently, until he's better," she told them.

ঌ২

Gracie brought the Turner twins, Tish and Tyne, and had expected to be the first to arrive at the agreed-upon end of Ferris Road. But Les was already there and had set up a large sandwich-board caution sign. He greeted them cheerfully as he took a carton from his van, "Good morning, ladies.

"There's everything you'll need here, Gracie," he told her. "Now I'll take the rest of this stuff down the road to the other half of our gang."

"Fine. We might as well get going!" Gracie was grateful that he had organized things so well.

"We'll be working our way back in this direction." He looked at the debris along both sides of the shady road, then back at her. "Everyone needs to wear one of these reflective vests and use plastic gloves, and each of you should be sure to carry an extra trash bag or two."

Tish was already pulling on her gloves, as was her twin sister. "We'll begin right here. . . ."

And Tyne added, ". . . on the left side of the road."

Gracie never failed to find amusement in their twinnish habits, like finishing each other's sentences. Though they were married, both women expected their husbands to understand just how powerful their own particular brand of sisterhood was.

Now Amy pulled up, accompanied by Mark Canfield, a friend of hers whose mother, Sally, was a former choir member.

Gracie greeted him with affection. She'd taught him for several years of Vacation Bible School, back when he was a towheaded boy given to keeping frogs and little lizards in his backpack. *Where does the time go, Lord? Now he's practically a man and more interested in pretty Amy than in what he might fish out of a stream.*

"So you want the two of us to take that side of the road?" Amy asked, donning her plastic vest.

Mark added, "Sounds good to me. We'll help on whichever side we're most needed." Gracie couldn't help but feel proud of their willingness to help by getting up early and giving up their Saturday morning.

Two other vehicles arrived, and Les talked to their drivers before returning to his car and calling through the open window as he eased by, "Don's leaving his car here and Barb's dropping off hers near the one-mile mark. They will ride the rest of the way with me, and when we meet halfway, Barb will drive me back for mine. We'll have plenty of room in the two vehicles for all of us to get back here."

Gracie dropped a sticky Styrofoam box and two beer cans into her trash bag as she straightened. "That sounds like an excellent plan." *Thank You, Lord, for making sure that when we, Your humble hearts and hands, start a project we also have a head to organize us.*

After the others left, conversation in Gracie's group first centered on the task at hand and then on the lovely mid-October day. Naturally, however, they were soon off on other subjects. "How's your mother, Mark?" Gracie asked.

"Good—she really likes what she's doing at school."

"She's still a personal aid to that little Macfarland girl?"

"*Um-hmmm.*" He was down in the ditch picking up shards of a broken jar, empty cigarette wrappers, soda cans and soggy newspapers. "But Lynn's not so little anymore. She's ten—and Mom says she's doing a whole lot better with her school work."

He was energetically rooting amidst overgrown grasses and weeds for more junk. He looked up at Gracie. "Mom spends most of her time with Lynn. It's really her major responsibility."

"I recall how hard she worked to become fluent in sign language."

"Yeah. But she doesn't use that as much now. Lynn's also gotten pretty good at reading lips, and that means she's caught up with her class in most subjects."

Gracie smiled her approval.

"But she hasn't caught up with math," Mark added. "And she doesn't speak a lot—not *yet*, Mom says."

Gracie would never forget the child's bout with meningitis when she was only two years old. Up until then, little Lynn Macfarland had been a happy, chattering youngster with a bright and bubbly personality.

Everyone loved Lynn, Gracie recalled. *There must have been hundreds—thousands!—of prayers going up to You, God, from all of us while she was so sick. There were times at the beginning when she didn't seem to respond at all, when we feared she'd remain little more than a vegetable, and it seemed You maybe weren't listening or caring.*

Thank You, Father, for Sally's steady assistance and for the Macfarland family's faith and love—and for Lynn, herself. For her courage and the example she sets. And please help her to make the progress she needs in math.

Gracie now picked up a crumpled, dirty, child's coloring book. How did it wind up here? Possibly some boy or girl had thrown it from the window of a passing car? Gracie couldn't resist glancing at the pages but, seeing no name or other identification, she dropped it into her bag along with her other "finds."

She enjoyed listening to Amy and Mark talk about their high school and community activities as they worked. The gloves Les had so thoughtfully provided were much appreciated when they came upon a partially eaten, decayed groundhog!

Mark had just rolled a car tire up the bank when Gracie suggested, "Let's combine all the junk we've collected so far. If we set it by the roadside with the tire, whoever comes with the truck this afternoon can get it."

They passed a large farmhouse as they strolled out Ferris Road, and then three new ranch-style houses. Gracie exchanged greetings with a woman who was working in her garden and a man repairing a fence, and received in turn their appreciation for helping to beautify the area.

A stretch with tall corn growing along both sides of the road seemed especially long to the group as they kept at their surveillance, moving slowly. Tish started to pick up a weathered cardboard box filled with beer cans which, not surprisingly, fell apart. "It can't really be that much harder to dispose of these properly."

"One wouldn't think so," Gracie agreed.

Then Tyne suggested, "Well, I think the law says an underage drinker better not be found with any alcohol in his vehicle."

"That's the big reason so many empties are dumped like this," Mark agreed. He had stepped back from the edge of the road to gather the remains of a forgotten picnic from a field.

Gracie now saw the other half of their group in the distance. Hooray! Mission nearly completed! She offered her help to Amy and Mark, who were gathering scattered nails and a heap of miniature plastic blocks.

"What a mess!" Amy was indignant. "People coming here must just open their doors and throw stuff out!"

Gracie had many times noticed and been annoyed by the paper, boxes, glass, metal and other junk left out in plain sight in God's gorgeous countryside. The incivility of tossing anything and everything out of car windows and not caring how it looked to others seemed just another indicator of the rise of bad manners when folks should know better.

They'd hardly begun picking up a tangled mass of muddy rags when a car slowed and came to a stop. She felt a moment of guilty pleasure when she heard a familiar voice request, "Hey, everyone, wait a couple minutes before picking up anything else."

Rocco Gravino, editor-in-chief of the *Mason County Gazette*, was climbing out of his small black car with his camera. "I thought I would have been able to get here earlier—but what we've got now looks like it'll work just right for before-and-after shots, to let readers know what a great job you did."

Tish fluffed her blond hair a bit with her fingertips, and Tyne did the same. Mark and Amy reached out at the same time to knock a leaf from Gracie's bright red hair, then both laughed. She thanked them for their attention and for helping her remain respectably tidy for Rocky's readers—but, inwardly, she was wishing for a mirror and a lipstick. Undoubtedly, she told herself, I'd look better covered with leaves and therefore anonymous!

"Abe told me you were out here with some other choir members," Rocky was saying to Amy. "He says you almost never ask for time off, and he felt if you were willing to get out here and muck around, the least he could do was cover for you there."

"Was it awfully busy?"

"Sure, it's a Saturday morning, isn't it?" He dropped a stray bottle into her trash bag. "But no one griped, even jokingly, about the missing waitress. Everyone he told respects you for doing this."

Gracie listened as Rocky teased Amy about her Saturday morning regular customers. But she teased him right back, telling him how she could always tell what he was going to order by looking to see which of his eyebrows was cocked when he walked in the door.

Rocky had just taken his last shots of several completely stuffed black bags, with the Turner twins bookending them when Mark moved beyond where they'd been working and picked up another can.

Gracie saw him do a doubletake and reach back down among the grass and weeds to pick up something. "Wow!" he exclaimed, holding it out on the palm of his hand. "Look at this!"

Amy, glancing over, seemed puzzled by his astonishment. "Okay, I see it, but what is it?"

He looked from her back to the coin, then toward Gracie. "Well, it's not one of those gold-colored dollars—those Sacagawea ones that came out some time ago. That I can see."

He rubbed it against his jeans, trying to clean it. Gracie now walked over to examine it. "It most certainly isn't! Look here, on the back, it says twenty dollars! You know, I suspect it's the real thing, from back in the days when coins were what everyone used instead of paper money."

Amy examined the find. "You're *right*. It says 1930. And it has sort of a squiggle—an *s*—on it."

A large grin appeared on Mark's face as his fingers closed around the coin. "I hope this will be one of those times when the finders-keepers rule prevails."

He looked earnestly at Gracie, and she smiled back encouragingly. "Maybe so. And your doing community service when you found it should be an additional point in your favor!"

Everyone was talking at once, and now it was Rocky's turn to examine the gold coin. He called it a "double eagle." Mark turned it back and forth before pointing out, "There's only one eagle on this, not a double one."

The older man explained, "The ten-dollar coin already had an eagle on it, and was dubbed an eagle. Since the twenty was twice as valuable, people started calling it a 'double eagle.'"

"Oh! That's neat!" Mark continued to turn it around in his fingers.

Tyne handed him a clean handkerchief as he started to put his find in his pocket. "Wrap it in this, just in . . ."

Her sister chimed in, ". . . in case you might have a hole in your pocket, or something."

Gracie laughed. "Then if someone else found it, would it be a doubled double eagle?"

Amy joked, "I think Uncle Miltie is finally starting to wear off on you." She was referring to Gracie's elderly uncle, who lived with her and was famous for his love of corny jokes.

Gracie noticed suddenly that Rocky had moved off and was using his cell phone, but she decided not to call attention to his actions.

Mark now reminded them, "As interesting as this is, we'd better get back to work. We just have a little ways to go."

"Guess what!" Amy shouted, as Les and the others approached. "Mark's found a valuable old gold coin!"

"If I'm not mistaken, this is an especially good date, and in excellent condition." Lester whistled as he peered at the gold surface.

"Do you have any idea what it could be worth?" asked Gracie.

He shook his head. "My dad has a pretty decent coin collection, subscribes to all the magazines and buys the yearly price guides. But, myself, I can't say as how I know much about it, except that a nickel's worth more than a penny."

Barb asked, "But you just indicated you thought this coin might have real value."

"It's only my hunch, based on years of listening to my father and his numismatic pals." He hesitated before adding, "Remember, anything I'd suggest right now would be guesswork."

Gracie saw Mark's eyes brighten. He reached for the wrapped coin in his pocket, touching the outside of it with his palm, making sure it was still there. "Well, any amount would sure help my college fund!"

Gracie nodded. "We all hope we're not raising your hopes." *Dear Lord, remember how impressed Elmo was by this boy, back when he was in Cub Scouts. And Little League. Mark was a fine youngster then and he's a splendid young man now.*

Rocky caught her eye and motioned with a tilt of his head for her to join him a few steps from the others. "I just called the newsroom and asked Sue to check on the value of a 1930-S double eagle."

"And . . . ?"

Both his bushy eyebrows rose, and he grinned. "If it's actually in as good condition as it appears to be—and only a dealer will be able to judge—Mark probably has stumbled upon a coin worth upwards of thirteen thousand dollars, maybe even a bit more."

She stared at her friend. *"Thousand?"*

He repeated the single word. "Thousand."

She turned to look at Mark, who was back at work picking up trash with the others. He and Amy seemed to be in a race to see how many aluminum cans they could lob into an open bag.

When their temporarily adopted stretch of Ferris Road was pronounced immaculate, everyone rode back to the church. There, Tish and Tyne tried at the same time to tell Pastor Paul Meyer the amazing news concerning Mark's double eagle. Then Mark held out the coin for him to see.

"Wow." Paul told him, turning it over several times, staring at the details of the raised printing on it.

Les joked, "Now we truly believe, Paul, in keeping our eyes cast down in humility, especially when there are rare coins on the ground!"

There was a bit more joking before Mark said, "I've got to go. I've got a number of lawns to mow and need to get one or two taken care of before midday."

He was almost to the edge of the parking lot before Paul hurried after him. Gracie overheard Paul offer to keep the coin in the church's safe until the bank would open on Monday. Good idea, she thought.

Gracie drove Fannie Mae, her aged and faithful blue Cadillac back to the house, eager to tell Uncle Miltie about the coin. However, the note lying on the kitchen table informed her he had headed off to the senior center.

She hardly thought of lunch until, after taking a shower, hunger suddenly reminded her she'd had a long morning and little food. Yes, there was quite a bit of the lamb roast left from the day before, as well as smaller quantities of peas and limas. Cold sliced lamb sandwiches were just the ticket! There was a jar of Joe Searfoss's home-grated horseradish and a loaf of multigrain bread she'd defrosted the day before.

She was just tossing the left-over vegetables in a mayonnaise dressing and adding cherry tomatoes for color when Uncle Miltie walked in the door, leaning lightly on his canes.

"I feel pretty spry today, my girl," he told her, smacking his lips. "If those are lamb sandwiches, I can eat three . . . at least!"

He went to wash his hands at the kitchen sink, but grinned at her over his shoulder. "That's one of the many pleasurable things about your meals, Gracie. One good one always leads to a better one."

She blushed, even though she knew he was right. She was a legendary cook and caterer in Willow Bend but never tired of her own imaginative menus or of her uncle's praise of them.

"I wish I could have helped this morning," he told her.

"Maybe next time. . . ." But she doubted that, even as she answered him. His osteoarthritis was unpredictable, and though he'd gotten back to using his quad canes instead of his walker, leaning to pick up trash over a couple of miles of country road could hardly be considered medically indicated.

But she didn't say that. She diverted him with news of the coin that Mark had discovered. "At least we have the date," she finished. "It's almost as clear as if it was freshly minted."

"Sounds good." He dried his hands and started across the kitchen toward the phone. "While you put my sandwiches on a plate with some chips and salad," he said, winking, "I'll make a quick call to Bernie Jenson. He claims he's not a real collector, but he is. Anyone who can blithely spend a bundle on a single coin, like he's liable to, has got to be pretty serious about it."

Two

G RACIE LIKED GETTING to Sunday school and church on time—a practice that Uncle Miltie dubbed "bird early"—which was why they hadn't seen the feature story on the choir's trash pickup until they arrived.

Estelle had brought in the second section of the Sunday *Gazette*, just in case the picture of her with the very large bag might go unremarked.

"You can tell who was working hardest," she declared proudly.

This brought a hoot of derision as Les insisted that the bulging bag to her right was the one he'd just tied off, having filled it himself.

"Children, children!" Gracie mock-scolded. "Everyone worked so well out on the job, let's not mess it up now."

They laughed, and Les reminded them, "It was really fun, though, wasn't it?"

"Yes, it was," Estelle admitted. "More than I expected. To be honest, I had to talk myself into going, but I'm glad I did." She looked as if she had even surprised herself.

Amy had already seen the newspaper article before leaving home. "I wonder why there's no picture of Mark and his double eagle."

"Maybe Rocky didn't take one," Barb said. "I didn't see him do it."

Gracie shook her head. "I'm sure he didn't—probably deliberately."

"Why wouldn't he?" Amy asked her.

Gracie shook her head. "I'm not sure. It certainly would have made the tale of our good deed a lot more colorful!"

It was the church's custom to invite congregants to share their harvest bounty. Looking out over the baskets of produce and flowers from the gardens of Eternal Hope's members, Gracie thought their morning anthem, "The Fruit of the Land Declares God's Glory," to be especially appropriate. The profusion of tomatoes, peppers, squash, eggplants, and melons, as well as the asters and mums, was indeed glorious.

From her vantage point in the choir loft, Gracie hadn't at first noticed Mark seated below with his mother. Sally Canfield was a regular attendee and had once sung in the choir. But her son had stopped coming when he was about fifteen. Gracie understood the irregular habits of teenagers, even when it came to something as important as worship.

And now, today, Mark Canfield was here! *I wonder if Amy's bringing him yesterday has something to do with his turning up today, Lord. I hope it's not just because of his finding that double eagle.* But then she reconsidered. *No, that's not right. If that should turn out to be his reason, then it's because You have chosen his path of return. The coin is just that—a mere coin—while Yours is the gold that never dims or tarnishes.*

✥

Heading home, Gracie decided to detour by Ferris Road. The massed trashbags were still awaiting pickup, as she'd hoped. She wanted Uncle Miltie to see what the choir had accomplished.

"Gosh!" he told her, "And golly! It's what I call a *haul* lot of junk!"

"Pretty funny!" Gracie retorted. "Les has arranged for someone to come and cart it away tomorrow morning, I believe. And I'm still feeling it in some muscles!"

"Was the coin found right out in the open?" Uncle Miltie now was curious.

"Not really. With the weeds and grass as tall as they are, if Mark hadn't been looking for something to pick up, he might not have seen it."

On the way back to town, her uncle suggested stopping at Abe's Deli.

"You may be Willow Bend's best cook," he said, chuckling, "dedicated to feeding me and one very large cat, along with all your catering clients . . . but a cheese danish or a poppy-seed bagel just aren't in your repertoire!"

"My friends." Abe Wasserman's face was one big smile as he came around from behind the counter to hug Gracie. "The service must have been longer than usual."

"It was the route from the church to here that was longer," Uncle Miltie told him. "Gracie took me out to see where they were uncovering treasure yesterday along Ferris Road."

"I heard from Amy about the coin Mark found—and then there was that great spread in this morning's paper! Some people sure have pull!"

Her uncle was smug. "It's her lemon cake, or maybe her chili! No, seriously, our Rocky is simply a good editor, you know, with that finely tuned sense of what people like to read."

"You're right about that! Everybody who's come in today has been talking about it." He chuckled. "Of course a couple of Harry Judson's fellow Presbyterians were annoyed about their never having been written up during all their years of doing the policing out there—and now you folks getting it the very first time!"

Returning with the blintzes and applesauce Gracie had ordered and Uncle Miltie's scrambled eggs with toasted bagel, Abe looked at them quizzically.

"Know anything about that gold coin that was found?" he asked while pouring coffee.

"Only that it's a double eagle." She was sure he was savvy enough to understand its possible value.

"Amy seems to like Mark a good deal. I know her well—and the fact that she asked him to accompany her is indicative of her feeling for him, I'm certain," said Abe.

"Are they seeing a lot of each other?" Uncle Miltie wanted to know. "Going out together?"

"Well," said Abe slowly. "I'm not keeping tabs on what she does when she's not helping out here, but Mark has waited for her often over the past few weeks."

"I understand he's trying to save money for school," Gracie put in.

"Could be." Abe moved away to refill the cups of several other patrons and to chat before returning. He continued, "And Mark's a good worker, you know. He's mowed my yard for me at the house these last two years, and is meticulous about trimming around bushes and walks."

"That's good to know."

"I'd give a positive recommendation to anyone who might be considering hiring him."

"Huh!" Uncle Miltie snorted, seeing their neighbor emerge from her house just as Gracie was pulling to a stop. "She's been watching for you."

Gracie smiled at him, opened her door and got out, calling, "What's up?"

Marge Lawrence looked conspiratorial as she joined them. "How close were you to Mark when he found that coin?" She winked.

"How *close* were we?" Gracie repeated, wondering what that had to do with anything. However, with her best friend appearing so serious, she answered, "Well, he'd been down in a ditch—well, not a ditch, actually, more like a shallow trough or something—where the run-off from the road goes. There's a lot of grass and weeds there, so he was checking all that out while taking a step or two back onto the road."

"Was the coin on the road itself?"

"We-e-ell, Ferris Road's one of those where each year or so they put down another layer of gravel and tar or bitumen or whatever, but there's space along the side that's loose pebbles and stuff. . . ."

"Yes," Uncle Miltie put in. "A lot of our less-traveled roads are like that. We used to call 'em 'tar-and-chip roads.' "

"So that's where he supposedly found the coin?"

"Supposedly? What's going on? I think it was more where there's grass or weeds growing, just beyond the hard surface."

"Then you didn't actually see him find it? You didn't see him pick it up off the ground?"

"I don't like the direction these questions are going," Gracie frowned. "You were out there, too, yesterday morning. Did you actually watch where each person was as he picked up each can or paper?"

"Of course not—but I hoped you had this one time."

"Okay, spill it." Uncle Miltie was annoyed at her taking so long to get to the point. "If we have to deal with some problem, we need to know what it's about."

Marge's lips pursed. "Pastor Paul asked me to have you call as soon as you got back."

Gracie wondered what their minister wanted, and she wished

Marge wouldn't make them drag what she had to say out of her, sentence by sentence.

They were inside the house by the time she got it all out. "Miles Stevens—you know him, of course, since he worked at the First National Bank just about forever. Well, he's heard about Mark's finding the coin, and now claims it's *his*, that Mark stole it from him."

"That's absurd!" Gracie came to a full stop and stood there staring at her friend. "He was with us, and Miles wasn't. And that boy did find the coin out there."

"I never did trust that man," Uncle Miltie declared, "even if he did work in a bank."

First National's board of directors obviously had considered Mr. Miles Stevens trustworthy. Gracie herself, however, had sometimes felt he was a little sneaky-seeming. "There's got to be something going on here that we're not aware of—that we don't understand." She looked at Marge. "How did you hear about this, Marge?"

"It was Pastor Paul. I saw him stop here a while ago, so I came out and asked if there was anything I could do—if I might give you a message when you got back."

"We went out to Ferris Road, then stopped at Abe's for lunch," said Gracie. "I'd wanted to show Uncle Miltie where we were working and how much we'd picked up."

Gracie knew the parsonage number almost as well as her own, so it was only a few seconds before she heard, "Pastor Meyer speaking. Can I help you?"

"Paul, this is Gracie. Marge just gave me a strange story about Miles Stevens claiming that Mark's coin is *his*."

"That's what he's saying."

"That's ridiculous!" But then she remembered hearing Paul's offer to put the coin in the church's safe. "He hasn't seen it, has he? You didn't show it to him?"

"Of course not! But he's heard that Mark has a 1930-S double eagle, and he claims he had one, which is now missing. And that since the choir sponsored the clean-up, *I'm* responsible."

"And just how would that coin get from Miles Stevens's possession to the weeds along Ferris Road?" Gracie demanded. "Was he strolling along out there and dropped it? It's unChristian of me to doubt him, I know, but it seems, shall we say, highly unlikely."

"I guess. . ."

"For that matter," she went on, unintentionally interrupting, "I've never seen Miles out walking at all. And as you know, I do a lot of that."

"That's true."

"This whole thing sounds fishy to me!" Gracie's eyes flashed. Uncle Miltie pretended to cower, while Marge gave her a thumbs-up.

"What he's saying is that he'd brought a few coins home from his safety deposit box last week. He says they were on the kitchen table last Saturday—a week ago, that is—and Mark was mowing his lawn at that time.

"For some reason or other—oh, yes, Mark came into the house to tell him he needed more gas. Miles says he was 'careless enough' to leave those coins right out there in plain sight while going into the other room to get some money. "So he came back out, gave Mark the money and told him to go over to the Gas-'n'-Go and get the gas can filled."

Gracie now understood. "He claims Mark Canfield just walked out of his house with that particular coin in his pocket?"

"That's what he says. That Mark must have done exactly that."

"And Miles didn't happen to miss this exceedingly valuable coin," she paused for effect, "for a whole week. Until he heard that Mark had found a 1930-S double eagle!"

"Right you are, dear Gracie. But, like you, I wish it weren't the case."

"Does he know that you actually have the coin in your possession?"

"I didn't think it wise to tell him, not just now. He's already insisting that I get it from Mark and give it to him. Or else be accused of obstructing justice."

"How awful!" she exclaimed. "He can't be serious!"

"Gracie, listen to me. You know I wouldn't do what he was asking, not without talking to Mark and to Herb."

"Do you believe there's a chance Mark might have taken it?" She hated even asking the question.

"No, I don't." A second or two passed before he added, "Let's face it, though, I don't know either of them very well."

Her mind was racing. She suddenly realized that she was trusting Mark completely, believing his version of events, not just because of her own longtime fondness for him but also because of her late husband's judgment regarding the boy's character. Elmo Parks had rarely made any mistakes when it came to assessing a person's moral fiber.

"So Miles thinks Mark just pretended to find the coin along the roadside? That his coming along with Amy to help us was just to give him a useful cover situation?"

"That's his thesis."

An unhappy sigh completely emptied her lungs, and she stood there trying to decide what was best. "So you'll talk to Herb about this? Maybe even before Miles Stevens gets a chance to?"

"Do you know if he's on duty today? I hate to bother our chief of police on his day off."

"I think he was off last weekend. Wasn't he in church? I didn't see him, this morning." She decided to take the plunge and offer to talk to Herb herself. "If you'd like, I could call him."

"Thanks, Gracie." Paul seemed relieved. "I'd be glad to discuss it with him, should he want that. But of course I wasn't there with you yesterday."

♪

Herb Bower was in his office and told her to come over right away if that was convenient. Gracie felt it best to go alone, even though both Uncle Miltie and Marge offered to join her. Admonishing them both not to tell anyone where she was headed or about Miles Stevens's claiming the coin, she strode out resolutely to Fannie Mae, determined to convince Herb Bower that Miles Stevens was accusing Mark unjustly.

Herb met her at the door. "Let's sit here, since nobody's around on this beautiful Sunday afternoon," he suggested, turning around one of the comfortable waiting-room chairs so that they could face one another.

She took her seat, and began straight away. "You know about our cleaning up the Ferris Road trash yesterday?"

"Of course." He grinned as he added, "When you rate the entire front page of the *Gazette*'s second section, that's pretty hard to miss."

She made a wry face. "Rocky was going around taking pictures, but we had no idea he planned to do *that*. However, it's because of what happened yesterday that I'm here right now."

She'd known from previous times when they'd worked things out together that he was an excellent listener. And on this occasion he proved to be so again. He sat there apparently relaxed, leaning back in his chair, ankle crossed over his knee. Even when she'd finished, his manner appeared casual.

"Do you think it at all unusual that Mark decided to go along with Amy's invitation to help pick up the trash?" he finally asked. "Are they especially good friends?"

Could he be thinking Miles's story was true? But she cautioned herself against jumping to conclusions. "Amy said he came into the deli while she was working after school the other day. She'd just been talking to Abe about coming in late on Saturday, so she turned and asked Mark if he'd ever participated in any cleanups, and he said the only time he'd done so was back when in Cub Scouts, when El had gotten all of them involved."

Herb's eyes and face softened, as did his voice. "That husband of yours touched the lives of so many people in ways we're still realizing."

Unbidden tears threatened to fill Gracie's eyes. El's death had robbed her of her best and most loving friend, the man she respected above all others. She and Herb rested there in sad silence for a moment. Then Gracie sat up straighter and looked him in the eye.

"El thought Mark was a very promising youngster."

"I gather he's an ambitious young man with a lawn-care sideline."

She nodded. "I understand he's got a lot of contented customers—like Abe Wasserman, for instance. He has his mind set on going to college, you see, and he's smart enough to realize his mother's not in any position to give much financial help."

"He's a good student?"

"Good enough. And, as I say, strongly motivated."

But this wasn't dealing with their problem, at least not directly. She drew in a deep breath and asked, "So what should we be doing about that coin?"

Herb regarded her somberly. " 'So what are *we* going to do?' You're beginning to sound like a hardened operator, Gracie, thinking that a little carefully applied muscle can carve out a straight path to the correct resolution. Believe it or not, my friend, sometimes things do work themselves out without our involvement."

"Herb," she assured him, "I accept your line of reasoning. I just wanted to weigh in—not meddle. I promise you."

He stood up, extending his hand to help her to her feet. "I'm glad you did. Had Miles arrived here first with his story, I'd have had to check it out. Now, if and when he does, I'll have more reason to be cautious in questioning him."

"I appreciate that—and you."

She appreciated him even more as he walked her to the door saying, "I do thank you for coming, Gracie—and for your caring so much about the welfare of Willow Bend. It's folks like you who make people like me want to never leave this little corner of Indiana."

She turned and gave him her most engaging smile. "I hope you and Marybeth never do leave, Herb—at least not as long as I'm around."

Three

MARGE AND UNCLE MILTIE were in the middle of a fast-paced game of double solitaire, so Gracie didn't interrupt, although her fingers did slide lightly across her uncle's shoulders. He could sometimes sound curmudgeonly, but she knew all too well that his crustiness was just the container for a very soft cream filling.

Undoubtedly he had realized that Marge wouldn't leave until Gracie got back and so, to distract her, had suggested the one game that Marge was able to win much of the time. She could drive him mad with her fidgety ways, but he knew how to handle her when he felt like it. Now, when she played her last card, a red queen on a black jack, she crowed, "I beat you again. I've got two games to your one!"

"*Aw*, I wasn't really trying. You know what a gentleman I am," said Uncle Miltie. And then with a pretend leer, "Always wanting to give the guest—especially such a pretty woman—the chance to win."

"*Ho!* That'll be the day." She made a face at him, but she was pleased.

"So how did you make out, Gracie?"

The reply came from the living room doorway, "I could only give him what little information we have so far to work with. Now we have to see if Miles comes to him with that story."

"I hope he was horrified!"

"Herb Bower wasn't born yesterday," Uncle Miltie stated firmly. "He'll know what to do . . . or not do."

Gracie hurried upstairs. *Well, I think my uncle's right. Herb will have*

You behind him if Miles goes to him with that story. And of course if there's something You want me to do, please give me the wisdom to recognize what it is.

She caught a glimpse of herself in the mirror and was almost surprised to see a slight smile on her face. *Thanks, Lord, for recharging my spirit each and every time we talk.*

By the time she returned to the kitchen, the pair already there were nearing the end of the current game. "The very last one," her uncle declared firmly. "I can't stand to lose any more."

"You're such a poor sport!" Marge teased.

"Sticks and stones," he replied, then glanced toward Gracie. "She promised to play Scrabble with me if I'd sit through one more game of this stupid double solitaire."

"I was just trying to give him another chance to even our score—but, of course, he's not winning."

She dramatically laid the final card on the pile where he'd just placed one of the several he still held. "Can I help it if he's so slow?"

He ignored her and said loudly, "As you can see, my dear Gracie, she's not smart enough to realize I'm letting her win this quickly so she won't back out of her agreement. Scrabble's a serious game."

"You two!" Gracie laughed.

"You know you'd miss it if we were boringly agreeable all the time, with none of this spice and seasoning! It'd be like a bland meal!"

Marge made no effort to hide her laughter as she got up and went to the counter for the Scrabble box. He was methodically separating the playing cards by color, and as she started to get the other game ready—turning the lettered wooden squares face-down upon the table—he was carefully fitting the decks into their proper boxes.

A threeway game ended with Gracie fitting her final *f* below the *i* of the horizontal word *lit*—thus forming the two-letter vertical word *if.*

"I can't believe it!" Marge cried. "You've been behind this entire game . . . and now you've won by one lousy point!"

She glanced at the antique school clock on the kitchen wall and pushed back from the table. "Can you believe it's nearly six already? I need to see if I had any calls."

Uncle Miltie also was getting to his feet. "Sometimes it's better getting messages on the machine. That way, you don't get bogged down with long conversations."

"But then *I* have to pay for returning the long-distance ones."

He headed toward the living room. "Let them call back. If they don't, you'll know it either wasn't really important, or they didn't care enough."

"But that unreturned call might be just the one that could have turned my social life around," she said, going out the door.

Marge had spoken lightly, as though amused by the possibility. But Gracie knew her friend missed having a male friend in her life. As she returned the cards and Scrabble to their cupboard, she sighed.

Seeing the stack of games suddenly reminded her that it had been a whole week since she'd talked with her own son, Arlen, her daughter-in-law Wendy and her wonderful grandson Elmo. It was true she'd been busy, as always—and they were, too—but for the Parks family, that wasn't a good enough excuse.

"Hello, Elmo," she greeted her grandson less than a minute later. "I've been thinking about you and your parents, and just had to call."

"Hi!" his voice was as clear and as real as though he were right here with her in her Willow Bend kitchen. "Mommy! Daddy! Grandma's on the phone!"

She waited, then heard him say, "I've been thinking about you too, Grandma. We went to the zoo today."

"Still like the monkey house best of all?"

"Well, the snakes, they're pretty cool."

As much as she treasured her relationship with her grandson, she couldn't work up much enthusiasm for snakes! "How about the elephants? You thought they were special, too."

"I still do—but then, *every*thing's special, and I know 'cause you told me that."

And then Arlen was on the phone with, "So how's the center of the universe, I mean Willow Bend, Mom?"

"Perfectly beautiful, right now!"

"And you and Gooseberry have been watching the season change during your morning walks," he prompted.

"Yes, we have. Then yesterday morning some of us in the choir went out to gather bags and *bags* of trash from along Ferris Road."

"I didn't realize your choir was adopting that stretch of road. Whose idea was that?"

"Well, in a way mine. And we haven't, really. But the church that had been doing this hasn't taken care of it since early spring. Since I'd noticed how awful the area looked, we wound up organizing to take care of it this one time."

"At least that's something that shouldn't get you in trouble. You're not involved in any major legal or other messes as of now, are you?"

"Of course not. And just because I've been involved in one way or another with a few mysterious happenings doesn't mean I'm trouble-prone, I'll have you know."

Arlen chuckled. "It's important to those of us who love you to make sure that that's the case."

Gracie had anticipated telling him about finding the coin and about Miles Stevens trying to claim it, but now decided to give only the first half of that information.

"Have you any idea how much the coin's worth?" he asked. "Since 1930 seems rather late in the production of gold coins, I'd guess this one's probably not going to wind up valued at more than several hundred dollars."

"There's been no opportunity to have it professionally appraised," she admitted, "but one of Uncle Miltie's friends checked values in the *Blue Book* or *Red Book* or *Green Book*—whatever it is that comes out each year to give current market prices. He says if the coin's determined to be in as good condition as we think it is, it could be worth as much as nineteen thousand dollars!"

"*Oops!* I mean thirteen!"

She smiled as his laughter at having so badly missing the mark came across the wires and into her cozy kitchen.

A moment later, he suggested, "Be sure to persuade Mark to find a secure place for that coin, Mom. Should it be lost or stolen, it'd be almost impossible to prove ownership."

"That's why Paul already has it in the church safe."

"Does anyone else know that?"

"I have no idea."

They were both aware that Willow Bend was a place where everyone was interested in what was going on in the lives of others, though usually not for the wrong reasons. *And let's face it, Lord, I recall a number of times when I've been very grateful for the concern and generosity of these people.*

Gracie now described the sudden appearance of Gooseberry, twining his orange body around her ankles. She looked down and grabbed his tail for an impromptu massage. Gooseberry loved getting a good tail rub.

Arlen chuckled. "I hope nobody ever tells that pet of yours that he's a cat, not a dog. You'd have a thoroughly traumatized feline were he to learn how abnormal he is."

"*Abnormal?* How can you possibly think such a thing?" She bent down and lifted the topic of their conversation one-handedly onto her lap, not the easiest thing to do since he was so large and so entirely relaxed that it was like picking up an inadequately stuffed rag toy. "He's just so much superior to the average cat that poor humans like us haven't got him figured out yet."

"Heaven help us if and when we do!"

His affectionate laughter was joined by hers.

Gracie awoke to the sound of pounding rain and, rolling over, pulled the covers up over her head. No, she didn't expect to go back to sleep, but at the same time had little urge to bound outside for her prayer-walk on a morning like this.

And I don't have a single thing that absolutely has to be done this morning, she crowed. That seemed so unusual that she forced herself to do a mental rundown and realized that, first of all, she needed to write a note on the birthday card she'd bought for 101-year-old Amanda Bixler.

She'd had every intention of doing that on Saturday, but with the trash duty, she hadn't got around to it. She also had intended to whip up an angel food cake, which she and Uncle Miltie could take over to Pleasant Haven this afternoon. With this in mind, she pushed back the covers, got out of bed, and began her day with a hot shower.

Gracie didn't consider pride to be one of her major faults. It was just that she got such satisfaction from using her own recipes, creating desserts and confections from scratch—most of the time, that was. However, there now was one exception to this self-imposed rule, thanks to a visit to New York City.

When at Arlen's the year before, she'd congratulated Wendy on her delicious, perfect angel food cake—and her daughter-in-law had shown her the boxed mix she had used. So when Gracie returned to Willow Bend a few days later, the bottom of her suitcase was weighted with a number of these boxes. She had two left—soon to be only one after she made Amanda's.

Had anyone asked, she'd have shared her "secret." But, as it was, she just smiled and said, "Thank you," when later she received raves from the elderly ladies at Amanda's end of the hall who were enjoying slices of cake with sliced strawberries and a scoop of ice cream.

After they had visited for over an hour, Gracie dropped her uncle off at the senior center and detoured around by way of the police station. Lucille Murphy, the daytime police dispatcher, greeted her in friendly fashion. "As far as I know, he can see you right away, Gracie, but let me call back there."

It was only a second or so later that Herb came down the short hallway to give a hearty welcome, "Good to see you, Gracie! Come on back to my office."

"I was over at Pleasant Haven to take a birthday cake to Amanda Bixler, and thought I'd stop in here for a few minutes."

She smiled at Lucille, who asked how old Amanda was. "One hundred and one—but doesn't look or act a day over ninety!"

Lucille laughed. "And there aren't many about whom you can say *that.*"

Gracie cocked her head thoughtfully. "To me, it's amazing to find as many as there are. Centenarians were extremely rare back when I was a kid." A mere fifty or so years ago, she thought.

As she started down the hallway, she heard the other woman's reply. "When I was a child, I considered everyone over thirty or forty to be an antique—and probably hadn't a clue how much unmapped territory lay between that and being a centenarian!"

"You certainly will never be old, Gracie, not to any of us who know you." Herb laughed as he pulled a chair around to the side of his desk. "And I suppose the fact of my aging at the same rate should make me more aware of my own mortality. But it doesn't, I'm afraid."

"I pray I'll age as gracefully as dear Amanda," Gracie said as she took the indicated seat. "She didn't have a particularly easy life as a child or adult, yet is such a sweet and forgiving person. Or maybe I should say accepting."

He looked at her with affection. "Don't worry, Gracie, you're all of those things and much, much more."

"Thanks, Herb." She was touched. He was, she knew, not a demonstrative man. To break the mood and return to a more business-like atmosphere, she asked quickly about the coin.

"Miles has made an appointment to see me an hour from now, but didn't mention what he wants to discuss."

"I—don't suppose you'd be allowed to tell me much anyway, would you?"

He leaned back in his chair and sat there looking at her. "That depends on what's happening, and also what you need to know. After all, it's not like we've never before been on the same team together."

"We-e-ll . . ." She shifted position. "I probably shouldn't be here right now, but something was said over at the home this afternoon that I figured perhaps should be shared. You know Marjorie Printz, who now lives there, don't you?"

"Of course. Even though she was already retired from elementary school teaching by the time I came, I soon got to know her. For that matter, everyone seems to."

She nodded agreement. "One of the aides mentioned that article in the paper, and then another visitor said she'd heard something about a valuable coin that had been found, and asked about that. I was as evasive as possible, but the reference to a gold coin got Miss Marjorie to reminiscing.

"She told us her father had saved a whole bunch of these—mostly eagles and double eagles—even when they were supposed to have been turned in back in the thirties, when President Roosevelt got the government to pass that law.

"And then she talked about what a godsend they'd been, since teachers didn't make much money thirty years ago. She said that 'nice man,' Miles Stevens, gave her double their face value when she used them as the down payment on her little house on Third Street, where she took care of her dad after his strokes."

"*Hunh!*" Herb snorted. "How generous!"

"It was all I could do to keep from blurting out something to that effect." Even talking about it now made her angry. "Marjorie added that the so-helpful bank officer told her to keep this a secret, so her father wouldn't be sent to jail for disobeying that terrible law about melting down all the gold currency.

"So to this day she's still thankful for Miles's being so considerate, for taking on himself the risk involved from owning those coins, and assuring her she need never again worry about the possibility of her father being imprisoned!"

"Some benefactor!"

She nodded. "I got to fretting on my way home that if he still has all of those—if he hasn't already sold them for scads of money, that is—that that might give more credibility to his claim that he's the owner of Mark's coin."

Herb came and sat on the corner of the desk nearest her. "Perhaps. But if that does seem to be happening, I may ask for his entire list of the coins, which I doubt will make him very happy."

"Herb," she began, looking thoughtful, "is it logical that he'd bring home just a few at a time from his safe deposit box, as he's apparently claiming?"

"I suppose that makes as much sense as it does for reclusive art collectors to have guarded, secluded, air conditioned galleries in which to keep their most treasured works. They evidently go in there all by themselves to enjoy looking at—and gloating over—what they own." He looked thoughtful, then glanced at his watch.

Gracie would have enjoyed staying longer, but Herb's time was valuable. And she had been grabbing more than her share over the past couple of days.

The sun was trying to break through the clouds, and the sidewalks had dried off. At home Gooseberry came to meet her at the door. He looked up at her with those innocent wide eyes and gave a slightly pitiful, "Meow."

Gracie weakened. "Okay, big guy, you win," she told him, laying her purse on the counter and putting the house key in her pocket. "However," she said, letting him lead the way out of the kitchen door, "to be perfectly honest, I need to get out now and get some exercise every bit as much as you do.

"But don't get your hopes too high, dear friend, for this may be just a break in the clouds. After all, the TV weatherman stated it was probably going to rain off and on all day."

Four

SHE'D TOLD HERSELF HERB would be too busy to bother with reporting to her anything about his interview with Miles Stevens. Yet as she neared home after her walk, she began to walk faster. She opened the door, went inside—and saw no blinking light on her answering machine.

Oh, well, I have no badge, she reminded herself. My capacity is purely unofficial.

Things had looked quiet enough while she was there, but he undoubtedly had mountains of paperwork, as well as myriad phone calls and people coming and going. He could have gotten called out, too, for some reason.

Gracie smiled a little, remembering when he'd first come to Willow Bend as an officer. Back then, he had been even more reserved in his dealing with people. But it made sense. Since he'd been fairly young and there might have been some attempts to take advantage of his inexperience.

There were, of course, always going to be those citizens of Willow Bend whom he'd catch doing things outside the law who wouldn't like him much. But for the most part there was only respect and gratitude. As for Gracie herself, she knew beyond a shadow of a doubt that he was sincerely trying to be the best policeman, and the best Christian he could be.

Thank You, God, for sending Herb here. I know, because Marybeth has confided in me, that he's had opportunities to go to bigger places where he'd earn more money. But Willow Bend is their home, and the people who live here are their brothers and sisters. Do keep him safe, Lord. He has a difficult job and sometimes a dangerous one. Whenever there are ways in which I can be of assistance to him and his family, please help me see what they are.

Uncle Miltie had said he'd get a ride home, and he did—at 3:15. It had slipped her mind that this was a day when he and two others from the senior center were going to the school to read to the littlest kids. But he talked of nothing else while she put dinner out for them.

After offering the prayer of thanks for the food, he added, "And thanks also for all those youngsters we spent time with this afternoon and for their teachers and the helpers. Some of those kids need so much help, like that deaf girl, Lynn."

Realizing that the child he mentioned was Mark's mother's charge, Gracie asked about her progress.

"You should see Sally's hands and fingers fly as she signs!" he exclaimed. "Even though Lynn's lip-reading is improving, Sally signs as a back-up. I was tickled pink we got the chance to stop by her classroom after our reading session. It was only because Sid's daughter, Liz, is her teacher. I asked her how Lynn's getting along, and she told us that this year she's near the top of her class academically."

"That's wonderful."

"Sure is." He finally helped himself to the salmon croquettes and Gracie's special dill sauce. "I didn't get to hear her talk. Liz says she can now, though not everyone can understand her.

"But you know what? Liz and Sally agreed it might be good for Lynn to practice her lipreading with a new person, get used to different speech patterns. I've got the time, so I said I'll go over there at least twice a week, and she and I will work on it during part of her study-period. I start tomorrow. Should be a snap. I'll just tell her jokes."

"George Morgan!" she said sternly. "Be careful! That could set her back! Seriously, though, when will you do it?"

"Sally's going to get back to me. Right now, it'll probably be at 10:05 tomorrow morning. Then I could also do it one afternoon."

It was only later in the evening that Gracie understood how very important this project was to him. Her uncle had been thinking hard about the responsibility he was accepting.

"You know, Gracie, I'm beginning to think I should never have volunteered for that lipreading stuff! It seemed like such a good idea—but I was just looking in the mirror and saying different words. They all look alike! It's not going to be as easy a job as it sounds. If

I exaggerate to make each word clear, it won't be natural. How can I be any help, really?"

"It does seem formidable," she agreed, looking up from reading the paper, "but it must be possible, since so many people do it."

He was nearly to his favorite recliner, but stopped and looked at her, then back at the door of the bathroom. Neither of them said anything else, but there was a smile on her face as she realized that he was turning around. Soon she could hear his murmuring, as he practiced in front of the mirror, telling himself jokes.

Going to the police station again the next morning, near the end of her walk, Gracie tried to ignore the label her own mother might have applied to her: "nosey posy." And there were other equally unflattering ways to describe those who took too active an interest in the business of others.

She preferred thinking of it as "being genuinely concerned." But was she only fooling herself?

And wasn't it possible that Herb just might have called when she was out but didn't want to leave a message?

"Wow, twice in two days!" Lucille greeted her. But then, she added, "That must mean things aren't going well in Willow Bend."

It's too close to the truth to be funny, Gracie thought. But she laughed anyway. "It's nothing important. Gooseberry and I were just going by, and I saw Herb's car out back. There is something I'd forgotten to tell him."

Her big orange cat, however, never one to stand on ceremony, had already strolled the short distance to Herb's office and proceeded inside. She heard Herb's voice greeting, "Well, well, Gooseberry, so you've come to visit me this morning. Shall we go out and welcome Gracie and invite her back here, too?"

Lucille gave a wave of her hand. "Might as well do as the boss suggests."

"I guess so." Laughing, Gracie headed down the hall. "I don't want to bother you if you're real busy, Herb."

"You're not. For that matter, I was just thinking that I should call you and this is much better." He added, "There's not much new, really. Miles Stevens merely wanted to repeat his claim that Mark, and Mark alone, had the opportunity to see the coin and to steal it, since no one else even knew that he had the gold."

"There's Marjorie Printz," Gracie pointed out. "Maybe she's an elderly cat burglar who leaves Pleasant Haven late at night to sneak around reclaiming whatever she thinks is rightfully hers."

He grinned. "As an officer of the law, I'm supposed to keep an open mind concerning opportunity when it comes to the commission of crimes . . . but *that,* my dear Ms. Parks, goes beyond even the limits of my fertile imagination!"

"Well, you can't say I didn't try!" Gracie pretended to puff a pipe à la Sherlock Holmes. "Seriously, though, Herb, if he actually did bring home just a few of his treasured coins, wouldn't he have noticed if one was missing?"

He shrugged. "I asked him that, and he explained that he'd covered all of them with a paper before going into the other room for the money to give to Mark for the gas. And afterward, when the boy had gone outside, Miles just gathered up what had been on the table and put it all into one of those semitransparent glassine envelopes, which he then put in a locked drawer.

"And," he said, noticing her troubled expression, "he didn't check them again until he heard about Mark's finding a gold coin."

"That sounds more plausible than I wish it did," she finally admitted. "But I still don't believe Mark stole anything from anyone!"

*

It was late that afternoon when Gracie called Sally Canfield at home, on the pretense of discussing her possible rejoining of the choir.

"We've missed you. I'll bet you can't say truthfully you haven't missed us!"

"I loved singing with you, you're right," Sally admitted. "But I've got so very much on my plate right now, Gracie, what with working at school and keeping things under control here at home. I *am* still teaching the young teens class there in the Sunday school."

"I'm truly grateful for that," Gracie reassured her. "If there's ever an age when children need encouragement and tender, loving care, as well as good biblical teaching, it's those early adolescent years."

"My sentiments exactly! And I want to again thank you for your part in making it possible for me to continue teaching them."

Gracie winced inwardly, remembering when there had been some discussion about Sally's removal from her Sunday school class when she was divorced. It wasn't as if she'd been the guilty party, for goodness sake. It had been her husband Arnold who had done the leaving and forced the dissolution of the Canfield marriage.

"You're more than welcome, Sally. I think you're terrific and you know it."

"Yes, I do . . . and I'll confess that I've been holding onto that assurance especially closely the last day or two."

That sounded as though she had a special need, but Gracie wasn't sure just how to respond. Fortunately, Sally went on, "Mark was so excited when he found that gold coin on Saturday! He's such a good boy, Gracie, and such a hardworking student. He's been saving to get a little nest egg together toward going to college. So this at first seemed like a godsend to him—and to me—until Miles Stevens started accusing him of stealing that money from him."

"I'd—heard about that."

"Oh, dear!"

She was obviously distressed, and Gracie hastened to add, "I'm pretty certain nobody believes it."

"I wish I could believe that, Gracie, but I've had personal experience as to how little it takes in Willow Bend to start rumors and keep them going."

That was all too true, unfortunately. "Well, I certainly don't believe it, nor does our chief of police!"

"Herb!"

"Yes, I stopped in to talk to him for a couple of minutes, and he told me Miles had been to see him."

"What about?"

I'm not sure Herb's going to be happy about my telling her this, Gracie thought, but she has to know. "That the double eagle was there on his kitchen table, with other coins, and that Mark must have seen it and taken it when Miles went into the other room to get him the gas money."

Gracie heard a long intake of breath. "That's what he insisted when he came here."

"Miles? He came to your home?"

"He most certainly did! It was awful, really, and he was insisting that Mark give the coin to him right then and there."

"Gosh," Gracie was thinking out loud, "it's a good thing Paul has it in the church's safe. Miles doesn't know that's where it is, does he?"

"I'm sure he doesn't." There was the briefest of pauses before

Sally added, "But I wasn't aware until now that anyone knew that except Paul, Mark, and me."

Gracie hastened again to give reassurance. "I happened to overhear Paul make that offer, and was pleased when Mark agreed. Under the circumstances, it's probably the best thing if nobody else learns where it is."

There was the sound of a worried sigh. "You . . . don't think there could be a break-in, do you?"

"Well, Paul's offer was to keep it only until the bank opened on Monday, but I guess Mark has seen no reason to move it. I suspect that the main reason Miles came to your house was his hope of bullying you and your son into handing the coin over right then and there."

"Well, we might have considered it! Let's face it, Gracie! It was awful having him threaten us! And he did! With a lawsuit!"

"Well, until this all gets sorted out, I'm going to be doing a lot of praying!"

"That's wonderful, Gracie. I do thank you for that, and for your friendship."

She was about to hang up when she suddenly remembered something else she'd wanted to mention. "Uncle Miltie's really excited about the possibility of helping with Lynn's lipreading."

"He's such a fine man, so generous with his time."

Her voice had softened with the change of topic, and Gracie went on. "He's concerned as to whether he can actually do it, however. In fact, I heard him practicing in front of the bathroom mirror, trying to make his mouth do whatever's necessary in order for her to 'see' the words."

"I know just how he feels!" Sally chuckled. "My first thought was that it wasn't possible—then that it *might* be possible, just not by me."

"Uncle Miltie says she's very bright."

"She is. I have high hopes for her and her future."

"And I'm sure she senses that, which gives her additional motivation to keep on doing her best for you."

After mulling over the conversation with Sally for a while, Gracie decided to call Herb, in case he wasn't aware that Miles Stevens had actually threatened Sally and Mark. But, missing him at the police station, she left a message that, although it was no emergency, she'd appreciate a call at his convenience.

Taking her at her word, Herb didn't get back to her for over twenty-four hours. Gracie managed with no trouble to stay busy, but her mind kept going to Sally's story of Miles's threat. The next day the phone rang bright and early.

"Good morning, Gracie. I know it's early, but I was afraid I'd miss you, that you'd already be out with Gooseberry for your ramble."

She glanced at the clock. "I had several things I wanted to do first."

"Look, if this is a bad time, you can get back to me later."

"Actually, it's a good time, and I'm glad to hear from you. What I wanted to say probably isn't too important, anyway. But I simply didn't know if you were aware that Miles had gone over to the Canfields' and threatened them with legal action if they didn't hand over *his* gold coin right away."

"They didn't, did they?"

He sounded so concerned that she had to reassure him before asking, "If he should find out that it's in the church's safe, do you suppose he might make trouble for Paul or for our church? Maybe it's the right time to turn it over to the bank. To put it there for safekeeping."

"I suppose so."

She suggested, "Since this coin is the center of so much contention, is it possible—is it ever *done* to have the item held by the chief of police or someone like that? Forget the bank?"

"Really, Gracie . . ."

"I don't mean to ask you to consider doing anything improper."

"Dear Gracie, don't you think I know that, after all this time? I was just about to say that I might have offered to do it myself. I didn't want to take the chance, though, that Sally might think I believe her son to be a thief."

"Oh!" Gracie appreciated Herb's tact.

"What do you feel is best now, at this stage—for me to make that offer, or you?"

Life sure comes with lots of decisions, Lord! "I can, if you'd like. She already knows we've been in touch, so Herb's offer shouldn't come as a surprise. And I suppose she'll want to talk with Paul, too—she'd have to, I guess, since he's the one keeping the coin now."

⚘

The coin transfer was made early the following morning, before Mark and his mother had to leave for school. At the station Herb took the coin from Mark and Paul. Then the police chief carefully sealed it in a marked envelope and placed it in his safe. Closing the heavy door, Herb spun the dial, then requested each observer sign a document as a witness to what he had done.

Gracie realized she wasn't the only one who had been holding her breath.

"There!"

Sally was standing taller, as if a load had been removed from her shoulders. "I appreciate your taking care of it up until now, Paul," she told their pastor, "but I suspect you are glad no longer to have the responsibility for it. I wouldn't blame you."

Paul looked at her gravely. "I didn't lose sleep over its being where it was, but, yes, I'll confess to being relieved it's here."

Choir practice that night went remarkably well. Rick Harding, one of their tenors, who'd been unable to make the cleanup on Saturday, claimed he was ready and able the next time if he could be promised as much excitement as this one had engendered. Not to mention the media attention!

Lester immediately whipped out a pen and piece of paper. "Okay, you can sign up right here, right now. This way, we'll be ready should Harry Judson's fellow congregants not follow through on its commitment to fill in for him."

"If I were *they*," Marge stated dramatically, "I wouldn't let anybody else even have a chance at it! Harry'll probably recuperate faster, too, so he can resume cleanup control of the area, without any help! Who knows what'll turn up next."

"What about that coin Mark found?" Amy seemed concerned. "He does get to keep it, doesn't he?"

"Well," Gracie began. "What happened . . ."

Marge interrupted, "Everyone seems to know that Miles Stevens is insisting it's missing from his collection, that Mark stole it from him and planted it by the roadside."

That rather bald announcement was obviously upsetting to some. Tish immediately came to Mark's defense, "Sally's son is such a nice boy. I can't believe he would ever do anything like that."

"We're quite sure he didn't," Gracie stated flatly. She glared at Marge.

Don Delano spoke up from the baritone section, "I can't believe that of him, either! He's in one of my classes, and I can tell you I've never seen or heard anything about him to indicate he's got an honesty problem. He's a good kid."

Marge added, "I heard Miles has actually already threatened legal action if he doesn't get it back." She was ignoring Gracie's look of entreaty.

Herb's wife, Marybeth Bower, said nothing, and Gracie knew that Herb was far too professional to confide in her any troublesome work issues. She did not interrupt for another minute or two, then deliberately asked Barb something about the anthem they'd be singing on Sunday.

The director looked at Amy. "You'll be here, won't you?"

"Sure. My mother and I were planning to go to Chicago, but that's next weekend."

"Good!"

Barb dreaded changes in any of her plans, especially when it involved solo parts. However, Gracie sensed Estelle's restless movement beside her, and realized the older soprano would never lose her desire to outdo Amy in solo parts whenever possible. But Amy's reassurance to Barb meant that Estelle now was foiled again. Gracie stifled a guilty chuckle.

Amy sang her part beautifully, even on the third page with its tricky change of key and extra-high notes. She had such natural talent and true pitch that Gracie marveled, as she always did, at the girl's ability.

It was after practice that Marybeth took Gracie aside. Herb, it seems, had asked her to tell Gracie that he'd appreciate a call at home. No, she didn't know what it was about, but he'd implied that he'd hoped it could be tonight, if possible.

Gracie thanked her friend and said she'd phone as soon as she got home. Uncle Miltie was glued to the TV, so she had plenty of privacy when she seated herself in the kitchen.

"Marybeth said she gave you my message." It was Herb who'd answered. "I'm glad. It wasn't necessary to talk tonight, but I wanted to make you aware of another new development.

"Have you by any chance heard of a young man called Clark Harrington?"

"I—don't think so, Herb. Should I?"

"Probably not. I hadn't. But this guy came into the station just as I was getting ready to leave—and we now have a third person insisting that the double eagle belongs to him!"

"What!" Gracie could hardly believe her ears.

"It's not a very strong story, but his claim is he inherited it from his grandfather. He says he carries it in his pocket as sort of a good luck piece."

"So, how did it happen to wind up on Ferris Road?"

"His explanation is that it must have dropped out of his pocket when he was out walking in just that spot. What he told me is when he pulled his handkerchief out of his pocket, the coin must have come, too."

"Did he have the location right?"

"Sure, but at this point everyone from here to the Canadian border could pinpoint it on a map!"

She couldn't argue. "When does he say he first missed it? And why would he just walk around with something so valuable?"

"Sunday. But even then he figured it must be around somewhere. Once he heard about Mark's coin, however, he made a careful search for it. As for being heedless with something so valuable, the short answer is, people are like that. That's all."

"Where does he live?"

"He gave an address in Akron, but he's been in Willow Bend for about a week, staying at Cordelia Fountain's tourist home. He's here on business."

"Oh, dear." To her, this sounded more probable than Miles Stevens's claim. Still, doubts lingered. "Can he prove he ever even owned such a coin? Is it insured or anything?"

"He didn't say, but we didn't talk long. I'll undoubtedly be seeing him again soon."

"Oh, dear," Gracie repeated.

Five

GRACIE DIDN'T ENJOY a restful night. She fell asleep fairly quickly, but was wide awake by 1:30 A.M. After that, her mind was racing.

Thank goodness this doesn't happen often, she thought. She kept going over and over the same questions and concerns as she tossed and turned. She felt particularly lonely—something she kept thinking would cease to bother her this way.

I still miss you so very much, Elmo, physically and mentally and even spiritually. You were so much a part of me, and so wise, and so close to God. How I'd love to talk to you—you with your cool head and your warm heart. About this coin business: I'm sure I'm not seeing something important. There seemed little possibility that each of the three claimants honestly believed he was telling the truth, which meant two of them probably were not.

But which two?

She still couldn't believe that Mark ever would have plotted to hide the coin in his pocket, then pretend to find it. It was true that the coin hadn't seemed terribly dirty when she first saw it, but then she distinctly remembered his rubbing it on his jeans. Could he really be such a clever actor . . . and thief?

Miles Stevens she knew she didn't trust, but this new claimant, this Clark Harrington, was an unknown entity.

Gracie considered herself to be, by nature, a person who looked for the best in others. Her dear Elmo, her loving El, used to tease her about it. But, sometimes, even he would be exasperated if she'd persist in "always arguing for the defense."

She was still awake at 3:45. Yet she didn't feel like starting her day that early. Turning on her bedside light, she reached for her Bible and began scanning some of the italicized words at the beginning of chapters.

When nothing caught her attention right away, she went to the concordance and looked for the references under *coin(s)*. There were only a few listed, most in the Gospels. The first Gospel reference concerned someone's bringing Jesus a coin. The second was about a woman who, having lost and found a coin, invited all of her neighbors to celebrate with her.

The third reference was to Jesus' commendation of the very poor woman who gave to God the last coins she had. The last recounted Jesus' anger at the temple moneychangers who had been stealing from the worshipers. He caused the villains to spill their coins onto the floor before He chased them away.

She pondered these lessons for a time. Although she could certainly understand and appreciate each of them, the only one that felt emotionally right at the moment was the final one.

She decided to pursue her biblical investigations further and check all the references to *money*. Suddenly, she closed the book, remembering the perfect verse without reading it: "The love of money is the root of all evils."

Her hand lightly caressed the soft brown leather as she remembered El's giving this Revised Standard Version to her the first Christmas after they were married. Slowly reopening it, she turned to the sixth chapter of Paul's first letter to Timothy and read, "There is great gain in godliness with contentment; for we brought nothing into the world, and we cannot take anything out of the world; but if we have food and clothing, with these we shall be content.

"But those who desire to be rich fall into temptation, into a snare, into many senseless and hurtful desires that plunge men into ruin and destruction. For the love of money is the root of all evils; it is through this craving that some have wandered away from the faith and pierced their hearts with many pangs."

How true, how very true, dear God, even two thousand years later.

She turned off the light and snuggled down under the covers once again. It was still dark, and she didn't look at the clock to see what time it was. She was content. And she surely felt loved—by God, certainly, but it was also as though El had been there to reveal those words to her.

Morning arrived soon. It was another beautiful autumn day, as shown by the leaves outside her bedroom window. She got out of bed and dressed quickly, eager to be outside with Gooseberry for their walk. Sometimes she listened to music or even, occasionally, to recorded books. Today, however, seemed so special that she wanted just to savor the sights and sounds of nature.

Anxiety over the much-disputed coin kept trying to intrude, but for the most part she was able to ignore it, if only temporarily. This was a time for enjoying the glorious and grand outpourings of nature's bounty around her.

Then, without realizing it, she found herself walking at the edge of town. Her path had taken her out to Ferris Road. There she saw signs that winter was stalking the brilliant landscape. In the sky, birds were massed and fleeing south.

It was hard to believe that the simple act of trying to restore the roadside to its pristine state had turned out to have such sinister results.

It was too distressing.

She was now strolling along, forcing herself to concentrate on the brilliant yellow of the goldenrod along the sides of the road, and the conical red spikes of sumac. "Both of these are considered unwanted pests or weeds by most people," she mused, "but God most surely must appreciate them, for there are so many growing wild."

A few freshly tossed cans, bottles, and papers were visible, but she tried to ignore them. She was especially disappointed, however, to arrive at that farm lane where they'd spent so much time, and see how messy it had become in less than a week.

Right there was where that controversial coin had been found. Wasn't it strange the way it all had turned out!

Soon Gracie and Gooseberry were back at the main road again, and shortly within the town limits. It would be about the same distance to detour past the police station on her way home as to take her regular route, but she disciplined herself to choose the latter path. "There have been times when I've had to keep in close touch with Herb," she murmured to her four-footed friend who was leading the way, "but I feel there's no need to interrupt his work today."

Back at the house, though, she wasn't so sure. Uncle Miltie greeted her with the message that Sally had already telephoned from school. Twice.

"She sounded perturbed, Gracie, as though she really needed to talk with you."

"Did she leave her number?"

"No—and she said you shouldn't call her there. She'll try to break free for a few minutes later in the morning to try you again."

"Well, I expect to be here." She tried to look and speak calmly. "I was going to take my shower right away, but I'll weed the flower bed by the porch, instead."

"Do you think it's about the coin?" he asked nervously. "What else could it be?"

"I'm afraid it's likely to be the double eagle, but it could be about Joe and Anna's party a week from Sunday. Sally was kind enough to offer to help out in any way she can, even though she really only was related to them by marriage."

He looked more relieved than she felt, and she tried to discipline her thoughts, to take a break from mysterious goingson and try to think about her plans for that meal.

Anna Searfoss, who was the hostess and who had asked her to cater it, had described it as an "ordinary kind of meal, celebrating our many, many friendships." Anna's nearly sightless eyes had been brimming with happiness as she gave Gracie instructions, knowing how perfectly they would be carried out. They were dear friends and loved to plan parties together.

"Is this your wedding anniversary? Or birthday?" Gracie had asked her friend, certain that those occasions had come and gone already in the year for both Searfosses.

Anna had reached out to lay her hand on her husband's. "Joe and I talked this over a whole lot." She beamed. "We're just doing this as a thank-you, to acknowledge the generosity and loving helpfulness of the people who never fail us."

The couple smiled at Gracie, and Anna said, "What we most like is your plain, simple, old-fashioned cooking. You know, your special fried chicken, baked beans, scalloped potatoes, cabbage salad, apple sauce and . . ."

"Or maybe serve melon chunks instead of the applesauce," Anna said.

Joe put in. "Not those ritzy-ditsy little round balls, but honest-to-goodness chunks. They look more homey that way."

Gracie's glance toward Anna wasn't seen by her, for she had been

186

going blind for years as a result of diabetes. However, her gentle smile and little nod gave agreement.

"And now where were we? Oh yes, we'd like pickled beets and hard-boiled eggs, too. You know, Gracie, Mama grew up in Pennsylvania Dutch country, and she always served pickled-beets and eggs for get-togethers."

"I like them, too," Gracie assured her, "and remember how you would bring them to church dinners. However," Gracie paused thoughtfully, "I'll need your recipe for the beets, in order to get the just-right degree of sweet-and-sour."

"We-e-ell, that could be a problem," the elderly woman admitted. "I don't actually have a recipe—I just go by 'guess-and-golly,' as Mama used to say."

Gracie laughed. "A woman after my own heart! My own mother creatively adapted many of the recipes handed down from her grandmother and mother, and I'm delighted to have had them passed on to me. But when my daughter-in-law asks what it means when it says 'add vinegar to taste,' there's no way to explain that without letting her make and taste it!"

"And I'll bet you still don't use a recipe or measure ingredients for making pastry," said Anna, chuckling appreciatively.

$$\sim$$

The phone rang a few minutes after eleven. Gracie went to answer it with a tremor of apprehension. Better to know than not to know, she told herself. She picked up the receiver.

"Gracie." It was Sally, not even troubling to say hello. "I have only a few minutes. Mark went out and got one of those electronic metal detectors. With money he can ill afford to spend, I might add."

"Why?"

"Well, he's been going back out there to Ferris Road whenever he has even a second's free time. He's making himself ill with worry that Miles will publicly accuse him of stealing that money or even try to take him to court."

Gracie wondered what that had to do with the metal detector. "But . . ."

Sally went on, "He's hoping that if he can possibly find another of those coins, and if only one of Miles's is missing, then that would prove he had nothing to do with it."

"I guess this way he at least feels he's doing something to help himself," Gracie replied sympathetically.

"But he's not sleeping much, and it's hard for him to keep his mind on his studies. In fact, he barely passed an important test yesterday. . . ." Sally sighed heavily. "Maybe you or Herb could talk to him? I'm afraid he's not listening to me."

"I'd gladly do anything I could, but I'm not sure I'd be of much assistance at this point. I've already made it clear to everyone that I saw him find and pick up that double eagle. This business with Miles has come from way, way off in left field, as far as I'm concerned."

She wanted to mention the information Herb had given her last night, about the second claimant, but felt she shouldn't without permission. They talked for another few minutes, and Gracie suspected that when Sally went back to work, her mother-heart would still be as troubled as when she'd picked up the phone to dial Gracie.

Uncle Miltie asked as she went through the living room, "Was that Sally?"

"Yes, dear, it was," Gracie replied. "She's a mother, and I know how mothers feel, especially when circumstances make watchful waiting and its accompanying worry the only course of action."

Uncle Miltie frowned. "Gracie, you'd better get to the bottom of this mess, or I'm going to have to take your private detective's license away!"

"I don't think you're joking—at least not with that glum expression on your face."

"If anyone can make this come out all right, it's you. And pardon me if I'm a stubborn old coot to believe that! But I just *do*."

"I'm proud you have such faith in me," Gracie told him. "But I just haven't got your confidence right now." Shaking her head sadly, she left the room.

⚬

"I'm as nervous as a groom!" Uncle Miltie said the next morning. "But I was once a groom, and I don't remember being so agitated!"

"She's just a little girl who's going to be thrilled to have you helping her. Lynn is going to be a wonderful project for you, you'll see."

"But I'm untrained and I'm just going to make things harder for her when I goof up."

Her head was cocked to the side as she challenged, "Did it totally destroy Arlen's self-confidence and verbal development when I couldn't make out his first words as a baby? Or he, mine?"

"Well, no, but . . ."

"And he wasn't even consciously aware of my trying so hard to communicate. Lynn has already come so far, and Sally's been working with her. She's old enough to understand that you have to practice before becoming perfect."

He looked somewhat relieved. Still he fretted, "I'd be satisfied with adequate, forget perfect."

"Then let's leave it to God, okay? You know as well as I do that He's going to be there with you. He's promised that. You'll be doing your best and Lynn's going to be doing her best. That's all it takes, along with the Lord's blessing.

"So today's just your first day. There'll be many more to come, and all along the way you'll see change and improvement. Progress doesn't arrive overnight. It's a process."

As he listened to her, his shoulders straightened. "Thank you, Gracie. So let's get going, right?"

"Yes, Uncle Miltie, let's get going." She followed him out onto the porch. "Right!"

She stopped in front of the school's main entrance, got out his walker and helped him from the front seat. She'd planned to leave the car there while going inside with him, but suddenly two cheerful youngsters of about Lynn's age appeared. "I'm Susan and this is Louise, and we've come to take you to Lynn, Mr. Morgan."

"I'm pleased to meet you, Susan and Louise, and appreciate your doing this. I'd neglected," he told them as he started toward the door, "to learn ahead of time just where I needed to go, and was hoping someone would be around so I could find my way."

Susan ran ahead and held the door wide open, so Gracie suggested, "I'm going to leave since you're in the hands of such capable guides. I'll be home, Uncle Miltie, so just call when you're finished."

Louise looked confused. "I—thought your name was George Morgan."

"You've got it right, Louise," he reassured her. "Uncle Miltie is just a nickname."

Gracie heard the girl ask, "Then—is the lady your niece or not?" Now he'd have to explain how long ago friends had started calling him by the sobriquet given to Milton Berle, a popular old-time entertainer of whom these kids had never heard.

Leaving the school, Gracie found herself once again tempted by the proximity of the police station. But as she drove though the alley, she saw no sign of Herb's car. However, he was coming down the street when she slowed to a stop at the next intersection. Tapping his horn lightly, he beckoned her to follow him back to the police parking area.

"I just dropped Uncle Miltie off and came around this way on my way home. I'm glad I found you."

"And I'm glad I found you," he teased. "Who's the detective around here?" They walked through the back door and down the hall to his office.

Gracie went straight to the point, since it seemed Herb was giving her permission to stay involved with the coin controversy. "Have you found out anything more about our newest claimant?"

"Not much." He shook his head. "Clark Harrington is apparently who he says he is. At least he is working out of Akron, Ohio—that I found out."

"Anything else?"

His grin was a little crooked. "Well, he's relatively new with his company, but he started there with good references. Even the personnel chief doesn't know much about him, but he's found no reason to do further checking."

"Where was he before?"

"Illinois. In Springfield." Herb crossed his right leg over the left and leaned back in his chair. "As of now, I'm not planning to check further, either."

"But what about Mark and the coin?"

"Well, I'm not sure. What we know about Harrington isn't a big help, is it?"

Gracie sighed, then leaned forward to tell Herb what Sally had told her about Mark's theory that if he could find more coins, he might be able to clear himself of suspicion.

"It's a good try, whether or not he finds anything," he agreed. "It could demonstrate his innocence—although, should he find another, there's always the possibility Miles will insist he must have taken more than one coin."

"Wouldn't that look more suspicious on Miles's part than on Mark's? Didn't he say he'd brought home only a few coins from the bank? Wouldn't he know if a second one was missing?"

"It would seem that way, wouldn't it?"

She tossed her head. "Well, I'm rooting for Mark."

"I know you are." He was smiling now. "And I appreciate your loyalty. Myself, I need to stay neutral, of course."

"Of course! But I can guess, I think, where your sympathies lay."

As Gracie got to her feet, Herb did likewise. "With a problem like this one," he said, "we need to view things from different perspectives, with multiple what-if's."

She agreed, but, being Gracie, she couldn't resist sending up a silent prayer that Mark's perspective prevail.

And she couldn't keep from adding a loving thought to strengthen Uncle Miltie's resolve as a lipreading companion. If he learned to tell jokes in sign language, that, too, might provide benefit for the greater community.

Six

GRACIE WAITED RESTLESSLY for her uncle's return. Not knowing just when that would be or even if he might have decided to eat lunch at the school, she'd decided on waiting before fixing anything.

It was after 12:45 when an unfamiliar tan car pulled up in front of her house. Uncle Miltie got out, then reached back in for his folded walker, which he opened and set up, all the time talking to the driver. He then closed the door and waved as the vehicle pulled away from the curb.

He looked buoyantly at her as she went onto the porch to greet him. "Your morning must have gone well."

"So much better than expected!" There was a sparkle in his bright blue eyes. "That Lynn is a little sweetheart! She and Sally certainly made me feel welcome. I was glad to be there, glad to be able to help."

"You're positively beaming."

And he was. It had seemed earlier as if he'd really needed his walker, leaning into it with each step. Now it was just something being pushed in front of him.

Why haven't I been aware of his reliance on his walker as a sign of anxiety, God? But then, that thought led to Gracie's turning her insight into a question about her own behavior. How do I unconsciously reveal my own unhappiness or stress?

The answer to that came instantaneously. *By talking things over with You, Lord, just like this. . . .*

"You know what?" Uncle Miltie was saying. "It turns out I wasn't a stranger to everyone. As soon as we got inside, Susan said to me, 'I brought my little sister to the library several times when you were there reading children's stories. We do read to her a whole lot, of course, but she loves sitting there on the carpet with all the other kids and listening to you.'"

He chuckled at the memory. "And, boy, did I work up an appetite!"

Gracie was already getting out the bread for sandwiches. She told him, "They get you without the jokes, so of course they love listening!"

She and her uncle both chuckled. He attempted to look indignant but failed. He was in too good a mood.

"We didn't get to even try much lipreading," he said as he watched her heat a container of frozen homemade pea soup, "but at least I can say 'hello' and 'goodbye' and a couple other things with finger spelling." He demonstrated these for Gracie, then asked, "Can you guess what they call doing this? It's *dactylology*—you know, from *dactyl*, meaning a finger or toe."

She smiled encouragement, and then he did something else with his hands, as he asked, "Want to guess what I just said to you?"

"I have no idea."

"I just said, 'I like you.'" He was proud of his prowess in a new arena, and Gracie was proud *of* him. "That's the sum total of what I've learned thus far—since I haven't yet found out how to say 'I love you,' I'll just repeat that last one a couple times, okay? For extra emphasis!"

He offered to help with the dishes, but as Gracie got to her feet she reminded him there were few dishes from a meal like this. "Go on in the other room and rest," she suggested. "You've had a big morning, and I'll bet you didn't sleep well last night, worrying about how it would go."

"Ah, Gracie, you know me too well." A delighted grin came to his face. "We're a good pair, looking out for each other the way we do."

She came around the table and leaned down to kiss his cheek. "I think I'm going to lie down now, too, and read. Then, when we're both refreshed, we can take a short walk together."

He looked at her with mock concern. "Only if you promise we won't go out Ferris Road."

She laughed. "It's a deal."

Gooseberry had obviously not been consulted about agreeing to rest for a while. He kept going to the screen door, his claws scratching noisily across the irregular metal at the bottom. "I know," Gracie told him. "I promise we'll head out later on."

She went into her bedroom and stretched out on top of the handmade quilt she used as a spread. Ah, it felt good to relax, even for a few minutes. . . .

She awoke, somewhat disoriented, to the ringing of her bedside phone. "Hello?"

"Grace Parks?"

The voice sounded somewhat familiar, but she couldn't place it. "This is she."

"Well, Mrs. Parks, I guess it's about time we talk."

She pushed herself up on her elbow. "Who is this?"

"Miles Stevens."

She was wide awake now, all senses alert as she sat up and swung her legs over the side of the bed.

"Hello, Miles, how are you?"

"What do you think you're doing, encouraging that young Canfield to. . ."

"*Mr.* Stevens," she interrupted firmly, "you called me in my own home, and I answered. However, neither courtesy nor hospitality requires my listening or responding to rude or arrogant messages. If or when you wish to call again, I shall expect an apology as well as a calm and businesslike conversation."

And she hung up.

All urge to sleep was gone.

She became more uncertain about whether she'd used the best tactic when seconds, then minutes passed. Finally, telling herself that a watched phone seldom rings, she went down into the kitchen for a glass of iced tea.

Still no call back.

Please, Lord, help me know what to say or do.

Well, she decided, I'm not going to just stand here like a lump of unleavened dough. She went to the utility closet for the broom. The kitchen floor could use some attention. There were cat hairs, bits of grass that must have stuck to her shoes or Uncle Miltie's, and about the usual amount of crumbs and spills.

She noticed several small spots near the sink and refrigerator, hardly enough to justify mopping the floor. Opening the top drawer to the right of the sink, she took from it a large rag, folded it once, dampened it under the faucet, then laid it on one of those spots. Placing her right shoe on that, she moved it back and forth several times, then went on to do the same with others.

Suddenly, in the midst of her floor-cleaning, she was remembering Elmo. Although they had loved one another dearly and did so much together, they had different tastes in many things, including books. El preferring science fiction for what he described his escape from reality, and she, mysteries. He had loved to tease her about her habit of cutting paper towels into smaller squares to avoid waste, and she, in turn, had fondly mocked his inability ever to throw away even the most mended article of clothing. Your stitches make this old shirt more precious to me, he would tell her.

Gracie sighed, then shook her head in an effort to clear it. How do I let myself get into this state, this remembering? Over five years gone, and there are times like today when it seems as though he's just got to be coming home, walking in through that door.

There was a knock on the front door! From where she stood she could see through the sheer curtains that a man was standing there. For a split second she was filled with joy, for this man looked to be was about as tall and well-built as her husband. But that moment of unrealistic, instantaneous happiness was replaced by a surge of awareness. El was not out on their—*her*—porch. He was not waiting for her to come greet him at the door.

Instead, awaiting her was a confrontation she dreaded, with Miles Stevens.

Her right hand felt cramped and, glancing down, she saw her fingers tightly gripping the back of the chair in which El used to sit. She was further brought back to reality by a second knocking, this time louder and lasting longer.

All right, she told herself, you are going to settle down and face him. She marched over to open her door and greeted him with a polite, "Hello, Miles."

He moved a step nearer, and she knew he was expecting to come into her house as he angrily informed her, "We were apparently cut off. . . ."

She pushed her shoulders back and her chin forward. She was ready for battle. He must have registered her stiffening, because his tone changed as he said, "Look, we need to talk about this."

She said nothing, just stood there looking at him through the screen door.

"Okay, I apologize for my—brusqueness, but you have to admit I have reason to resent your attitude."

She answered firmly, but still courteously, "As I have every reason to resent yours."

His eyebrows rose slightly. His mouth tightened. Then his face, without warning, relaxed into a large but definitely suspect grin. A grin that bordered on a smirk.

She suspected this might be just how he'd looked when he'd convinced Gracie's friend Marjorie Printz to believe he was doing her a wonderful favor when he paid her "twice the value" for her father's gold coins.

"Really, Gracie, this misunderstanding can be cleared up in no time at all if we just sit down and talk about it."

She knew she needed to allow herself to listen to what he had to say. Unlocking the screen door, she stepped outside onto the porch and pushed the door closed. "Very well." She took a wicker armchair and indicated the one to her right for him to sit in.

He began with a statement that surprised her. "I understand you're quite fond of Mark."

"I've known him for a long time," she replied, "and have always been impressed by his character."

"But you do know that he's determined to save money to go to college. That's quite a sum."

"Yes, he's worked hard at mowing lawns and doing other jobs that don't interfere with his schoolwork. I find it commendable."

"I, too, appreciate that." He leaned forward a bit. "Mark has taken care of my yard both last year and this. He's always made a good job of it and that's why I trusted him. In fact, I even recommended him to many of my neighbors. That's why I find it so distressing that he took something very valuable that doesn't belong to him."

He was sounding quite reasonable. Gracie knew she had to make her argument carefully. "I understand you had a number of coins there on the table."

He nodded. "There were five."

"Were they all gold coins?"

He nodded. "Yes."

"Why did you have them there? Why did you bring them home, leaving behind the others at the bank?"

"What others?"

He stared at her.

"Are you saying those were the only gold coins you own?" she asked.

He gave a little laugh. "Really, Gracie, I understand your loyalty to a young man you like, but I do think just how many gold coins I possess is my own business."

She spoke deliberately, to control her rising anger. "I'm sure you must recall that it was you who brought up the subject in the first place. It was you who called me on the telephone and came here to my house to talk about the missing money. Since that's the case, I think my question's perfectly justified. How many gold coins do you own—and where are they?"

She felt that the retired banker now was on the defensive, although he answered smoothly, "I came to discuss one particular coin, and that's what I intend to do."

"I assume you have them insured, right? You have an inventory list for your records?"

"May I remind you again that that is no concern of yours?"

"And may I remind you that you're accusing Mark of stealing something though you won't offer proper proof that you ever owned it in the first place?"

"My entire career was in banking, Gracie Parks, as I think you well know. I have never before been accused of dishonesty."

Gracie spoke evenly. "And all my life has been spent with people, and I've learned a great deal about what makes them tick. Everyone has different motivations, and does things for many different reasons. So, Miles, what is your motivation for being here right now?"

He looked pained. "Folks here call you a helpful, loving person, the kind who always sees the best in people. So I came to you with the hope, the expectation that you'd be able to see reason. That you would want to help persuade that poor boy to stop his charade. This fable of his innocence is only that: a pretty story.

"You can't really want this to go to court, can you? Don't you realize that he'll be marked for life by the stigma of his thievery?" He pounded the arm of the white wicker chair with his fist, and his voice raised. "Is *this* how you prove your friendship?"

She got to her feet, and so did he.

"Come now, Gracie! You know you can't be certain that I'm not correct."

His voice and expression were now patronizing. She resented that, as well as everything that had preceded it. She even disliked the sound of her own name, hearing him speak it. The man was really too much.

"I think we'll have to agree to disagree," she told him. "And I think there's nothing more to discuss."

He took a step nearer, reaching out for her arm. "You're being unreasonable."

Suddenly they both heard the slam of a car door. Then came the sound of Herb's deep voice. The Willow Bend police chief strode up Gracie's front steps. "Good afternoon, my friends. Is there any trouble here?"

Miles Stevens shook his head. "No, no trouble at all, Herb. I just dropped by to talk with Gracie for a bit. We had a few things to discuss."

Gracie bit her lip.

Miles looked from one to the other, started to say something, then shrugged his shoulders, turned, and walked off the porch.

Neither Herb nor Gracie said a word until Miles's expensive black sedan had purred its way down the street. "Thanks, Herb," she told him. "Can I give you a cup of coffee?"

"Is it ready now?" he asked.

"It won't take long."

He glanced at his watch. "I'm expecting someone at my office in about fifteen minutes."

She opened the door as she reassured him, "I promise not to keep you more than ten, okay?"

"Sure."

"And in place of coffee, I do have iced tea," she offered, heading for the refrigerator.

He sat down at the table. "Well?" he said.

Gracie poured the tea and brought the glasses with her, talking all the while.

"I hung up on him this morning, which is one of the few times in my life that I've done that." She shrugged. "I guess I shouldn't have been surprised when he showed up here a little later."

"He's used to having his own way."

"But, Herb, what he wants is for me to talk Mark into giving up that coin, to hand it over to him."

"And you didn't agree to do that."

"No. It wouldn't be right."

"So what's the situation now?"

"The same as before, I guess. Except that he now knows for sure he can expect no help from me." She drew a long, slow breath. "Of course if it should end up that Mark did steal it, I'll owe Mr. Miles Stevens a great big apology."

"But I take it that, meanwhile, you're not losing sleep over that possibility."

She smiled. "For the time being, I'm resting well. But what might buy me a few extra hours of easy slumber is your telling me anything more you've learned about Clark Harrington."

"No luck there, Gracie," he said ruefully. "Sorry."

"Well, I know it's not for want of trying."

He nodded. "I've been making calls. But just don't have anything more that seems useful."

Gooseberry had come from the other room, and circled Herb's legs, rubbing against him. The policeman stooped to pet him, then walked outside with Gracie.

"What about Ohio, Herb? Or Illinois? You said he had connections there. . . ."

"I'm still waiting to hear. But I think if they had anything to tell me, I'd have heard by now."

She watched him drive off. Just as she was about to wave at a neighbor, she heard Uncle Miltie's voice. "Gracie, who was the visitor?" he called.

She started toward him, smiling. "I just walked Herb to his car, and was thinking how blessed our town is to have someone like him looking out for our welfare."

"*Humph!* I never heard a sound, I'm sorry to say. I'd have liked to see him, too. Did he have anything to say about our coin controversy?"

"Not much—and he was only here a few minutes."

"What did he stop for? He's so busy, he doesn't seem to have much time for social calls."

She now filled him in about her earlier guest. His eyes widened.

"The thing is, I never knew Miles all that well before. Oh, I'd seen and spoken to him at all sorts of meetings and activities, but I'd never had a real conversation with him. And, you know, I just always had this sense he was sneaky. I can't explain it."

"Woman's intuition." He went over to the cookie jar, and took a molasses crisp she'd baked two days before. Taking a bite, he informed her, "You always manage to put the *cook* into cookie, Gracie, my girl."

"That's one of the many reasons I enjoy having you here. You don't take me and what I do for granted."

"Well, you have to admit that having a proper attitude keeps me well supplied with delicious treats."

She raised a fist. "Hey! I always thought your compliments were totally sincere."

"Uh oh!"

"Well, don't worry." She was heading out of the kitchen as she spoke. "I love baking, as you know, so you're going to be stuck with having home-baked goodies."

"*Whew!*" Uncle Miltie now reached into the cookie jar and grabbed a handful.

Seven

G UESS WHAT, GRACIE—the weatherman goofed for a change."

She hadn't really been paying attention since she had been busy going over, once again, the Sunday school lesson she'd be teaching in another two hours. "Which way did he err this time?"

"Much colder than predicted. Down to twenty-seven degrees, it says here." Uncle Miltie was checking the outdoor thermometer. When she didn't respond to that, he continued, "Poor old Fannie Mae has a white frosted roof and hood this morning."

"Well," she replied, still trying to keep her mind on the lesson, "then we'll need a few more minutes, won't we, in order to scrape windows?"

"They appear clear along this side—but the front and back ones usually take more time."

"*Um-hmmm.*"

"And we mustn't forget the mums," he reminded her.

"*Um-hmmm.*"

"I like that big bouquet of mixed asters you fixed last night."

"*Um-hmmm.*"

There was a brief pause before, "I especially like those black and green ones."

"*Um-hmmm.*"

"Aha!" he cried. "I didn't think you were listening."

She looked up, questioning. "What?"

He snorted. "I've been talking away here and you kept saying, '*um-hmmm*,' as though you were actually listening. So I decided to trap you with some black asters!"

"Black asters?" Gracie laughed. "I'm no botanist but I'm pretty sure we don't have any like that, unless you somehow sneaked them in."

"You're safe on that count," he reassured her. "I just said that to see if you were paying any attention at all to your poor old uncle."

"I'm sorry." And she was. "But I do have to go over this lesson again."

"What's it about?"

He seemed to be missing the message that she still needed time for study. "I've read Acts more often than any other book in the Bible—except for the Gospels, of course—but the commentary for this lesson points out some interesting aspects about money, or the love of money, that is. It reminds us how mistaken we can be about what we think it can buy or give us."

"That is pretty appropriate right now," he commented.

"And it's nothing new! Here we have Ananias and Sapphira, for example"—she indicated Chapter 5 in her open Bible—"who were probably a well-intentioned couple who wanted to do good for the early church, and *did*.

"They sold property they owned, which may even have been passed down from generation to generation. They doubtless had the right to sell it if they wished, as it was also their right to do whatever they chose with the money received from it.

"They must have given far more than a tithe—or just a tenth—and those present when they brought it to the apostles must have been impressed and grateful. But the problem was their motivation. Their attempt to use the money in order to gain the esteem of others was wrong."

"Yeah, I remember when I first read that, I thought it seemed almost unjust of God to punish them when they were giving so much."

"Well, that's what's been troubling me—which angle to emphasize most strongly to the class. And then, once I'd decided it had to be motivation, that led me, again, into wondering about what's really going on in the minds of these three fellows—all so different—who are claiming the disputed coin."

Uncle Miltie lifted an eyebrow. "Well, Mark would undoubtedly say he hopes to be able to use the proceeds from the coin to help fund his college education."

"So the main question in his case is whether that desire of his could be strong enough that he'd actually steal in order to reach that goal."

Uncle Miltie nodded. "I'd guess Miles's motivation is simply the idea of possession, owning something valuable enough to make him feel privileged above others. People who collect such things are covetous . . . and tenacious."

"I got to thinking that I can relate to that," Gracie said unexpectedly. "It's sort of like that picture I have above the couch in the living room. It's an oil painting that Elmo inherited, and people have often admired it, even offered to buy it were I to tire of it. But it's mine and I'm afraid that I'm proud to have it there where others can admire it and even hope to possess it."

Uncle Miltie didn't reply, only smiled.

"The only thing is, I at least am displaying this possession in public, not hoarding it secretly like Miles Stevens."

He patted her hand. "But neither of us can make even an uneducated guess as to our third contender's motivation."

Estelle Livett was waiting at the door of the Family Activity Center, her voice husky. "Make Barb listen, Gracie. I've told her that, with the antihistamine and the orange juice I've taken this morning, it's okay for me to sing those two brief solo parts in our anthem."

"I'm sure she doesn't want you straining your voice," Gracie soothed. "Remember last year about this time? Your allergies were acting up so badly you lost your voice entirely after singing that Sunday. . . ."

"I had a cold then, not just allergies."

"Whatever it was, you ended up unable to sing at all until after Thanksgiving, when we were well into our Advent and Christmas anthems." She put her hand on her friend's amply rounded shoulder. "Barb just doesn't want to risk not having your lovely soprano voice to count on this fall."

"I'll bet she's already asked Amy to sing my part!"

Gracie laughed. "As I recall, you had the chance to sing her part last summer for a similar reason. That's one of the good things about our choir. We do have backups."

Unfortunately, this innocent comment led to Estelle's stopping to extoll the marvels of the *very* large and wonderful choir back east in which she had sung long ago.

One of the things Gracie most appreciated about her vantage point from the choir loft was getting to see who was in church. This was especially true when it came to latecomers. Among them today was Rocky, who arrived while everyone was singing the second verse of the first hymn. Looking in her direction, he gave an unobtrusive thumbs-up as he took an aisle seat near the back.

He was an "occasional" attendee, at best, so it crossed her mind to wonder exactly why he had chosen this service. It didn't matter, though, she was simply grateful he had chosen to be here today.

She always enjoyed Pastor Paul's children's sermons, with all the kids coming forward to sit in the front seats. Today's topic was "Making Choices." After Paul had greeted them, he picked up a baseball bat from among some items placed at the end of the pew, then asked, "What is this?" Almost all of them answered correctly, as they also did when he held up a shuttlecock.

"Let's play badminton, Eric," he said to an intently listening six-year-old. Tossing the shuttlecock upward, he took a mighty swing with the bat, slashing at the lightweight feathered cone. One part shattered, drifting down to the floor, while the heavier, plastic covered nose-portion flew quite a distance.

Several children looked upset. Others giggled. Paul leaned down and picked up a part of the broken object and examined it. "*Hmmm*, something seems wrong here."

Eric had chased after the other half in the aisle. Now, bringing it to the pastor, he said, "You're supposed to use a *racket* for badminton."

"You know, you're exactly right." Paul reached for one of those, but also lifted a basketball, tossed it into the air, and used the racket to propel it gently into the lap of a nearby girl.

Eric reached for the basketball and handed it back to him, patiently explaining, "You don't use a racket with a basketball. You use your *hands*."

"You're right again, Eric." He smiled down at the youngsters. "And I appreciate your patiently explaining my errors—not yelling at me or anything, just giving me the right advice as to how to improve."

And then, taking a single step backward in order to include the whole congregation in what he was saying to the children, he elaborated on his theme—which was the need to choose the right actions and words when dealing with others.

". . . Because if we don't, we can hurt the feelings of people we care about, or even people we don't, and make them sad. Or," he picked up more pieces of the broken shuttlecock, "what's even more harmful is that we can even break their spirit—making them afraid to trust *anyone* again.

"And we wouldn't want that to happen to anyone, would we?" he asked. His congregants murmured their understanding, although a few of the littler ones seemed more interested in the broken shuttlecock, which he then set carefully down.

One of the smallest girls saw her opportunity. As Paul remounted the pulpit, she followed him, tugging at the sleeve of his robe. "Here, Pastor Paul. Here's your shuttlecock. I'm sorry it's all broken."

He reached down to receive her gift. "Thank you, Angela, for bringing this to me, and for your concern. I truly appreciate it."

From where Gracie was sitting, she was almost sure there was moisture in Paul's eyes as his gaze for a moment remained on the file of youngsters now proceeding out of the sanctuary.

But then he cleared his throat and quoted, "And a little child shall lead them. . . ."

Paul should have children of his own—a wife and family. Gracie had thought that many times, and now again, she knew it was so. *He's such a loving person, and the little ones respond to that, as do so many of us—of all ages. Couldn't You arrange for him to find just the right life partner, Lord? Everyone who worships You here at Eternal Hope Community Church would sing* Your *praises even more loudly than usual!*

※

It was after the benediction that Uncle Miltie came up to her. "Hey, Gracie, how about our going over to the deli right away—maybe beat the crowd?"

"Sounds good to me. Rocky's here and you know he'll want to join us."

"Here he comes."

As they arrived at Abe Wasserman's well-loved local institution, Uncle Miltie said, as he always did, "*Hmmm,* smell that! Nothing finer than a diner!"

Rocky corrected him. "You ungrateful wretch, you've got Gracie's cooking to inhale every day!"

Gracie laughed. "Not all these wonderful aromas on any one day."

He started to respond, but Abe was welcoming them. Gracie gave him a hug. Abe beamed. Gracie was a special favorite of his. Abe now motioned to an empty table, but Gracie shook her head. Abe had an odd expression on his face.

"The way I figure," Uncle Miltie was saying, "is that she's the performer and I'm the audience. All I have to do is make sure she never gets tired of encores!"

As Gracie started to sit down at their regular table, Rocky suggested, "How about the booth in the corner? It's quieter, and you know sometimes it's nicer to eat our scrambled eggs with salami and blintzes with sour cream and applesauce without my having to share you with everybody who needs your advice or wants to discuss a recipe. . . ."

"Well, Gracie is popular," Abe agreed. "But so is Willow Bend's esteemed newspaper proprietor!"

He beckoned to Amy, who'd also just arrived, to bring over tea and coffee and take their orders. Before heading back to the kitchen, however, he said in a low voice, "I couldn't tell you while we were standing back there, or while Amy was nearby, but I'd been trying to steer you in the vicinity of that young guy sitting over there."

Gracie now examined from a distance the profile of a slender, dark-haired man who seemed to be about thirty years old. "I don't think I know him, Abe. Should I?"

"Probably not. Yet."

"Yet?"

"His name's Clark Harrington."

"Oh. I see now."

Rocky exclaimed, "Our third contender for the double eagle!"

After Abe left them, Rocky mused, "I wonder how well Abe's gotten to know him. He didn't say if Harrington's been coming in regularly." He stood up.

"Come to think of it, I should probably go wash my hands before eating." Rocky grinned as he sauntered off.

Gracie smiled as she watched him move purposefully between tables and stop near the stranger. She had no way of knowing what was said, but Clark Harrington seemed not to resent the intrusion on his meal.

Rocky then stopped again for a few moments to speak with the stranger on his way back to the table where Gracie and Uncle Miltie were ignoring their food as they eagerly awaited his report.

"Seems like a friendly chap," he commented. "He says he's updating the computer system and computer labs at the high school, and will probably stay at Cordelia's for another week or so."

"Good work, Rocky." Gracie was thoughtfully considering what she'd just heard. "Does he know you're the editor of your paper?"

"Yep, he does. That's how I explained my curiosity."

"So what else did you learn?" her uncle asked impatiently.

"Well, he likes the town and is comfortable enough at Cordelia's and thinks we have a good school." He paused to look each of them in the eye. "And no, neither of us mentioned a gold coin."

"Does he seem, ah . . . sincere or open or—oh, you know what I mean."

He shrugged. "I'm not clairvoyant enough to gain that kind of insight in only a few minutes. I wish I were."

"Well, I thought maybe with your newsman's instincts, you might have made an educated guess."

He took a bite of scrambled egg before responding, "All I can say about Clark Harrington right now is that he appears to be friendly and straightforward."

Uncle Miltie was getting bored. No new facts—and he was still hungry. "You two ordering anything else?"

"Is that shorthand for 'Let's have some cheesecake?' "

"Your newspaperman's nose must be working now! I guess you saw the blackberry one on the counter as we came in!"

"And the cherry, too," the editor answered modestly.

Gracie laughed. "I'm too full," she told them.

"Not us!" her menfolk responded. "Amy!"

The teenager brought her pad and pencil to their table. "That's what I like—patrons who are easy to keep happy."

Amy giggled. Then a cloud crossed her face.

Gracie sensed something wrong. "You've had a bad experience recently?"

"Well, sort of." Amy glanced around.

"Tell me about it."

Amy shook her head. "I must get on the ball. I'll have your cheesecake for you in just a moment."

Gracie began to watch the girl as she went about her work. Was she avoiding Clark Harrington? It was hard to tell.

Still, Gracie thought she could see her intentionally walk around another table so she'd be approaching his from the far side when offering a beverage refill.

What did it mean? When Gracie got the chance, she quietly asked, "Has Clark done something to offend you, dear?"

Amy looked startled. "I'd—hoped it didn't show, and that Abe doesn't realize it."

Rocky now leaned forward. "What's he done? Harrington, I mean."

"Nothing, really. But he knows I'm Mark's friend and about our picking up trash that Saturday. So he's been making small talk to me about it when he comes in."

Amy hesitated. "That's probably why it bothers me, plus he's been hinting that he'd like to take me out."

Gracie was purposely calm. She didn't want to upset her young friend in any way. "You're a very attractive young woman. He should, though, have enough common sense to know how inappropriate that would be. He's too old, he's a stranger, and you would have given him no encouragement, I'm sure."

Amy looked at Gracie with gratitude. "I'm just trying to do my job. So I've tried to stay polite."

Gracie reassured her, "Being courteous isn't any kind of invitation."

"I'd like to think that was right," Amy said anxiously. "But I'm kind of worried that he might have followed me home last night."

"What did you do?" Rocky asked, looking grim.

"I deliberately drove back out to Main Street, and stopped right under the light there at the Willow Mart. I went inside just long enough to buy a magazine, staying up front so I could watch my car."

"And the other car?"

"I'm not very good at recognizing them. I can't really tell the difference." She looked apologetic now. "But some car I didn't know followed me."

Gracie prompted, "Followed you to your house?"

"Thank goodness I have one of those electronic garage-openers, so I drove right in, and closed it behind me."

"And you didn't tell your folks?" Uncle Miltie demanded.

"The thing is, I'm just not positive about it. If it turns out to have been a coincidence that a car stayed behind mine, I don't want to get anyone in trouble."

"You really must tell your folks, dear."

"I don't want to bother them with worries that might be my imagination." She looked uncomfortable. "I shouldn't have mentioned this to you."

Gracie disagreed. "Yes, dear, you should. We're your friends, you know. And your parents are your friends, too."

Amy sighed. "I must get back to work."

Rocky stopped her. "First of all, you must tell Herb. Do it right away."

She shook her head. "I can't, not now."

"Then I'm going to, my dear. You're far too precious to us to let anything happen."

"Please don't!" She looked panicked. "I knew I should never have burdened you with this, but. . . ."

Gracie now asked, "What time are you finished?"

"Not until five-thirty."

"And you walked over from church?"

"Yes, but. . . ."

"I'll be here at 5:35," she promised. "Don't leave until I get here, okay?"

Seeing Amy's face, Gracie fished in her purse for the small pack of tissues she always kept there, and handed it to the anxious girl.

Amy accepted it gratefully.

Eight

FROM ABE'S DELI, Gracie, Uncle Miltie and Rocky headed directly to the police station. But Herb Bower wasn't there. Gracie then tried to contact him on his cell phone but, after leaving a message, had to wait an hour before he responded to her S.O.S.

"What's up, Gracie?"

"Maybe nothing, Herb, but still I wanted to run it by you."

"Well, you've got my full attention now."

She briefly told of her concerns. At the end, he asked, "Did you chat at all with Clark Harrington?"

"No. But I trust Amy when she says there's something about him that makes her uncomfortable."

"*Hmmm.*"

"Have you found out anything more about him yet?"

"No."

"Well, that may be good news."

"Yes," he agreed. "But it still won't hurt for both of us to keep an eye on him."

"My feelings exactly!"

Gracie now felt restless, so she invited Gooseberry for a walk.

He looked up at her from the carpet, stretched, then meandered to the kitchen, for all the world as though he was deigning to do her a favor. She laughed. "You can't fool me! You want to go out every bit as much as I do!"

She'd already let him out when she remembered to scribble a

note, "Back soon—we've gone for a walk," which she laid on the kitchen table. Looking at the door, she crossed the porch and went down the steps. Gooseberry had been rather impatiently pacing but now, after a brief, wide-eyed stare which his mistress interpreted as "It's about time you got here!" he stalked down the sidewalk, head and tail held high.

"Okay, kiddo," she told him, "you map our route today. If you stay within reasonable bounds, you can determine where we go and when we return."

He continued walking ahead of her, not even looking around to make sure she was following. He did, however, wait each time she briefly stopped to speak to people enjoying the lovely afternoon.

"Did you know from the beginning that we were headed for Ferris Road?" she asked as they got there. "Are you feeling your sleuthing bones acting up? Or do I mean whiskers?"

Gracie wished she had thought to bring a camera, since the leaves were glorious in all their autumn color. She'd walked quite a ways when she saw someone step out onto the road from a side lane. The moment he saw her, he ducked back and a second later she heard a car door closing.

Suddenly, he emerged out onto the road again. It was only then that she realized who it was. "Mark!" she called, "Hi!"

He waved, also. "Hi, Mrs. Parks!"

"Have you found anything with that metal detector?"

For a split second he looked startled. "Metal detector?"

"The one your mother told me you'd been using out here, the one you must have just put in the car." Gracie didn't wish to seem like she was checking up on him. At the same time, she wanted to hear his version of his actions.

She at first thought he was going to deny it, but then he said, "You know I found that double eagle. You were with me."

"But what about after that?"

He looked sulky. "Well, I *did* find one more," he told her reluctantly.

"One more what?"

He still hesitated. "An eagle, a ten-dollar coin. Two days ago."

"My goodness! Your hunch was correct then!"

"That's right," Mark suddenly looked pleased. "I thought there might be others and there were. At least this one. I tried to get a book giving current values, and found a place on the Internet where they offer coins for sale. Since my eagle's one of a fairly small minting, and not too many are known to have survived, it's worth a lot, too."

"Oh, my!" Gracie didn't know what to say.

"What's Miles Stevens going to say about this, huh?"

"Well, they almost have to be from somebody's private collection, if not his, don't they?" Gracie mused. "But from whose? And how did anything this valuable come to be here, of all places?"

"I keep wondering, too. Isn't it interesting that nobody's ever mentioned this second one? But," he was frowning, "nobody ever mentioned the double eagle, either, not until after I found it."

She looked around at all the trampled-down growth. "Where did you find your eagle, Mark?"

"Right over there," he said, pointing to some thick undergrowth. He stopped her from moving nearer. "Be careful, Gracie! That's poison ivy!"

"Oh!" She shivered. "It sure is!"

"Is that why you bought your metal detector?"

"Well, yes. I'm allergic to poison ivy, so I couldn't go pawing around through all these leaves. I figured that if I wore boots, like today," he said, sticking one foot out toward her, "and poked around with the detector, if it told me something was there, then I could put on the long, heavy plastic gloves and find what was making it act that way."

"So that's how you found the new coin!"

"*Um-hmmm.* And that's of course why I'm here again this afternoon, hoping I might find yet another!"

Gooseberry had been unusually patient with Gracie's staying in one place for so long. Now, however, he was circling her ankles and edging toward the road. He stopped there, looking back to check whether or not she was obeying his instructions.

As she and Gooseberry started back the way they'd come, she turned around to call, "You do have that in a safe place, don't you, Mark?"

"I—hope so."

She took a couple steps back toward him. "Might it be a good idea to put it with the other one?"

"Probably—but I didn't want to bother him."

"He was the one to make the offer before," she reminded him.

"Yeah, but . . ."

"So how about my asking him about it?"

"Well, I suppose you could. You're good friends, aren't you?"

"Yes, we are. And his wife sings with me in the choir." She was nearly back to him when she asked, "You don't happen to have it with you now, do you?"

"Well," with what appeared to be a sheepish grin, he said, "it just so happens that I do."

She resisted the impulse to scold him, telling him how unwise that was. Instead she merely said, "How about driving us back to town? If Herb's at the station, we could get it taken care of right away."

He agreed. Then, at the edge of town, he asked, "You didn't get a call from Mom today, did you?" He looked worried.

She shook her head. "No. Do you know what she wanted to talk about?"

"Well, she may have to give up her Sunday school class."

She turned to stare at him. "She does such a good job with those children. It would be a shame."

He shifted a bit on the seat. "She thinks maybe she'd better, since she got that letter."

"What letter?"

"Oh." There was a pause before he went on. "I maybe—should let her tell you."

"All right." Gracie knew she needed to be patient.

He exhaled completely, and pushed his fingers through his thick, dark brown hair. "It was on the screen door this morning, folded over once and fastened there with tape."

It was all she could do to keep from asking questions, but she waited, hoping he'd go on, which he finally did. "It was written in funny letters on regular white computer paper, and it wasn't very pleasant. What it said was that she's not fit to be a teacher of any sort and if she doesn't voluntarily give it up, then there's going to be trouble. I right away thought it meant her work with Lynn, but Mom feels it's about the church and her Sunday school class."

"There was nothing else?"

"Well, nothing that's going to be of any help."

"Would you be willing to tell me what it is?"

He looked even more uncomfortable than before. "Mom says it's a Bible verse from somewhere in Matthew, though I don't remember where. It goes something like, 'Outwardly you appear righteous to people, but inwardly you're full of lawlessness.'"

Gracie looked fiercely indignant. One question remained. "Was the note handwritten? You said 'funny letters.'"

He was keeping his eyes on the fairly empty street. "It was a computer-generated font."

They were approaching the station, so she suggested, "Perhaps you should mention this to Herb."

He was giving his full attention to turning into the parking lot. "Isn't Mom the one to do that—if she wants to?"

She knew he was more worried than he was showing. But he was also being sensitive to his mother's feelings.

"You're right, of course. I'd probably be upset if Arlen or anyone else went over my head like that." She sighed. "I do hope, though, that you can get her to talk with Herb or with Paul. Or even me."

They walked together up the slanted ramp to the door and went inside, Gooseberry again marching, head and tail high, through the short hallway. Gracie turned toward Herb as he came out to greet them, "He's come to turn himself in," Gracie announced.

The police chief bent to stroke the large orange cat between his ears and along his back. "Mouse murder, I suppose," Herb replied. "You can be sure I'll get him the best defense attorney possible!"

Gracie laughed as she led the way inside his office and slid the chair beside his desk. "We're here to ask a favor."

He smiled at Mark. "Which is . . . ?"

"You already know about Mark's buying the metal detector."

Herb glanced toward him and nodded, and she went on, "Well, his search was rewarded. He's now found another gold coin, an eagle.

He reached across to shake hands. "Congratulations!"

"It was a long shot," Mark admitted.

Herb's glance shifted to hers for a moment, then back to Mark, who was explaining his reasoning while taking the coin from his pocket and handing it across the desk. "Gracie says maybe this should stay with the first one, in your safe—if that's okay with you."

"Good idea. But whether or not it's kept here, I'd suggest your telling nobody else at this point—other than your mother, that is."

"I found it yesterday, and Mom and Gracie—and now you—are the only ones who know about it." He then asked anxiously, "You haven't had a report of anyone's missing it, have you?"

Herb shook his head, and Mark sank back into the chair, obviously relieved. "Then maybe there won't be so much conspiring this time, everyone trying to claim it."

Gracie sighed. "I sincerely hope not!"

Once again she and Mark signed papers stating that the coin was being placed under the protection of the chief of police. As Herb closed the safe's heavy door and turned the knob, he asked, "You're planning to continue searching for more?"

"Whenever I have the free time."

The two adults shook hands with Mark as he left the office. Then Gracie made her way home.

Gracie couldn't get the threatening letter Sally had received out of her mind throughout the evening. *What would I do if I received an anonymous message like that? Lord, I'm glad You have blessed me with friends and loved ones who have never tried to hide behind an unidentified threat. I believe it's just someone blustering, but there's no way to be sure. Help me to help Sally face this crisis. She surely has enough on her hands with Mark's situation.*

Everything she knew about Sally was positive. She'd been a loving, faithful wife and mother. It was her husband who'd taken himself out of the marriage, with hardly a look back at his wife, son or two daughters.

Thank goodness Sally had been able to keep the house! The child support payments she received were hardly enough to meet expenses, so she did have to work. She'd been in the beginning of her sophomore year in college when she got married, and when Mark, her first child, was born she'd dropped out. Therefore, despite her love of teaching, she didn't have her certification and could serve only as an aid.

During her first two years working in the school system she had served as the companion of a boy with severe physical and emotional problems. She'd loved and cared for Larry, and had been dismayed when his family decided to place him in an institution.

But then came Lynn. Sally had undergone special training to prepare for working with a hearing- and speech-impaired child, and was now with her for the fourth year. Everyone was delighted with the girl's progress and development.

What possible justification could there be for threatening to put a stop to *that?*

On the other hand, why would anyone want her to quit teaching her Sunday school class, if that's what the message meant?

Gracie recalled the short-lived furor when one of the older women in the church—one who'd never been married nor volunteered to teach a class in her life—decided that it wasn't "fitting for someone divorced to be teaching those innocent young children in Sunday school!"

Hattie Bomboy had threatened even to quit Eternal Hope Community Church if Sally wasn't removed from teaching. But, then again, she'd threatened that for years while trying to get her own way about a variety of issues.

She still hasn't left us. Unfortunately! Gracie thought wryly.

Might this be Hattie resuming her old crusade? If so, why? Could it be because of rumors concerning the ownership of Mark's coin? Was there any chance that she was a friend or relative of Miles?

Gracie decided she'd be much more concerned about that possibility if she could even remotely imagine that ornery octogenarian using a computer!

※

She didn't get up right away when awaking early the following morning. Instead, Gracie kept going over—as she often liked to do—small details of the celebration being hosted by Anna and Joe Searfoss. It was coming up so soon. But it looked to be a pretty straightforward catering job and it had the added appeal of being for the Searfosses, whom she adored.

She'd ordered the chicken when picking up those dozens of eggs, which she'd hardboiled yesterday. Uncle Miltie always enjoyed helping remove the shells, cracking each egg by lightly banging it against the sink, then rolling it between his palms. He frequently demanded Gracie's attention when he was able to get the entire shell off in one piece. "Who's the eggspert now?" he would crow.

The beets had come from their own garden, for her uncle liked growing the green leaves of spinach and the red-veined leaves of beets among her many-hued flowers. And now the beets had been cooked, skinned, cut up and packed into large jars, along with the eggs, vinegar, seasonings and the dark red juice in which the beets had been cooked.

Other than this, however, nothing had actually been completed for the big day. Reaching for the tablet and pen she always kept in the drawer of her bedside table, she began jotting list after list of what was to be done, and by whom. To most people, this might seem a huge undertaking, but Gracie knew from experience that the individual or team heading each list could be relied upon.

Gracie picked up the annual *Daily Guideposts* devotional book, read the selection for the day, and spent time praying for her family, friends, church, town and nation. She closed with special prayers for Mark and for Sally, for Lynn and her family, for Marjorie Printz and the Searfosses, and for Clark Harrington and Miles Stevens, too. No one was beyond the reach of prayer.

And it was then that Gooseberry strolled into her room, meowing the message that it was time for his mistress to be up and around, facing the day ahead.

Nine

A RE ... YOU ... (SOMETHING) ... to ... the (something) center ... to-day." The studious frown left Uncle Miltie's face as he crowed, "I've got it, Gracie. You just asked, 'Are you going to the senior center today?'"

"That's great! You're coming along well with your lipreading."

"... you're ... coming along well ... with your lipreading."

"Fantastic!"

"I didn't get that word, 'cause your mouth changes shape when you're laughing. Try something else."

"Okay, but just this one more time. Then you can take those plugs out of your ears!"

Grinning, he reached up and removed them, having obviously understood what she'd said, though not repeating it. "You know, Gracie, I've often been concerned about not always hearing as well as I should. But now I'm beginning to think I must have been doing some lipreading all along, and just didn't realize it."

"I wouldn't be surprised. It reminds me of Sally's saying how quickly Lynn took to it."

"I've got a whale of a lot more practicing to do before I'm anywhere near as proficient as she is."

"Of course. Just remember, though, you haven't been doing it very long." She transferred the breakfast dishes to the dishwasher and brought back with her both her cell phone and the paper on which she'd been working before getting out of bed. "And now I must make some calls for Sunday."

"Are you too busy to talk?" she asked Marge, having reached her at her shop. "I tried you at home first."

"I came in early."

"So what are you doing? Cleaning up?"

"Who, me?" She laughed, as did Gracie, who suspected the truth. "I have a new book from the library, and sitting here in the early morning is a surprisingly good way to get a bit of peace and quiet. No one's looking for me to be at work yet."

"Except me." Gracie smiled to herself. "Is it a romance you took out?"

"What else?"

Gracie responded with, "I like them, too. I even don't mind if there's a romance in one of my mysteries."

"And I'm generous enough to admit that a mystery's acceptable in one of my romances, too."

They often passed on books they knew the other would like. Now they had a few new titles to recommend. But, suddenly, Marge changed the subject.

"Just one more thing—did you hear that Sally's giving up her Sunday school class? That might mean she'll have the time to come back to the choir, especially now that her daughters are older."

"Who told you that?" *Has Sally really given in to the demand, Lord? I was hoping she'd hold firm, knowing how You were holding her in Your love.*

"I heard it from Comfort. Rick found out last night when doing his ambulance duty."

"Was there an accident?" Gracie didn't remember the Volunteer Fire Company's sirens blowing. So she knew there hadn't been a fire.

"Not this time. Miles Stevens was having pain in his chest, and dialed 911. Rick was on call, but apparently didn't have to do much. They took Miles to the ER, though."

"Do you have any idea how Miles is now?"

"She said Rick checked this morning, before leaving for work. The hospital told him that tests didn't seem to indicate that he'd had a heart attack. He'll be back home later today."

Gracie put the phone down slowly, wondering if it had been Miles who, despite his own distress, had passed on the news of Sally's giving up her Sunday school class. On the other hand, it might have been someone else with the ambulance crew or there in the emergency room who'd mentioned it to Rick. The truth was, people in small towns were full of information and usually all too willing to share it.

She kept going over and over this small puzzle without feeling certain she'd arrived at any solution.

She found that she was grateful when Uncle Miltie came back to the kitchen to tell her he was ready to be off for his scheduled practice with Lynn.

Gracie stopped at church on her way home from taking him. In her care were boxes of foodstuffs to be used at the Searfoss dinner. Carrying in the first load, she found the church secretary in the kitchen fixing herself a cup of tea. "Hi, Pat. How are things going?"

"Fine, thanks. What about you?"

"Great. I had to stop at the store for some stuff, so figured I might as well bring the potatoes in now, rather than unloading them twice, at home and here."

"Good idea. Is there more to be brought in?"

"Well, yes—but I can handle it."

"I'm sure you can, Gracie, but I'm going out with you anyway, and help carry."

As they returned with their arms filled, Gracie asked as casually as possible, "I didn't notice Paul's bike. Is he in his office?"

"He walked over this morning."

"Oh, Pat, didn't you once work with Miles Stevens? I just heard he was taken to the hospital by ambulance last night."

"Oh, dear! What's wrong?"

"Possible heart attack. But probably not. Do you know him well?"

"Does anyone?" Pat gave a wry smile. "When he was at the bank, he always seemed to be so—I don't know—sort of officious and pretentious or something. I was never that comfortable around him."

Gracie now had her supplies stacked neatly in a corner of the big kitchen. "I think I'll go pester your boss for a few minutes," she said to Pat Allen.

She found Paul seated at his desk, a picture of concentration as he studied his computer screen.

She cleared her throat to get his attention, and the young pastor glanced up, a smile lighting his face as he rose from his desk chair. "Good morning, Gracie. And welcome."

She slid her hands into his outstretched ones. "I'd brought some things to the kitchen, and thought I'd stop in to talk with you."

"I'd have been sad if you hadn't."

"You looked totally engrossed."

"I'm never too busy to see you."

She did believe him. That was one reason she usually made the effort to not take too much advantage of his generosity when it came to sharing her thoughts with him. "There are several things I thought I should mention. Just stop me if you already know them," she began.

He nodded encouragement. She began by telling him about her conversation with Mark, then about those with Herb and Marge. "May I ask, Paul, if Sally's said anything to you about giving up her class?"

"No, she hasn't—and I hope she doesn't! Those kids really do love and respect her!"

"What's your feeling about the anonymous note? Who might have written it?"

"I'm as unwilling to make a guess as I think you are."

"Is it probable, or even possible that the writer might have been referring to Sally's work with Lynn, instead of her teaching here?"

"I don't feel I have enough information even to make a guess."

"*Hmmm.* It would have been so easy to write a clearly understandable message that its not being done raises the question as to whether the ambiguity was accidental or deliberate."

"Sally's kept the paper, hasn't she?"

"I didn't ask. One's impulse, I think, would be to throw away such a thing instantly. However, if you're thinking of fingerprints or anything, they'd undoubtedly be badly smudged by now."

"Well, I'm no FBI lab technician."

"Neither am I. But maybe I could go see her after school. Just talk to her to let her know she's not alone. We all need to know that. And, of course, we never are."

Paul smiled. "Your faith is one of the things I love most about you, Gracie."

He leaned back in his chair, then said unexpectedly, "How would you feel if you were Sally?"

"I hope I'd appreciate knowing I had a friend on whom I could rely. But I'd also appreciate all the tact and sensitivity that that friend could muster."

"I think that says it all," Paul said, looking at her with an approving expression. "God bless you, Gracie Parks."

She blushed.

They went on briefly to discuss Mark's situation and Miles's stubbornness, but she didn't tell Paul about Mark's discovery of the second gold coin. Don't feel too proud of yourself for keeping one little secret, she reminded herself. You've told him just about everything else.

She got up from her chair. "I hate even to suggest it, but is it possible that someone knows something else about Sally, or thinks he does, and is using that against her?"

He stood up also. "I can't imagine what it could be."

"Me, neither, dear friend. Me, neither."

At home Gracie was still distracted. She got out the sweeper and sought out some of Gooseberry's favorite spots. He'd know them again even without the fluffy markings, that was certain. What she needed right then was something to keep her busy, something that required little concentration.

It was late in the afternoon when she decided to call her niece Carter Stephens in Chicago. She was a lawyer whose job was in the district attorney's office. The phone rang five times before being picked up by a man. "This is James Riley, a colleague of Miss Stephens. She's unable to come to the phone right now, but perhaps I can take a message?"

"Hello, Jim Riley," she greeted the familiar voice. "This is Carter's Aunt Gracie from Willow Bend, Indiana."

"Well, hello to you, Gracie Parks from Willow Bend, Indiana."

She laughed. "What a memory!"

"What an aunt our Carter has! She's kept us up-to-date with all your local mysteries. We have cases far less interesting around here, I promise you."

"Willow Bend's a real crime capital," she agreed, then heard a chuckle from the other end of the line. She went on, "I'm in something of a quandary right now, and thought perhaps Carter might have some ideas that could help."

"She's tied up with a big court case just now, and probably won't be back at all today. If she is, it will be rather late. Would you like me to leave a message for her to call you as soon as possible?"

"Thanks, Jim, I'd appreciate that."

"No problem. Look, I'm not trying to interfere if this is something related to family or anything. But if there's anything I can do to be of any use, I'd be glad to try."

"I appreciate that. And I'm going to take you up on it." She said thankfully to herself, I can see why Carter says Jim's like a second father to her, or a dear uncle.

Briefly she told him about the coin and the two men who were trying to claim it.

Jim said, "So tell me again, what do you know about this Clark Harrington?"

"He's apparently a computer expert. The trouble is, nobody seems to know anything else for sure about him. Our chief of police. . ."

"Ah, yes. How is Herb?"

"You don't forget anything, do you?" She laughed. "Herb's just fine." But then she became serious again. "He actually checked with someone in Illinois who said Clark's record was a tiny bit iffy—but not enough to make him persona non grata here in Willow Bend."

"Well, how about giving me a little more to go on, Gracie? What's he look like and how old is he, where does he live and/or work? Whatever you can think of."

She was almost embarrassed to admit how little she had to give him. But Jim just told her he happened to have some time right now to follow up on a few things which, from his perspective, could turn out to be most interesting.

Gracie hung up, feeling somewhat relieved but also worried if there was something else she should be doing. Suddenly it occurred to her. She and Gooseberry could take a walk in the direction of Cordelia Fountain's. The redoubtable tourist home proprietor was pretty observant and might have noticed something she'd be eager to report.

But, after her visit with Cordelia, Gracie was no more enlightened than she had been. Cordelia had been the one first to bring up the subject of Clark Harrington. According to her, her boarder was "such a nice young man, so gentlemanly and quiet." She added, "You'd never know he was in the house if you didn't see him come in, or notice the bit of light showing under his door at night."

"Aren't you ever a little nervous, Cordelia?"

"Not at all." She laughed. "I've run this place for well over a quarter-century, and never lost so much as a bath towel."

"Does he use your phone much?"

"Not at all. He explained when he first came that he'd be using his cell phone to make business and other calls."

"That's good, especially if he's going to be here a long time."

"Well," he told me that his work at the school, his updating computers and putting in new things, should be finished in seven to ten days of actual work—and *that* was almost two weeks ago."

Gracie tried to get the wording of her next question just right. "Since he evidently goes from place to place to work, I wonder if he has mail forwarded?"

Cordelia informed her, "He has his laptop computer with him, so he relies on e-mail."

"Has he mentioned a wife and children?"

"No. And I haven't asked."

Gracie felt stymied. What to try now? The good news was that the one message on her answering machine when she got home turned out to be from Jim Riley, as she'd hoped.

"Greetings to you, Inspector Gracie. This is your humble deputy checking in. Here's what I've learned thus far about Mr. X. The address you gave me for his employer is that of a mailing service, one of those businesses that, for a fee, provides a 'mailbox' along with your personal box-number. I haven't given up, mind you, but that's all the time I have for this project today. Perhaps your highly efficient niece will have the opportunity to do better. Good-bye for now."

"*Hmmph!*"

Gracie was standing there staring at the machine when Uncle Miltie interrupted her thoughts. "I thought I heard voices. What's going on?"

"That's a very good question." She turned to face him. "But I don't have a good answer."

He frowned, perplexed. "What's that supposed to mean?"

"I wish I knew!"

"C'mon, Gracie, out with it!"

"Okay, but have a seat here at the table while I get us each a glass of water."

Sitting down across from him, she told how she'd reached Jim Riley when trying to find Carter, and then of his phoning her back. "Doesn't it seem strange to you that Clark's so—secretive?"

"Most people don't go around broadcasting their business, you know."

"Well, he's not so reticent that he isn't demanding that Mark give up that double eagle!"

"He's not going to get it, is he?"

"Not if I can help it!"

The phone rang, and Gracie hurried to answer it, hoping it would be Carter. It wasn't, but it was a caller she could cheerfully greet. "It's good to hear from you, Anna. I hope you're not anxious about Sunday's dinner."

"No, dear," Anna Searfoss reassured her. "At least I hope I don't need to be. You remember, of course, that we didn't send out invitations, saying only that anyone from church was welcome to come, as well as any of our other friends who wanted to."

"But we are trying to keep track of just who's planning to come. I think it's going to be a lot of people!"

Gracie was confident of her planning abilities. "We've made arrangements to feed at least a thousand people," she teased.

"The multitudes, I guess," Anna responded affectionately.

"You've got it. I've been meaning to call you about something else, dear. I know you asked Sally to bake the cake. . . ."

"She *offered* to make and decorate a big sheet cake, and I said I'd appreciate it—and I do. But," now Anna's voice sounded troubled, "will that be enough?"

"Several of the women are already planning to bring extras, including two large frosted cakes. I'll talk with Sally after she gets home from school today. If she thinks we might need more, I'll ask around for another volunteer, or maybe bake a couple myself."

"But you have so much else to do right now, Gracie! With Joe's help, I can mix up a package-cake or two."

"Well, don't buy the cake mix or ingredients until you hear from me, Anna," Gracie suggested. "I'm almost sure Sally and I will decide we have plenty."

But as she headed home, Gracie was mentally going over the rest of the menu. Yes, she'd better order more chicken thighs and split breasts. And she'd pick up another large seedless watermelon, as well as more honeydews and cantaloupes.

You could never have too much, she knew, because whatever was left would be joyously shared with those who would most appreciate the bounty.

Ten

GRACIE HAD GONE OUT to help Uncle Miltie with the flower beds and was on her knees pulling weeds from the narrow bed alongside the garage when a car pulled into the driveway.

"Hey, George, how about going with us to the senior center for some pinochle?" It was Lou Simpson, Willow Bend's retired police chief, and Joe Searfoss.

"We-e-ll, I should finish this deadheading." Uncle Miltie stood there looking at the difference between the flowers to his left, which already had their spent blooms removed, and those yet to be trimmed. "You know it's a jailable offense to let all the plant's energy go into producing seeds instead of more flowers."

Lou laughed. "You're right. I'd have thrown the book at you!"

Gracie looked up at her uncle, knowing how much he enjoyed the fellowship of the men. "I doubt it will make much difference if you trim them now or this evening when it's cooler. For that matter, I'm going in fairly soon myself. The temperature must have risen at least a dozen degrees since we came out."

His face lit up, though he wouldn't admit that he was pleased with this reasoning. "You're right about that, Gracie." He raised his arm in order to wipe his forehead on the sleeve of his shirt, then reached for his walker, which was parked behind him. "Tell you what, fellows, give me a minute or two to wash up, and I'll be with you."

The two men got out of the car to keep Gracie company as her uncle hurried back to the porch steps. She noted that he wasn't leaning on the walker at all, just pushing it ahead of himself. He did, though, use the sturdy handrail as he went up the steps.

Lou observed, "He seems to be getting along better this summer, doesn't he?"

"Yes, he is—actually. But he's usually better in the summer. It's partly because of the heat, but he's also more active physically, and outside a lot more, working here in the garden and helping with the yard trimming."

Joe now cleared his throat. Looking at Gracie with affection, he said, "Anna and I sure appreciate all the work you're doing for our party."

She smiled at him. "It's fun doing it for people like you."

"Like us?"

"Sure." She got to her feet. "I like engineering a meal for the people I care about. Friends and feasts go together. And it's even nicer when those friends are so easy to work with."

"Do you have many who are—ah—disagreeable or grumpy?"

"More than you'd expect—although each party tends to have a different version of any transaction," she admitted. "You two told me what you wanted, and that's what you're getting. There are always some who keep changing their minds from day to day, or have to have every single detail spelled out. Then they lean over my shoulder all the time, making sure I'm doing the right thing at the right time in the right way."

He frowned thoughtfully. "I couldn't handle that kind of pressure, Gracie—and you shouldn't have to, either!"

"You sound like Elmo," she replied, but she was smiling. "My dear husband sometimes got even more upset than I did when that happened, and was quite disturbed with me on several occasions—as well as with the troublemaker."

"I can see why!"

"I assured him, however, that I really did have the upper hand. I could stand someone's being difficult one time—but there was no way I'd do a repeat catering job for that person!"

He appeared about to say something, then switched to a different subject. "Who do you think is the rightful owner of that double eagle, Gracie?"

"Are you interested in what I can prove? Or in my female intuition?" she teased.

He grinned. "Your sleuthing abilities undoubtedly have more to do with the latter. It was Lou, when he was police chief, and now Herb, who have to do the proving."

His friend chuckled.

"Well, I was out there picking up trash with Mark at the time he found it, Joe, and I doubt *very* much that he was faking his surprise— or his sense of gratitude for the possible bounty it could bring him."

"He's always seemed like a good kid, and an honest one. I'm hoping he gets to keep that coin."

Joe had lived here all his life, so this seemed a good opportunity for Gracie to ask, "Miles is a native Willow Bender, right?" Lou and Joe both nodded.

"Yep, he was born here, and as far as I know the only time he's been away much was when he left for college, in New England somewhere. He and Hattie both went there." Joe looked to Lou for confirmation.

"Hattie Bomboy? That was the only Hattie she knew. Are they related?"

"Step-brother and -sister. His mom died when he was real little, and his dad married Hattie's mother maybe two or three years later." This was Lou's contribution.

"Oh."

"Why did you ask?"

"Well, you mentioned that both of them went East to college, so I wondered if there was some connection. . . ."

Uncle Miltie was now coming back out onto the porch, so even-tempered Joe just added, "And they both have something of the same dour disposition, don't they?" Gracie looked at him thoughtfully.

Lou and Joe then waited for their friend as they started back to Lou's car. "Let's go, George!"

Gracie bent to pick up her uncle's extra clippers and decided to trim the two butterfly bushes before going inside. They'd been blooming profusely for weeks but now were rather raggedy with their long brownish seed-spikes protruding.

It was nice of the men to come for Uncle Miltie, she thought. Actually, he had made many good friends here in Willow Bend and, though he sometimes spoke nostalgically about friends in his old hometown, he'd made little effort to keep in touch.

She found herself humming a tune she didn't at first recognize, one that had a pleasant meter and rhythm. Oh, yes, now she knew—it was one that Barb had included in an informal program back in June. It had something to do with friendship, or having friends. Gracie hummed through it, trying to recall some of the rather simple but affective words.

Sometimes—usually!—simplicity made for the most meaningful expression of any sentiment, Gracie thought. That was because it allowed your own heart and spirit to supply the emotion.

There were a lot of lines ending with rhymes to *friend*, like *mend* and *send* and even two-syllable ones like *amend*.

As she continued working on the second of the tall butterfly bushes, some of those almost-forgotten words started to come back.

> "When you're lonely, need a friend,
> Someone on whom to depend,
> Reach out to your neighbor in your pew.
> Do not be too proud or shy,
> Look at others in the eye,
> Maybe they've been longing to know you."

Gracie knew that wasn't exactly right, especially those last two lines, though they didn't sound so off when sung. There were several other verses, yet they continued hovering elusively just out of reach somewhere in the recesses of her mind. However, the last three lines of the final verse she remembered well, so she hummed, then sang them to herself here in her yard:

> "I know if at life's end
> I should die without a friend,
> I'd be the poorest person in the land."

Thank You, God, for my many wonderful friends. I don't know how I could get along without them—and that goes especially for Uncle Miltie, whom I originally invited as an act of loving kindness to him. What a blessing he's become to me and to the church and to the community of Willow Bend—exactly what we needed! Even with all of his terrible jokes!

Long after she'd gone inside, those words from the song stayed with her, and she found herself singing them in the shower, something she always did.

It was perhaps an hour later that she called Barb.

Gracie asked, "Do you still have the music to that song we sang about friendship several months ago?"

"You mean the one starting, 'When you're lonely, need a friend' . . . ?"

"*Um-hmmm*, that's the one. What would you think about our choir's surprising Anna and Joe with that song on Sunday?"

"In church?"

Gracie heard disapproval in Barb's voice. She knew the choir director hated changing the music, once planned, so she hastened to reassure with, "I was thinking about maybe doing it during the dinner or afterward—something completely informal."

"That would be a lovely tribute! I'm sure I have the music here, so if I take it over to the church before Pat leaves—or Paul could take care of it, for that matter—copies could be run off for everyone to use at tonight's choir rehearsal."

"Great! I'll see you there."

Gracie always enjoyed choir practice, and this was an especially lively one. As a bonus, Tish had brought two of her county fair-winning apple-plum dumplings to eat afterward.

"Choir practice always gives me an appetite!" sighed Marge.

"Amen to that!" said Rick.

As for the plans to sing the friendship song, even Estelle hadn't seemed miffed that others would have parts equal to hers. Gracie thought this was a good sign—an indication that Joe and Anna inspired harmony and that the party would be one where everyone's best spirit was engaged.

Gracie told them, "This is going be a surprise for Anna and Joe and everyone else. So if anyone happens to be wearing an apron when serving, I'd suggest he or she just keep it on for the singing, too."

"I don't know if I'd go that far," Estelle stated. Nobody troubled to remind her that she wasn't one of those who usually helped much with serving.

"Since the majority of my clothing's washable these days, I seldom need to wear an apron anymore," Barb explained rather unnecessarily. "But I understand that you want us to make the tribute as natural a moment as possible." She went to the piano and got the group again intent on rehearsing Sunday morning's worship service.

They warmed up with several voice exercises, followed by the hymns Pastor Paul had chosen to go with his text and message. The anthem turned out to be somewhat difficult, but Barb insisted, "You can do it, my friends. Just push yourselves a little harder!"

There was again a small amount of grumbling about the choice. Don looked worried, and Marybeth was frowning.

"That's a lot better," Barb assured them, "but you altos were just a little late in coming in there on the middle of page three.

"First, though, I'd like to go over the bottom line on page two. Notice the change of key there, tenors. You have a two-beat rest, then come in firmly, solidly with, 'Come! The Master is calling. . . .' "

She started to play those notes again, but Lester asked her to back up a few measures, since he was still having trouble making that transition. This time the tenors were more sure of themselves.

"Fine!" Barb pronounced. "And now, everyone! We'll make a quick stab at a couple of those anthems that we'll be using during the next month or two."

A muted rustling accompanied low voices as they searched through their choir folders. Estelle sniffed as if issuing a critical comment that only she could hear. That was a change, thought Gracie. I wonder if she realizes her responses are so obvious. Then, guiltily, she added to herself, But what about my own?

"And now, Gracie," Barb said, breaking into her reverie, "would you please pass out the photocopied sheets?"

It may have been because the clock showed only a few minutes more, but that number went almost flawlessly. Once, twice, three times: They had it down cold, and all cheered as the last note died away.

It had been Marybeth's suggestion as they were enjoying Tish's treat that met with universal approval. "Look, Gracie's in charge of the dinner and will be the one to best decide the right moment for the song. Let's keep an eye on her and let Gracie indicate when that should be."

"That's okay with me." Gracie laughed. "But only if you promise not to leave me just standing there all by myself."

Marge reached out to squeeze her friend's arm. "No *way* would we let that happen, Gracie. We intend to be in on the fun, too."

Eleven

SATURDAY HAD COME QUICKLY, and passed even more speedily. Gracie had spent a good part of it in the church kitchen, figuring she could get much more done there than if at home. What she hadn't considered, however, was that Uncle Miltie would insist he wanted to help, too.

Even Rocky had showed up in the early afternoon and was given an apron to protect his clothes while he chopped cabbage. "Hey, Gracie, this has to be enough already!" he griped as he dumped a mound of slaw into the large container. "I've done four loads!"

She agreed. "Then you can begin working on these carrots," she told him, sliding a couple of bags across the counter.

"Why didn't you buy those little ones that are already cleaned and ready to use?" he grumbled.

"Why, indeed?" She couldn't resist grinning at him. "Maybe I guessed that you'd be here and would need something more challenging than just opening a bag of prepared ones. Anyway, they'd be even more work to shred!"

He turned toward her uncle. "You've got to be a saint, putting up with this woman!"

"Perhaps there could be an editorial addressing the matter! Which do you think would appeal more to people: 'Saint Miltie' or 'Saint George'?"

"I suggest you stick with the first, to avoid confusion. I understand 'Saint George' has already been taken."

Gracie just shook her head as she transferred the shredded cabbage and carrots into plastic bags, ready for the refrigerator, and began making her special dressing, which would be added to it tomorrow.

Rocky had been with them for almost an hour when he got a call from one of his reporters on his cell phone. "What do you mean, Miles Stevens is going to sue?" he demanded. "Where's the information coming from?"

The other two stood there staring at him. Then Uncle Miltie whispered, "Maybe it's just a threat, just something to say." But even he looked upset. Gracie's mind was racing.

It turned out that a lawyer for Miles Stevens had just made a public statement that if the 1930-S double eagle was not returned to his client by Monday noon, legal action was going to be taken.

The clock was ticking!

2

Gracie had expected to pay Sally a visit on Sunday, stealing a moment between church and cooking—not late Saturday night! However, as she rather groggily reached for the phone, she found herself a moment later sitting on the edge of the bed, demanding, "What did you say?"

It was Sally. Her words were frantic. "There was someone here, demanding the coin!"

"Who was there, Sally."

"I'm not sure who it was. I didn't really see him."

There was the sound of crying, and excited, terrified voices in the background, and Gracie asked, "Was it too dark to recognize anything that might identify him?"

"Yes. He threatened Mark. Mark tried to convince him the coin wasn't here. He refused to listen."

Gracie tried to keep her voice composed. "He left then?"

"Y-yes. None of us knew he was here till Mark woke up and found him standing over him."

"Have you called the police?"

"No-o-o! And that's what I should have done, isn't it? Instead of bothering you like this. . . ."

"Don't worry about that—but call them right now. And tell the kids not to touch anything, especially in Mark's room!"

233

Gracie seldom used the police chief's home phone, but now was the time for it. "It's Gracie, Herb. I just got a call from Sally, who's at this moment calling your office. There was an intruder in their house demanding the coin. He appeared in Mark's room—and it was too dark and Mark was too sleepy to recognize him."

She gave Herb what little additional information she had, then suggested, "Don't you think it's time to make public the finding of that second coin? Perhaps say that the person who can identify *that* gold coin without seeing it, giving the year and mint mark of course, might be considered as having some claim upon both of them?"

They discussed this course of action briefly before agreeing to meet at Sally's as quickly as possible.

Uncle Miltie wanted to go, too, but Gracie asked that he stay home and call Carter, despite its being so late, to see if she'd found out anything.

"That's just an excuse not to let me go with you," he challenged through her bedroom door as she hurriedly changed back into the clothing she'd so recently taken off and left lying over the chair by her bed. "You shouldn't be going over there alone at this time of night!"

"I'll be okay, I promise." But she doubted that her smile, meant to be one of reassurance, looked any more real than it felt. "You hold the fort here, and I'll do my best there."

She gave him a brief hug on her way out the door. Every light at Sally's was on, inside and out, and all four family members were waiting in the kitchen. Kate, seven, and Jennifer, eight, were hanging onto their mother, thoroughly frightened, while Mark was indignant and upset.

After hugging Sally, Gracie asked first to use their phone. When Cordelia answered on the second ring, sounding half asleep, Gracie attempted to disguise her voice. "May I please speak to Clark Harrington?"

"Do you realize what *time* it is?" the other woman demanded.

"I'm sorry, but this is *very* important."

"Well!" the tourist home owner's displeasure was evident. "It had *better* be, waking up decent, law-abiding citizens like this. Hold on a minute and I'll call him."

Gracie could hear her voice, "Mr. Harrington—Mr. Harrington, you're wanted on the phone!" There was a brief pause before an even louder, more insistent, *"Mr. Harrington,* someone's on the phone, and it sounds important."

Gracie heard a banging, which she assumed to be Cordelia's pounding on his door. Then there was a pause followed by a somewhat breathless, "He doesn't seem to be here. Can I take a message?"

"No, thanks."

"He does have e-mail, you know."

She'd sounded a little more cooperative, so Gracie asked, "Can you give me his e-mail address, so I won't need to bother you?"

"Well, no . . . I don't have that, but if you leave your name and number, I'll have him call if you'd like."

"Thank you for your help, Mrs. Fountain. Perhaps I can phone him later."

"A *lot* later, you mean," the exasperated voice rejoined. "In the morning!"

Gracie rubbed her ear for a moment. "She really slammed down that receiver!"

There was a racket out on the porch. Gracie looked at the panicked expressions worn by the Canfield family. Somebody was pounding on the door and rattling the knob. And then Uncle Miltie was demanding, "Open up in there, Gracie. It's me and Rocky!"

Seeing her newest visitors, Sally asked, "What are you two doing out there at this hour?"

"Uncle Miltie called me about the problem," Rocky put in quickly, "and we decided we should be here to help. So what's happening now?"

Gracie was frowning at her uncle. "I thought you were going to call Carter."

"I did—but she'd gotten back too late and hadn't had enough time to check for you. She will tomorrow, though—I mean today," he added, glancing at the clock on the stove.

Herb arrived then. Gracie now phoned Miles's house. The phone was answered on the fifth ring. By now, if it *had* been Miles who'd so frightened this household, he'd have had plenty of opportunity to get back to his house.

"Ah, so you are home again, no?" she said in a deep voice.

"Who is this?"

She knew he was trying to identify her, and she had to be quick. "Don't do it again!" she commanded and hung up.

"What was that all about?" Uncle Miltie wanted to know.

"I—may have made a mistake on that call," she admitted.

"In what way?"

"It occurs to me Miles might be the kind of person who has caller-identification for phone calls, like we do at home."

"Oh."

Herb was looking at Gracie. "Did you tell Sally what you suggested to me?"

She shook her head. "I was waiting for you to get here."

"And we're *all* here now . . . ," Rocky smugly pointed out. "The game's afoot!"

Gracie looked startled, then recognized the allusion to Sherlock Holmes.

"We're Watson and Watson II," Uncle Miltie informed her.

Gracie now nodded at Herb. He explained that it was probably time to let word out that a second coin had been found. And that he and Gracie thought that those claiming ownership of the first coin should be obligated to put in writing what each one looked like, including specific identifying marks.

"Our printer might be able to make a change for the next edition if I get hold of him right away," Rocky immediately declared. "But what should I have put on the front page?"

"Just the basic facts, and the idea of the challenge," said Gracie. "In what you call a 'sidebar'—a boxed announcement, I think."

⁂

Uncle Miltie had gotten up a bit earlier than usual for a Sunday, so he was already sitting at the table with a bowl of cereal when Gracie appeared in the kitchen.

He tried to carry on a conversation unrelated to the events of the previous night, but as far as Gracie was concerned, what she needed once again was a little peace and quiet.

Yes, she only had one more trip out to the car with things for this afternoon's dinner.

No, she didn't need help, but thanks anyway.

Yes, they'd get to church on time.

No, it didn't seem strange at all for Anna and Joe to have this big party for everyone. As they'd said many times, they greatly appreciated the way everyone was so helpful and took them places and did things for them, and this was merely one way of saying a special thanks.

The church was full, as was Sunday school. The congregational singing of some of the old-time hymns rang forth in joy, and the choir members of the Eternal Hope Community Church didn't miss a note or a beat in their anthem, "For Love of Thee We Bring Our Praise."

Gracie had at first found herself sitting bolt-upright in the old, usually comfortable wooden chairs there in the choir loft. Then, aware of feeling more relaxed, she was able to listen attentively to Paul's sermon on "Love for a Lifetime."

She'd seen that title in the church bulletin at the beginning of the service, but it had hardly registered in her racing mind. After all, there was the dinner to finish preparing, the aftershocks from her dramatic late-night summons to the Canfields' and her curiosity about what Rocky had put on the front page of today's paper.

Hers was usually delivered before she left for church on Sunday morning. The changes to the front page must have pushed everything back.

But now, temporarily, Gracie found herself at peace, resting in the arms of God.

❧

The kitchen was abuzz with the energy and enthusiasm of friends who'd for years worked harmoniously together. Tish and Tyne, their houses on a different paper route from Marge and Gracie, had both read the front page, as had Eleanor McIver.

"Can you believe it, Gracie?" Eleanor was arranging chicken pieces on broiler trays. "Someone's recently found another of those gold coins. But they're not telling whether it's like the first one, or who discovered it!"

"Isn't that too much?" Tyne put in. "I'm amazed anyone could keep such a thing secret!"

"We certainly couldn't!" Tish agreed.

"I wonder if it was found out on Ferris Road, like the other one," Eleanor said. "I often drive that way, you know, and have seen different people searching around. For that matter, the whole area near where Mark found the double eagle now looks like it's been the stomping ground for a herd of elephants."

"Yeah, I've heard of elephants." That came from Uncle Miltie, who was coming into the kitchen, looking innocent except for a certain sparkle in his eyes which Gracie recognized. "A few elephants have even heard of *me*."

Tish, however, was trying to straighten out what she thought was an innocent mistake. "We were talking about the place out on Ferris Road that is all trampled down as though it was run over by a *herd* of elephants."

"Oh, *that* kind of herd." He patted her shoulder as he headed on to where Gracie was standing. "What can I help with here?"

Glancing out into the large room, she saw several of the men starting to set up tables. "It's time to get out one of those seating arrangements I saw you working on. The tables could use your supervision."

Reaching into his shirt pocket, he brought out and unfolded a sheet of paper on which were sketched two different arrangements. "I'll go over there and show them what will probably work best." He headed out of the kitchen door.

Eleanor looked quizzically at Gracie, who smiled. "It takes something like this to remind me that my uncle spent most of his career as a building contractor."

Rocky now stuck his head in the door. "So, Gracie, how did you like the layout and story in today's paper?"

When Gracie admitted she hadn't had a chance to see it yet, he went to his car for a copy.

After reading it, she told him, "My hope is that nobody new will turn up to claim that second coin." Then she added, "But it will be very interesting to see what happens!"

Sally and Mark now arrived, carrying in the huge white-frosted cake Sally had so beautifully decorated with autumnal flowers and fruits. Green vines of frosting formed the words:

WITH LOVE, PRAYERS, AND GRATITUDE
FOR ALL THOSE WE LOVE
From: ANNA and JOE SEARFOSS,
YOUR SISTER AND BROTHER IN CHRIST

Gracie wiped her eyes after reading the lovely sentiment, and suggested placing the cake on the corner table farthest from the entrance, at least until the official host and hostess arrived. Should they wish to have it on display somewhere else, it could then be moved.

Marge, who'd just returned, having gone home after church, commented softly, "It's a beautiful cake, but those words sound so final, as if they're leaving us."

Sally explained, "That's what they asked me to write on it, so that's what I did."

Anna and Joe soon arrived. They began greeting everyone, and expressions of mutual gratitude filled the air with each new appearance of a Willow Bend friend or neighbor.

Gracie was too busy to keep track of who arrived when. She was surprised to see that Cordelia had brought Clark Harrington with her. She went about introducing him, and, when people learned he was staying with her, he was cordially welcomed.

Sally came to tell Gracie when Miles Stevens appeared. "What do you suppose he's up to now?" Sally asked.

"I have no idea," Gracie replied. "I'd suggest that we both keep our eyes on him and on Clark."

She hadn't noticed Lynn coming toward them. But the girl was now signing something to Sally, and giving Gracie an understandable greeting of, "Hello, Mrs. Parks."

"Hello to you, Lynn," she responded slowly.

Lynn then noticed Uncle Miltie across the room and hurried over to be with him.

"Aren't they sweet together?" Sally asked. "It's a good thing I'm not jealous as her helper, for those two have bonded beautifully. She eagerly tries anything he suggests."

Added Sally, laughing. "We'd better be careful. There can no longer be private conversations when she's around—or your uncle, either, unless we turn our backs on them."

Gracie was nearly finished when Pastor Paul raised his voice above the happy hum of conversation. "Please take your places, everyone."

Gracie had no doubt that Uncle Miltie's choice as to where to sit was deliberate. He and Lynn were one table over from and facing Miles, who was seated next to Clark, of all people, at the end of their table. Sally and her daughters, being relatives-by-marriage of Anna and Joe, were at the head table, while Mark was helping to serve.

Thank goodness enough chairs had been set up for everyone.

There couldn't be more than fifteen empty ones in the whole room! Paul led everyone in saying grace, then requested additional blessings upon the friendships they all shared.

Now came the infectious happy sounds of contented people eating together and thoroughly enjoying one another's company.

Twelve

GRACIE SUGGESTED that her helpers and some of the students, including Mark, now go sit with their families, at least until time for serving dessert. With so much to do and so much going on, she was too busy to pay much attention to the guests whose behavior most interested her. She did, however, touch her uncle's shoulder as she stopped to refill his coffee cup. "Everything okay here?"

He nodded so. Giving him a fast peck, she went on to the next table. When she came to Miles Stevens, she responded to his comment about her organizational skills with, "Things do seem to be going well, don't they?"

But why was he so friendly suddenly? she wondered. It didn't reassure her to know she'd find out eventually.

The phone in the kitchen rang, but by the time Gracie finished filling Clark's cup, Paul had pushed back his chair and was striding to answer it. After he had hung up he walked outside instead of returning to his seat.

A few minutes later she glanced toward the door and saw Paul coming back in, but not alone. A beautiful blonde was with him— Carter!

Setting the pot on the table, she rushed across to greet her niece with a big hug and kiss. "I'm so glad you're here!"

"I am, too! As soon as I got to the edge of Willow Bend, I tried calling your place, then here. Paul told me to come on over and eat with everyone."

"Wonderful!" Gracie wanted to ask if she had specific information concerning Clark, or if there was some other reason for coming now. But it was not the time or place for that. "Paul, how about taking her over to speak with Anna and Joe while I fill a plate with warm food from the kitchen?"

Many of Gracie's friends and neighbors knew Carter, and greeted her with friendly words. At the end of the table just before her great-uncle's, her blue-eyed, steady gaze met Clark Harrington's.

Paul said, "Carter, this is Clark Harrington, a computer and electronics expert originally from Chicago."

"Is it possible we may have met previously, Mr. Harrington? Your face seems somewhat familiar."

"No, I don't believe we have." His voice was level.

She shrugged lightly, and turned her attention toward Miles. "And I believe you are Mr. Stevens."

He actually looked shocked for a moment, before saying, "I suspect you must be Mrs. Parks's niece, from the DA's office in Chicago."

Ah-ha, he's giving Clark a warning signal! Gracie realized. What she said, however, was, "Is that an extra seat, Uncle Miltie?" indicating the one on the other side of him from Lynn.

"Afraid not, Gracie, Harry's probably coming back."

Just then Harry Durant did arrive, saying, "I've got to go. I thought I'd be back to the garage before this. With all the Sunday afternoon drivers, we get pretty busy about now."

Then, when Gracie looked across at the other table, Miles was still there—but Clark was gone!

She was distracted when Paul stood up and presented Anna, who got to her feet, saying, "Joe and I want to thank all of you for being with us for this very special day. And I believe we also need to give a little explanation for having invited you here.

"A number of people have wondered if this marks the occasion of one anniversary or another, while others have asked—mostly indirectly, of course—if perhaps we've decided to move away or if one or both of us is sick or dying. The answer to both questions is no—at least as far as we know right now, although we're obviously not growing any younger.

"We have been to many funerals these last years, and got to talking one night about the especially large crowd who'd just come to one of those held here in our church. How pleased our late friend would have been had she been able to visit with all those people who came to bid her farewell, many of whom she hadn't seen or heard from for years.

"Well, one thing led to another, and we decided we'd much prefer having people come while we're both alive and well and capable of hugging and kissing and talking to them. But we didn't want anything real formal or fancy, or anything people would feel obligated to attend. So we decided that, if Gracie and others would take care of the cooking and serving, we'd like to have a nice sit-down, family-style meal together. . . ."

She continued speaking for a minute or two. Then Joe stood up and just said, "As always, I agree with my wonderful wife. Nothing could please us more than being here with all of you today, sharing food and the good Lord's plentiful love."

Next Paul asked if any guests would like to say a few words.

Sally Canfield reached out for the microphone and thanked Anna and Joe for all they meant to her. When she'd finished, Paul carried it to one after another of the guests. Gracie was pleased to see that Rocky was discreetly photographing each testimonial.

Paul finally said, "We are especially grateful for all of you who've so eloquently shared in words what this wonderful couple means to you. And now at the end of these public testimonies, I would like to ask the creator of this splendid feast to close with prayer."

Gracie accepted the mike, and spoke into it, at the same time beckoning to the other choir members to join her as she walked toward the head table. "Your church, your Sunday school and your choir rejoice in this time spent with you today, Anna and Joe. You have truly been trusted, special, and much-loved friends, and we honor you.

"There are so many things we would like to put into words in order to try to let you know how much you are appreciated and loved, but we'd still run out of time before they were all said. And so those of us in the choir decided to sing for you not a ballad nor timeless classic, but a simple little composition that was sung here in the church some months ago.

"Perhaps you will remember it," she said with a broad smile. "It's called 'Friendship.' Perhaps the rest of us need to hear it again more than the two of you do, but Barb is going to play the piano and we're going to sing it."

The Turner twins cleared their throats in unison while Rick Harding waggled his fingers at his giggling daughter Lillian, who sat on her mother's knee.

The group had sung the first three verses before Gracie glanced in the direction of Miles Stevens, who was looking down at the tabletop in front of him.

Then the voices of Eternal Hope's choir came to the last verse:
"Are there fences I should mend?
Broken friendships to attend?
Guide me, Lord, please lead me with Your hand;
For if at this life's end
I should die without a friend,
I'd be the poorest person in the land."

People applauded, but before the choir separated, Gracie picked up the microphone and bowed her head. She had an active prayer life and occasionally was asked to open or close a business or other meeting with prayer, but still this occasion was more moving than most. She closed her eyes and drew in a deep breath.

"Dear Lord, what a privilege You've given us to be here today for this blessed occasion of celebrating Anna and Joe, and what they mean to us. Thanks for letting me and others of their large circle of friends prepare this food of which we have partaken, and thanks for each one who lovingly journeyed here today at the invitation of this couple.

"But, Lord, I'm right now going to ask another blessing of You, that You will help each of us—every single one of us as we leave here today—not only to remember the love and fellowship and food, but that we are all one in You. Please help us to look around at those who may feel outside of our own little circles of friendships or family ties, and not only welcome them when they come—but invite them in, as Anna and Joe did today.

"I'm sure everyone here joins me in praying for them to enjoy many more healthy, happy, contented years, dear Lord. We ask this in the name of Your Beloved Son, Jesus. Amen."

She did not look into the face of her pastor or Carter or anyone as she hurried to the kitchen, fearing that if anyone said a word to her right then, she'd burst into tears.

Thirteen

E LEANOR MCIVER HAD BEGUN washing dishes, and several people were already drying and putting clean things away. Gracie decided she wouldn't be missed for a few moments if she went in search of her niece. But she found Rocky hurrying down the hallway toward her. "You're the one I was looking for."

"Oh?"

"We're all in Paul's office." His hand was on her elbow, though she was walking as rapidly as he was. "Your uncle and Lynn just began telling us what was said, and you need to come with me."

There in Paul's study they found Uncle Miltie trying to quote as nearly as possible the things he'd lip-read while Miles and Clark were talking to one another. Every so often he stopped to check something with Lynn.

But the girl seemed a little frustrated, causing Gracie to ask, "Would you like Sally here with us, dear?" Gracie realized that Lynn needed a surer interpreter than her struggling uncle.

A smile lit her face and she nodded. So Gracie headed out to look for her friend. She saw Mark first, and asked that he tell his mother to come to the church office right away. "Perhaps," she added, "you should plan to stay, also."

Lynn made out better in sharing her account once Sally was there. It seemed Miles Stevens had been startled to find Clark there and hadn't been pleased that the younger man was seated at his table.

Apparently Clark had been offering the older man a deal. He was prepared to get out of the picture in order to make it easier for Miles, with his local connections, to claim the coins. But Clark would do that only on condition of Miles's promising to split any proceeds evenly with him.

Miles, however, couldn't bring himself to agree to such a proposal. But he didn't exactly refuse it, either.

Carter turned to face Lynn directly. "May I ask a few questions, dear? From what you overheard, to which of the men do you think the coins might really have belonged?"

Lynn looked from Carter to Sally, and started rapidly finger-spelling. Sally listened, then asked aloud, "You are sure Clark said he knew Miles was as much of an impostor as he was, when it came to any claim to the coins?"

The child looked at them and tried to the best of her ability to say the words, "If I were Mark, I'd be very angry at people trying to take what I'd found away from me!"

"Well, I was!" Mark burst out.

"Yes, you were," his mother agreed.

"But even though the other two were making their claims and tried to appear upset, somehow they just weren't able to pull it off— they weren't angry enough," Gracie pointed out. And it was true.

Sally looked around the group. "I just want to know which of them was at our home last night."

Lynn looked very upset. Sally paid close attention. "I think it was Clark, and then Miles accused him of being a young whippersnapper!"

"How did she know how to sign 'whippersnapper?'" Uncle Miltie whispered to Gracie.

"Well, she may have been able to come up with that one, but I think the operative word is really *cahoots*. Those two, however they knew each other, were in both a tug-of-war and a conspiracy!"

※

Clark Harrington had been questioned by Herb, but Miles Stevens was now back in the hospital. The diagnosis this time: more heart trouble. She was pondering the issue and chastising herself for having so little sympathy for a sick man—yet, she was also having a harder time than usual feeling guilty for being judgmental.

At the deli, Abe came walking over to Rocky and Gracie after they had sat down at their favorite table. "What's your choice going to be this morning?" Gracie was keeping her thoughts about Miles Stevens to herself.

"Some tea, first of all," she told him. "And then one cookie."

"A cookie?" he repeated. "You want just one cookie?"

She nodded and sat up straighter. "Yes, dear Abe, one cookie. You can choose it."

"So, you want to live dangerously today?"

"The kind of chance I'm taking is one that puts me in the hands of someone I love. Miles Stevens and Clark Harrington took chances without honesty, without trust, without faith. Only greed drove them. And so they failed miserably at gaining what they sought. Asking for one cookie shows I'm not greedy, at least, dear Abe."

Rocky chuckled. "You find your lessons everywhere, Gracie," he said fondly.

"Well, I'd rather find lessons than coins any day. No one fights over them, for one thing. We may never know where those gold pieces came from, but what's truly golden is friendship."

And, at that moment, Abe returned and ceremoniously presented Gracie with a large piece of apple strudel.

"I didn't have a cookie worthy of you," he announced.

They all laughed.

GRACIE OVER THE NEXT FEW DAYS found herself worrying more about Miles Stevens's condition than she'd have expected. One thing that bothered her was that, although she had readily asked God for the banker to have a change of heart—to become the kind of person who could truly love fellow mankind, she still had to discipline herself to pray, to really pray for his well-being.

On the fourth morning, after learning of his heart attack, she finally called his stepsister. "How's Miles coming along now, Hattie?"

"I—don't rightly know. I haven't gotten over to see him yet."

Perhaps she hasn't had a way to get there since she had to give up driving, Gracie thought. "Do you need a ride? I could drive you over this afternoon, if you'd like."

"Oh, I wouldn't want to bother you."

At least she didn't say she'd rather not go. "Look, Hattie, I need to pick up a prescription refill at the pharmacy, and should stop at the grocery store for a few things. How about my coming by for you around 1:30? We'll go to the hospital and then you could come with me if there's anything you need at either of those places—or anywhere else for that matter.

"However, if you'd prefer, I could take you home before running my errands."

There was silence for an extended moment before, in a small voice, Hattie replied, "You—don't have to do that."

"It's not a matter of 'having to,' Hattie." Gracie gave a little laugh.

"I'm taking the car out this afternoon, and it's no more difficult to fit two women into Fannie Mae than just one."

"Wel-l-l, I suppose. . . ."

"I'm assuming that means yes, so be ready when I arrive at half past one, okay?"

Gracie arranged miniature chrysanthemums in a small milk-glass vase to take to the hospital. *I don't know if this whole idea is what You want me doing, God, but it does feel right. I have no way of knowing whether Miles will even talk to me, or if he might command me to leave. Should that be the case, Lord, please give me the grace to not create a scene.*

I realize that he has no reason to welcome me, for I was incredibly rude to him when he called and when he came over.

๛

Hattie carried the vase as Gracie drove, and the older woman reminisced a little. "We weren't close as children."

"What about as time went on?"

"Well, never as close as some stepbrothers and -sisters. It can be a difficult relationship, sharing parents. We were practically strangers, and then suddenly we were related!" Hattie shrugged.

Gracie glanced toward her companion, who was staring out the windshield. "I'm curious. When you did see Miles in recent years, were you able to become closer?"

"Not entirely." There was another pause, which Gracie made no effort to fill.

"I think I understand," said Gracie. "Miles seems to expect to run everything his way." Hattie nodded as they turned into the hospital's parking lot. "In loving, mutual relationships there has to be give and take. Not just take!"

Even as they got out of the car and went inside the three-storied brick building, Gracie was uncertain what she should say to Miles. *Help me, Lord—please guide my tongue and my manner. Help me to do whatever You know is best.*

They rode up in the elevator. Then Gracie saw one of the physical therapists she knew walking an elderly, somewhat stooped man in hospital-issue pajamas down the hallway. She heard the hushed voice of the woman beside her asking, "That's—Miles, isn't it?"

"Yes, I'm sure it is," she agreed, and was grateful she'd made no effort to rush Hattie. They watched him enter room 209.

The therapist was encouraging him. "You did much better this afternoon, Miles." She was helping him back into bed.

He sighed heavily. Then he became aware of the two women and, holding on to the arms of the chair, he sat up straighter.

"Hello, Miles," Hattie said as she moved to the foot of his bed. "How are you feeling?"

His gaze flicked from her to Gracie, then back. "They say I'm better."

"Miles, then let's believe them!" Hattie said sharply. She looked at him. And Gracie watched them both. Neither of them is an easy person, she told herself.

Liz Eckard, the therapist, smiled at Hattie and Gracie and said, "He's coming along well." Then, turning at the doorway, she told her patient, "I'll be back in the morning. In the meantime, remember to keep doing your leg exercises."

Miles had been ignoring Gracie. Or seeming to. So she said nothing while moving the straight chair from the other side of the bed, and indicated Hattie should sit down close to him. She now set down the bouquet. "I hope you're not allergic to mums—but these are from my yard. Uncle Miltie and I thought you might enjoy them."

He nodded, just a little. "Thanks."

That didn't seem like much of a response, but she kept on talking to him. "We'd decided not to buy more varieties, but this dark pink fringe on the white blossoms looked so pretty in the catalogue that we couldn't resist."

That got little more response. "Yes. They're pretty."

She smiled at him as she sat on the side of his bed, but said nothing more for a while. Sadly, he and Hattie seemed to have little to say to one another, either. Gracie finally decided to bring up the celebration that had taken place on Sunday. "Wasn't that a lovely event? Anna and Joe have so many friends!"

Hattie now complimented her, "You really know how to put on meals—catering them, I mean. Everything went along just as it should."

"Thanks, but I had wonderful helpers. All of the volunteers worked so well together. I could never handle all of it myself!"

"Volunteers?" Miles unexpectedly repeated. "You don't even pay them?" He sounded scornful.

"Oh, I do expect to be paid—and pay others—when it's something like a Rotary dinner or a wedding reception, but I'd never accept money for helping with something like this. After all, we're friends, and have been for decades."

Again there was silence.

Her stepbrother's taciturnity seemed to embarrass Hattie. Gracie decided to offer her the opportunity to come with her for her other errands, as she'd earlier suggested.

As Gracie followed Hattie from the room, she heard the man in the bed say faintly, "Gracie—Mrs. Parks . . ."

She turned. "What is it, Miles?"

"Would you—would you please come back to see me sometime? There are things I think—I *need* to talk to you about."

She stood there looking at him, trying to discern his motivation. *But I know, Lord, that for Miles Stevens to ask any favor is pretty difficult, so I'll take a chance.* "Yes," she said softly. "I will return—if you want me to."

"I'd—appreciate that. But next time, could it be just you? You and me?"

Hattie had walked as far as the next doorway and was standing there waiting for her, so Gracie just said, "Certainly."

Hattie asked, "What was that about?"

"He was grateful for my bringing you," she said, hoping that to be at least a partial truth. God must have some good reason for prompting her to ask Hattie to come here with with her, and she assumed He must have a reason for her return.

It turned out that Hattie did need a few items at the pharmacy, and several bagsful of groceries. "I don't get to the store much," she explained. "So I take advantage of it."

Hattie didn't seem aware of the helping-hand services offered by the senior citizens task force in town. Gracie knew they could make a big difference to Hattie's life if she would only accept their outreach.

She carried most of Hattie's purchases inside her rambling old house. She'd many times admired the early Victorian exterior, which badly needed paint. Now she saw that the interior, particularly the kitchen, needed major work.

Gracie started back home, but kept feeling nudged to return to the hospital. "I don't know why I should right now," she said out loud. But at the next street she turned around and headed back.

She walked down the hall and stopped in his doorway, wondering how to explain her presence again so soon. But Miles was still sitting where she'd left him a good two or three hours earlier. She thought she hadn't made a sound, but his head turned and, not looking surprised, he said, "Come on in."

She did so, and he went on, "I've been doing an awful lot of thinking."

"Medical crises can do that to us."

"I understand that, but there's more to what I want to tell you."

"Oh." *What can I say now, God?*

But Miles only expected her to listen, and he went on to admit that he'd been so despondent after the party that he'd considered trying to kill himself. Then the chest pains struck.

"Don't tell anyone, Gracie. It was just that—well, for the first time it hit me that if I did what Anna and Joe did, invite anyone and everyone to a party, and if you were catering that, it might very well be just you and me there. And I'd be paying you to come."

She couldn't argue that, so she just seated herself in the chair his sister had recently vacated. "I'm sure Hattie would have come."

Suddenly the conversation took a different turn. Miles insisted to Gracie that he'd honestly thought Mark had taken his coin: It had been there on the table, then was gone. "It wasn't until days after I made that accusation that I went through everything again, all the newspapers and other stuff there in my kitchen—and it was then that I found my own double eagle.

"But I'd already told my story to everyone, and—and couldn't bear the thought of everyone laughing at me."

She sighed. "So you let everyone continue to wonder whether or not Mark was a thief."

He nodded glumly. "I was so afraid of people thinking me a fool that I decided to carry out whatever I had to do to make people believe me the victim."

"Even going to Sally's home to demand the return of the coin?"

His weary eyes opened wider. "I didn't do that. I confess to not doing what I should have, but I swear I had no part in anything like that!"

"But it wasn't Clark, either, not if what Lynn told us is correct."

"Lynn? How can that little girl tell you anything?"

He seemed genuinely to want to know, so she explained the conversation in the church office. "But what about that note on Sally's door?" Gracie waited for his reply.

She somehow believed his claim that he knew nothing about that, either and, since Clark evidently believed Miles responsible for the confrontation at Sally's, they together tried to figure out what anyone else could have to gain.

It was on the way home that Gracie put everything together and realized she needed to make one more stop, one she dreaded. *Is it really necessary for me to be the one, God? Couldn't I just go to Herb and tell him all I know—and what I surmise?*

But that feeling was still there, that urging that she must do what was right, that nobody else should be given the responsibility of accomplishing what she knew had to be taken care of.

Almost reluctantly, she made a right turn several blocks before her own home, and another one a little later. This had once been the finest part of town, where the wealthy lived in large houses with expansive lawns and enough servants to keep everything well cared for. But now the very biggest of those original mansions was a nursing home, and another had been renovated into a nonmedical residence for a number of elderly women who needed personal care.

Most had been torn down and replaced by smaller houses on smaller lots—now measured in feet instead of acres, or even fractions of these. Gracie sighed as she pulled into a driveway still somewhat protected by a not-too-stable-looking *porte cochère* that had definitely seen better days.

She turned off the engine and got out of her car, then stood there just looking around for a few moments, trying to picture what this would have been like when everything had been in excellent condition and well maintained.

Well, I'm here, Lord—and now for the hard part. She disciplined herself to walk around the car and go to the massive entrance with its two large doors and twin cast-iron knockers. She raised and lowered the one on the right, making as loud a noise as when she'd stopped there earlier in the day.

She waited for what seemed a long time before repeating her summons, and was about to press the small button set in the side of the doorway when the door was pulled open far enough for Hattie to peer through the crack before opening it a little further.

"What's wrong, Gracie? Is Miles worse?"

Gracie pushed the door open far enough to walk inside. "I need to talk with you about something, Hattie."

They were standing in the shadowy reception hall, but Hattie did not suggest their going into one of the adjoining rooms. "What did you . . . ?" But then she changed her mind and said simply, "What about?"

There were long pieces of walnut furniture with spindled arms, backs and legs—what Gracie thought of as deacon's benches—along the two sides of this space, and Gracie moved toward the one on the right. "Could we sit here for a few moments? I won't be staying long."

Hattie left the door standing open as she seated herself beside her visitor, who was saying, "I just came back from the hospital, where I talked some more with Miles."

"He is worse then, isn't he?"

"No, I don't think so, Hattie. But we did discussed matters, and now I'm wondering about several things."

Hattie shifted position. "What things?"

"Well, first of all, why did you put that note on Sally's door?"

"How did . . . I mean, what are you talking about?"

"The note you taped to their screen door, the one that implied that Sally's a terrible person."

"Well, she *is*—she has to be! Why else would she let that son of hers get away with his thievery? Why doesn't she see to it that he gives back that coin to my brother?"

Okay, she's admitted that. Now for the major question. Gracie drew in a full breath before saying, "And that's why you disguised yourself to frighten Mark Canfield. You wanted to make them give you the coin so you could return it to him."

Hattie, eyes wide behind her glasses, reached out as though to stop her. But Gracie went right on, "You just wanted to scare them into giving up the coin."

Hattie sank back against the spindles, looking every bit her age and almost in despair. "It was all I could think of—but they wouldn't give it to me. It would have been so simple if only they'd done what I asked."

Gracie reached out to touch the other woman's arm. "They couldn't give it to you, Hattie, because they knew it was never your brother's. Mark did not steal it from him, or from anyone. He found it, just like he said."

"But Miles says . . ."

Gracie nodded. "It turns out that Miles, too, was wrong, and I'm sure he will now tell you that. He at first did think it stolen, and that's when he accused Mark—but he later discovered it had just been misplaced."

"He has it now?" Her voice quavered.

"He has it now."

"Oh, my . . ." Gracie could see Hattie was stricken.

"If you have any doubts about what I'm saying, dear, how about our calling Miles right now? He can tell you himself."

Hattie was twisting her fingers as she attempted to explain to Gracie why she had behaved so recklessly. "Miles helped me out financially a number of times when I almost lost this place. I—thought that this time I could be helping him. I really did."

"I'm sure you did."

"But I just made things worse for him and for me. And for everyone. . . ."

Gracie knew that to be true, but she said only, "However, you are now the single person who can solve the problems, Hattie. It won't be easy, but it's up to you to straighten out this situation, to put all the false accusations to rest."

It was the following morning, and Gracie and her uncle were waiting at the restaurant's door when Abe first turned his sign from CLOSED to OPEN.

"It's about time you let us in," Uncle Miltie grumbled.

Abe looked at Gracie with raised brows. "Is he always this grouchy when you get him up early?"

She laughed. "He'll calm down once he's got coffee and a bagel in his tummy."

"It'll take more than a bagel to soothe me if you're going to give me such a hard time," he protested.

"Well, we'll see what one of my fresh-from-the-oven raisin-pumpernickel bagels can do in the tranquilizer department."

Abe was chuckling as he headed around the counter, leaving these long-time patrons to seat themselves. He returned in less than a minute with a mug of coffee, a pot of tea and three of the still-warm bagels. He didn't usually have time to sit with them, but nobody else had strolled in yet. "So what's new?"

"More than you could possibly imagine!" Uncle Miltie announced, and proceeded to give a rather extensive summary of what he'd learned from Gracie.

"So Sally and Mark know?"

"Yep, Gracie took Hattie over there last night, and they got everything straightened out."

"And what about Miles? How did he take it, finding that Hattie had gone to such extreme lengths for him?"

Gracie answered that. "Please don't tell anyone—but he cried like a baby when Hattie went back over to the hospital and told him. And she was crying even harder. They were hugging each other like they'd never stop."

Uncle Miltie explained, "They've evidently both felt lots of love for one another—but neither knew that the other felt that way, and each one was too proud and persnickety to show it."

Gracie added, "I suspect we're going to see those two doing a lot of things together from now on!"

There was a twinkle in Abe's eyes as he stated, "I want to be around when Rocky hears about this."

"But he only gets to know the mushy stuff if he promises not to print it," Uncle Miltie reminded him. "Which is like showing a starving man a—a raisin-pumpernickel bagel and telling him he can smell, but not taste it."

Her uncle looked at Gracie. "For that matter, I saw you pick up your cell phone and put it in your pocket. Let's call Rocky now and invite him for a warm bagel, my dear."

Rocky arrived within five minutes. "Wait till you hear what news I have for you!"

Uncle Miltie choked on a swallow of coffee, giving Gracie the opportunity to say, "That condition seems to be catching."

"What?" Rocky didn't get the joke.

"You go first," she said in reply, smiling at him.

So he did. His news was startling. "Clark Harrington is wanted in Wyoming and Nevada—and goodness knows where else—for illegally using his considerable knowledge of computers to run several different scams. His legitimate jobs just serve as a screen."

"So, do you think it's possible this might mean those coins just could have been his?" Abe asked, looking askance.

Gracie stared at Rocky, hardly breathing until he said reassuringly, "I doubt he'll try to claim them now. He's certainly smart enough not to want the law looking into more of his activities than they already know about."

Then he added, "Now you have to spill your beans. Time's a'wasting.

The news waits for no man . . . or bagel . . . which reminds me—I'll have a poppyseed one. Make that two, with cream cheese."

Gracie read the following morning's paper before even drinking her first cup of tea. Rocky, she was pleased to see, had handled all the details involving Miles and Hattie's involvement with commendable discretion.

When she called his office, she left a message on his answering machine. "This is a brief message for an excellent editor and a truly great man. Thanks for being you, and for being my friend."

She was surprised, however, when he arrived less than a half hour later, asking, "You were pleased with the write-up?"

"Very, very much so." She had just taken from the oven a dish of stuffed French toast. "There's jam inside—do you want cherry or blackberry? I can make you a peach, if you like."

"How about one of each?"

Then, when she joined her uncle and her friend at the table, even Rocky looked thoughtful as Gracie prayed simply, "Thank You, Lord, for all the good things in life, especially for wonderful people who truly love their fellow men and try to live uprightly."

She paused for a moment before adding, "Thank You for blessing me with two such fine men sitting with me here at this table this morning." They echoed her soft amen, and Rocky reached for his fork with an expectant grin. "Boy oh boy!" he said happily.

There was fun and laughter as they finished their food. Gracie had expected to drive her uncle to the senior center, but Rocky insisted he'd do that, since it was on his way back to the office. She followed them out onto the porch, then turned to find her cat there at the door.

"I agree, Gooseberry, it's time to go for our walk. It's another beautiful day in Willow Bend, Indiana, and I feel refreshed. Come, let's enjoy it to the fullest."

She took his *meow* for an eager assent.

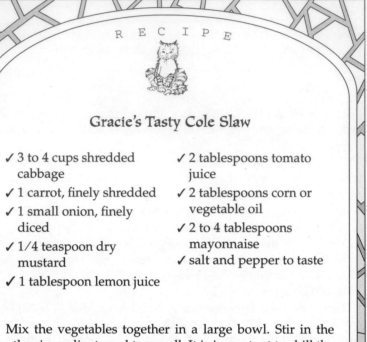

Gracie's Tasty Cole Slaw

✓ 3 to 4 cups shredded cabbage

✓ 1 carrot, finely shredded

✓ 1 small onion, finely diced

✓ 1/4 teaspoon dry mustard

✓ 1 tablespoon lemon juice

✓ 2 tablespoons tomato juice

✓ 2 tablespoons corn or vegetable oil

✓ 2 to 4 tablespoons mayonnaise

✓ salt and pepper to taste

Mix the vegetables together in a large bowl. Stir in the other ingredients and toss well. It is important to chill the mixture well before serving

Gracie says, "For an extra zing, sometimes I peel a Granny Smith apple and cut up half a cup of matchstick-fine slivers to throw in."

GUIDEPOSTS

The Doubtful Doctor

GUIDEPOSTS

CHURCH CHOIR
MYSTERIES™

The
Doubtful
Doctor

Eileen M. Berger

Guideposts®
CARMEL, NEW YORK 10512

www.guidepostsbooks.com

Guideposts Book & Inspirational Media Division
Series Editor: Michele Slung
Cover art by Stephen Gardner & Edgar Jerins
Cover design by Wendy Bass
Interior design by José R. Fonfrias
Interior cat illustrations by Viqui Maggio
Printed in the United States of America

*This novel is dedicated to our
three wonderful young granddaughters,
Mackenzie, Katherine and Dorothy Berger,
who aren't yet interested in reading it
—or are not yet able to—
but I hope someday they will want to do so.*

* * *

*Your grandfather and I are so very grateful
for having you in our lives,
and we love you dearly!*

Acknowledgments

WHAT A PRIVILEGE and joy it has been to get to know and to work with the wonderful people at Guideposts Book and Inspirational Media Division! They're not only excellent at their profession, but are approachable and helpful editorially and in other ways—including lifting up members of my family in their prayers.

Thank you, Elizabeth Kramer Gold, Michele Slung, Stephanie Castillo Samoy and Brigitte Weeks for your skill, patience and know-how—and for giving me the opportunity to write this, my fourth "Church Choir Mysteries" novel.

The
Doubtful
Doctor

One

GRACIE PARKS HATED BEING late for choir practice, but she remained in the doorway of her church's Family Activity Center as Marybeth Bower's car squealed into the parking lot and stopped. Her friend ran toward her. "Thanks for waiting, Gracie! I just got back from taking the twins to the doctor, and almost didn't come, since Barb makes us so aware of every split second when we're late. If we didn't have to sing, I'm sure she'd make the offenders stand in the corner!"

Gracie sympathized. "At least you've got a better excuse than I do. I had a long-distance call from a friend and could have hung up, but didn't."

"Of course not!"

Then Gracie thought to ask, "Are they very sick?"

Marybeth shook her head. "It was just a follow-up visit—but Dr. Hanley had been called earlier to the hospital for an emergency, so his office was full and we had to wait."

"I don't know how Al keeps up that pace! He really needs someone else in that practice. He even cancelled his vacation last summer, when everyone had that awful flu. He and Jean only managed to take a few days off later."

"Let's hope he gets away *this* year!"

As they entered the church, Barb Jennings, from her seat at the piano, called out, "Thank goodness you two are finally here! Hurry to your places, and just share with your neighbor as we finish going over the *second* of the hymns for Sunday."

Lester Twomley, seated directly behind Gracie, whispered as she took her seat, "Feeling pretty brave tonight, aren't you?"

She grinned at him, then quickly shifted her attention to singing the alto harmony for the last verse of "For the Beauty of the Earth."

"That was fine," Barb approved, now in her benign choir director persona. Everyone knew latecomers brought out the despot in her. "Do that well with 'Abide With Me,' our last congregational hymn, on page 137, and we can get right into practice for Sunday's anthem."

Gracie had always thrilled to this particular hymn. But there was sadness there, as well, for it had been the accompaniment to too many funerals, including her beloved mother's. Tonight, however, the choir sang the first and second verses so smoothly that Barb pronounced happily, "Splendid! Now get the purple book from your folders and turn to page. . ." She was flipping through her own copy. "Yes, page twenty-six."

There was a rustling of pages, accompanied by several soft groans about the new selection. Amy Cantrell asked, "Do we have to do all that 'Oo-ing' and 'Ah-ing' on page twenty-nine?"

"Of course we do. That's how it's written, so the composer wants it that way. But," Barb added kindly, "you're going to like it, once we finally get it right."

Tonight, there was less talking and joking than usual. Therefore the choir director had an easier time keeping them on track. Gracie knew Barb both loved her role as curator of the musical spirit of their church community and was exasperated by the need continually to ride herd. The choir was made up of so many personalities!

Barb looked around with a stern expression even though there was a warm twinkle in her eye. She knew her singers well. They still needed to go over one small section where several choir members weren't sure of their parts, but then they'd be finished.

And so they were.

Gracie walked down the steps from the choir loft with Marybeth. "Do you think Al and Jean might get out of town for a much deserved break?" she asked Marybeth.

"Well, they're scheduled to go to California next week to visit their son and daughter-in-law. Then they are all flying to Hawaii, where they have a time-share for a month. Isn't that great? I just hope my kids are completely over all their coughing by then!"

Gracie nodded. "I remember how I used to fret when Arlen could hardly sleep for all the hacking his poor little body was going through.

It's no fun having a sick child, and a willing doctor on call is what every parent wants and needs! But that means twenty-four hours a day, seven days a week, in order to be responsive to all the families in town for every 'emergency' sneeze or sniffle. It can't be easy—that much responsibility! No wonder real vacations for doctors come few and far between."

"Well, you're right, of course. But I think things are going to be different this time. Al and Jean are determined to make it happen. It'll take more than the twins' follow-up to put a crimp in their plans. Anyway, Al's made arrangements to have another doctor in for the month, a retired physician from Indianapolis. A Dr. Elder, I believe his name is."

Gosh, Gracie thought to herself, that's interesting. She'd long ago had a dear friend by that name who became a doctor. "Did he give a first name?"

"I think Al said it was Tom."

Tom Elder. Dr. Thomas Elder. *Hmmm*. It's a common enough name, I suppose, Gracie considered. She now asked, "Is he a general practitioner, like Al?"

"Al didn't say—just that Tom was an old friend and an excellent physician. It seems this Dr. Elder retired a bit early. The story is, I believe, that his wife had been quite ill, and he chose to care for her himself.

"At this stage in his career what he does is go out for a month or more at a time to 'spell other doctors'—that's how Al put it—if they need a break for some reason."

∾

It was a lovely evening, making Gracie almost wish she'd walked to church just to have the pleasure of strolling home again. However, she also enjoyed slowly driving Fannie Mae, her trusty old blue Cadillac, through the peaceful streets of Willow Bend, and in no time she was pulling into her driveway.

Entering her kitchen, she was warmly greeted by her uncle. George Morgan was an octogenarian known to one and all as Uncle Miltie, owing to a certain fondness for bad jokes, like a long-ago comedian of that name. He'd come to live with his niece after his wife had died, when Gracie already was a widow living on her own in this large, comfortable house.

The two of them had settled into a relationship that was a joy to each. He provided the sense of humor, not to mention his former contractor's handyman skills, while Gracie took care of his still-zesty appetite with all the culinary love she could muster.

"You're early! Is that a good sign or bad?"

"Very good. Everyone was on his or her best behavior, and we whizzed through even the most difficult numbers."

"No high-faluting attitude from la belle Estelle, our own dumpy diva?"

"Not a one! Nor from Barb, though both Marybeth and I managed not to arrive until the middle of one of this Sunday's hymns!"

He set the carton of peppermint ice cream he was carrying on the kitchen table, leaving the scoop sticking up as he headed for the wall calendar. "*That* deserves to be recorded."

She laughed as he put a big exclamation point on the square for the day. "Just you and I will know what it means."

Marge, looking her usual carefully made-up and coiffed self, breezed in a few minutes later, after parking at her house next door. "Why'd you leave in such a rush?" she wondered, as she tucked back a stray hair.

Gracie smiled at her best friend. "I don't know. Does there have to be a reason for everything? I was talking to Marybeth and then, *wham*, I was home. I guess Fannie Mae was eager to rest her tires and enjoy the beautiful evening, or maybe she was reading her owner's mind."

"It is a glorious night, isn't it? A full moon and so many stars!" Marge's own eyes glowed brightly, and Gracie knew that their brightness owed as much to Marge's zest for life as to her new mascara.

"Speaking of stars, how would you like one of these sugar cookies? I bought some wonderful old cutters at a yard sale last weekend. There's a man in the moon, too." She offered the jar to her two companions. Marge helped herself to a large heart while Uncle Miltie took three stars, wrapped them in a napkin and stuck them in his sweater pocket.

"Speaking of stars," began Uncle Miltie, "reminds me of Sherlock Holmes."

His two listeners groaned and rolled their eyes.

"It seems Holmes and Dr. Watson were one night forced to camp out," he told them. "Some hours later, Holmes awoke and nudged his faithful friend.

"'Watson, please look up and tell me what you see,' requested Holmes.

" 'Millions and millions of stars,' the good doctor replied.

" 'What does that tell you?'

"Watson thought for a minute. 'Astronomically, it tells me that there are millions of galaxies and potentially billions of planets. Theologically, I can see that God is all-powerful and that we are small. Meteorologically, I suspect that we will have a beautiful day tomorrow. What does it tell you, Holmes, old chap?'

"The great detective was silent for a minute, then spoke, 'Elementary, my dear Watson. Somebody has stolen our tent.' "

With that, after adding chocolate sauce to his dish of ice cream, Gracie's uncle headed for the living room. The two women, watching him fondly, could hear the overexcited tones of a sports announcer.

When he was past earshot, Marge said to Gracie, "He's doing a lot better, isn't he? I haven't noticed him using his walker as much recently."

"You're right. His arthritis was bothering him a lot over the winter, but he's much better now that it's warm. Although his jokes could use improving," she said, smiling.

They discussed a catering job that Gracie had agreed to take on. Loving to cook as she did meant she could contribute to the community, enjoy herself and earn money at the same time. Left comfortably well off at the death of her adored husband Elmo—in an awful car accident—and able always to count on her son Arlen, living in New York with his family, Gracie nonetheless liked feeling entrepreneurial.

Marge, who ran a small, eclectic gift shop on her own, understood her friend's need for a sense of independence—and challenge. Gracie was involved in the activities of Willow Bend at every level, giving of herself generously. Her catering was the frosting on the cake—and Gracie's cakes, of course, were legendary locally.

Then Gracie asked, "Had you heard that a retired doctor from Indianapolis will be coming to keep Al Hanley's practice going while he and Jean are vacationing?"

"Really? How old is he? Is he married?" Inadvertently, Marge fluffed her hair. "*Hmmm?*"

Gracie tried not to grin. Her friend's normal curiosity about any newcomer went off the charts at the possibility of a new male in town, and a professional one at that. "Marybeth mentioned his having taken early retirement in order to care for his sick wife."

"Wasn't that sweet of him?" Marge became dreamy-eyed at the thought. "I don't know many men who'd do that."

Gracie agreed. "He must love her very much. But he also may have wound up missing his work and feeling needed by more than one person. So he's willing to fill in at other doctors' offices."

"When's he coming? And where will he stay?"

She laughed. "I've shared the full extent of my knowledge, Marge, but we'll soon learn more."

꠸

Gracie didn't think to mention to her uncle the coming personnel shift at Dr. Hanley's practice until lunch the following day. Casting about for subjects to divert him, she came up with the news she'd heard from Marybeth.

Uncle Miltie, upon hearing the new doctor's name, sat there mulling over the information. "Thomas Elder. Tom Elder. Didn't you used to date someone by that name?"

Gracie had gotten up from the table and now responded while still facing the sink where she was putting their dirty plates. "For a while, during the last year or so of high school and beginning of college."

She turned to smile at him. "That's impressive, that you remember. You couldn't have met him more than a time or two."

"Nice guy, as I recall." He nodded, apparently satisfied his recollections were correct. "Tall, broad-shouldered. Wasn't he a football star or something?"

"If you remember him so well," she said dryly, "I'm glad there's so much on the plus side!"

"Your mom liked him—but told us that since you two seemed to be getting real serious, she was happy you'd decided on different colleges. She thought you needed to be exposed to more people before you decided for sure he was the one."

Gracie looked thoughtful, but didn't reply.

"Is that how it turned out? It must have, with each of you finding someone else. It's not unusual. . . ."

Gracie still did not respond, asking instead if he was planning to go to the senior center later in the afternoon. As for herself, she had a long list of tasks, many related to the catering job that she and Marge had discussed the previous evening.

"I'll be heading out soon," Uncle Miltie told her. "I think I'll stop at the library if Joe, who's picking me up, doesn't mind." Joe Searfoss and his wife Anna were among their closest friends, and hearing Joe's name reminded Gracie to call Anna later that afternoon.

Her large orange cat Gooseberry seemed restless. Maybe it was the siren call of the mild spring day—except he didn't seem to be able to decide whether he wished to be on the same side of the kitchen screen door as the birds or not.

This, however, was often a problem with cats.

She ignored his indecisive meows for fifteen minutes or so, then reached down to scratch his ears as he once again wove his way around and between her legs. "Yes, I do understand," she told him. "I need to get out and enjoy the glory of the afternoon as much as you do."

Seeing that her uncle had already left, she locked the door and slid the key into her pocket as she went down the steps. Gracie sighed, remembering how she and her late husband Elmo had seldom ever had to lock up. But things were different now, even in a small town that Uncle Miltie called "as close as you can get to heaven this side of the Pearly Gates."

On her walks, Gracie usually led the way. Sometimes, though, Gooseberry got to choose by a whiskery whim whether to go right or left at intersections. On this occasion it was he who made the turn that would take them past Cordelia Fountain's tourist home. The voluble—and occasionally volatile—blue-haired owner was out sweeping her porch and looked up as she saw Gracie and Gooseberry approaching.

"What a perfect day this is!" Gracie said to Cordelia.

"It certainly is," the tourist home owner agreed. "And I'm inspired to get everything just right before the doctor gets here."

"The . . . doctor?" Gracie was confused for a moment. Could Cordelia be ill? She looked fine and was, in fact, sweeping with what seemed like extra vigor.

"Oh, yes—didn't you know?" Cordelia loved the privilege of passing on news. "There's a physician coming from Indianapolis to take over Dr. Hanley's practice while he and his wife are on vacation.

"Laura—that's his nurse, you know, Laura Felix—called to ask if he—Dr. Thomas Elder—might stay here. Of course I said he could. The big front room, that one on the right," she motioned toward the two big lace-curtained windows on the second floor, "is all ready for him."

"That's nice," Gracie said. "I just hope it won't be too trying for you if he gets a lot of night calls, the way Al apparently does. Doctors do, you know."

"I don't think that'll bother me much. After all, if he's willing to help people who are sick, I should be able to put up with getting awakened by the phone during the night—especially since it's only for a month."

Besides which, Gracie thought, Cordelia would have more scoops as to what was afflicting the town's citizenry. "Telegraph, telephone and tell Cordelia" was Uncle Miltie's updating of the ancient joke that was old even for him, but still rang true.

Cordelia was, as Gracie well knew, never malicious in her fondness for gossip. The problem was, too often gossip seemed to have a life—and an agenda—its own!

They talked for another minute or two before Gracie and Gooseberry proceeded on. But she was now distracted from the spring scene and the beauties of the day by the what-if's of her Tom Elder's coming here to Willow Bend.

What if, indeed? She tried to rein in her growing curiosity. She told herself there had to be many men—other doctors, for that matter—who shared the same name.

Tom Elder. What *if*?

She was somewhat surprised that he'd be staying in a "tourist home"—as they all used to be called before becoming today's "bed-and-breakfasts." True, there was no motel right here in Willow Bend, and the only hotel had burned down sixty or seventy years earlier.

Still, if these two doctors were old friends, as people were saying, it seemed to her Al and his wife would have made their own house available.

The rest of her walk was uneventfully pleasurable. Since the mild weather had drawn many Willow Benders out into their yards, Gracie's greatest challenge was to get a good pace going and actually exercise.

Even Gooseberry seemed in an unusually sociable mood. She leaned over to scratch his ears as they entered the home stretch. "I saw you eyeing that bird, and I'm delighted you decided to show some self-restraint. After all, you don't see me chasing every neighbor I come across!"

2

"Want a piece of fruit or something to hold you over till supper?" Gracie asked, hearing the front door open. "I've got chicken stew I'll be reheating—but first I have a bit of correspondence to take care of."

He shook his head. "Joe brought me home by way of The Sweet

Shoppe, and I treated both of us to those delicious peanut butter shakes."

"In that case, we probably should eat dinner sometime in the middle of the night!"

"I think not!" He chuckled. "I got us the kiddie portions. So it was merely an appe-teaser!"

She looked at him and shook her head. "Okay, I'll assume you're not starving. Otherwise, we might have to turn you over to a medical school for scientific investigation."

Uncle Miltie looked at her in mild indignation. "What's Plan B? You obviously have more than letter-writing to attend to. Normally, my little indulgences don't put a crimp in our dinner plans. What's a tiny shake between friends? That's what I want to know!"

"I guess I should be grateful it wasn't a banana split!" Gracie laughed. "And your appetite is a marvel!"

He grinned at her.

"It's just that I've a lot of catching up to do and I'd like time to sort out just the right cards to send to Eternal Hope's shut-ins. Plus, I realize I neglected to send one to Paul, whose birthday's this Sunday."

"It is?" He looked shocked. "It hardly seems more than a couple months since our pastor last celebrated a birthday!"

Gracie looked at him with a wry expression. "It keeps taking less and less time for a year to pass, doesn't it?"

"You said it!" There was a sparkle in his eyes as he straightened his shoulders proudly. "Isn't it great that it doesn't show on you and me?"

"We'll keep on pretending it doesn't, won't we?" she vowed as she left the room.

Soon, as she was selecting cards from her collection of special greetings and prayers, she heard the steady buzz of her uncle's drill emanating from his workshop in the garage. She doubted it was a coincidence that he was out there right after she had mentioned Paul's imminent birthday.

It was fun to choose the right card for each of the three shut-ins and to write them personal notes, which she signed from both her uncle and herself. However, when it came to selecting the best and most appropriate sentiment for Paul Meyer, their young and boyish minister, she was having a hard time making up her mind. She decided, instead, to write a few of the letters she owed, including one to her little grandson Elmo.

The evening meal was in preparation by the time Uncle Miltie appeared again. He announced, "They could have used me for Dr. Pavlov's dog experiments. Even after that milkshake, I started salivating when I smelled that chicken heating up!"

She smiled as he went to the sink to wash his hands. "I have a favor to ask when you're done—or after we eat, if you'd prefer. I can't decide whether to send Paul a Scripture card or one of those two humorous ones lying beside your plate. Most people would probably opt for one of the religious cards, just because he's a preacher, so that makes me think a funny one might be a better choice. Why be so predictable? It's not as if being a minister means you don't have a sense of humor!"

"That's a mighty weighty responsibility to have hanging over my head," he said, picking up the top card. A grin covered his face as he read it, and he glanced her way as he reached for the next one. It, too, made him smile broadly.

Chuckling, he held out the second. "Truthfully, they both are fine, but I like this one."

"You sign it first," Gracie told him, handing him a pen from her apron pocket.

He frowned thoughtfully before scrawling a few lines under the inside drawing of an angel with a lopsided halo and a missing front tooth. "How's this sound?" he asked, reading—

"These two older codgers,
(one of whom admits to being firmly in that category)
are wishing you a most enjoyable birthday and year
—and we know what 'enjoyable' is!"

Gracie laughed and took it from him. He'd signed his full name, George Oswald Mason.

Below that she placed a simple *Gracie*, followed by *So go for it, Friend!*

Two

ROCKY GRAVINO APPEARED as if by magic at the front door just as she was serving dessert. With his usual lack of hesitation, he accepted Gracie's invitation to join them. "Why don't you have some of this chicken first," she urged him, and met with little resistance.

Taking the seat across the table from hers, he announced, "Cordelia called me about the new doctor who's going to be staying at her place. Sounds like an interesting fellow, so I thought I'd check him out myself."

"With so much curiosity building up about Al Hanley's replacement, you may find yourself arriving on Cordelia's front porch alongside a delegation! Especially if she keeps sending out bulletins!"

"Well, the press takes precedence," grandly proclaimed the proprietor of the *Mason County Gazette*. "I may sleep, but the news never does. And editors have sharp elbows when it comes to nudging aside the competition. First, the news, then the Welcome Wagons."

"*Hmmph!* Sometimes you might as well call it 'snooze!' That's 'news' with an *s*, in case you missed my point," Uncle Miltie chortled.

Gracie now broke in. "Has Dr. Elder actually arrived in town yet?"

"Nope." Rocky took a bite of chicken before adding, "Cordelia's not sure just when to expect him, but she's going to let me know when he arrives. She seems to think that the sooner I receive the call, the better the chance of having a good spread in the paper that will include prominent mention of his choice of lodging, not to mention his hostess."

"She's probably praying he gets there immediately," Uncle Miltie observed. "I've never known such a tireless publicity hound in all my born days!"

"It's more than just dollars and cents to her," Gracie reminded him. "It's the history that's involved in that lovely old house of hers. That's what means so much to her and why she craves continual coverage."

"Yeah. She's insatiable," Rocky agreed. "And I'm the one to know it! What's more, anything that gets published is only incentive to think of something else to merit yet another article."

Both Gracie and Uncle Miltie sighed simultaneously in commiseration. In a small town like Willow Bend, Indiana, one's friends and neighbors had habits, virtues and vices that were all too familiar.

"Anyway," Rocky went on, "it's not like Gracie, whose mystery-solving talents deserve more column inches than she'd ever permit me to devote to her."

Gracie blushed faintly.

Her uncle reached over to pat her hand where it lay on the edge of the table. "We're just grateful that, at least thus far, that this household's amateur sleuth is one who's suffered no dire consequences from her adjunct police work."

Gracie sighed again as both men watched her affectionately. It wasn't her fault. She was always just minding her own business when troubling events occurred and, somehow, with her generous spirit and sympathetic manner, she found herself drawn into other people's problems!

Now Rocky asked, oblivious to the effect he'd already created, "Do you know for sure if this doc's your old beau?"

She glared at her uncle. "Someone's been speaking out of turn. . . ." If she'd been faintly pink before, she was rosy now. Even her ears gently burned. Uncle Miltie, how *could* you? she silently railed.

"Not at all," he insisted. "I just mentioned that Tom Elder was easy to remember 'cause you used to date someone with that name."

Rocky now looked at her, started to say something and stopped. Then he grinned.

This is too much, Gracie thought. I've not even had time to examine my own feelings about the possibility that Tom Elder might be coming to Willow Bend, and here they both are, watching my reactions as if I were under a microscope!

Pushing back her chair, she got up and headed for the kitchen counter. On it was the apple crisp she'd made to use up the last of the season's winesaps she'd been keeping in storage.

As casually as possible, she changed the subject. Her mother, she told them, had made this dessert using fruit from old gnarled trees in their back yard. "She never did it often enough to suit me. Sometimes just a whiff of cinnamon and apples baking is like having a glimpse of her spirit. Smells and memories are so mingled, you know."

The two men agreed that this was so, and Gracie knew they had silently agreed to drop the subject.

At least for the time being. *Whew*, Gracie thought.

During the night it began to rain. It stayed damp and gray until midnight Sunday. At the service, the choir's anthem, as well as their special selections honoring Paul's birthday, went stirringly. For her part, Gracie felt recharged. *Thank You, Lord*, she murmured. *Sometimes singing is truly a gift of joy, and Your love makes the harmony perfect.*

Just before the congregation stood to leave the sanctuary, Paul invited everyone to join him for the regular coffee and cake in the activity center, adding the fact that extra treats had been laid. "If you don't help me celebrate, I might have to dip into the collection baskets to buy larger trousers! I mean, I'm grateful you want to make my birthday special, but just remember I've got no clothing allowance!"

"I'm so glad you're here today, Gracie," Cordelia Fountain said, as she stopped Gracie en route to the coffee table.

"I almost always am, Cordelia," she replied. "You know that. Just about as regular as clockwork."

Suddenly Gracie's smile wavered as her eyes met the incredibly warm brown ones of a tall man standing between the tourist home owner and Barb Jennings.

"This is Dr. Thomas Elder, and he enjoyed the music so much this morning, he's wondering if it would be possible to sing in the choir during the month he's here. I told him we'd love to have him."

Could this be businesslike Barb Jennings—she of the drill sergeant demeanor when it came to errant members of her choir—now batting her eyelashes? "Well, Cordelia," Barb said, "even though I'm the choir director and you're not, I have to say I agree with you entirely."

The newcomer reached out and took Gracie's hand. "It's good to be here in Willow Bend, Gracie. And thank you, Barb, for agreeing to have me."

Gracie looked at him and said, "We think the world of Al and are grateful you'll be filling in for him while he's away."

"I know from experience how difficult it can be when a town's busy practitioner leaves for a month."

He met her gaze. She pulled her hand gently away from his clasp. Was that the hint of a wink? Gracie thought it had been and, inwardly, she chuckled. Her old and once very dear friend had changed very little. But where was his wife? Was she too much of an invalid even to attend church?

Yet, if he was staying at the tourist home, he might very well be on his own. After all, Cordelia had not mentioned a reservation for a Mrs. Elder.

Other members of the congregation now began to gather around Dr. Elder. This gave Gracie the opportunity to slip off to begin helping in the kitchen. She'd presumed that Marge would turn up to help, then thought what an unrealistic expectation that was. Here was a good-looking new man, albeit a married one, and Marge liked window-shopping almost as much as she did buying things to take home.

"We're always young as long as we keep learning from experience," a voice next to her suddenly said.

Gracie recognized the words and replied, "I remember that line, Tom. It's from our senior play. You were the hero's best friend, who kept dispensing wisdom."

"Well, I may not have been wise myself back then, but at least I knew my lines."

"Mine was only a bit part."

"You were cute enough to steal the show, as I recall."

"*Me?*" She looked around.

"You are the only one I see here from that off-off-off and way-beyond-Broadway production."

He could always make her laugh, she remembered. As Tom was beginning to say something else, Rocky suddenly materialized next to him, asking, "Any chance of my getting a cup of coffee, Gracie?"

Even if he wasn't a regular attendee at Eternal Hope's Sunday morning worship, Rocky turned up there often enough to know that the custom was serve-yourself.

But her intuition told her his interruption wasn't entirely about coffee, so she filled a cup and handed it to him.

He nodded his thanks to her and said, "I'll come with you," then nodded curtly at Tom, who looked startled.

At the refreshments table there was a steady stream of people arriving and departing. Gracie, seeing that she could be useful, began replacing slices of cake and setting out more cups as quickly as they were removed. As a reward, she drank in the sound of happy conversation and laughter, a harmony that was as precious to her as music.

She was so busy she didn't notice that Tom Elder had left. By the time she'd helped clear away everything, there were, in fact, only a few people remaining.

Seeing her, Paul came over and embraced her. "So far this is one of the nicest birthdays I've ever had, Gracie, and I can't thank you and the other kitchen helpers enough."

"You have already," Gracie told him. "You have a special place in the heart of each person here, and seeing your pleasure in our celebration of you is all the 'thanks' necessary."

"I was hoping there might be something I could do to help, but I don't see anything left to be taken care of." Marge now joined them, and both women assured the minister that no one expected him to be pitching in with the clean-up on the occasion of his birthday.

As Paul went off in the direction of his office and Marge and Gracie headed out of the building, Marge noticed the absence of Fannie Mae in the nearly empty parking lot.

"Would you like a ride home?" she asked.

"This has turned out to be too lovely a day not to be walking," Gracie answered. "I'll get home under my own steam, thanks."

"How did you get here, anyway?"

"I wanted to walk, so Uncle Miltie went to the phone and asked Rocky to pick him up. That's one way to get that old sinner to attend services."

Gracie wasn't surprised to discover Marge and Uncle Miltie already playing Scrabble by the time she arrived home. The unexpected sight was finding Tom Elder with them, sleeves rolled up almost to his elbows, and as deeply involved as they.

Her uncle, however, was loudly protesting, "That's unfair, Doc, using Latin names for parts of the body!"

"No more unfair than your using that whatever-it's-called type of commercial screw! And *mallei* is the plural form of the name of the outermost bone in the middle ear, not just a Latin term."

Since no one was hungry after all the pastoral birthday treats, Gracie joined the game and the four of them played one more round. Marge won by just two points when she added her final *J* to a free *O*.

"Are you sure JO is a real word?" Tom challenged. But together, all three, who played frequently, declared it to mean *sweetheart* or *beau*.

Their visitor now got up, apologetically covering an obvious yawn with the palm of his hand. "I'd better get myself back to my room and start unpacking and organizing."

"Have you seen much of our town yet?" Marge asked.

"Not really. It was after dark when I arrived last night, and then I went to church this morning."

"Well, look . . . ," Marge began.

But Uncle Miltie was pushing back his chair. "What about my riding around with you and filling you in on places and things?"

"We could all go!" Marge looked hopeful. "The more the merrier!"

Tom's smile took in everyone around the table. "I'd like to take a raincheck, if that's okay. Right now, I think it's best for me to just go back to the tourist home, get settled in and hope for a good night's rest. I need to be fresh and ready to go with Al to the hospital for rounds in the morning, then spend the rest of the day with him in his office.

"Thank goodness his nurse will be on duty with me all month, for every practice has its own way of doing things."

"Well, Laura Felix will keep you straight if anyone can!" Uncle Miltie said. "You can bet on that."

Tom stood there by the door looking quizzical. "Should I take that as comfort? Or a warning?"

"That'll depend," Uncle Miltie replied with a sly grin. "She's as sharp as a dagger, but less likely to draw blood."

Gracie raised an eyebrow. Marge giggled.

"For that matter, she could probably handle the office herself if she were licensed to see patients—at least *she* probably thinks she could."

"Well, then, I can only do my best—and also pray for guidance. Thanks for the heads-up."

"You have the right idea," Gracie told him. She had followed him out onto the porch and down the steps to the walk. "We'll all be praying for a good beginning to your work here."

"I appreciate that." He draped his arm loosely around her shoulders in what she was sure was just a friendly thankyou. "Bye for now, Gracie. And thanks."

Marge was standing in the doorway. "What a dreamboat—and a doctor, too!" She looked accusingly at her friend. "And you never even mentioned him to me."

"Nothing to mention," Gracie said as off-handedly as possible. "We knew each other all those years ago, before meeting the people we married. And that's both the long and the short of it. Do you want me to start digging up some of those forgotten skeletons in *your* closet?"

"But . . . ," Marge began.

"Period," said Gracie firmly. "End of discussion."

"Well," said Marge, her eyes suddenly gleaming with mischief, "I don't care. If any of my skeletons looked like that, I'd be handing you the shovel, that's all I can say!"

Uncle Miltie was already ensconced in his favorite recliner in front of the TV. Marge now asked, "What have you got planned for the rest of the day, Gracie?"

Gracie glanced up at the antique schoolhouse clock on the wall and told her, "First of all, I'm calling Arlen and Wendy and little Elmo to find out how things are going in New York City. I sent them a tin of cookies last week and I want to get my grandson's verdict: Does he like chocolate or butterscotch chip the best?"

"I wasn't thinking about that every Sunday activity of yours." Marge sighed. "I guess I ought to go home and phone my cousin, as well. I keep thinking I'll get over to Indianapolis to visit her, but the problem is I'm busy all week, and then there's choir on Sundays."

After Marge had helped herself to a couple of licorice drops from the bowl in the hall, she left with a cheery wave. Gracie realized it was a relief to be alone, yet no surprise. Old friends and new friends: Suddenly she was feeling it all to be too much, and she knew just the antidote.

"Hi, Grandma!" She'd dialed her son's Manhattan number and now heard Elmo's beloved voice. "Hey, Mom—Dad! It's Grandma!"

"It certainly is, my darling. How are you?"

"Good, Grandma. I saw Mommy dancing." Wendy, Gracie's daughter-in-law, had her own studio where she taught, in the apartment building where they lived.

"That's lovely. Was it fun?"

"I wanted to dance, too," he confided.

"You're growing up to be such a wonderful boy, Elmo! No wonder we all love you so much!" She laughed with unalloyed pleasure. Being a grandma was about the best job she could imagine.

Then, before she could say a proper good-bye to the child, Arlen came on the line, teasing, "What crimes are crying out to be solved in Willow Bend at the moment?"

She laughed. "Not a thing wrong in this corner of·Indiana, dear. The only mystery here is Uncle Miltie's appetite. How about up there?"

"All under control, as far as I can tell."

"That's the way I hope it always will be for you, even if, when we talk about 'control,' we mean what the good Lord's wishes are for us."

He said with audible pride, "You'll be happy to know, Mom, that we haven't missed church and Sunday school for weeks and weeks now. We even went this morning, though I'll confess that it was such a heart-stopping first-breath-of-spring morning that my attention wavered a bit. Central Park has some pretty beautiful spots."

"Little Elmo and I explored quite a few of them on my last visit. Just remember, we have the good Lord to thank for springtime, as well as every other blessing."

Gracie heard her son chuckle.

She added, "I'm pleased that you enjoy going, dear, especially when I remember how often you used to balk, especially on bright spring Sunday mornings like this. All in all, though, I don't think your dad's and my insistence hurt you too much."

"Praise the Lord, it didn't." He was laughing as he said that, and Gracie joined him.

Suddenly Uncle Miltie appeared in the doorway, asking, "Is that my great-nephew you're talking to?"

She nodded. But when she handed the phone to him, his first comment to Arlen was, "Did your mom tell you about the old boyfriend who's suddenly come on the scene?"

Gracie reached for the instrument. "If *that's* what you wanted to say, I'm taking this back!"

As he lifted the receiver beyond her reach, she managed to hear her son. "Hold on tight to that phone, Uncle Miltie. You've got my curiosity up! What's *really* going on down there in Indiana?"

It was only after another few minutes that she could retrieve the telephone and attempt to tell her side of the story. "It's true that Tom

Elder and I knew one another back in high school . . ." She took a breath. "And we did go out together . . ."

"And that's practically the first she's admitted to actually dating the guy," her uncle shouted loudly enough to be heard all the way to New York, even without benefit of the telephone.

She rolled her eyes. "And we were in one play together. . . ."

"My mother the actress!" Arlen teased. "I'm learning all kinds of things."

"He's a retired physician and is filling in for Al Hanley, who's finally managing to get the time off he so well deserves. Dr. Elder's got a room at Cordelia's for the month, and she brought him with her to church today.

"And it certainly wasn't I who invited him here for Scrabble this afternoon. I arrived back home after a nice walk, and you could have knocked me over with a feather when I saw the three of them huddled over the table. Marge was all wide-eyed and flirting shamelessly, even though she knows full well Dr. Elder is married, with a sick wife. Your uncle couldn't pull off looking innocent, that's for sure."

"So he's the little guy with the bow and arrow?" Arlen chuckled.

"If so, he's the most unlikely looking Cupid in the world! Right now Uncle Miltie has on a blue denim shirt and red suspenders and his smelly old house slippers."

Arlen asked more seriously, "So what's his story now? How does he fit into your extremely full and proper life?"

Gracie was serious, too. "He doesn't need to. We were friends those decades ago, but then I met and fell in love with your father. And Tom married his wife. I've neither seen nor heard from him until now, so you can rest assured, dear son of mine, that there's no fitting 'into' involved. Don't worry."

"Oh, I wasn't worrying." Arlen hesitated a moment.

"Yes?"

"Just one more question," he said. "What does Rocky think of Dr. Elder?"

"I'm sure they'll be great friends once they get to know one another."

"Ha!" exclaimed Uncle Miltie. "Well, I asked him to join us after church. But when he heard I'd invited Dr. Elder, too, he unceremoniously and discourteously suggested I ride with my new friend, instead."

"Uncle Miltie!" Gracie protested.

Arlen, who'd been listening to the exchange, could be heard coughing.

"You two!" she exclaimed. "I'm going to hang up, Arlen, and go shortsheet your uncle's bed. Unless you think of something more drastic that isn't illegal."

Arlen Parks was definitely his mother's son. "I'm praying for you, Mom," he told her.

But he couldn't keep from adding, "Just remember, if you land up there, the food in jail won't be up to your peerless standards!"

Three

GRACIE WAS ON THE SCHEDULE to deliver the flowers from the church service to shut-ins, which took most of the following morning as she visited three different Mason County nursing homes. *Lord, thank You for bringing me to these new and old friends. They remind me that the golden years shine the most brightly when Your love provides the illumination.*

Jennie Butzak, at her last stop, was so frail at ninety-five that she rarely got to church anymore.

"I don't want to bother people, making them pick me up and bring me back again," she'd just said to Gracie. "I don't hear half of what's said from the pulpit, anyway. But, oh, how I miss worshiping with those people I love!"

"I know what you mean. Even though I go to church with my son's family when visiting them in New York, and the sermon's always good, it's just not the same when the congregation is made up of strangers."

"Gracie, I take comfort from the fact that I had perfect attendance in Sunday school and church for fifty-three years. I hope you don't think it's too prideful of me."

Gracie nodded, feeling moved by her friend's devotion. "Of course not. I remember the standing ovation when that was announced."

"It wasn't necessary, of course, but I . . ." Deeper wrinkles creased Jennie's forehead as she sought the right words. "I just hope it made some of the younger people see that it can be done."

Gracie had reached out and gently squeezed the thin, blue-veined, arthritic-knuckled hand, leaning over to kiss Jennie's wrinkled cheek.

The hospital was also on Gracie's schedule. Phyllis Nickolson was there with her son Darren, who'd been brought in two days before, so dehydrated and lethargic from flulike symptoms that he needed intravenous liquids and constant observation.

"It's so good to see you, Gracie," Phyllis said in an almost-whisper, so as not to awaken the little fellow.

She'd stood up to hug her friend. "I understand that Paul's birthday party went well."

"Very well indeed. He's a son and brother to all of us, truly a pastor to feel proud of."

Phyllis looked at Gracie, glad to be reminded of the normal goings-on beyond the hospital walls. It was one thing to be the switchboard operator here, and another to be tending a sick child of her own within its precincts.

"Here we are!" came a cheerful voice from the doorway. The women turned as Dr. Albert Hanley came striding in and reached for Phyllis's hand.

"I understand from Nancy," he said, motioning toward the nurse who'd followed him and Tom Elder into the room, "that Darren's doing great."

He beamed. "And I'm happy to take a little of the credit, while giving the rest to our dear Lord."

Phyllis looked down upon her still-sleeping son, lying there so motionless. "I do hope so." She brushed her hand tenderly against his flushed cheek.

Al now introduced Dr. Elder to her, and started to introduce Gracie, as well. But Tom, who'd already shaken hands with Phyllis, said, as he accepted Gracie's, "I know this friend of yours from decades ago."

Nancy Bixler looked fascinated by that bit of information. Dr. Hanley, meanwhile, was checking over the child's chart and explaining to Darren's mother about Dr. Elder's temporary duties.

"We'll be back here in maybe thirty minutes," Al added, "which will give our boy a bit more rest before we examine him. No sense waking him now, since we still have several other patients to check on before heading for the office."

Gracie sat down to continue her visit, but made a point of leaving before the half-hour was up. She saw the doctors again as she neared the lobby. They came down the hallway from the other wing and Tom waved.

She waved back, and they disappeared into the elevator.

On the way home, she almost didn't remember to stop at the post office to buy the stamped post cards Uncle Miltie had asked her to pick up. The problem was, he'd never asked her for them before, so it was easy to forget now.

Uncle Miltie's involvement with the mail had changed abruptly after Harold Mayhew, the elderly fellow who still did maintenance work at the town hall, had last fall won a ten-day Caribbean cruise with his very first entry in a sweepstakes! Of all people in town, he'd seemed just about the most unlikely to enjoy such a windfall. However, friends had lent him luggage and helped him get outfitted for the trip and off he'd gone!

He'd come back with not only a wonderful tan but countless stories of places he'd been and things he'd seen, with awed accounts of the food, entertainment and people aboard the ship.

From what Gracie understood, ever since then a number of the men at the senior center were now spending much of their time trying their luck with entering sweepstakes and contests!

Certainly, this was what had begun Uncle Miltie's "addiction," as his niece now referred to it when teasing him. He'd even signed up for one of those newsletters written for serious sweepstakes participants. Thus far, his total winnings consisted of a stuffed brown plush walrus, a bright orange cap with the logo of some kind of motor oil, and a T-shirt advertising a well-known laundry product—size extra-large and coming down below his hips.

Gracie gave him his fifteen dollars' worth of postcards before checking the refrigerator. She was grateful she'd prepared far more spaghetti sauce than they could eat two days earlier. Now she needed only to simmer it slowly with additional seasonings. A cut-up onion and a large can of chili beans, and it was transformed into a tasty lunch, bringing not only compliments from Uncle Miltie but also a request for seconds. And thirds.

Crisp soda crackers were the only accompaniment he desired. "I'm not saying I won't maybe eat a bowl of ice cream later," he told her when she inquired about dessert, "but, as of right now, I'm not only stuffed, but totally satisfied. Three helpings will do it, no question.".

As she walked behind his chair on her way to take the dishes to the sink, she paused. "I've been blessed in that both you and El have always appreciated the simple dishes I prepare as much as you would after an elaborate banquet."

"I've concluded, my dear," he replied, "that love is the single greatest ingredient in cooking, just as it is in relationships. If someone enjoys cooking for those they cherish, it shows."

"You're right, Uncle Miltie."

She added one more word. "Again." He blushed with pleasure.

Then they both laughed as he pushed his chair back and got up. "Anything you'd like help with?"

"Not a thing. After all, you did a lot of work out in the yard this morning."

Looking down at Gooseberry, who'd finished his lunch as well, she told him, "I don't expect you to help with the dishes either, my furry friend."

Soon, Gracie was finished cleaning up and ready to bring the phone to the table to start making calls, the first one to the church office.

The secretary answered with her usual brisk efficiency, "Eternal Hope Community Church, Pat Allen speaking. May I help you?"

"Hi, Pat. This is Gracie."

"Hello, Gracie! The choir outdid itself yesterday, and I think, food-wise, we really gave Paul a rousing vote of confidence. There was practically a cake for every year God's blessed him with to date."

"Well, at least he didn't have to blow out candles on each and every one of them!"

Pat laughed. Then her voice changed. Obviously someone else had just entered the office.

"It's Gracie on the phone. . . ."

"Ah, then I want to talk with her, too—when you're finished." Paul's tone was respectful. "Don't worry, I can wait."

Pat spoke again to Gracie, "Paul just came in and would like to speak with you."

"Fine, put him on."

She waited until she heard him take the phone. "Hi, Paul. How are you feeling now that you're a whole year older?"

"Definitely heavier, if not wiser. But, really, the joy for me comes in sharing my birthday with all the church members. So I don't care how often they come on the calendar!"

"Well, as one of your flock, Paul, I can tell you that it wouldn't suit me—or any of us—if you were to age at double or triple the rate we do."

They both laughed. Then Gracie got down to business. "I think, despite her protests that it's too much trouble, we should occasionally help Jennie Butzik get to church. I know how it is to miss that special warmth and blessed feeling one gets worshiping in a well-loved church. Just because someone's old and weak doesn't mean he or she isn't any longer a full-fledged member here. Jennie misses us. And we miss her!"

"You're right," Pastor Paul agreed. "I can see that we must make more of an effort to convince her to come."

At that moment Uncle Miltie came into the kitchen and motioned to the phone. "Is that Paul you're talking to?"

After assuring Paul she would work on it, Gracie told Paul Uncle Miltie wanted to talk to him, too, and handed the phone over.

She was surprised to hear him say, "I was wondering if you could stop by here on your way home, Paul. . . . No, nothing's wrong. It's just that I made a little something for your birthday and would like you to have it. . . . Oh, it's not much, but I just didn't want to bring it with me to church."

Gracie now recalled having heard sawing and hammering in the garage, and she'd smelled paint, too. But she hadn't asked what he was up to since he obviously meant for her to be surprised, as well.

Late that afternoon, Paul leaned his bike against the front porch. "*Yoo hoo!*" he called out, only to see Uncle Miltie emerge from the garage carefully carrying a large square structure.

"That's beautiful," the young minister declared, seeing what Gracie's uncle was carrying. It was a five-tiered, green-painted martin house with its silver-gray shingled roof.

Uncle Miltie held it out, cautioning, "Better hold it by this wire at the top. I think the paint's all dry, but no use taking chances."

"You made this for me?" He looked at Gracie's uncle with respect. "You know, you could sell these as fast as you could make them."

"But then it would be work." The older man was trying not to show his pleasure. "I've constructed houses and garages and all kinds of buildings most of my adult life, and I think I'm entitled now to make things for people I love, just 'cause I love them."

"I will treasure it always."

Their pastor turned the gift around, examining it from all sides.

297

"But I'm also going to need your advice as to where to put it in my yard. From what I understand, I *think* this should be up on a pole, and not too close to trees or tall structures, right?"

"Right! And look, if you're heading home now, I could maybe come with you and we could make that decision. We could determine just how long that pole should be. . . ."

Gracie smiled, watching them leave together, talking nonstop as Paul pedaled and Uncle Miltie walked alongside, the martin house cradled on the handlebars. All her life she'd known Uncle Miltie as a builder, a man using tools to make things. Since he'd come to live with her, he'd repaired and fixed and done any number of projects here at her house as well as for many neighbors and friends.

But she had not known him to put together one of these martin houses, which looked exactly like the one he'd made for his wife a good fifty years ago. Perhaps that one even still stood on the pole in the backyard of the house he'd sold when he came to live with Gracie.

She brushed a tear from her eye, realizing that, yes, he certainly did love this earnest young man, as he'd come to love this town and this church.

The martin house would be right at home on the property of the man who cared for the souls and spirits of the Eternal Hope Community Church members, Gracie and her uncle included.

෴

It was after breakfast the following morning that she had her first look at a different project he'd been working on. He came in from the garage carrying a somewhat kidney-shaped, highly polished flat object that was at least two and a half feet long and only about half that wide.

"Here's something else I've been doing, Gracie."

"Well, it's made of lovely cherry lumber, and the finish looks great, but—I'm afraid I can't figure out what it's for."

"Come with me." He walked across the kitchen and into the other room, toward the larger recliner.

"You know that's my very favorite chair, where I like to sit much of the time. But, when I'm working on sweepstakes entries and contests, I've mostly been doing that at the table.

"However, I had this idea for making a handy laptop desk." He arrived at his chair and sat down, carefully lifting his project and laying it across the arms of the chair, the smaller concave curve close to his abdomen and the outward-curving one above his knees.

"As you see," he told her, tilting it upward a bit, "I've designed it so it's stable and so papers, postcards, envelopes and pens won't fall off into my lap while I'm working."

"Wow!" she said, whistling. "Pretty clever."

"Yep, and I'll be able to work on entries and still see TV."

He picked up his copy of the lists and descriptions of current sweepstakes from the floor.

Gracie asked as he started to turn from one page to another, "What are these entries with X's through them?"

"On that particular one, it's to show that I'm not interested. But on this one," he said, pointing, "I can only send one entry per household, which I've done already."

He then indicated one on the opposite page. "However, for this, which I'd really like to win, I've sent in three for me and three for you and two each for Arlen and Wendy and little Elmo."

"That's very generous."

"I'll be every bit as happy if you win."

"Well, I for one will certainly split the goodies with you if I do," she declared, then laughed. "Unless it's another of those caps!"

"Hey!" he told her. "We can share—you wearing it one day and me another. No need for either of us to get sunburned or cold!"

"Okay. But it's a good thing I'm no fashion plate like Marge! Sweepstakes style leaves a lot to be desired!"

Her uncle chuckled. "I love you, Gracie, my dear, and think you look gorgeous, whatever you have on."

⁂

What Uncle Miltie had said stuck in her mind. The unconditional love families gave was what made them such powerful forces. She'd certainly been blessed by having parents who'd deeply loved one another and their children.

She could hardly remember her father coming into the house without calling, "Dot, where are you?" if her mother wasn't right there in the kitchen. When her mother would emerge to greet him, they'd always hug and kiss, and somehow Gracie got the idea that all families were like that.

After all, Gracie and her brother William Arlen Stephens, who'd died of cancer in middle age, had always experienced unconditional love and support.

Tom Elder's family had not been like that. Gracie had been

shocked, almost horrified even, when Tom had taken her home with him for the first time. She had listened embarrassedly as his parents made belittling comments and nasty remarks not only to their kids, but to one another.

Tom, though, had not seemed aware of it—not then, anyway. But after being in her home a number of times, he'd stopped inviting her to his.

And another important thing: Neither he nor any of his family went to church, while everyone did in hers. At the time, this hadn't bothered her as much as it did her parents. Now she understood why, without consciously realizing it, she'd been surprised to see him in church on his first morning in Willow Bend.

Had he come because his landlady asked if he'd care to join her and it seemed only polite? Had he somehow learned from Cordelia that she, Gracie, went to that church? She remembered his vibrant singing voice. Was he now so committed to the Lord that joining a choir for a month seemed desirable to him?

Help me, Lord. I know You see into Tom's heart as You do into each and everyone's. Is he someone who's come back into my life for a purpose? Should I ask what's been happening in his marriage? I could tell him how gloriously satisfying and enriching my time with Elmo was. But who am I, even as an old friend, to meddle? All I know is that he seems kind and glad to be here and to see me. And he seems . . . alone.

She realized, to her surprise, as that day ended and the next began, that she was having difficulty keeping from thinking of him. For example, while fixing waffles for breakfast, she wondered if Tom was eating at Cordelia's. Or was he leaving there early to sit in the coziness of Abe's Deli? Or was he forced to drink the insipid coffee and cellophane-wrapped cakes of the hospital cafeteria when he made early rounds?

This is getting ridiculous! she scolded herself.

As this was a morning when Uncle Miltie went to the library to read to preschoolers, Gracie took him there a little before 10:30, then stopped at Miller's Feed Store. Hammie, who fortunately never seemed to mind that Hamilton, his given name, had been shortened to something that could have an unfortunate connotation, was lugging a heavy sack out to Mac Medline's car when she arrived.

"Hi, Gracie," he called. "Be right with you!"

"No hurry, Hammie. I just have to pick up some cat food."

He slammed the trunk closed, waved to Mac, and started up the ramp to the loading area where she was waiting. "I haven't seen Gooseberry for a while. But he must be happy as a clam, except he's a cat—what with the amount he's eating these days."

"Not really. He's always been big." What's Hammie talking about? she wondered.

"Maybe it just seems like only a little while since your uncle was here for more of these." He headed for Gooseberry's preferred brand and turned to grin crookedly. "Things do tend to get hectic around here! I lose track of time!"

"I can relate to that!" But her curiosity was up. "Did Uncle Miltie buy anything else while he was here?"

"Sure did. That's why I remember it. We'd just got a load of pet supplies, and I know he bought a flea collar, some vitamins, and let's see—also a toy or two from that rack over there."

Gracie had never suspected Hammie of being untruthful. But her uncle buying a toy for her cat seemed improbable. Especially since she'd seen nothing like that around the house. Also, it was Uncle Miltie who'd specifically reminded her to stop here for cans of food. Could Hammie have George Morgan confused with someone else?

But who else told such bad jokes that an entire town groaned at the punchlines before he could get them out? For someone to imitate his bad puns while buying cat food and toys would require motivation that Gracie simply couldn't imagine.

Vitamins? For Gooseberry?

That cat could run them all into exhaustion. And then some!

Four

GRACIE WAS STARTLED out of sleep by the boom-crack of an electrical storm she'd not heard coming. Gooseberry undoubtedly had been startled also. He moved slowly up along her blanket-covered form and waited until he was almost to her ear to give a loud, questioning, "Meow?"

"It's okay," she soothed, reaching out to stroke his head.

She turned to check the clock, surprised to find it was just a little before five. "I don't know about you, buster, but I'm going to try going back to sleep."

Which goal she didn't achieve, though she lay in bed for another half hour while the worst of the thunder and lightning passed. The torrents of rain continued falling, however.

"Well," she murmured, pushing back the sheet and sitting on the edge of her bed, "I doubt that the two of us will be going for a walk this morning, Gooseberry."

He raised his eyelids to half-mast, then yawned. Stretching lazily, he went back to sleep.

"You obviously don't care that I'm up. I suspect your cat dreams seem pretty important to you. But I know when you hear me in the kitchen, you'll remember that cat food is what matters most to you."

He opened one eye.

Gracie headed downstairs. She was followed by the soft thud-thud of a soon-to-be-breakfasting feline.

It was later that morning when the phone rang.

"It's for you, Gracie," Uncle Miltie called out to his niece, who was folding towels.

"Thanks. I'll take it from here."

It sounded as though he chuckled, but she wasn't sure why until after she'd picked up the phone.

"Hello?"

"Hi, Gracie."

It was Tom.

"I was just thinking about choir rehearsal. I should be able to make it. However, since this will be my first time, I wondered if I could pick you up, just to help smooth my way."

She laughed as she leaned against the window sill. "Sure."

"Thanks very much."

"You know it'll be my pleasure."

"Great! What time shall I pick you up? 6:45?"

"That would be fine. When do you think you might finish at the office?"

"Hopefully 5:30. But who knows? Yesterday it was over an hour later. Doctors never have exact schedules, you know!"

"Well, how about my holding dinner until about six o'clock—or 6:15 for that matter—which would still give you time to eat before leaving? Should you be really late, I'll simply slice off some of the roast and make a sandwich for you to eat while driving to the church."

There was the sound of a long sigh. Then he said, "That's the best offer I've had for ages. I'll be there as soon as I possibly can."

In the window's reflection, she caught herself smiling. She asked how his day had gone.

"Okay, so far," he told her. "And I now have an even better reason to buckle down and keep things moving."

She was about to respond when he added, "Thanks for the invitation, Gracie. I'll do my best to be there by six o'clock. With bells on."

"Honestly, there'll be nothing in this meal that will suffer if you're later than expected," she reassured him.

⚓

He arrived at 6:04. She figured it was buying the box of fancy chocolates that had kept him from getting there before the top of the hour.

She thanked him with the promise, "We'll sample these for dessert."

The laugh wrinkles at the outside corners of his eyes deepened. "You may do so, Gracie, but I've got a hankering for that pie on the counter. I smelled its delicious aroma even before coming through your door. I'll confess to hoping that's going to be offered as a far superior dessert."

"She's the best baker in Willow Bend!" Uncle Miltie said joining them. "Almost always wins a blue ribbon at the county fair for her fruit pie and maybe her coconut custard."

Ignoring his public relations push on her behalf, Gracie asked her uncle to lead them in prayer. "So," Uncle Miltie began promptly after the amen, "was I right about Laura Felix?"

Tom grinned crookedly. "I think I'm doing fine with the patients and most of the time I do well with Mrs. Felix, but," the right corner of his mouth turned up in what looked like a decidedly rueful smile, "I'm not sure she'd say the same. She's set in her ways, that's for sure."

"She's been with Al for over thirty years, and believes he's the greatest doctor in the world," Gracie told him as he passed her the broccoli. "I suspect she wouldn't be amenable to going along quietly with any changes of protocol, medication or manner."

"Well, you've got that right!" He idly poked several pieces of broccoli around on his plate before spearing one. "The first time, she even corrected me right there in front of the patient."

"Oh, my!" said Gracie.

"Now she writes things down on paper and insists on going over each complaint later. I must say it's a trying way of doing things."

"Al didn't warn you?" Uncle Miltie was curious.

"Oh, he mentioned that it might take awhile for the two of us to become a team. Still, he obviously appreciates her knowledge and concern for his patients."

"*Hunh!*" the older man snorted. "I'll tell you one thing. I don't expect to live long enough to see her choose to be a team with anyone but Al!"

"Oh, I don't know," Gracie put in. "She can, when she wants to, get along fine. She's been on the board at church and seems to have done a good job there."

"Then you must have a very firm chairman of that board, and treasurer and pastor—or whomever else she's accountable to. Otherwise, I'd have predicted she'd have taken over completely by now."

"She's tried to at times," Gracie admitted, "but there are others equally strong and determined."

He looked at her in awe. "And you are all still alive. And your church seems to be thriving!"

She laughed. "Alive, thriving and I, for one, try never to let her see my bruises and vulnerability."

He reached for the roast and transferred a slice onto his plate. "So . . . I shouldn't let her see if I'm upset or angry?"

"Preferably not, in my humble opinion. If you consider her way to be better, by all means go along with it. But if you know it's not, then just tell her that's the way it's going to be."

"And if she argues?"

"I assume she already has," Uncle Miltie muttered, while continuing to butter one of the warm dinner rolls that had come from the oven only a few minutes earlier.

"Let's just say Miss Felix doesn't hesitate to display her disapproval. Right there in the outer office."

"The patients won't have any confidence in him, Gracie," Uncle Miltie now pointed out.

She chewed her lip. This didn't sound easy.

"And I've also indicated," Tom said, "although not right then, that I'm keeping a running account of how everything's going, so Al will receive a full report upon his return."

He flashed a grin. "Things have improved somewhat since we got that on the record. Besides, when all's said and done, it's only a month."

"Well, even a month can be a long time," Uncle Miltie stated.

Dear Lord, Gracie prayed silently, *let Laura Felix have the benefit of Your healing spirit, so she won't strive to be so bossy and competitive. Her resentment of Tom is natural enough, since she's set in her ways, but it serves neither the patients nor her own well-being.*

At the church, Gracie and Tom arrived for choir practice the same time as Tish, Tyne and Rick, all of whom greeted Tom warmly.

Barb had already seated herself at the organ. After saying, "It's good to see you could make it, Dr. Elder," she added, "And now you can just take a seat next to . . . ah, you're a tenor, aren't you?"

He seemed to hesitate before qualifying, "I've got a better baritone range, but can hit almost all but the very highest tenor notes."

Marge replied before Barb could respond, "We probably need tenors more."

Barb wished to make a different point. "Well, doctor, what we'd really like is for you to be where you're most comfortable, so why don't you sit next to Don Delano, over there?"

Don, grinning, slid over one seat to make room for him. "Welcome to our illustrious Eternal Hope Community Church choir, doctor."

Looking around, Tom replied, "If I'm to be part of this choir while I'm here in Willow Bend, I expect to be called Tom."

Gracie smiled. Barb, cueing them to begin the first hymn, thought how lovely Gracie looked when she smiled. She caught Gracie's eye and grinned back.

Practice went so smoothly—Tom's voice was still strong and pure, Gracie noted—that Don Delano issued a mock-warning. "We're not going to allow you to quit at the end of the month."

Tom looked pleased. "Thanks."

Barb gave Tom copies of the anthems they'd be singing for the following three weeks. As they were packing up to leave, Marge called out, "Who's up for stopping at The Sweet Shoppe on the way home, so we can welcome our new member with a few frivolous calories?"

"Why not Abe's?" Don asked. "He's not quite closed for the night yet."

Soon eight members of the choir, including Tom, were entering the delicatessen. Abe Wasserman greeted them. "Good evening, everyone. Choir practice must have finished early."

Tom glanced at Gracie, and she grinned. "Abe's pastrami sandwiches are what keep us in good voice. Being a doctor, you know what they say about apples, but here in Willow Bend, it's his bagels we rely on."

"You must be Al Hanley's vacation replacement," Abe said to Tom, shaking his hand. "Al himself is a two-bagel-a-day man."

"Hey, guys!" Rocky now walked into the deli, as the already short-of-table-space choir members made room for him.

"I have to be back at the office in a few minutes, but I needed a break and a cup of strong coffee and," Rocky said to Abe, "something sinfully big and full of flavor. Maybe a hunk of cheesecake?"

Abe thought for a second. "Cherry? Blueberry? Or what about my new flavor, cranberry? There may be a slice of pineapple left, too."

"I'll let you choose. That way I won't feel so guilty." Rocky looked at his friends with an innocent expression. "Am I right?"

Tom looked at Abe and said, "I'll have one of whatever he's having. I can tell he knows the ropes here. Attitude is everything. And that's my medical opinion."

"Yes, but in your musical opinion," Rocky asked, "how did the choir perform?"

"I think it would be more to the point to ask Barb here how we performed."

Barb Jennings, who didn't often join them in after-choir fellowship, stated firmly, "Tom did very well indeed, especially since it was a first run-through for him."

Tom looked at her. "Thanks, Madame Choir Director, and despite your kind words, I promise to do even better next time."

The banter continued until Rocky started to push back his chair. "By the way, Tom, I'm working on a piece about your filling in for Al at his office. It'll be in either the Saturday or Sunday edition, if that's all right with you."

"Sure." Tom shrugged. "If there's anything you want to know, just call. Do you need a bio?"

"Well, correct me if I'm wrong. You were born in Kentucky and raised in Indiana, the oldest of three siblings. You went to college in Michigan and med school in Ohio, where you also did your internship and residency. You have two kids—a daughter, Millicent, who's also a physician, and a son, Bob, who's an electrical engineer."

Rocky pursed his lips. "How am I doing so far?"

Tom sank back in his seat. "That's scary! How did you find out all of that?"

"We're all open books these days, thanks to the Internet. The problem is not how to find the information but how to stop it once it starts."

"*Phew!*" Tom mopped his brow in exaggerated concern. Then he smiled at Rocky.

Marge felt the need to add, "No computer can match Gracie's sleuth sense!"

"What?" Tom looked baffled.

"You don't know about our Gracie's mystery-solving?"

Gracie found herself squirming. "It's nothing, really—just that I've sometimes helped out with little problems in town, even some when crimes were committed."

"She's Jessica Fletcher and Nancy Drew all rolled into one," Marge said loyally.

"Gracie, will you tell me about some of your cases?" Tom asked her.

"Maybe some time when I'm not so exhausted. Look, I think I'll go home now." As quickly as she could, she headed out, stopping only to give Abe a good-bye hug.

Uncle Miltie was in the kitchen pouring himself a glass of milk when she walked in. "You must have gone out to eat after practice."

"Yes." She covered a yawn with the palm of her hand. "To Abe's."

"Tom went with you?" He cocked an eyebrow.

"*Umm-um.*"

"That would be a good introduction to the town for him."

"I agree, especially since everyone was on their good behavior." She filled a glass with water from the tap as she added, "Rocky dropped in for a bit, too."

"Oh," said Uncle Miltie casually, "protecting his interests, was he?"

She glared at him. "More like protecting his stomach! He was there taking a cheesecake break."

"Don't get riled up. If your face turns any redder, it'll be the same color as your hair."

"You're incorrigible and you know it!" Gracie declared. "As of this moment, Gooseberry's the only man in my life, and that means you, too!"

Five

ROCKY ISN'T IN CHURCH TODAY, Gracie realized. She had come to expect him since he'd shown up the last several Sundays, and she was disappointed to realize he was absent. She'd wanted to tell him she'd enjoyed his piece on Tom Elder's arrival in the community. But his attendance was irregular, and wishing would never bring him there with any faithfulness. She knew that.

While she was removing her robe after the service, Uncle Miltie suggested that they go to Abe's for lunch, and added that he'd already invited Tom.

She was just a little annoyed at his taking it upon himself to make plans without having first checked with her. But then she did that all the time and her uncle never fussed about it. For that matter, they frequently went to Abe's following church, so why should he have to ask her?

Amy Cantrell, the choir's youngest and very talented soprano, had left immediately for her part-time job and was already busily waitressing by the time the trio arrived. She waved her order pad in acknowledgment when she saw them walk in. A few moments later Rocky arrived at Abe's. "Ah, I'm not late," he sighed. "Good. I was trying to get something straightened out at the paper."

Tom nodded. "I suppose that's a fairly frequent situation for an editor."

"You said it!" This sigh was even more protracted than the previous one. "For any of a hundred reasons."

He didn't amplify that, and Gracie handed him her menu. "A

good meal and no additional caffeine in your system for a while will make you feel better."

He frowned at her before turning toward the other man. "See for yourself, Tom. Here she is, again practicing diagnosis and treatment—and without a stint in medical school or an internship!"

The physician laughed. "At least this particular prescription won't have any potentially harmful side effects!"

"Well, I hope you're right," Gracie said, laughing. Then she looked at Rocky accusingly. "You, my friend, should have been at church this morning to hear Tom's debut performance."

"I hope my voice blended into everyone else's," Tom quickly broke in. "My intention is to be just one of the gang."

"You know what I meant," Gracie said. "It's just wonderful to have another strong male voice. Anyone new changes the mix."

"I enjoyed myself, I really did. It's been a long time since I've done much singing, and I hadn't realized how much I've missed it."

There seemed something different about the way he said that—wistful, almost—but Gracie didn't feel it her place to ask a question or to push for information. Nor did the others. She was grateful for Amy's reappearance at that moment with their plates. Soon they were launched into a discussion of the origins of the dill pickle. Abe's own half-sours, Tom learned, were famous as far away as Milwaukee.

Abe stopped at their table. "I liked Rocky's profile of you, Dr. Elder. Most of the time he can be relied upon to get the facts right, so I hope you'll agree it gives us Willow Benders a pretty good picture of the man who'll be patching us up for a while."

"I haven't had a chance to read it yet, but I doubt that it will keep you from recognizing the guy holding the tongue depressor," Tom answered, smiling.

In a few minutes, however, he got to his feet. "Sorry to have to run, my friends, but I have rounds to make."

Uncle Miltie had made it clear that today was his party, so after he had taken care of the bill, they all walked out together.

At home, Gracie changed into her walking gear and started out with Gooseberry, allowing the cat to pick the direction they'd take. Not everyone would enjoy having a feline guide, but Gracie appreciated how nice it was just to meander along without consciously thinking about anything.

After some clever twists and turns through a few of Willow

Bend's more interesting alleys, Gooseberry led Gracie past the police station. But Herb Bower's car wasn't there, so she kept going.

Had the chief of police been in church this morning? She didn't think so, although Marybeth Bower had been in her usual place in the soprano section. Gracie had forgotten to ask how the twins were doing, she realized.

Arriving home, she found her uncle on the couch and, since a golf match was in progress on the television screen, she was fairly sure he'd been asleep for quite a while.

There was a lined yellow pad on the floor beside him. She could see that he'd scratched out much of what he'd written. She was mildly curious as to what he'd been up to but made no attempt to find out. They were best friends as well as relatives, but each respected the other's privacy.

She sat down in her own recliner and tilted it back a ways as she picked up the mystery borrowed from the library a week ago. She was in the middle of the seventh chapter when her uncle awoke, and said sleepily, "You're back already."

"*Um-hmmm.* And you've had a nice long nap."

He appeared ready to argue until looking at the clock. "How about that?" He pushed himself up to a sitting position and moved his sock-covered feet from the couch to the carpet.

"I was working on one of those contests, and got so drowsy I must have dropped off." He scratched his head and looked at her with a slightly sleepy smile.

"It's a good day for that," she agreed. "Church, followed by a good meal, then a nap. I feel almost like taking one myself."

"Why don't you? Just lie down here. Or go to bed. I'll take responsibility for answering the phone or the door."

She started to say she didn't actually need any extra sleep, but changed her mind. "I'm going to take you up on that, Uncle Miltie. I'll stretch out on my bed and read some more of this book. And should I drop off before I figure out whodunit, who cares?"

He assured her that he considered that a very sensible way to spend the rest of the afternoon. And then he turned up the sound of the golf match.

2

They were midway through supper on Tuesday evening when Rocky arrived. Noticing that he looked troubled, she nonetheless greeted him saying, "I'm glad you've come. It was going to be a 'Musgo' meal. You know, when all the leftovers must go. But there are too many even for us, so all outside help is welcome!"

"Never let it be said that I'm not willing to help out good friends." Though he smiled as he responded, Gracie was aware he was hiding some distress.

What could be wrong? The strain she was sensing in Rocky, even as he engaged in his usual joking with Uncle Miltie, was worrisome. Still, she knew he would tell her what was bothering him when the right moment presented itself.

It was only after Uncle Miltie excused himself to go watch the news that Rocky seized the opportunity to let Gracie know what was on his mind.

What he told her was indeed distressing. "I got a really strange note in the mail today."

"At work?"

"*Um-hmmm*. It had an Indianapolis postmark and came in an ordinary business envelope. There was no return address, but I thought nothing of that when slitting it open—until I pulled out a single sheet of legal paper ripped messily from a pad.

"Such things are common enough in newspaper offices. Plenty of folks like to write in with complaints or tips, and they don't mind how it looks. All they care about is getting their point across. And sometimes a letter that looks like this will contain scurrilous information or an accusation, most often anonymously."

Gracie listened patiently.

Rocky looked at her, his face a study in unhappiness, and said, "I'd like to believe this unsigned note was as loony as most of them . . . but, Gracie, I just don't know."

Alarmed now, she sat there just looking at him.

Slowly he explained. "What it said was 'You are a fool to believe him. Thomas Elder is NOT a widower. Check with Clearview Terrace in Allendale for Elizabeth Elder.' "

"Oh, dear," Gracie said. "I'd been waiting for Tom to bring up the subject of his wife. Anyway, I just thought she'd been sick and that he did these temporary jobs because it was simpler.

"Well, this particular man wrote in an article in his very own newspaper that Dr. Thomas Elder of Indianapolis was a widower. That's what I understood from a follow-up conversation we had, after our little exchange in the deli. At least, he never corrected me about his wife being dead when I said it to him. And nothing I found on-line contradicted it."

"Oh, dear," Gracie repeated. Her mind was racing. Was the note Rocky had received correct? What was the truth about her old friend's marriage? *Lord, this does matter to me. Please help us make sense of it.*

She reached for his hand. "I'm sorry, Rocky."

And she was sorry. For him and for her . . . and even for Tom, who must have deliberately given the implication that his wife was dead.

"I telephoned Clearview Terrace," Rocky told her gravely. "Mrs. Elizabeth Elder has been a resident for almost two years."

"Rocky, oh, no!"

"I have all sorts of ideas about what it means. It's the lack of facts that's making me crazy. And I've broken a cardinal rule of journalism, to always check sources. *That's* what's driving me up the wall."

"But . . ."

"Maybe I'm getting too old for this job!" He'd pushed himself up from the table to begin pacing. "I like Tom—at least I did. And the fault resides with me. People mislead journalists, whether consciously or unconsciously, all the time.

"I wanted the piece to function as a good introduction of him to the town, as well as a thank-you to him from Willow Bend for his coming to take over Al's office." His fingers pushed back once again through his tousled salt-and-pepper hair.

"Even if I failed to check my facts, Tom Elder was not completely forthcoming, and the result is, I feel like a fool."

He continued to pace as Gracie asked, "Don't you think a simple misunderstanding might be possible? Maybe there was never an intention to mislead us?"

"Are you implying I jumped to a conclusion I shouldn't have, that wasn't justified by the facts I did turn up, did check?"

"I never did read that article," Gracie admitted. "Let me get it now."

She went into the other room, where she saw the folded paper. Bringing it back with her, she asked, "Shall I read it aloud?"

He smiled somewhat crookedly. "I appreciate the offer, but I already know too well what it says."

She read it through carefully. "But it's excellent, Rocky, dear—a real portrait of a dedicated physician and a fine family man. That he's not actually a widower puts a different light on what's here, but it also isn't really a criminal affair. Couples do get divorced or live separately, and though it's odd he hasn't mentioned his wife in any way, we have to suppose he has his reasons. Simply because you received an anonymous note doesn't ensure that there's been wrongdoing."

"Gracie, your fair-mindedness is admirable."

"I think we need to come right out and ask him, that's what I think," she said slowly.

She realized that learning the truth about Tom Elder mattered more to her than she might have supposed before this unsettling conversation had begun. Why had she been so content to be incurious about his marital situation or his wife's whereabouts? In a different way, her oversights were as guilt-inducing as Rocky's.

"I'll ask him," she said suddenly. "I want to."

"Good girl."

"But only on condition that you'll double-check whatever I find out—and that you promise to be praying for me."

He'd started to nod at the double-checking part, then looked decidedly uneasy. "Maybe we'd better get Pastor Paul or someone else in on that latter request. That's more his department than mine."

"Oh, really?" She cocked her head to the side and looked him right in the eye. "None of us is ever not in the praying 'department,' as you put it, Rocco Gravino. And since you brought this problem to me, if I ask you to pray, then pray you should."

"Okay, okay," Rocky protested.

He sat down and put his hands on his knees. "Well, I did ask to speak to Elizabeth Elder when I phoned this Clearview Terrace."

"And?" She saw that, once again, he had an odd, troubled expression on his face.

"I asked to speak to Mrs. Elder. Not a great idea, as it turned out." Apparently realizing she was about to ask why, he held up a hand.

"Here's the reason."

Gracie sighed.

"I finally got shunted to the office of the administrator. What I eventually learned was that Elizabeth Elder is a patient in the Alzheimer's unit. You can imagine how I felt, after demanding to speak to her and after accusing the first nurse I talked to of conspiring to keep that from happening. I was playing the tough-guy reporter, you see."

"Oh, Rocky! Oh, poor Tom! And poor, poor Elizabeth!" Gracie fell silent, and a shiver of sadness ran through her body.

"You know, Gracie, trying to put myself in his shoes, which of course I can't, I suppose such an illness might come to seem like a death. And, since we don't know what his life was like with her before she became ill, or during a long decline, he might be almost justified in wishing she were dead.

"But it's still not the same, and it's not what I've led people here in Willow Bend and Mason County to believe."

Oh, dear God, what if that had been Elmo's fate? Or mine? I hope we'd have been strong enough to handle it, but I'm so very grateful that neither of us had to find out.

Their disturbing discussion had so distracted Gracie that she had lost track of time. Suddenly Uncle Miltie appeared to tell them that the weather forecast for tomorrow was rain beginning in early morning and continuing until evening.

"We sure do need it," he pronounced. "If we don't get some soon, I'm going to have to start watering, which seems ridiculous this early in the season."

Gracie was amazed that he failed to notice the stricken expressions on her face and Rocky's. It was not like canny old Uncle Miltie to be so unobservant.

Gracie awakened before it was light to the sound of rain thickly pounding on the porch roof. She rolled over and went back to sleep, dreaming of cat toys and cookie cutters bobbing along the currents of a swollen river.

Eventually, though, Gooseberry made sure she was awake by giving a familiar "*Yee-ow*" right by her ear.

She groaned, and buried her head under the covers. But he was persistent, tucking his right paw at various places along the top of the blanket, then the sheet, until he reached her. When she rolled onto her back and squinted at him, he offered the cat version of a smile, his purr becoming almost melodic.

"Okay, you win," she told him as she stroked his back and scratched under his chin. "I suspect you already realize that we're not going for a walk in all this rain. I know you don't enjoy getting soggy any more than I do."

That it was time to get up was made more evident by the distant faint *ding* of the microwave. Uncle Miltie was heating a cup of water for his pre-breakfast mug of tea.

Yes, it was officially morning, and she'd hop to it. She'd promised to help Pat Allen prepare the church's monthly newsletter to go out, so she needed to be ready the instant all the photocopying was completed.

Thinking of her spiritual home, Eternal Hope, made Gracie wish she could talk to Pastor Paul about the problem Rocky had brought to her. But she knew she wouldn't share it with him, at least not yet.

She wondered how soon Tom would be back in his office after making his hospital rounds. Perhaps the best thing would be to ask him over for the evening meal. There would be nothing out of the ordinary about that. Besides, she'd simply say that they could then go together to choir practice.

She took an ultra-lean tenderloin roast from the freezer so it could begin to thaw and decided to make a raisin pie for dessert. Uncle Miltie liked to call it by its old Pennsylvania Dutch name, Funeral Pie.

Lots of the older folks she knew, like her uncle, remembered when raisins were always kept on hand for pie-making, when no other fruit was available. It wasn't just quaint, though, it was delicious.

"*Umm*, I don't even have to guess," Uncle Miltie said, sniffing the kitchen air a little later. "That aroma of raisins and lemon cooking together ought to be bottled and sold as an air-freshener! It'd wipe out all competition!"

"There's your chance to make a fortune," she told him. "Get working on it!"

Taking a spoon from the drawer, he scooped out some of the sweet, bubbling mixture and blew on it several times before pronouncing, "Takes me back at least a millennia or two, to when I was a boy. You might say, when I was 'a-raisin.'"

"I might," Gracie said dryly. "But before you got so wrinkled, there's the possibility you could have been a mere grape!"

The pie was nearly ready when Pat telephoned. Gracie told her she'd be there as soon as it was on the cooling rack.

She then rang Al Hanley's office. But Laura Felix informed her Dr. Elder was still at the hospital.

"I'm always waiting for him," she told Gracie sourly.

"Well, it must be very difficult to keep to a schedule if you're a busy doctor. People don't take sick on a timetable!"

"Well, Dr. Hanley never had any problems keeping a strict schedule!"

"But Dr. Elder's new to town. Surely, that makes a difference!"

"For him, each patient seems like an emergency, is all I can say."

She sounded in a real huff, and Gracie decided it would be better to let well enough alone. Given Laura's tone and volume, every patient in the waiting room was already well aware of her displeasure.

"I'll be leaving for a while, but will call back later," Gracie said politely.

There was a slight pause before the woman answered more courteously, "You're not sick, are you? Do you need an appointment?"

"No, I'm okay." It occurred to her that Laura might be disappointed at her answer, so she politely added, "But thanks for your concern."

Gracie said a quick prayer for Laura's impatience and one of thanksgiving for her organizational skills.

Six

WORK ON THE CHURCH BULLETIN with Pat Allen took well over an hour and a half. Gracie called Tom again from the phone in the hallway before leaving for the grocery store to get milk and a few other items, including a roll of film for her uncle.

This time, fortunately, Laura was able to connect her with the doctor right away. But since there was no sound of her hanging up, Gracie decided to speak guardedly, "Good morning, Tom, this is Gracie. Uncle Miltie and I were wondering if you might be free to come for dinner this evening."

His reply was equally restrained. "That would be lovely. I'll call, Gracie, if by any chance I'm running late."

"Good. We'll expect you about six, and after dinner we can head over to choir practice together."

She heard the sound of his hanging up, but kept her own receiver to her ear until hearing the rather muffled sound of the other office phone being returned to its base.

Dear Lord, I hate to ask a question like this, but did You know Laura Felix was an eavesdropper? Is she also a gossip? Does she share with others what she knows or thinks she knows about what goes on in that office?

Might she even be the one to have engineered that anonymous letter about Tom's wife? Oh, Lord, I do hope not. If she read Rocky's article, and if she somehow knew about Clearview Terrace, could she have arranged for the letter to be mailed from Indianapolis? Don't think ill of me, please, oh, Lord, for imagining one of my acquaintances so malicious.

I'm just so concerned about the situation—about Tom's marriage and how he might have let Rocky mistakenly assume his wife was dead, but also about the deteriorating relationship between Tom and Laura Felix.

When she got home, she felt inclined to talk to Uncle Miltie about her worries. But it was time—past time actually—to be getting lunch on the table. Ham sandwiches, baby carrots, sliced tomatoes and re-warmed baked beans. Was she forgetting something?

"No pie for lunch?" her uncle asked, sounding plaintive.

"There are two kinds of cookies in the container—molasses and iced lemon—and unless you already ate all those sticky buns that were left, I don't think you're in imminent danger of starving this afternoon."

She told him that Tom would be there for the evening meal.

"Will Rocky be here, too?" he wanted to know.

"Not by invitation."

But then she laughed. "He doesn't need one, though, does he?"

"It's really his second home, or maybe I should say his second kitchen—even if I'm not certain I want to imagine what he does in his first one."

"Do you think he's lonely?"

"Maybe. Just remember, he's got a job that keeps him more in-volved in every bit of the town's business than almost anyone but Mayor Ritter or one of the ministers. So there are almost endless opportunities for him to be with someone, talking about this problem or that project."

She nodded, but still wondered. Weren't there people who regu-larly attended church services yet didn't seem to actually give or re-ceive the fellowship and love she found there? At the same time, "alone" didn't have to mean lonely.

"Being busy isn't a substitute for being happy, or even truly en-gaged," she finally pronounced.

"Are we talking about the same person?" Uncle Miltie regarded his niece intently, as though truly questioning what she'd said.

"Who in Willow Bend has more opinions on more subjects and knows more about what's going on than Mr. Newspaper Proprietor Rocco Gravino?"

She let out a deep breath. "But how many people can he really confide in or trust completely?"

"For that matter, how many people do you know about whom you can say that?" responded Uncle Miltie.

"Oh, lots of them—you and Paul and Herb and Marge."

"Slow down there, missy. Is there even one on that list to whom you could tell every single secret of your heart and know beyond the shadow of a doubt that it would go no further?"

"Wel-l-l-l," her voice trailed off, for she realized what he said was true. Paul would be closest to that ideal, she was quite sure, and Herb had been wonderful as they'd worked side by side to help resolve various upsetting local incidents. Marge, of course, would be the most likely of the bunch to be careless with privileged information.

"See?" he crowed, obviously pleased with himself for making her consider his opinion. "By the way, I wonder if I shouldn't be insulted that you didn't say right off that you'd trust *me*."

She refused to take his swipe seriously and, instead, she just reached out and patted his shoulder. "I don't think you have anything to worry about in that department."

Their dinner guest arrived about three minutes before the designated hour.

Uncle Miltie had opened the door for Tom, and led the way to the table. "Might as well have a seat, doc. As you see, the table's set and all you need is . . ."

Tom finished the sentence for him. "My appetite!"

Gracie now made her appearance, her face rosy from the oven heat and a few curls sticking charmingly up behind her ears.

"Welcome, Tom. Would you like to wash your hands?"

He looked at her admiringly. "Yes, thanks."

"Right over there."

"As it turns out," he admitted, "today was pretty hectic. I got to the office from the hospital a little late this morning, and was never able to catch up with the incoming patients and phone calls! And then I had one fellow who arrived in pretty bad shape, so I had to call for the ambulance to take him to the hospital. The upshot was, I didn't get to see everyone waiting in the office and I went to check on him before coming here."

"Is it—ah—permitted to ask who that is, Tom? Obviously, we know almost everyone in town and would be eager to know who needs our prayers."

He nodded. "I understand. You undoubtedly do know Harold Mayhew."

"Harold?" Uncle Miltie's eyes widened. "Is he real bad?"

"Since everyone either already knows this—or will in a short time—I can tell you he'd been having recurring pains in his left shoulder and neck for at least twelve hours. Unfortunately, he felt scared and kept reassuring himself it was only a sore muscle or something."

"It's his heart?" Gracie asked. "I'm not surprised, really."

"Well, if he'd gone to the ER or come to me right away, I think we might have prevented it."

"Harold has never liked going to doctors, isn't that right, Gracie? Remember when he was trimming around the courthouse, using one of those gizmos with the plastic cord that goes whirling around so fast it even takes out thistles or brambles and brush? He cut his lower leg real bad, but never told anyone till a couple days later, when it was so swollen and infected that he couldn't walk on it. He almost lost that leg, as I recall."

Gracie agreed. Then, glancing at the clock, she asked, "Would you like to offer the blessing this evening, Uncle Miltie?"

He bowed his head and gave thanks, finishing with "Please, God, look out for Harold tonight and tomorrow and ever after, as he is in need of You and Your eternal grace."

The meal went quickly, even with dessert and loading the dishwasher. Choir practice was still twenty minutes away. Tom had enjoyed the raisin pie. For some reason, Gracie felt reluctant to tell him it was also known as Funeral Pie. Uncle Miltie, amazingly, failed to mention it as well.

"Would you mind if we left a little early, Tom?" she asked. "I just have to comb my hair."

"Not in the least." He'd remained in the kitchen, even though her uncle had invited him to watch the start of the news with him.

Gracie walked to the mirror in her small downstairs bathroom.

Am I being ridiculous, Lord, still keeping my hair this red? It started back when El first died, and I was so devastated. I didn't see how I could go on day by day, not to mention year by year, without this man I loved so much, the man I was convinced You'd joined together with me in an indivisible bond.

Then one day as I was calling out to You for help—and for the stamina to keep on keeping on—it was just as though You were taking me in Your arms and assuring me, "Lo, I am with you always, even to the ends of the earth."

At that moment I determined to change my outlook, and color came back once again into the grayness of my life. Yes, I was a widow, but You'd promised to be with widows and orphans, so I'd better shape up. With Your help I would be a complete person again.

She wondered what Tom had thought when first seeing her like this. Undoubtedly, he remembered that her hair had once been a medium brown, though she'd liked to think there had been reddish highlights after days spent in the sun.

She turned off the bathroom light, went back to the kitchen, and picked up her purse. "Ready?"

He nodded, smiling. "You look lovely this evening."

"Thanks." She'd have liked to say something more, something lighthearted, but the words simply wouldn't come.

Whatever she was going to say—and she'd now have to wait until after choir practice—she was counting on God to be with her. Tom's situation saddened her beyond measure, and she intuited that he would be relieved at unburdening himself.

Rick Harding had pulled into the lot just ahead of them, and he waited to walk inside with them.

"How's Harold doing, Tom?"

"As of 5:30, he was stable." Tom stopped to look Rick in the eye. "I was pleased you were one of the crew to come to the office for him. Your manner is efficient and friendly in just the measure it needs to be."

Rick smiled his thanks. "I'm the newest EMT in the Willow Bend Volunteer Fire Department. It's my way of helping out in this town my wife and I have come to love. I usually don't take calls so soon after my working day's over, but because my hours are flexible, I fill in more often than some."

"Do either of you know if Harold has family?" Tom asked. "He was in such pain at first that the information sheet wasn't a priority."

Rick looked questioningly at Gracie, who said, "I don't think so, but, now that I think of it, I realize I don't know for sure."

Rick added, "He lives alone and, as far as we know, he doesn't participate in any of the churches or organizations or groups."

"Pretty much of a loner, then," Tom murmured. "Look, we think he's going to make it, but we really should find out who to contact in case of any emergency."

They all agreed. But now it was time for silence in the choir loft. Barb brought them to attention, saying, "Everyone's finally here, and we're already seven minutes late!"

Marge leaned over to whisper when the next break came, "Gracie, how about you and Tom stopping over at my place afterwards?"

Normally, there'd have been no reason not to agree. But Gracie understood there could be no further delay in confronting head-on the issue of Tom's wife. "I don't think I can tonight, Marge. Perhaps next week?" She smiled and tilted her head regretfully.

Marge shrugged, smiled back and now repeated her invitation to Tom alone. Looking toward Gracie, he noted her almost infinitesimal head shake.

"I'm not free tonight, either, Marge, but I do appreciate the thought."

She looked disappointed, but repeated Gracie's words, "Perhaps next week."

As it turned out, Gracie and Tom were among the last to leave, and a teasing smile came to his face as he turned the ignition. "So, if you don't think we can go to Marge's tonight, what do you think we can do?"

"Well, there's something I very seriously need to talk to you about, actually."

"*Hmmm*, somehow that has an ominous sound to it."

She nodded. "Rocky stopped by yesterday."

"I take it he does that quite often."

"Yes, he does. The three of us have become close friends over the years."

"And . . . is he wanting me to back off our friendship—yours and mine?"

It had not entered her mind that Tom might think that! "Not at all! It had to do with that profile of you he ran in the paper."

A frown creased his forehead, but he waited for her to continue. "He regrets that he didn't double-check some of the facts before publishing it."

His head cocked slightly toward the side, indicating to Gracie that her companion still had no idea where she was going with her thoughts.

"I considered it a fine article, perhaps too flattering, actually, but I probably wouldn't have asked for changes." Tom grinned.

"Did you read the entire thing?"

"Well, I may have just scanned parts of it." He grinned again. "After all, I already do know a lot about me."

"You saw no errors?"

"Not that I recall, and I'll admit to being grateful he didn't ask for nor print the date I graduated medical school. When we get to our age, there seems little point in deliberately helping people pin down how old we are."

"I won't comment on that."

"So what's the problem with the article?"

"Rocky received a note stating that one thing was very wrong. It came from Indianapolis."

"Indianapolis? Someone contacted him from *there?*"

He looked perplexed. "Who? And how in the world would that person have even known about a feature article in the *Gazette?*"

"It was anonymous, and Rocky often doesn't bother taking seriously things like that. But he did this time. What it said was that Rocky was wrong to call you a widower. Your wife is alive, in fact, and in a home outside of Indianapolis."

He became very still, with not a muscle moving. There would have been no more change in his expression if he'd been turned to stone.

Then, suddenly, his shoulders sagged a bit, and his right hand appeared to tighten convulsively around the wheel. When he still said nothing, she added, "All we want is to understand why you let him continue to believe your wife Elizabeth had died when it isn't so."

"Did Rocky phone the home? Have you been checking up on me?"

"Rocky was hoping to prove the writer wrong. He is a committed journalist, you know. His phoning was more his effort to prove you'd told the truth, rather than the opposite."

Tom drew in a deep breath before saying, "Actually, Gracie, the Elizabeth Elder to whom I was married *is* dead. Although I didn't tell Rocky she was no longer living, I have to say that, to me, it often feels like the case."

Tom looked at Gracie for an instant, his gaze utterly intense. "That woman in the home may bear a remarkable resemblance to her physically, but in no other way.

"I'll confess to not at first recognizing the symptoms, though I should have, of course, for they were classic. Forgetting not only the names of people she'd known for years, but frequently not recognizing them. Losing items she'd set down right out in the open, as well as those she'd put in the wrong places, like a new package of nylons in the freezer and a half-gallon of ice cream on the shelf with boxes of cereal.

"She locked herself out of the car with the keys still in the ignition at least five different times, and left all of her credit cards in a restaurant, and in a store and at the gas station we often went to.

"The deterioration seemed to happen incredibly fast, but it's probable that, with my very busy practice, I didn't pay enough attention to what was going on at home. When I finally did, I took her to the best specialists I could find. She was institutionalized, at first only for an extended period. When she came back home, it was with round-the-clock help and supervision.

"It was then I took early retirement, thinking that if I spent enough time and effort on the day-by-day effort to encourage and guide her, I might be able not only to keep her from getting worse, but also to help her regain some of the ground she'd already lost."

He shifted on the seat and glanced again toward Gracie. "I'll admit that up until then I'd never given stay-at-home parents anywhere near the credit they deserve.

"I now have much more appreciation for their dedication and love, for I had to do almost everything for Elizabeth. What she could manage for herself one month or one week kept changing. Never for the better. And I discovered not only how very difficult, but also how lonely it can be for a care-giver."

Gracie didn't know whether to speak or not. If she did, would it make it easier for him to continue, or would it cause him to pull back?

He went on. "Also, the truth is that there was so much I didn't know about her life in the period before she became ill. She'd left home over three years earlier, you see, and the good-bye note she wrote to me back then was pretty blunt. She was tired of me and the city, and she hated my practice. She'd so often declared that I seemed to consider it more important to me than she and the kids were."

Sensing the pain that admission caused, Gracie reached out for his hand. "So she returned to you? Did she ever talk about what had happened?"

He shook his head. "And I didn't push her. Though she'd apparently left me for another man, I—well, I wasn't sure I could handle learning the details of her life during her absence." He shrugged slightly.

"Physically speaking, since that's more my area of expertise, she'd lost a huge amount of weight when she was gone. She was nearly emaciated, in fact, so I tried not only to get nourishing food into her, but vitamins and minerals, too. In addition, because she seemed so depressed and lethargic, I wanted her to see a psychiatrist, which she refused to do.

"When I finally got her to agree to be seen by an excellent internist we both knew, tests were run, showing her blood count to be very low and her liver enzymes elevated—but other than that she seemed fairly healthy. As her antibodies and genetic studies were within normal limits, and viral studies came back negative, we concentrated primarily on trying to get her built up physically."

"You continued working during all of that?"

"For the first six or seven months. But she continued deteriorating, mentally and emotionally. When she smashed my locked medical cabinet and tried to kill herself, I decided to quit work rather than send her away."

"But you eventually had to do so." Gracie murmured, heartsick from all she was learning.

He nodded. "I'd checked out all nursing homes within fifty miles, and finally decided on Clearview Terrace. But before I could arrange her admission, she somehow found the car keys, overdosed on painkillers, and crashed the car into a tree."

"It was—intentional?"

"It almost had to be, even though she never admitted it."

"Do you often get to see her?"

"That depends on your definition of *often*." He shrugged. "At first it was almost every day, with me trying to work with the doctors and therapists. Later, it dropped to three or four times a week. Now it's more apt to be every week or so, for she doesn't recognize me and barely acknowledges my presence."

"And your kids—how have they reacted to this?"

"Millicent goes once in a while, and we talk. She's a doctor, too, and so I don't get to see her often enough. We've both had our share of schedules that kept us from our families. Like father, like daughter."

Gracie sighed.

"Rob has little use for any of us, unfortunately," Tom continued.

"He's an electrical engineer, and apparently an excellent one. It's just that his family seems pretty far down on his list of priorities, I'm afraid."

This time Gracie's sigh was even longer. She closed her eyes in sadness. *Oh, dear God, help me to help this man.*

Seven

TOM WALKED HER TO THE DOOR and Gracie went in alone. "Hey, you're running late," her uncle called from the other room. "Did you stop at Abe's?"

"Not this time."

"Barb kept you late again?"

"No, things went quite well, but a couple of us got to talking—you know how it is."

"Did you hear any more about Harold's condition?"

"Rick was the EMT who rode with him to the hospital, but I learned nothing beyond what Tom told us at dinner."

"I sure hope he's okay!"

"Me, too. But we know he's got good care now and there'll be people watching over him until he's better. That's what hospitals are for."

Then Uncle Miltie remembered to ask, "When you were out today, did you get that roll of film I asked for?"

"Yes, I did. I'm sorry I forgot to give it to you." Pulling it from her purse, she handed it to him. "Why do you suddenly want all these pictures of Gooseberry and you?"

"Hey, don't think I've gotten vain or anything!" He looked a little sheepish, however. "It's just for this contest I keep entering, not only do they want a verse or a saying that they might conceivably use for a *Lucky Kitty* commercial, but also a picture of the cat and one of its masters included with every single entry."

"You must send a different picture with each entry?"

He nodded. "Plus, if I want the shot returned, I'm to send five dollars for postage and handling."

"That's a lot!"

"I think so, too. But I don't want them keeping my only copy."

"Well, remember that where I get film developed you can order two prints of each picture for a very small additional charge."

"*Hmmph.*" He looked even more sheepish. "I'd forgotten that."

She'd started to turn away when he said, "Would you mind listening to what will probably be my next entry?"

"Sure, why not?" she told him. "We should probably get Gooseberry in here to hear it, too."

Uncle Miltie held the paper at arm's length and began reading.

"Treat your cat like royalty,
Buy your pet the best—
Give him *Lucky Kitty*
And you will pass the test."

He looked at her expectantly. Gracie opted for diplomacy. "That sounds fine. But do you suppose we could play around with that last line?"

"Like—what?"

"I don't know exactly. There's nothing actually wrong with yours."

His brow furrowed in thought. "Gee, you know, I wasn't all that satisfied with it, either. I just couldn't think of anything to improve it. I even tried, 'And he will do the rest.' But that didn't sound any better."

"Well, why do you think Gooseberry might actually want *Lucky Kitty*, rather than some other brand?" she asked, attempting to jog his creativity.

"I don't know that he does. He just eats it as well as any kind."

"You mentioned about something not seeming any 'better.' Might that word work in your last line? Perhaps, 'Better than the rest'?"

He now tried it with her suggestion, "It's better than the rest." A big smile came to his face. "That's it, Gracie. That's exactly right! Much catchier! Willing to hear another one?"

"Okay."

"This is one I've already sent, with a picture and the five bucks:

"Keep your kitty happy—
That's easy, you can see.
Buy him *Lucky Kitty*
At your grocery."

Eagerly, he went on, "And I'm working on one more that isn't right yet."

She understood her part now. "Let's hear it."

He cleared his throat.

"For cats you think are snoopy,
And that's a great big pity,
What you need to fix the problem
Is to buy *Lucky Kitty.*"

Uh, oh, they're getting worse rather than better, she thought to herself.

Feeling pretty certain none of Uncle Miltie's entries were going to prevail, Gracie started for the kitchen. "Keep working at them!" she called back to him.

"You bet!" Then he added, "Please remember if you go to the pharmacy or grocery store, whichever gives back two prints of each picture, that we have another roll ready to be developed."

How many more hapless verses would she have to listen to? It was enough to make her plead with her uncle for more of his corny jokes.

◦

Gracie padded into the kitchen in her nightgown and slippers. She'd been aware that the day was beautiful, but now found that the temperature was already seventy-seven degrees at 6:15 A.M. "Okay, Gooseberry," she told her companion, "you've got your walking outfit on, but I don't. Just wait for me."

She caught herself humming as she changed. "Today I'll set the pace," she informed her cat as they started out. "And our route."

It was at least forty minutes later when she stopped at Abe's Deli. "*Umm.* What delectable smells!" she told the owner as he came to greet her with a hug.

"Date and almond pinwheels are what you're sniffing, and what you'll have, if you say the word."

"Exactly!" She went over to sit on one of the high red vinyl-covered stools at the counter. "I hope that was the right word!"

"Of course," he stated, setting down the plate on which were two large cookies. "Myself, I'm feeling especially cheery because Sophie left yesterday afternoon." He poured her a mug of coffee.

"Come on, Abe, you know you're always as glad to have your sister come for a visit as to have her leave."

"How well put!" He gave a wry smile. "I love her dearly, but she drives me crazy! She apparently doesn't know how to relax—not here, anyway. From the time she comes till the time she goes, she's busy trying out different recipes, or scrubbing any scrubbable surface, or taking down all the curtains in my apartment and washing and ironing them, or systemizing all my spices alphabetically, even though some of them I rarely use, or. . . ."

"Stop!" She covered her ears with her hands. "I'm sitting here getting more and more convicted of laziness with each additional task."

"*You're* convicted? Imagine sharing my upstairs living quarters with that hurricane! I don't usually get up until 4:30 or five o'clock—except when Sophie's here and out of bed and starting to bake an hour before that.

"And she can't just work at any one task without planning for the next one and the one after that, ad infinitum. It's enough to exhaust a person even before beginning any of it!"

"At least with Uncle Miltie, we're not competing with the cooking. Actually, not with anything else, either."

"He's quite a guy. I'm glad your arrangement's worked out so well for both of you."

"Me, too." She took a bite of her pinwheel and chewed it slowly, savoring the flavor. "Delicious! Whoever made these has my unqualified admiration."

"It's Sophie's own recipe. Actually, she says she ate something similar to this at a party, and kept experimenting at home till she got it just right."

Leaving, she bought several of Sophie's pinwheels to take home to share with her uncle. She stopped at the newspaper office on the way home. Gracie was talking to several of his employees when Rocky came hurrying in.

He practically screeched to a halt upon seeing her and Gooseberry.

"Hello, Gracie."

"Gooseberry and I were coming back from our constitutional and stopped at Abe's. I thought you might like a taste of something delicious."

"Sounds great!" He took a pinwheel. "Wow."

They laughed companionably.

"But you're really here about the note, right?"

She nodded.

"So what's the story?"

She filled him in on what she had learned, and then he asked, "Tell me, Gracie, do you believe that everything he said is true?"

"I have no reason to doubt that he was being honest with me. His story is certainly plausible, isn't it?"

"I agree. I think it's all been a misunderstanding, and a very sad one."

He looked at her for a long moment before asking, "You like him a great deal, don't you?"

Is he jealous? Of Tom? To Gracie that seemed incredible but, just in case, she chose to give reassurance. "I like a lot of people, Rocky, including, in a very special way, a certain editor who's been a wonderful, faithful friend for many years."

"Well, the feeling's mutual, my dear."

But then he was saying, "I'd still like to know why, though, Tom and his son are at such loggerheads."

"Isn't that something that could be none of our business?" Gracie asked him. "Not all parents and children get along, terrible as that is for me to imagine."

Rocky looked thoughtful. "So, what you're trying to tell me is that it looks like Dr. Tom Elder is who he says he is: a good guy who took early retirement, then missed being a practicing physician enough that he covers for some friends who want temporary respite from their medical practices. And that he has a wife with tragic emotional and physical afflictions is just part of the package . . . ?"

"Yes," said Gracie softly, "I guess that's what I'm saying."

He turned to face her directly. "I want you to know that I do not make a practice of checking up on the friends of my friends."

"If you ever do, I'll always believe you have a reason."

"Thanks, Gracie."

She sighed. "Listen, the Rocky I've come to know has integrity. If he does searches, it's because those searches need to be made. If you're curious to learn more about Tom's estranged son, then you have my blessing. I trust you."

She got to her feet. "But I must be going. I still need to drop off a roll of Uncle Miltie's film. This time the pictures are mostly of him and Gooseberry."

Hearing his name, the cat stood up, as did Rocky, who asked, "Some special reason why most of a roll of film is of those two?"

"*Um-hmmm*. There's this contest he keeps entering, one requiring not only a slogan or verse about *Lucky Kitty* cat food, but a picture, too, with each entry. I just learned about that, so am taking this roll to Robertson's Pharmacy, where I can request that two pictures be made from each negative."

"I hope he wins something more than another baseball cap!"

"Me, too. Although I could use one of the supersized T-shirts he's acquired for summer sleeping, if he feels like sharing the wealth. Still, it sounds like it's getting to be an expensive hobby."

Gracie agreed, but didn't mention the five dollars demanded of those wishing to have their pictures returned.

⁓

Uncle Miltie was standing by the microwave as she entered the kitchen. "Want some water heated for you, too?"

"Not right now, thanks. But Gooseberry and I brought you something." She handed him the box.

"It smells good." His eyes brightened as he lifted the lid and reached in for one of the cookies. "They look like little pinwheels!"

"They are, baked with love and bossiness by Sophie Glass."

"Well, if they taste as good as they smell, then I'd have to say bossiness will qualify as the mystery ingredient."

"You're right," Gracie told her uncle. "Even if I had the recipe, they probably wouldn't taste the same."

"Thank goodness for that, my dear," Uncle Miltie replied with a smile.

Eight

ON FRIDAY MORNING Gracie returned home after driving her uncle to the library. She was so busy she didn't notice that well over the usual two hours had passed before she received his call.

"Sorry I didn't phone before this, Gracie, but Joe stopped at the library for some books on tape for Anna, as well as a new book he wanted for himself. Since I was done with my story-reading with the kids, I came home with him and they've invited me to stay for lunch."

"Tell them I send my love."

"That I'll do, even if they know already that they have it."

As it turned out, she was grateful he was happily occupied at the Searfosses' because just before noon, Tom Elder telephoned. "Would you happen to be free right now?"

"Well, yes, I am."

"Would it be okay if I came there for a few minutes?"

She glanced at the calendar. "You're not working today?" He sounds upset, she thought.

"Yes. But I need to get away for a bit."

Is Laura Felix listening in on this conversation? Gracie worried. Just in case, she decided to be cautious. "Look, I'd already planned to have just soup and sandwiches for my uncle and myself, so why not come share that? It would save time, since I know your schedule's always full."

Gracie felt there was no harm in failing to mention that Uncle Miltie wouldn't actually be eating the lunch she'd prepared for him.

"Great idea. I'll be there within a few minutes."

Again today she heard his connection being closed, but she once more stayed on the line herself, waiting for a second possible click. What she heard was Tom's voice, faintly saying, "I'm going out for . . ." That was first.

Then came the ominous and decisive click.

2

"You're tired," Gracie greeted Tom.

He looked at the spread on the kitchen table with appreciation. "You're right," Tom admitted. "To be honest, though, I'm mostly tired of one particular woman."

"Laura Felix, I presume."

"You presume correctly."

He walked with her to the table as she murmured, "Have a seat. Uncle Miltie's actually having lunch with some friends, as it turns out. I'll just get some crusty bread to dunk in the chowder. Or would you prefer crackers?"

"Whichever. I'll gladly take either one. What I cannot take, though, is the highhanded attitude of that woman. How Al handles it, I'll never understand."

"I wish there were something I could do to help," she told him. "Did something especially trying take place this morning?"

He nodded grimly. "First of all, I should say that I was up much of the night. I was called in when Harold Mayhew took a turn for the worse around two this morning."

"Is he going to be all right?" As soon as she'd asked, though, she wished she'd waited. Telling her about Harold might keep Tom from getting on with his situation at the office.

But he said only, "I think so," before continuing. "So I got to the office a little late—which one would think is the worst of all criminal offenses, the way she acted—and right in front of the patients in the waiting room!"

"Was it what she said . . . or what she did?"

"Both! She held up her bent left arm to look most obviously at her wristwatch as she snorted, '*Humph!* It's about time you got here,' as if I were a tardy second-grader! Then she looked toward her audience with a martyred expression, sighed, and stated, 'We're already almost an hour behind! It's such a busy day, I don't see how we'll ever get caught up.'"

"What did you do?"

"I resolved to make the best of it by also looking at those patients and saying quietly, 'I'm sorry about being late, but there was an emergency in Intensive Care. I've been there since before 2:30 this morning, trying to save someone's life.' "

"Good for you!"

"Thanks." He gave her a fleeting smile. "And I was also thankful that one of the older women from your church, an Eleanor Something—her last name escapes me. . . ."

"McIver?"

"Eleanor McIver, yes, that's who it was. Well, she looked indignantly at Laura and stated to me, 'We're all very grateful for your priorities, Dr. Elder. And, may I ask, is the patient still alive?' "

He ran his fingers through his rumpled hair. "I'll tell you, Gracie, I could have kissed her feet! When I said he was not only better, but I thought his prognosis was improving, everyone in the room cheered. Several even made a point of saying that in that case they certainly didn't mind having to wait a little longer for their appointments."

"We really do have a lot of wonderful people in our town. I'm not one bit surprised at Eleanor's being the one to stand up for what was right."

"It didn't stop Laura from practically having an apoplectic fit!"

"Is that an actual medical term?"

"No, it's a figure of speech," Tom replied, now with a faint grin.

She was once again serious. "What happened next?"

"I asked her to come into my office—*Al's* office—and stated in no uncertain terms that I wasn't going to tolerate any of that kind of attitude while I was working there."

"And I'll bet she pretended not to have any idea what you were talking about. She's probably cultivating every single ruffled feather!"

"You're totally right!"

Gracie started to suggest they'd better begin eating the soup before it got cold. Then she remembered that they hadn't asked a blessing on the food—and on those partaking of it.

Tom gently shook his head at her invitation to say grace. But since Gracie loved bringing God to her table, she happily offered up her prayers. For a fleeting moment she wondered why her old friend was a singing but not a praying man, but then she decided to enjoy his company and work at getting to the heart of the Laura Felix dilemma.

They were halfway through the meal when she told him of her certainty that Laura was listening in on his phone calls. That's why she'd not mentioned that he and Gracie would be alone for lunch, she confessed.

This upset him as much as anything. "Do you suppose she does the same thing with Al, as well?"

"We can't know."

"He seems a decent, intelligent fellow, not the type to endure years of browbeating, not to mention eavesdropping."

"If it's so easy for her to eavesdrop on you with the phone, is there any reason to believe she'd not be doing the same with Al? And going through his mail and personal papers? And yours?

"For that matter, is it possible that something was included in your communications with Al that would have given some clue as to your marital status and to where Elizabeth is living? I've been worrying that Laura's the anonymous letter-writer."

"I—don't know. He and Jean and Elizabeth and I have been friends since Al and I were residents together long ago. I don't recall every phone call made to and from this office, but I may have said enough that she could figure out my situation."

When Tom left, after thanking Gracie from the bottom of his heart for letting him impose upon her, Gracie was pleased to notice a little more bounce in his step than there'd been when he'd arrived. Soon, having cleared the table, she decided to drive out into the country.

"I'd like to take you with me, Gooseberry," she said. "But I need to be able to just visit, not to have to keep track of your where-and-what-abouts."

Gooseberry gave what resembled a snort.

"Remember the last time we were there I caught you sneaking up on one of Eleanor's chickens," Gracie reminded him.

But the first chicken she saw today was already quite dead, and the farmer's wife was plucking feathers from the headless bird. "Come on back here!" Eleanor called out, spotting her friend.

"It's been decades since I've de-feathered a chicken," Gracie admitted, looking on with curiosity. "I suppose it's like riding a bike and you don't actually ever forget."

Eleanor laughed, "There's not much call for this skill anymore, and even I don't often do it. But this was one of the few laying hens we've kept in order to have eggs for our own use. I wouldn't have killed her unless I had to.

"She must have created a small tear when laying her last egg, causing at least a drop of blood. So when another hen saw it, she began pecking at it, and kept on making it bleed more. Then the others joined in until there was a virtual feeding frenzy, causing so much blood loss that this poor creature would soon have died, anyway. Barnyards are probably more violent than most people would care to know!"

Gracie said she was sorry. Then, since she knew Eleanor had been in the doctor's office that morning, she changed the subject and asked, "Are you okay? Your health in order?"

"Fine—all of us. And we've been very busy, but that's the way it is on a farm, especially during spring and early summer."

"And you're always doing so much for others, as well."

Eleanor looked up and responded with a smile, "Look who's talking! You're always doing for others, too."

Then she added, "I did, though, take one of my neighbors, Mrs. Castor," nodding in the direction of the farmhouse just west of them, "to Al Hanley's office this morning. And I was impressed with that Dr. Elder's way of handling things. He has a nice manner with patients. Elsie really liked him."

"That's good to hear. Did you know he was an old friend of mine, from long, long ago?"

"Is that so? Well, Laura was being her usual difficult self, having a bit of a tantrum about his being late getting to the office. He spoke up for himself, though, and told us folks waiting there that he'd just come from Intensive Care, where he'd been since the middle of the night."

Gracie wasn't sure just how far to go, but she ventured, "Do you suppose Laura treats Al like she did Tom today?"

"She's always been proud of working with Al—not *for* him, of course—so I doubt she'd deliberately try to embarrass him. But what do I know? Generally speaking, we're such a healthy crew around here that we seldom need doctors."

"What else do you know about Laura's background?"

Eleanor nodded. "Well, she wanted to be a doctor herself, you know, and practically idolized her dad Henry, who was a Mason County general practitioner. From the time she was little, Laura vowed she was going to grow up and be a doctor, too, and work with him.

"But he died far too young, while she was in her first year of college. Something seemed to go out of her at that time. Her spark and enthusiasm just sort of died. It was then she decided not to be a doctor, but a nurse."

She frowned thoughtfully. "Al had already come to practice in Willow Bend at least five years before Henry died—maybe ten, I don't remember exactly—and he promised Laura a job when she finished nursing school."

"So I suppose," Gracie wondered out loud, "*he* was okay, since he'd worked with her father, but nobody else quite makes the grade."

"It would seem that way." The work on the chicken was completed but, when Gracie said she'd better start back home, Eleanor invited her into the huge red dairy barn to see the newest addition to the herd, an adorable little wobbly-legged heifer born that morning.

Toward the middle of the afternoon Joe brought Uncle Miltie home.

"I'm going to take a nap," he told his niece. "I've been having too much fun."

"Well, I think I'd like to take a walk. I owe Gooseberry a stroll."

She loved this time of year. For that matter, she loved every season in Willow Bend. *Thanks, God, for planting me here in Indiana, where I have the best of all the seasons, with none so long that I take it for granted and forget to be grateful.*

But spring is so especially glorious! How I do love the changes from day to day, the earliest flowering of the crocuses on the south side of my house, then the other bulbs and bushes and trees and . . .

Gooseberry stopped to sniff at a mysterious clump of grass, then hurried to catch up with her once again before moving on ahead. The next time he crouched down at the edge of tall grass and weeds, she moved closer, but saw no sign of animal life, not even the slightest movement of a stem or leaf.

She suddenly heard a familiar voice behind her asking, "How are you, Gracie?" She turned around.

"Hello, Paul. Isn't this a perfect day?"

"It certainly is! I'd been in the church office this morning, then made some hospital calls. A bike ride with no particular destination is my plan now. If only for an hour or so."

"Who do we have in the hospital?" She was on the prayer chain, of course, but if there'd been an emergency other than Harold May-hew's, she hadn't heard of it.

He listed the mother of one of the parishioners and two people whose names were on the membership roll but seldom if ever came to church. As almost an afterthought, he mentioned Harold Mayhew.

"When checking over the chaplains' register, I saw his name, but no church affiliation was listed. I decided to stop by anyway."

"I heard this morning that he'd been taken to Intensive Care. Is he still there?"

Paul nodded. "And will probably continue to be for a while."

"How did he seem?" She always tried not to pump Paul for information that was better kept private, but her question seemed general enough.

"Hanging in there, Gracie. He's a pretty tough old bird."

She laughed. "That cruise he won made him the envy of many in town, and I suspect that was the first time ever in his life that he got to do something that many others would have loved experiencing."

"But now he's had a heart attack, and it's far from an enviable experience."

"How true. Life can change so very quickly, can't it?"

"Apparently, they've told Harold it could have been a whole lot more serious. The fact that they worked with him so long and that Dr. Elder stayed there for hours makes him figure it's more serious than they're telling him."

"Did he mention anything about family or friends?"

"I asked if there was anyone he wanted notified, but he just shook his head and closed his eyes." Paul looked away from her, but she doubted he was actually seeing the lilac bush on which his gaze appeared to be fastened. "I get the feeling he's afraid of death, Gracie. But he may be almost as apprehensive of life, of reaching out to others and maybe getting no response."

"Oh, Paul, can you even imagine how horrible it would be to not have anyone you could call upon when your life had been—well, turned upside down? Maybe near its end?"

He sighed. "I've never gone through that, and hope and pray I'm never separated emotionally from relatives and friends. And I sincerely believe God will never separate Himself from me, or me from Him, but I doubt that Harold has any such assurance."

"Did you pray with him today?"

"Of course. But I got the impression that made him more uncomfortable, rather than giving peace."

"Who knows? Perhaps being uncomfortable now will lead to his listening more closely later. Listening to the Word of God, that is."

"I'm sincerely praying it will."

She silently joined him in that prayer.

Nine

GRACIE AWOKE while it was still dark. Her first thoughts, strangely, were of Harold Mayhew. It must be terribly lonely for him if nobody came to see him, if he had no close friends or relatives. Could it be that he was so used to being alone that he no longer was consciously aware of the lack?

She rolled over and tried to go back to sleep, but couldn't. She tried to think of other things, but her thoughts kept reverting to him. None-theless, it surprised her when Uncle Miltie's first words as he joined her in the kitchen were, "I've been wondering how Harold's doing."

"Me, too, but I'm not sure whom to ask. Paul visited him yester-day, I know, and Tom had been caring for him in the wee hours. But his nearest-and-dearest list, for all intents and purposes, seems non-existent."

"I suppose Tom is bound by his medical oath not to talk out of school . . . I mean, hospital."

She poured some buckwheat batter onto the hot griddle and watched as the first small bubbles formed near the outer edges of the pancakes. "I wish there was something we could do to let Harold know we do care about him."

"We-e-ll, maybe I could go see him—if he's allowed to have non-family visitors. We've been talking more of late, you know, about contest entries and sweepstakes and his cruise and stuff. He just might like to have me come, if for nothing more than just relieving the . . . the sameness of being in bed all the time, and not really know-ing the people around him."

She nodded. "I'll be glad to drive you to the hospital if you decide you want to go."

He looked at her thoughtfully. "I'll think about it."

Soon Uncle Miltie murmured, "If we can find out for sure that he can have visitors, I think I should maybe go today."

"Morning or afternoon?" Gracie wasn't surprised. Her uncle's jokes were tin, but his heart had always been made of gold.

His right eyebrow quirked upward. "You're not going to talk me out of this, are you?"

She slid the spatula under the first pancake. "I doubt that you want me to."

"One part of me wishes I didn't have to go, but I know I should." He sighed melodramatically. "So how about right after lunch?"

"Sounds good." She flipped the pancake. "I'll check with the hospital after we eat. You know how it's really busy those first hours of a new shift."

What Gracie learned from Nancy Bixler, a nurse she'd known for many years, was that no specific notation had been made on the patient's chart about visitors being forbidden. "It would probably be good for him," Nancy confided.

An hour went by before Gracie picked up the phone again. She was puzzled when the number rang again and again. About to hang up and try again, she suddenly heard an impatient, harried-sounding "Hello?"

"Is this Dr. Hanley's office?"

"Yes—Dr. Elder speaking."

"Tom." She gulped. "Are you okay?"

"Oh, Gracie!" She was sure she heard a sigh of relief. "Things aren't at all okay! Laura didn't show up. . . ."

"Didn't show up?" she repeated. "Do you know why?"

"She didn't call until a little while ago, nor did she answer her phone. When she finally did call, she merely said she felt under the weather."

"And you doubt that?"

"Well, I think the weather she's under is a black cloud of resentment at my presence in her life!"

"Did something in particular set her off this time?"

"More like a bunch of little things. She apparently believes she can do anything here. The biggest incident, though, was when I said I would do the rebandaging of a bad wound I'd taken care of.

"She stated right in front of the patient that she would do that. That she always did it for Dr. Elder, who highly valued her skill. And then she sort of body-blocked me out of the way. I'll admit to having not handled that situation very well. I blew up at her."

"*Uh-oh. . . .*"

"So it's apparently payback time—on this, the very busiest day I've had scheduled here so far!"

"Al doesn't have a secretary, in addition to a nurse, does he?"

The sound was something like a snort. "I did wonder when Al told me he didn't, that it worked better this way. But I sure do understand now! Our office tyrant wouldn't be able to tolerate another employee here."

"I'm taking Uncle Miltie to the hospital to see Harold, if that's permitted," Gracie ventured.

Tom paused a moment. Then he stated in a neutral, professional-sounding tone, "That should be fine."

"How long do you think he should stay? Just a few minutes?"

"As long as he wants to, or as long as Harold seems to want him to stay. That's my professional opinion. I'll call there right away and, if he's still doing as well as when I saw him real early this morning, he'll be transferred out of the ICU before you even get there."

"Good! I've been thinking about him a lot and I am glad he's got you on his side."

"Thanks, Gracie. I need to hear that, I confess."

She walked outside to share with her uncle what she'd just learned. "So I'm going to wait a bit before taking you to see Harold. And I'm also changing out of these jeans. After dropping you at the hospital, I'm going to Tom's office to see if there's anything I can help with."

"That's ridiculous!" He had that stubborn look, which she'd come to recognize early on. Yet Gracie wasn't sure exactly what seemed so ridiculous to him.

"If you need to help Tom out, then go on. I'm sure one of the guys can take me to the hospital. And he'll either wait for me or I'll call someone else when I'm ready to come back home."

When Gracie showed up at the medical building, she knew all of the seven people sitting there in Al Hanley's office. Four were patients, it turned out, while the others were drivers or spouses.

"Things are really backed up today," one of the older men stated, and another added, "Laura's missing in action."

"She's never wanted a secretary or helper, Gracie," Maisie Carrothers declared. "I know for a fact that Al's brought it up a number of times, but she's always turned thumbs down on getting someone else in here."

John, her husband, nodded. "Finally a couple of years ago that girl from the hospital's medical records department started typing up his medical notes for him."

"Yeah," Maisie agreed. "Sylvia Plenning's a medical transcriptionist. She types up the information off of that little hand-held recording device Al always uses after seeing a patient. She gets it back here by the next morning, so it can be put on the patients' charts before they're filed."

"That must be a godsend for a busy office like this," Gracie commented. Then, though aware it was none of her business, she asked, "Does Sylvia take care of the bookkeeping, too?"

"I think someone else has responsibility for that. Or maybe Laura does it."

Tom did a double take when, accompanying his previous patient back to the waiting room, he saw Gracie sitting there. She rose and said softly, "When I heard Laura was off today, I thought I'd come ask if there was anything I could help with. I know nothing about your routine, but perhaps I could at least answer the phone or write down appointments."

"I'd sure appreciate that!" His smile was at first for her, then he shared it with everyone. "If the rest of you will continue being patient for just another minute or two, I'll go over the appointment book with Gracie. I have it back in the examining room with me, since I've been here all on my own."

He groaned as they walked through the inner corridor toward Al's office. "I've been going insane! None of the files had been pulled! It's impossible! It's no way to provide proper medical care!"

He turned the appointment book around on the desk. All the times for morning and afternoon were filled. "It would be a help if you could even get folders for the next couple of patients from those files over there."

"Of course."

"Have you entered any future appointments?" she asked hopefully, but wasn't surprised at the shake of his head.

"I didn't take the time. But I do have an appointment list for Laura to take care of as soon as she's back." He pulled a folded sheet from his pocket. "Perhaps you could also make a couple of these calls—if you're brave enough to face the possibility of raising Laura's ire."

She accepted the rumpled paper. "I'll see how things go. I should get at least some of this done. I'm sure we can keep up with appointments for those already here or headed in. We'll just continue to have a back-up, that's all."

She went to the waiting room to ask the next patient to come back to an examining room, grateful that Tom was looking over her chart, which he must have pulled when getting the previous patient's chart.

The first three incoming calls were for appointments, which she tried to schedule in time slots similar to the ones visible on existing schedules. The next call was from someone needing a prescription for medication he'd been on for several years. She managed to find that chart and clipped the message to the front of it.

She sent out for sandwiches, which she and Tom ate a bite or two at a time, between patients, as they drank coffee that got stronger as the day went on.

Uncle Miltie called at 4:45, asking if he should be doing anything in preparation for the evening meal. She thanked him for offering, but said there were leftovers in the refrigerator that she could warm in the microwave, and they could eat within fifteen minutes of her getting home.

She took time to ask how he'd made out at the hospital—and was surprised at his having stayed there over two hours.

"I didn't expect to, you know, but Harold didn't want me to leave. Since nothing else needed my attention, I stayed."

"Did he do some of the talking, or did you have to keep the conversation going?"

"He talked—about growing up in Illinois and coming here with his parents when in high school. The way it sounds, he didn't have a good time of it here. I guess lots of teens already have their friends made by that time, and he didn't fit in."

"That could explain a lot of things."

"Yeah, I think so, too."

"I'm afraid we take it for granted most of the time, but you and I are blessed by being able to encourage and keep friendships."

"Well put, my dear."

She glanced at the clock again and said, "I want to get all the charts out for tomorrow. Whether or not Laura's back, having them ready should make things easier."

"Have any idea what time you might be home?"

"I don't see how it can be before six."

"In that case, I'm going to have a bowl of ice cream. Since I'm telling you first, does that mean it's a *scoop*?"

Gracie groaned. Her uncle was still chuckling happily as he hung up.

Two hours later she stopped on her way home to pick up Uncle Miltie's pictures from the pharmacy. Handing them to him as she walked through the door, she told him, "I'll look at them while we're eating."

But he was impatient to have her reaction. "How about this one?" he said, holding out a print.

"Excellent!" she pronounced. "You and Gooseberry make a handsome couple, I admit."

"You know, I think I might have been handling this contest backward," he said, handing her yet another snapshot. "I've been writing the slogans and poems first, then trying to match a picture to them.

"With these, I'm gonna try making words fit the images."

"That sounds like a good idea," she agreed. But, in fact, she had little idea what he was talking about. The main thing, she figured, was that he was enjoying himself.

Soon after dinner was on the table, Gracie found her critical faculties once again being called upon. Looking at the verses he'd penned, she politely suggested, "Mightn't it be best to sleep on them before you make a decision?"

He must have realized her response was less than enthusiastic, because he gave a crooked grin. "That bad, *huh?*"

"Let's say they might benefit from a bit more polishing before being sent off."

"If you want to know the truth, some of those I like best actually never get shown to anyone at all."

"Well, knowing what to discard is part of the creative process, I suppose."

As they were eating, he asked, "Why didn't you ask Tom to come for supper? Your leftovers are always good enough for company."

"Well, I admit that I did ask, but he had to go back to the hospital. He sent a patient there this morning, right from the office, for various tests and X rays. He wanted to check her over again, and to look in on someone else, as well."

"He does seem like a conscientious doctor."

"I think so—especially since seeing him in action today. He genuinely cares about each patient, which is what got him sort of riled up this morning, when Laura never phoned to say she wasn't coming in until he'd been in the office for *over* an hour. She didn't even answer her phone when he called."

"If she gets mad and quits, maybe Al will be able to put someone less temperamental and obstreperous in there. She may be an okay nurse, but as a human being she falls pretty short."

Gracie sighed. "I suspect she loves her job—especially what she regards as the prestige it gives her. It's the new guy on the block she resents, the fellow who has the nerve not to appreciate her know-how and her important contributions."

Guess who just called."

It was Tom's voice on the phone, and Gracie responded, "It had to be Laura."

"No wonder you have a reputation in these parts for figuring out mysteries!"

She laughed aloud. "This one was too obvious to miss."

"Not to me it wasn't. Despite having left messages all day saying I'd appreciate hearing from her, I confess to being surprised when she phoned a few minutes ago."

"Did she ask how things went?"

"Sort of, though not in so many words. I just said I hoped she was feeling better, then told her how much I'd appreciated your helping out."

"So if she refuses to speak to me ever again, I'll be able to chalk it up to jealousy?"

"Jealous? You've got to be kidding, Gracie. She doesn't even like me."

She didn't want him to realize how funny that struck her. "I meant she wouldn't want to hear that I, or anyone else for that matter, was able to do what she prides herself on doing so expertly."

"We-e-ll, you may have something there. She's been the most unreasonable when I let her know I was going to do something Al probably lets her take care of. My problem is that I'm the one officially and legally responsible for the practice while he's away, and I don't know what she's capable of handling—of handling well, that is."

"Do you suppose you might be able to say that to her—you know, get it right out on the table? Maybe that would help."

"It might, I suppose. But it could work the other way, couldn't it? Isn't it possible that she'd think I missed her so much yesterday that I'm now forced to kowtow to her?"

"Well, maybe what we should do is pray for greater understanding. God always has a plan and a purpose."

There seemed a brief hesitation before, "You may if you want to."

"This does involve the rest of the month for you, Tom."

"Don't I know it!" There was the sound of a deep inhalation and slow release of breath. "I was beginning to wonder how I'd survive—but I *will* keep on trying my best."

"You already are."

"You truly think so?"

"Of course. You used to be that kind of guy, and nothing I've witnessed so far indicates to me that you've changed in any significant respect."

"Thanks, Gracie. Thanks a lot."

"You're welcome, of course." And she added, "I rather expect you'll see Laura there tomorrow."

"And if not?"

"Tell you what, my friend. If she's not there within a half-hour of the office opening, give me a call and I'll rush over. But I'm sending up another prayer that it won't be necessary."

"You have more faith than I do."

"I hope you can take this in the way it's meant. You need to look inside yourself to see why it is you doubt when it's so clear to me our Lord is with you every step of the way."

A long pause. Then, "Thanks again, Gracie."

Ten

GRACIE WAS OUT WALKING by six o'clock. "Look, Gooseberry! There's still all this sparkling dew on the grass and trees—where I wish it would stay, incidentally," she added, wiping off the water that had just fallen on her nose from the tree above.

Gooseberry, too, was moistened. But he seemed to enjoy it, rolling in the rich spring earth. "I think you'll stay outside for a while when we get home. If you climbed into my recliner, it would be like a mudbath when I sat down!"

His ears twitched, but he didn't look at her.

"I wonder what's going through your head right now, dear friend. Are you so busy checking out the nose-high sights that you hardly notice my talking to you?"

That made her think of El again, remembering that night when they were out over the middle of the Atlantic Ocean and had experienced one of the most terrifying electrical storms she'd ever seen.

El had been asleep beside her and, needing his calm reassurance, she'd nudged his arm. Looking out the window, he smiled. "Beautiful, isn't it, Gracie?" His voice and expression were drowsily appreciative, but not enough so to keep him from closing his eyes and starting to go back to sleep.

She was provoked by his unawareness of her mental state. "Just look out there," she told him. "What if we're struck by one of those bolts of lightning?"

Reaching for her hand, he had squeezed it tightly. "Gracie, my beloved, should such an unlikely thing occur, as long as we go to-gether I'll have no regrets."

But when your time did come to leave, you went alone, not with the crash of thunder and strike of lightning, but in that horrible auto-mobile accident.

She brushed away a tear, then deliberately studied her surround-ings, consciously determined to enjoy the beauty of this world. *For a while there, God, nothing appeared awesome or beautiful after El went to be with You, and I wondered if it ever could be again. But now, though I do still miss him and wish he were with me, You've given me peace and contentment and won-derful friends, as well as the opportunities to serve You in many ways.*

Thinking how terribly lonely she'd been as a new widow made her wonder about Tom Elder's state of mind when Elizabeth left him.

I don't know how I could have borne El's deliberately separating from me, Lord. It was only the knowledge that he had loved me without reservation that helped me go on—even though that undoubtedly made my sense of loss greater.

Back at home, she was sweeping the kitchen floor when the phone rang. "She's here," Tom Elder announced without elaboration.

She responded quickly, before anything more could be said. "I ap-preciate your letting me know right away, for I do have some things I didn't get done yesterday."

And she hung up. Just in case Laura Felix was up to her old tricks.

"That was abrupt," Uncle Miltie commented.

"Better safe than sorry," Gracie told him, explaining that Laura Felix had the unpleasant habit of listening in on the office extension phone.

"Goodness me!" said Uncle Miltie. "Are you sure?"

"I'm sure I wasn't imagining the extra clicks I heard. I told Tom, but it'll be difficult for him to confront her with it."

"You're right about that, Gracie Parks!"

She was surprised when Hammie Miller stopped by to deliver to Uncle Miltie another case of cat food. She waited until he'd left before asking, "Have you forgotten we now have enough cat food to feed an entire shelter? Gooseberry may have a healthy appetite, but he'd be better off eating less, not more, I'm sure."

Uncle Miltie looked neither surprised nor contrite. "Of course I remember. But don't worry."

"About what?"

"Well, since I took the labels off, I marked them with an indelible marker telling us the flavors." Taking a paring knife from the drawer, he began removing the new labels, as well. "They say no purchase is necessary for these entries, you know. It's the law. But I'm old-fashioned, or maybe just superstitious. If I'm going to do this, I guess what I think is having a real label to send along can't hurt my chances!"

After finishing lunch, Uncle Miltie asked Gracie if she'd take him to the hospital to visit Harold Mayhew again. "And don't bother about picking me up," he told her. "There's a good chance I'll run into some other visitor with whom I can bum a ride. If not, I'll call."

On her way home, she stopped at the *Mason County Gazette* building. Rocky saw her just before she got to his own office and reached to move a pile of papers from the single straight chair kept beside his huge desk.

"So your system of keeping people from staying too long still works," she noted. "At least I get to sit down."

They both laughed, and she asked, "You've eaten lunch?"

He glanced at the clock on the far wall. "Nope—I had no idea it was this late."

"That's what happens when you love your work."

"Or," he countered, "when you have so much work to do that you have little time for anything else."

"I just took Uncle Miltie to the hospital for a visit, and thought you might join me for a bite over at Abe's, or The Sweet Shoppe, if you'd prefer."

He threw down the pencil he'd been rolling between his fingers. "Lead the way, Gracie—before I change my mind!"

Abe Wasserman must have seen them coming, for he met them at the door. "Hello there! I was just thinking last evening that it seems a long time since you've been here."

"Not so long," Gracie reminded him. "Sunday after church."

"Ah, yes, you were here then, but I was so busy at the time that we had little chance to visit."

"Well, after you bring me a pastrami sandwich and a diet root beer, then we'll ask you to sit down with us," Rocky growled.

"Don't listen to him, Abe. You can rest your not-so-very-old bones next to me . . . and then bring him his pastrami!"

"Hey, I'm starving! And it was your idea to come out to lunch."

"But, cleverly, you see, I've already eaten. The only thing I need is some advice, and I think you give better counsel on a full stomach than on an empty one."

"*Hmmph!*"

At this, Abe decided to get the pastrami and give his friends some privacy.

"To be honest, I hadn't yet thought of asking you this when I invited you for lunch." She shared with him her suspicions about Laura's eavesdropping, then inquired, "So which way should I handle this? Advise her to think twice before doing it again? Say I think Al should hear about it? Tom knows, is appalled, but is basically powerless. He's temporary, she's permanent. Or so we believe.

"The more I've considered the problem, the more I'm sure this situation must be dealt with right away, though I'd prefer waiting till Al's back."

"Well, I'd want to be notified if this were an employee at the *Gazette*," he stated. "I'd need to know."

⁂

Her uncle didn't get back until nearly three, and again he appeared pleased at the time he'd spent with Harold. "You know, Gracie, he has more on the ball than I used to think. I still don't know why he's always been such a loner, but there at the hospital he does talk with other patients.

"Since he's now allowed to walk outside of his room, I found him in that lounge or social area, whatever they call it, right there at the end of the hall, only four doors from his room. They have this really huge, wide-screen TV there, and he was watching one of those game shows."

"Now that surprises me," she told him.

"Me, too, or at least kind of. There were other patients there, too, so I suppose one of them had turned it on, but Harold got real involved, rooting for one of the teams of four people who had to agree on an answer among themselves for each question.

"I didn't think they were very easy questions, but Harold came up with the right answer a good many times."

"Impressive."

"The really neat thing about this afternoon was that several patients and visitors came over and talked with Harold, too."

"How did he react?"

"Lapped up the attention like a kitten!" He paused for a moment. "It's really plain to see, Gracie, that this is the best medicine: friendship."

"Really, Uncle Miltie, dear," Gracie's eyes twinkled, "what you're referring to is the love the Bible instructs us to share. It's the giving freely of ourselves in fellowship. Love is the best medicine, to be sure!"

Uncle Miltie brought two more examples of his versifying with him when coming to the dinner table.

"Read 'em aloud, Gracie."

She didn't want to seem to hesitate, but so far they hadn't been getting any better.

"It really gets expensive
When buying this and that.
If you try *Lucky Kitty*
You'll have a happy cat."

"Now let's have the next one," he encouraged her.
Gracie read on.

"If you give food to your cat,
And he then turns away,
You'll find that *Lucky Kitty*
Will really save the day."

She cleared her throat. "Well, at the moment, I'd probably go with number one."

"What's wrong with the one you just read?"

"Nothing's wrong with it. I just happen to like the first one better."

"I don't suppose you'll like this one, either. . . ." He pulled yet another slip of paper from his pocket and recited:

"So it doesn't taste like mice,
Which make up some cats' diet,
Still *Lucky Kitty's* sure to please,
Just buy some soon and try it.

She laughed. "There are probably people who'd take offense at cats doing anything as crude as eating mice."

He stared at her. "That's what cats *do*."

"I realize that as well as you, and am thrilled always with Gooseberry's talents in that direction!"

After they'd finished dessert, he began bringing out the snapshots so Gracie could see if she thought there were any tie-ins he was missing between verse and photo.

"Do the instructions say there has to be a connection between the two?" she asked.

He didn't answer and, instead, just sighed at the number of photos left over. "Looks like I need to write some more if I'm going to mail in all these duplicate shots."

"Do you have any idea how many have gone out thus far?"

"I have all the poems in a file but," and his grin looked a bit sheepish, "I don't think I really want to know how much I've spent on this contest—especially when I was sending in all that money in order for them to send back the pictures."

"Oh, well, it's probably cheaper than playing golf," she suggested.

"Yep," he agreed, then added with an oversized wink, "or chasing after women."

⚘

Gracie had Tom Elder's situation so much on her mind that she wasn't startled when Marge, who came by to play Scrabble, asked her, "What do you think of Tom—as a doctor, that is?"

"As far as I can tell, he's doing a good job and is conscientious. You may have heard that I spent part of yesterday answering the phone there and doing a few things to help out, since Laura didn't come into work."

"She mentioned that she wasn't feeling so hot."

"When did you see her?"

"Oh, she stopped by the shop late today just before I closed." Marge hesitated. "It seems like she—*uh*—doesn't exactly trust him, and told me it might be better for you to not get too involved with him."

"What?" This was absurd! "I hardly think that helping out with things in the office for part of one day constitutes being involved with him!"

"Well, she asked if he's been here very often."

"What did you tell her?"

"Just that we'd played Scrabble together, and that I knew he'd been here a time or two since then."

"And . . . ?"

"Nothing much else."

"What did she say about his being here?"

Marge's brows drew closer together. "Well, she told me he's still married, that Rocky was wrong that he was a widower. And she said she didn't want you hurt if you were thinking of this leading, somehow, to a permanent relationship."

Gracie was indignant. "I trust you informed her that I am not looking for any kind of relationship. Not with Tom or any other man."

Marge shrugged. "Well, I didn't exactly put it like that, but I'm sure she got the point. She does know, of course, that he's an old—and shall we say *close*—friend of yours."

"Oh, my! I can't help the coincidence of someone I once knew turning up here . . . but I certainly didn't arrange it to put a thorn in her side. It was Al who hired him, anyway. She should blame him, not me, even if I know that's unchristian of me to say."

"Oh, Gracie," Marge said. "It is a bit of a mess! And all because Al and Jean deserved a holiday at long last!"

Eleven

GRACIE WAS IN BED reading her library book. Even though it was a well-written, fast-paced mystery, it would reliably soon send her off to sleep.

But another mystery kept nagging at her: Why had Laura Felix taken such an instant dislike to Tom? Why? He was only here for a month and yet she felt compelled to try and sabotage him? Why?

She must be missing something here. She felt certain her present regard for Tom was more than just the memory of past friendship. But could it be clouding her judgment?

Had Laura resented Tom's coming before he even arrived? Might she have wanted Al just to close the office for the month he'd be gone? Could she have wanted that month as vacation, too? In that case, was it possible she wouldn't have liked *anyone* who came?

But Laura was obviously not one to hide her feelings, so it seemed unlikely Al wouldn't have sensed her hostility. And since Laura had talked to Marge about Tom, and implied that Gracie shouldn't get involved with him, she must have told others in town the same thing.

Laura knew that she and Marge were best of friends, so her comments to Marge were undoubtedly double-edged, probably more aimed at hurting Tom than protecting Gracie.

Was there any possibility that Laura had, as Gracie had hypothesized before, orchestrated the anonymous note? But what could it matter whether Tom Elder was a widower or not, if he was only invading Laura's turf for such a short time?

She went back to her mystery and read on, realizing soon that she was so tired her mind wasn't actually receiving the messages being sent by her eyes. Why had the male protagonist's mother just warned the heroine to have nothing more to do with her son's young daughter? And why should that send shivers up the young woman's back?

She closed the book, laid it on the bedside stand, and got up. Gooseberry, who'd been quietly lying on the foot of her bed, got slowly to his feet, stretched mightily, then lay down again, now turned away from his mistress, and went back to sleep.

"Sometimes I envy you, Gooseberry," she whispered. "As far as I can tell, you can just turn off or tune out everything outside of yourself and enjoy your slumber."

As she finished dressing the next morning and started from the room, she looked back upon hearing the almost-silent sound of her cat's paws hitting the carpeted floor.

"Wouldn't you think after all these years, my friend, that I could tell when you're faking sleep?" She bent to rub under his chin. "In all truth, though, I realize that you could have been asleep. And if so, I commend your ability to awake with such instant awareness."

Waking with awareness. That phrase kept coming back to her as she and Gooseberry started out for their morning walk. *Are You trying to get my attention, Lord? At this point I haven't the vaguest idea what it could be, so if it's You, I'd sure appreciate getting some sort of clue.*

The sun had risen, and the night's dew clinging in sparkling splendor, even on fenceposts and electric wires, made the world almost incandescent. She realized she was humming, then singing,

> "For the beauty of the earth,
> For the glory of the skies,
> For the love which from our birth
> Over and around us lies,
> Lord of all, to thee we raise
> This our hymn of grateful praise."

She continued singing the other three verses, feeling especially stirred by the last one:

"For the joy of human love,
Brother, sister, parent, child,
Friends on earth, and friends above,
For all gentle thoughts and mild,
Lord of all, to thee we raise
This our hymn of grateful praise."

Her choir had sung that as an anthem two weeks before, and she'd commented to Tyne Anderson that she wondered if the author of those lines, Folliott Sandford Pierpoint, might have lived in a place similar to Willow Bend.

Or, put another way, how could he not have?

Uncle Miltie looked agitated as he came to the kitchen when she entered. "Are you by any chance going to the post office this morning or later today?"

She hadn't intended to. But she said, "I could use some stamps, so I'll be glad to go by if you need me to."

He gave a sigh of relief. "I just looked over those contest rules again. I don't know how I forgot that today's the deadline. All entries must be postmarked before midnight!"

"Well, I'm not on a schedule, so tell me when you have things ready, and I'll take them."

Things were very quiet the rest of the morning, with even the television silent. Uncle Miltie said little as he ate lunch, and, returning to his little work area he stayed only a minute or two before bringing a handful of pictures and papers back to the kitchen table. "Will it bother you if I spread this stuff out here?"

"Not in the least," she assured him. "Just let me know if there's anything I can do to help."

It was nearing 3:30 when he called up the steps while she was vacuuming. "I think I'm done here, Gracie."

"Okay, I'll be right down." She shut off the machine and went into the bathroom to run a comb through her hair. When he handed her his stack, she told him, "I think I'll put these in a plastic bag for safekeeping. There are so many envelopes, and I'd sure hate to lose a winning entry."

He tried for a grin, but she was alarmed to see he looked more tired than humorous. "Of course, then if I don't win anything, I could always blame you," he joked.

"In that case, I'm definitely going to stuff them in this bag," she informed him. "I'm not sure I could stand having that on my conscience the rest of my days."

He walked out on the porch with her, and as she drove away he was still there with Gooseberry rubbing up against his legs.

*

Everything seemed to proceed quite normally during the next week. Al and Jean Hanley called Tom to report they were having "the vacation of a lifetime," and Tom told them things were going fine at the office. When he reported this conversation to Gracie, she challenged his accuracy. But he just shrugged.

"Things really do seem better—or else I'm so appreciative of their not getting any worse that I'm not about to rock the boat."

"Has Laura really stopped her own peculiar form of employer torture?"

"Either that or I'm getting used to her." He gave that lopsided grin of his. "I think it may be a sort of truce, actually. She rarely smiles or says more than what's absolutely necessary to me. Patients fare a bit better, though. I suspect maybe I'm doing the same, though I hadn't realized it till now."

"Well, as long as it works," Gracie said.

*

Rocky had not mentioned the anonymous note with the Indianapolis postmark for some time. Suddenly, late one afternoon, the subject came up again.

"You're not going to believe this!" he exclaimed as he came through Gracie's kitchen door. "I've just gotten another of those notes about Tom Elder." He waved an envelope at her.

Gracie rose to meet him, but when she reached for what he was holding he drew it back. "Let's not touch the note itself—in case we need it checked for fingerprints."

"Did you do that before? On the other one?"

He shook his head. "I didn't think of it until after it had been handled a number of times."

Pulling the folded sheet from a nondescript white envelope, he laid it on the table. As he carefully straightened it with a pair of tweezers, she read the words boldly printed on it:

PRINT RETRACTION!
SOON!!
OR ELSE!!!

She looked from it to him. "Even without those exclamation points, I'd consider this a threat."

"Me, too."

"Do you suppose Tom has any idea what's going on here?"

"We'll probably have to show this to him. I'm not sure he realizes just how potentially dangerous an enemy he might have."

"Or else someone who's really off mentally." She frowned. "His wife Elizabeth evidently would fit that description. But if she doesn't even recognize him anymore, she'd hardly have been able to compose these messages, much less address the envelopes and put on the stamps, not to mention mailing them."

"Nor would she have access to the *Gazette*," he added.

Neither said anything more for a moment. Then she suggested, "I think it's time we talk to Herb."

Rocky started to shake his head, but then she added, "Not only is he our chief of police, but he's got a lot of common sense along with his professional know-how. He's often had ideas I'd never think of."

"I'd prefer not going to the authorities yet."

"That 'or else' on the note especially worries me."

"Me, too," he said again.

"Would you at least consider sharing this with Tom? I'm getting pretty nervous about leaving things as they are."

"If you think that's necessary, I won't stop you." He sighed heavily. "As though I could even if I wanted to."

She laughed, deliberately choosing to treat what he'd said as humorous. "Then, with your approval, that's what I'm going to do. I'll call him at the office and invite him here for supper."

"Oh."

He appeared less than happy until she added, "Why don't you come, too?"

He didn't answer at once but just sat there looking at her. "If you're sure you want me to."

She reached for his hand. "I always like having you here, and you know it."

He cleared his throat.

She smiled at him. "Do you have to go back to the paper?"

"Of course." He pushed his chair back, but didn't get to his feet. "I've already stayed longer than I should."

"Well, when could you best break for supper?"

"You don't have to . . ."

"I know that, my friend. I also know that if I ask Tom and he comes, I need you here to show him the message and hear what he has to say."

"What about Herb?"

"I'm not sure what's best as far as he's concerned. I believe he has to be told what little we know. But I also suspect that, were I in Tom's situation, I'd be more apt to share information if a policeman I barely knew weren't sitting at the same table."

She stood up and moved a step or two nearer, putting her arm around his shoulders. Leaning over, she rubbed her hand against his cheek, feeling the faint, rough, afternoon stubble.

He turned a little. "Gracie . . . ?"

She straightened. "If it's okay with you and Tom, we'll probably eat around six o'clock. As usual."

He nodded as he got to his feet and started for the door. "Without Herb?"

"As of now—though we still may need him in the end."

"What about Uncle Miltie?"

"He'll be here, too, unless—well, maybe I can think of something else."

That turned out to be unnecessary, for when he came to the kitchen a little later, after a nap in his recliner, he said, "Gracie, I was just thinking about Harold. He's at home now, but that means he's alone again. He did seem better there in the hospital, especially when people came to him." He rubbed his jaw thoughtfully.

"Were you perhaps thinking of taking supper to him? I'll be happy to fix up a basket of goodies for you to take."

"Are you sure that won't be too much trouble?"

"I wouldn't mind in the least," she assured him. "What do you think? Leave here maybe four o'clock or 4:30? You'd better phone him first, though."

Things worked out as planned, with Uncle Miltie visiting Harold, and Tom arriving only a few minutes after Rocky. As she sat down after putting dessert—chocolate pudding with a dollop of whipped cream—on their plates, Gracie said softly, "Tom, Rocky received another message today."

He looked at her with stirrings of alarm on his face. "The same message?"

Rocky held out a sheet of white paper. "This is a photocopy of the original."

"Why a copy? Why not the real thing?"

"I doubt it will be necessary, but we could need to check for fingerprints. I didn't think of that with the first note, but"—he gave a broad shrug—"who knows?"

"Who indeed?" Tom sat there looking at the paper for several more seconds before meeting Gracie's gaze, then Rocky's. "The woman I married is still breathing, sleeping, and waking. She can occasionally be coaxed to eat or drink a little, but is kept alive by the tube into her stomach, which most of the time she doesn't notice."

At this time, Tom rose from his seat and began pacing. "She hasn't known me or our son or daughter for over a year now and has not carried on a rational conversation for much longer."

"She'd claimed, and I'd convinced myself, it was true that I'd always been far too busy with my practice during our married life. How else could I account for not having realized she was so dissatisfied?

"Then, after finally realizing how much she was losing touch with reality, I closed down my medical practice and did my best to care for her.

"But my response was too late . . . and my guilt too great.

"I simply had to face the fact it was impossible for any one person, no matter how hard he tried, to care for her twenty-four hours a day."

He returned to his seat. "I do not know who wrote this message. Nor how this individual even knows about your paper, Rocky, or about that article, with its unfortunate misrepresentation.

"It seems to me that someone from here must have seen it and is now either writing these or sending word to someone else who's doing so."

Rocky asked, "Have you met anyone here you might have known from before?"

"Aside from me, that is," Gracie put in.

"Nobody! Even if I did, I can't imagine why that person might hate me so much."

Gracie sighed. "We do believe you, Tom, but maybe you can think of someone to whom you've talked here who's shown special interest in your personal life, or asked a lot of questions—present company excluded."

There was the briefest hint of a smile as she uttered those last words. "I can't think of anyone," he said.

"How about the ordinarily curious?"

"You mean, like your friend Marge or Mrs. Fountain?"

"Or Laura?"

"She may have been the bane of my existence when I arrived here, but personal questions are not her style."

"Never?"

"Nothing more personal than why was I late again today in getting back from the hospital!"

Rocky was frowning. "Was there anything in your phone or written correspondence with Al that could have predisposed her to dislike or distrust you? Perhaps about your wife being in that home or about your son?"

Tom looked at Rocky thoughtfully. "Not that I recall. Al knows about my situation, of course, and I suppose it's possible he'd have shared that with her. It's just that I doubt it."

Gracie sighed again. "I've told you I'm sure she's listening in on your conversations. And if she's doing that, isn't there a good chance she'd go one step further?"

Marge knocked briefly at the kitchen door and walked into the room, whistling to her little Shih Tzu Charlotte, who was following her. "I called you from the store a couple of hours ago, Gracie, and Uncle Miltie said you were at the post office. Do you honestly think he has any chance of winning with all his entries?"

"Hi, Marge," Tom said. Rocky waved his hand in greeting.

"Hi, guys."

Both men said their good-byes shortly thereafter, and Marge said, "What I really came for was to ask for your recipe for that casserole you prepared for our last church supper. You know, that one with frozen french fries and cheese and—and other stuff."

Gracie headed for the large walnut recipe box her uncle had made shortly after coming here. "I'll have to check since I've made it only that once." Pulling out the card, she brought it and a blank card to the table and handed her friend a pen.

Marge kept talking while copying the information, but Gracie successfully steered the conversation away from too much emphasis on Tom Elder's attractiveness.

"I can't help it, Gracie," Marge complained. "He's the type of guy I really go for. So what if it's only a fantasy? Besides, he's *your* old beau, not mine."

"Marge, dear," Gracie sighed, "you know I love you, but I'd just prefer not discussing Tom Elder."

With a mutinous glance, Marge now changed the subject as requested, mentioning the possibility of a visit to her cousin Nancy. "If I have to miss choir that Sunday, so be it. You know how regular I am, and Barb does, too."

It was shortly after Marge left that Uncle Miltie called for a ride home, and it was on the way back that Gracie told him about Marge's plan to see Nancy.

"Isn't she the one who's a nurse in Indianapolis?" he asked.

"I think so. As I recall, she's a little overweight and talks a lot. But Marge seems to enjoy her."

"*Hmm.*" She changed the subject again, and when they got home she handed him the chocolate pudding she'd saved for him. "Want to take this in to eat while you watch TV?"

He agreed that was an excellent suggestion and grabbed a handful of cookies as he headed out of the room.

Twelve

WHEN GRACIE AWOKE early the next morning, she realized that lodged in her mind was a full-fledged idea that had somehow developed overnight. She acted on it with a mid-morning call.

"Are you busy right now, Marge?" Her friend was at her gift shop.

"I wish I were! It's pretty quiet. But what important subject did you phone to discuss this beautiful morning?"

"Well, I got to thinking about your driving to Indianapolis this weekend. What's your plan for the trip?"

"It's actually only Sunday I'll be away. Nancy has concert tickets for that afternoon."

"Well, would you like a driving companion? It's ages since I've been to a really good concert, though Elmo and I used to go to Chicago for them often. Somehow it just didn't seem worth the effort after he was gone. But maybe Nancy could still pick up an extra ticket."

"Of course, Gracie. I'd love to have you along."

"That's great! It's not often I feel so impulsively inclined."

"At least this way we can share the burden of Barb's displeasure," Marge noted.

"Ah, yes. Well, since you're providing transportation, how about my breaking the news of our absence to her? She can only excommunicate us."

It was Uncle Miltie who told Rocky about the concert outing. When Gracie returned from her morning walk the next day, her friend was sitting in her kitchen staring into a mug of milky coffee.

"Need a dunker?" she asked him.

Rocky didn't answer. Instead, he looked at her and stated, "You think Nancy's the guilty party."

"I don't know what to think, but she's a connection to Indianapolis and that's why I have to go."

"You don't expect her to confess, do you?"

"If she's the one, I hope she'll admit to it. But I'm not going to hold my breath. I don't think Marge has a clue, though."

Rocky scowled.

Gracie went on. "I'm pretty sure Nancy must be a nurse in that home where Elizabeth Elder is a resident."

"And if she is?"

"I'm doing a lot of praying—for all of our sakes. Unhappiness is a part of God's plan I can do without. And I'm beginning to sense that it's the root cause of much of what's troubling us here."

"Does Tom know what you're planning?"

"I don't intend to tell him yet. There's no use getting his hopes too high."

"And you weren't going to tell me, either. Except that Uncle Miltie decided to spill the beans."

That was a statement, not a question, and she saw no point in responding to it. "I'll let you know when I get back. Well, not till Monday morning, probably."

"Be careful, Gracie," was all Rocky said before he left.

Gracie didn't notify Barb Jennings until Saturday evening, when she told the choir director that she and Marge would be leaving in the morning for Indianapolis.

Yes, they planned to be back that very evening and had every intention of being at the next rehearsal.

Gracie leaned back in the comfortable seat, gave full attention to her surroundings, and sighed. "I'm so used to driving that this is sheer luxury. What a delightful experience it is just to watch the countryside go by!"

Marge smiled at her. "I'm glad you suggested coming with me. Even if I'd thought of it, I probably wouldn't have asked, knowing how faithful you are to the choir."

Gracie smiled back. "Well, don't make me feel guilty!"

Marge now explained. "Nancy's less than a year younger than I, you know, and we used to have such wonderful times when we were kids."

"I know. You've told me."

"Nancy has been through a lot, and so have I, since those days!"

"Nancy's a nurse, isn't she?"

Marge nodded. "That's what she always wanted to be. When we were maybe seven and eight, Mom and I visited Aunt Ruth and Nancy at Halloween. Her mother had bought her a fairy princess outfit and I thought it was the most beautiful costume in the world. But Nancy liked my costume better. We traded, so she could be the nurse."

"Is Nancy married? I don't recall your mentioning a family."

"She was engaged back when she was still in nursing school, and expected to get married as soon as she'd graduated. Nick, whom I'd always thought was a really neat guy, became a state police officer. But then he fell in love with someone else and ended their engagement, which pretty much broke Nancy's heart."

"I'm sorry."

"I don't know that she's ever even looked at another man romantically, so it's good she enjoys her career."

"What's her job?"

Marge grimaced. "A tough one. I could never spend all my working hours with people who are mentally ill!"

"What sorts of mental problems?"

Marge suddenly had to pay close attention to a huge truck that had just pulled around her. "They make me furious when they do that!"

"Me, too. Some of these drivers are really nothing more than overgrown bullies. However, I, for one, am not about to challenge them!"

Nancy met them at the door of her small stucco house. The cousins greeted one another with obvious affection, and Nancy welcomed Gracie warmly before asking, "Is it okay with you two if we go out for brunch? The restaurant three blocks from here has a wonderful breakfast bar, where I go for a treat sometimes."

They enjoyed a delicious meal: Omelets and all the fixings were the main attraction. And Gracie went back for seconds on the fresh fruit salad.

While they were finishing their coffee, Marge excused herself to go to the ladies room. Nancy watched as her cousin crossed the restaurant before asking, "I've been wondering. Does she have a crush, do you think, on that Tom Elder who's subbing for one of your doctors? She always mentions him when we've talked lately."

Gracie thought carefully before she answered. Having Nancy bring up the subject herself was a wonderful advantage. "You know Marge. If they seem eligible, she's hopeful."

"That's why I asked. She's still on the lookout for Mr. Right, even with a string of Mr. Wrongs in her past!"

Gracie decided to take the plunge and confront Nancy with her suspicions. "You are the one who sent those messages to Rocky, aren't you?"

Looking flustered, Marge's cousin stammered, "I—don't know what you're talking about!"

"Yes, you do, Nancy. And I can appreciate how concerned you are, especially since you know Tom's wife."

Gracie thought she understood some of the thoughts going through this woman's mind, so she explained, "It took a while to figure it out, but I finally asked Marge if she'd sent that clipping to you."

Nancy looked around to make sure that Marge wasn't in sight. "I'd tried to get her to go slow, to promise she'd do nothing to encourage him, but she just laughed."

"And you had no way of knowing that the business about Tom Elder being a widower was simply a misunderstanding on Rocky's part. He's the one who wrote the article.

"The problem is, this has been more upsetting to Rocky, who's one of my dearest friends, than to anyone else. He's usually such a stickler for the facts! But he was so impressed that Tom would come to Willow Bend to take over a practice temporarily that he wanted everyone in town to know how blessed we are. And he also, unfortunately, thought it would be a splendid way to introduce Tom to Willow Bend."

Despite Gracie's explanation, Nancy was defensive. "I didn't want some guy like that to string her along. Someone who wasn't coming clean."

"I understand," said Gracie. "But is that an accurate way of seeing Dr. Elder? Was his reputation here a dubious one in any way? To me—and I've actually known him a long, long time—he seems a decent, hard-working man who's coping as well as he can with a terrible personal problem."

Nancy drew in a deep breath. Then she sighed slowly. "Actually, everyone at Clearview likes him. He used to come all the time, back when there was still hope we might stop Elizabeth, at least for a while, from slipping farther away.

"Unfortunately, it didn't work, and the truth is, he's not there as often any more. But I don't blame him, really, and he comes a lot more than most of the families do, if you really want to know. People can't stand it, and it's pretty awful to watch one's loved ones become strangers."

Looking relieved, Gracie nodded suddenly, to indicate Marge's approach. Nancy told her, "Thank you. I was wrong to meddle."

"Well, your note gave Rocky a bad shock, but it seems your heart was in the right place."

"I was thinking about Marge's susceptibility, I guess, not Dr. Elder," Nancy said, quickly adjusting her facial expression to greet Marge, who now stood beside the table.

"Well, there you are! And your make-up's perfect again. You put Gracie and me in the shade!" Nancy complained to her cousin.

"In a great big auditorium, no one will notice us anyway," Gracie said, laughing.

"That's not how I see it!" Marge retorted.

*

Both Gracie and Marge were still humming some of the music they had heard as they drove back to Willow Bend. When Gracie walked into her kitchen, Uncle Miltie looked up from the table to ask, "Have a good trip?"

"Wonderful! In every way."

"Good! Nothing much to report here. I'd call it uneventful, in fact."

"You make it sound as though I'd been away for a month instead of a day."

"Gracie, any longer and I'd have had to send out an SOS! Bring this man cookies!" he grumbled.

"You old faker! I left a full freezer, a stuffed fridge and a freshly restored cookie jar! Any more food and you'd have had to send out for a case of antacid!"

She made just two phone calls that evening. The first was to Rocky, leaving a message on his answering machine. The second was to Tom. But instead she reached Cordelia, who told her that she and Marge had been missed at church and that Tom had been called to the hospital an hour before.

"I'm going to read in bed for a while," she told her uncle. "If there are any phone calls and I don't pick up by the third ring, you'll know I've sacked out."

But the phone did wake her. Opening one eye, she saw it was already light, and she noticed her alarm clock indicated it was 7:03!

"Hello?"

"Good morning, Gracie."

It took a second or two to respond, until she had finished a massive yawn. "Good morning, Rocky."

"You sound sleepy. Don't tell me you're still under the covers at seven o'clock!"

"The truth is, I was exhausted by the time we got back."

"Well, I'm sorry to have wakened you, but I got in too late to return your call last night."

She propped herself up on both pillows. "I'm glad you did. I wanted to let you know right away that everything's okay now. You won't be getting any more anonymous notes."

"Way to go, Sherlock! I'm really glad it wasn't some grudge-holder's opening salvo. Every small town has too many secrets, as it is, without importing new ones. I'm glad Tom Elder came to town to take Al's place for a bit, but I wasn't happy to be the transmitter of erroneous information."

"I know that, Rocky," Gracie assured him. "And, for her part, Nancy Conway, Marge's cousin, was simply looking out for someone she cares a lot about. She chose the wrong way to do it, is all."

"I'll take your word for it," Rocky said solemnly.

"What time might you be free to meet me at Abe's?"

"Maybe about 9:30? I've got one quick early meeting here."

"Sounds good to me. Let's aim for that, unless you'd prefer calling when you're ready to leave your office."

"That's okay."

She headed for the shower. Going downstairs ten or fifteen minutes later, she heard sounds from the garage, and called, "Good morning!"

"And a good morning to you!"

"Have you eaten breakfast?"

Going to the refrigerator for the orange juice, however, she changed her mind and took out several kinds of fruit. That salad at brunch yesterday had been tasty. She was standing at the sink, looking out the window, when her uncle came inside.

She hadn't noticed that one of the kitchen chairs had been missing, but now, seeing him carrying it into the room, she asked "Something wrong with that one?"

"I saw night before last that it was a bit wobbly, so took it to my workshop and reglued it."

"Thanks. I didn't realize we had a problem."

"We didn't, but I figured I'd rather fix it before it became one."

Surprisingly, Rocky had already arrived at the delicatessen before she got there, very obviously checking his watch as she came through the door. "You are late, Mrs. Parks, by nearly a whole minute."

Abe, from behind the counter, called out, "Do you know what you want for breakfast, Gracie?"

"Just a blueberry or raisin bagel, with cream cheese, as usual."

"I'm starving, even if this is my second breakfast," Rocky said, smacking his lips. "I'd like two toasted English, with a big pot of jam, and an order of hash browns with ketchup."

"What a combination!" Gracie protested. "Why don't you add a dish of rice pudding to the mix?"

"Sounds like a great idea. And a rice pudding!" Rocky called out.

"I hear you missed church yesterday, Gracie," Abe said, arriving with their food.

Looking at Rocky, she teased, "Who needs a newspaper with Abe in business?"

"But, seriously," Rocky told her softly, after Abe had taken away the empty tray, "I did pray for you. And I guess it worked."

"Thanks, Rocky, dear. That means a lot to me. My success in talking to Nancy is probably owing to your intervention on my behalf. It was a satisfying solution, and a lovely concert, to boot."

"It's an honor for me to be your Watson, Gracie. And the praying part wasn't so bad, either."

"Believe me, Rocky, that's the nicest thing you could tell me. I won't forget it."

"More coffee?" Abe asked. "You two look pretty pleased with yourselves."

Thirteen

AL AND JEAN HANLEY CAME BACK from vacation, tanned and rested. Gracie was busy with catering projects, and Uncle Miltie was starting to put in more time digging up the garden.

The choir planned a surprise party for Tom on his last Sunday with them. Pastor Paul announced from the pulpit just before giving the benediction: "As always, there's a glorious bounty of refreshments made by our talented and creative cooks. So stop for a while to join us in thanking and saying goodbye to a special person who came to Willow Bend in the cause of healing. His care has made a difference to many of us, and what affects part of the community affects it all, in the end.

"You may not know him well, but you've probably at least seen him here and heard him sing. Many of us in town have come to regard him not only as an excellent physician but a good friend. This is certainly true for the choir members and for me. So I'd like to ask Dr. Thomas Elder if he has anything he'd like to say at this time."

Gracie was sure Tom was surprised. Yet he carried it off well by standing up behind her to say, "Thanks, Paul, for those kind words. On my first Sunday here there was a party for you, and now, on my fifth and last Sunday with you, there's another. I am honored to be so honored.

"I hope most of you will stay for the fellowship hour, since my stint here in Willow Bend has turned out to be a true blessing for me. Nearly everyone has welcomed me—has made me feel welcome, and I shall always look back with affection and gratitude on my month spent with you.

"I hope to maintain some of these friendships, and be with you again on some Sunday not far in the future." He smiled out at the congregation.

Amid the clapping of hands, he sat down. Gracie turned so that her gaze met and held Tom's for that moment before Paul gave the benediction and the choir led the choral response.

"We are going to miss you," she told him as they headed together toward the refreshments.

"Is that a generic we or a personal one?" he asked, gently taking her arm.

"Let me just say, you've worked your way into the hearts of many of us. Me included."

He was about to say something when Barb appeared at his other side. "Come back and sing with us any time! There will always be a place for you!"

Gracie was amazed to hear Barb then invite him to dinner. "If you're not already booked up, I'd be honored to have you come to my house tomorrow night."

"I do appreciate that, Barb," he told her, "but I plan to leave for home in the morning."

"Well, maybe later on today?"

Looking genuinely regretful, he shook his head. "That's kind of you, but I'm afraid I already have plans."

"Too bad." She smiled at him. "Well, I see I should have asked earlier. This means I really expect you back in Willow Bend soon."

"I look forward," Tom said, "and I thank you again for your musical encouragement."

"So you're all booked up for today," Gracie murmured.

"Well, I was hoping for an invitation to play Scrabble at your kitchen table, and I wanted no possibility of conflicting engagements."

He'd said that softly enough that Gracie thought nobody could overhear. But Marge had just arrived. "Did I hear the magic word *Scrabble*? Can I come too?"

Tom looked at her, but Gracie responded with, "Sure. How about coming over around two o'clock?"

"Great!" She scurried on into the kitchen.

Gracie started to follow her, but Tom stopped her by asking, "Am I on the same schedule as Marge?"

Gracie thought for an instant. Then she smiled.

"Not if you walk over from Cordelia's. Otherwise, Marge will see your car if you drive and she'll be in the door within thirty seconds of your arrival."

"How about going to lunch with me now?"

"You can't be serious!" She shook her head. A red curl bounced gaily on her forehead. Tom grinned.

"I'm planning to sample each cake, and I was just wishing for somebody to volunteer to eat the other half of every piece," she informed him.

He laughed. "You've talked me into it. We'll have double the fun and half the calories. We can fight over the frosting."

Tom did manage to sneak in to Gracie's house before Marge could spot him. "How grateful I am that you figured out who'd sent those notes to Rocky! I would have always gone on, somehow suspecting Laura."

"I'm glad I could help," Gracie said, setting up the Scrabble board.

By the time Uncle Miltie and Marge had joined them, Tom and Gracie were neck and neck. "This is getting ferocious," he said. "Let's call it a tie and start a new game, all four of us."

They each concentrated on making this last game of Tom's Willow Bend stay a lively one, which meant much arguing and waving of the dictionary.

After devouring practically an entire plate of homemade ginger-snaps, Tom reluctantly got up to go back to Cordelia's to pack. There were hugs all around, and Marge kept sighing loudly, but soon, with a last glance at Gracie, Tom Elder was out the door.

That night when she went to bed, Gracie whispered to Gooseberry, "I know he needed to leave now and that it's for the best that he leave now, but oh, I know I really am going to miss him!"

Tom continued to stay in touch with Gracie after returning to Indianapolis.

During one conversation, he described a trip his own church was sponsoring: "It's to the back country in the Dominican Republic. Mostly people will be doing construction at a mission school, but there's also a group of doctors and nurses helping at the mission hospital and seeing patients in outlying areas."

One bright, sunny morning a week later, when she and Goose-berry returned from a walk, Uncle Miltie told her, "Tom wants you to call as soon as you have a chance."

"Do you know why?"

His grin was accompanied by a shrug. "He likes you, Gracie. Why wouldn't he want to talk to you?"

She waited until her uncle had gone outside to work in one of the flowerbeds. The phone was answered on the first ring. "Hi, Tom," she greeted him. "Everything okay?"

"Certainly it is, now that I have you on the other end of the line."

But then his tone became serious as he said, "What I wanted to tell you is that I'm going to go on that trip to the Dominican Republic."

"Wonderful! You did such a great job here that I know you'll be a blessing there."

"I'm looking forward to it. I'm filling in for someone who at the last moment isn't able to go."

"When do you leave?"

"Five days from today. I've already got the first of my shots and immunizations."

"That part I don't envy you. I hope you're not getting any reactions."

"They make even a hardened doc like me a little bushed, but the effects that one notices are usually, and thankfully, quite temporary."

"I'm glad to know that."

"Can I write you from there?"

"Of course, Tom, you know that."

He told her more about the planned clinic and then about some of his traveling companions.

"It'll work out wonderfully, I know," said Gracie. "Experiences like this just go on resonating in your life. You'll see."

It was later that same morning that a call came for Uncle Miltie. On the line was a woman whose voice Gracie didn't recognize. She never tried to listen in on his conversations, but she couldn't help hearing his end of this one.

"Hello . . . Yes, this is George Morgan . . . *Um-hmmm*, I'm the one who sent in those entries . . . I think so—yes, I'll be here. . . ."

He just stood there looking at the phone in his hand until she asked, "Are you okay?"

"I think so—unless I'm hallucinating, that is. What I think I heard is that representatives of the Lucky Kitty contest are coming here about 1:30 today."

"What does that mean?"

"I don't know. It was such a shock I didn't think to ask." He replaced the phone. "Can you beat that?"

They ate lunch earlier than usual. All the dishes were cleared away and the crumbs, cat hairs and grass swept from the floor, so they were sitting peacefully on the porch rockers when a big black Lincoln pulled to the curb.

Both Gracie and Uncle Miltie went down the steps to meet their visitors. One was a short man, probably in his mid-fifties, and the other was an attractive middle-aged woman. A driver stayed in the car.

Gracie greeted them cordially and introduced her uncle, who was hanging back a bit.

"Call me Bertie," said the woman. "Everyone does."

Nathan Buckman and Alberta Coopersmith looked around with curiosity.

"It's for real, Nate. Look, there's the rose trellis where the orange cat had his front paws raised as though about to climb after that squirrel—and the rail fence where he was walking. And that's the window he was sitting in. . . ."

Her partner explained, "We've been seriously thinking about going national with our distribution. *Lucky Kitty* so far has been on sale mostly in Indiana, Illinois and Kentucky.

"So we got the idea of having a contest, just to drum up interest, really."

"But," Bertie jumped in, "what happened next was that we realized our packaging needed more pizzazz, if you know what I mean. We'd been looking through hundreds of cat pictures and checking with commercial sources, and then Nate came up with the idea of having everyone include a photo with his verse."

"Right from the beginning, Mr. Morgan, we were intrigued by your cat."

As if on cue, Gooseberry came around the corner of the house toward Uncle Miltie, cocked his head to the side, and gave a shrill "Me-e-e-o-w!"

"Meet Gooseberry," Gracie said. "He thinks Uncle Miltie—I mean, George—is his uncle, too."

Bertie looked ecstatic. "Gooseberry. Even his name's perfect. Though we may have to change it."

Uncle Miltie's brows raised a bit, a signal to Gracie that was apparently unrecognized by their visitors.

"Of course we'll have to put him on a diet. We can't have prospective purchasers thinking that *Lucky Kitty* will make their cat fat."

Her uncle's brows rose yet higher. Gracie felt obliged to contribute, "He's really not overweight, not according to our veterinarian. He's just a big guy, and his especially thick hair makes him look heavier than he is."

"Well, we won't quibble about little things like that, will we, Gracie?" Nate Buckman obviously felt it was time to act.

"We've decided your cat has a unique look. He's just the sort of cat we need for our promotion, so let's not beat around the bush. Here's the contract for you to sign."

"What does it say?" Uncle Miltie looked surprised. "Is it about Gooseberry or about me? He's my niece's cat, actually."

"Here, look at it. The cat can't sign for itself."

"Did I win that contest?"

"No, but . . ."

"Who did win it then?"

"That's not why we're here, George."

"What about my poems?"

"Listen, we've brought with us a cashier's check for five thousand dollars. And it's all yours when you sign this exclusive contract licensing us to use your—*ah*—Gooseberry pictures."

"I said, what about all those poems I sent?"

The pair exchanged glances. Then Bertie Coopersmith said soothingly, "We'll probably use some of them, as well. It's just that we've not yet determined how."

Uncle Miltie looked stubbornly at them. "I don't think I care to sign anything unless or until you clarify exactly what you have in mind. I'm a poet, not a cat's talent agent."

"Well," Bertie cleared her throat, "we just might be able to raise the amount to eight or ten grand, but that would be our final offer! And, of course, we'll buy all your poems, too."

Uncle Miltie now reached for the envelope, but didn't open it. "I do thank you for raising the amount. Unfortunately, I can't sign anything right at the moment, not today. And those poems were contest entries—that's what made 'em fun."

Bertie looked from him to Gracie and back again. "What are you talking about? All I know is, right this minute we are offering you good money!"

"My agent told me that any financial arrangements must be handled through him."

"Your—*agent*?" Nate seemed irritated.

Gracie wondered if she looked as startled as did their visitors, but she made every effort to look unruffled as Uncle Miltie said, "I'll see that he gets this right away. You'll hear from him soon."

And he walked away from them, holding onto the railing as he started up the steps. They called after him, but he neither turned nor responded even as he went inside.

"Well, I never . . . !"

Gracie was almost as amazed as Bertie, but she kept a straight face as she politely accompanied them to their car.

When she got back inside, however, she had plenty of questions. Her uncle explained that he'd talked with Joe and Anna Searfoss about sending in those entries. "She told me right near the beginning to put a copyright-sign—you know, that little *c* with a circle around it—on everything I sent out. And she even called that nephew of theirs in California, the one who's her agent for those children's books she wrote so many years ago that are now being republished.

"I followed his instructions, and now I need to go to the library or somewhere to fax him this contract."

He looked proud of himself, the canny old darling. "I just hope I didn't react incorrectly, and lose the chance at all that money, but I don't trust that pair!"

Uncle Miltie called from the other room, "I know you're getting supper, but could you come here for a minute, please?"

"Sure." Gracie dried her hands as she came toward him. "What's up?"

"Here's a message from Carter. I sent her one of those faxes, too, because she's in the Chicago DA's office. Look here at her e-mail. She's going to do more checking, but she thinks that contract's on the level—and could possibly be raised some.

"If it is, and since I've already written those verses and put the copyright notice on both them and the pictures, she says it's probably going to be a matter of personal choice. First, is *Lucky Kitty* a product with which I'd like to be associated and, second, do we really need the money?"

Carter Stephens was Gracie's much-loved niece, and her counsel had come in handy before, whenever Gracie found herself involved in perplexing situations with legal implications.

"I guess what she means is that if we accept the money, we accept the Coopersmiths and the *Lucky Kitty* crew into our lives, as well."

Tom called again that evening. He told Gracie that the wife of the man he was replacing on the trip had also decided to cancel because of her husband's health. "Any chance of your going with us, Gracie? I can have the group leader call and fill you in on specific things you could be doing there."

"I don't think so, Tom. Perhaps if you do this again and I can get in on it a bit earlier, when I'm not already so committed. I'm probably more set in my ways, too, than I know. But I like to think I'd hear the right opportunity when it knocks."

He wisely didn't coax, and they spoke of other matters, including Harold Mayhew's health and the choir's latest Sunday triumph.

"Your voice is still missed, Tom," Gracie told him.

"Well, now you're hearing it on the telephone," he teased.

"You know what I mean!" Gracie retorted.

"I do, Gracie, but even more than I'm missing those moments of harmony with the choir, I'm missing our own private moments of harmony."

"Well, I'm very flattered. Thank you for saying something so lovely." Good thing he couldn't see her blushing, Gracie thought.

"Wish me *bon voyage*," Tom said.

"I do, indeed, but what I'll say now is God be with you on your journey. Everything you are doing is in His name."

She replaced the phone carefully, as if it were a fragile treasure. Gooseberry then walked over to her, rubbing against her leg, and she leaned down to lift him in her arms and carry him with her as she went outside.

Uncle Miltie was working in the flowerbed beside the front walk. "You know what, Gracie? I've decided that if Anna's nephew says it's an okay deal, I am going to accept that ten grand, but only on the condition they promise not to starve Gooseberry skinny! He's a cat, not a supermodel!

"And who knows? Maybe if Tom Elder goes on another of those

working trips overseas or here in America, you and I can take some of that money and both go with him."

She decided not to tell him she'd just turned down the opportunity of doing that for free. "Right now, Uncle Miltie, I'm more than satisfied to stay at home here in Willow Bend."

"And if you're here, it's the right place for me, as well."

She put her arm around his shoulders. "Willow Bend may be a proper noun, but I think we can agree it's ten letters filled with contentment. Being here makes us both winners, don't you think? And I'm not talking about your contest!"

"Praise the Lord!" replied Uncle Miltie.

"*Meow*," added Gooseberry.

Gracie's Orange Baked Beans

- ✓ 2 tablespoons sweet butter
- ✓ 2 medium onions, thinly sliced
- ✓ 1/2 cup orange marmalade
- ✓ One 18 ounce can of brick oven-style baked beans
- ✓ 1 tablespoon Dijon-style mustard
- ✓ 1 teaspoon dried thyme

Melt the butter in a skillet over low heat. Add the sliced onions and cook gently, stirring from time to time, until they are soft and lightly golden. Push the onions to one side of the pan and add the marmalade, allowing it to melt over the low heat. Stir together the onions and the marmalade, then add the other ingredients and turn up the heat just a little. Stir well and cook until heated through.

Gracie says, "Stirring in some bits of bacon—fried crisply and patted dry before crumbling—just before serving perks up this tasty recipe even more. And throwing in a few toasted onions from a can, which I'll do if I happen to have one open, is another addition that provides zest to an unusual variation on a familiar side dish."

Words have always been a joy to EILEEN M. BERGER, who learned to read at an early age and could lose herself in books and magazines, particularly fiction. Raised on a poultry farm, she spent many hours alone, feeding and watering chickens and gathering eggs. During those hours she often reimagined the plots of existing novels she had read and played with "what-ifs."

"What if the author had done such-and-such in that third chapter, *then* what would have happened?" she'd ask herself. Or, "Suppose the author's lead male had a different personality or background, *then* how would the young woman react if he did the same, or other things?" From there it was a natural step to telling herself her own stories and to promising herself to be an author someday.

But she lived for many years and through many experiences before disciplining herself to write down her thoughts, and in the meantime earned degrees from Bucknell and Temple universities—in biology, chemistry and medical technology. She became head of a pathology laboratory in a large Midwestern city before returning to Philadelphia to work toward an advanced degree. But then she fell in love with a young Baptist minister, got married and went to live in a tiny parsonage in a small north-central Pennsylvania town.

It was there, as a preacher's wife and mother, reading and telling hundreds of stories to the three little ones who soon came along, that she began writing and selling stories, poems and articles for children and adults. The books came later.

Eileen and Bob still live just outside of that same community, which they love. In addition to their church and community involvements, Eileen is active in various writers' organizations, especially the West

Branch Christian Writers, the critique-support group she helped found twenty-some years ago, and is a longtime board member of St. Davids Christian Writers Association, which holds the second oldest annual conference for Christian writers in America.